Old School Ties

KATE HARRISON

An Orion paperback

First published in Great Britain in 2003
by Judy Piatkus (Publishers) Ltd
This paperback edition published in 2009
by Orion Books,
an imprint of The Orion Publishing Group Ltd,
Orion House, 5 Upper St Martin's Lane,
London WC2H 9EA

An Hachette UK company

5 7 9 10 8 6

A CIP catalogue record for this book is available
from the British Library.

ISBN 978-1-4091-0233-5

Typeset at The Spartan Press Limited
Lymington, Hants

Printed and bound in Great Britain by
Clays Ltd, St Ives plc

The Orion Publishing Group's policy is to use papers that
are natural, renewable and recyclable products and
made from wood grown in sustainable forests. The logging
and manufacturing processes are expected to conform to
the environmental regulations of the country of origin.

Forgive your enemies, but never forget their names.

John F. Kennedy

Do you really want to hurt me?   Boy George

Tracey Mortimer rules the skool and the world 4ever and ever! OK!

(Tracey Mortimer,
The door of Cubicle 3, girls' toilets, Humanities Block,
Crawley Park Comprehensive, June 1984)

CHAPTER ONE

27 Sunnyside, Bracewell New Town,
Berkshire, April 2001

Last night, when the third gin and tonic finally knocked the sharp edges off my day, I dared to look in the mirror. And there, just below the problem family of white hairs breeding in my fringe, were the eyes of Tracey Mortimer. The most popular girl in the school.

I thought she'd gone for good.

When I was Tracey Mortimer, the whole year group belonged to me. Kids gossiping on the bus would say, 'Guess what happened in Tracey's year . . .' One parents' evening, a teacher took my mum aside and said, 'We're all hoping that Tracey's year is a bit of a hiccup. Half the staff room would be applying for early retirement if we thought this was the way kids were going to behave from now on.'

If we'd had a yearbook, like they do in America, I'd have had a mention on every page, and I'd definitely have been voted the girl most likely to succeed. I'm not boasting. Look at me now – plain old Mrs Dave Brown – and maybe it's hard to believe, but I really was top dog. Not swotty – I would never have been head girl, but then we didn't have a head girl, it wasn't that kind of school.

What I had was the knack of being at the centre of everything, without pissing people off. Saying what everyone else was thinking, but making it loads funnier. Knowing how short we should be wearing our school skirts, or how thick we should be

1

tying our hideous ties, way before the latest trends hit the pages of *Jackie* or *Just 17*. And, of course, giving the teachers just enough of a hard time to wind them up, but not enough to get detention more than once a month . . . And I even made detention fun.

Those were the bloody days. They really were.

I poured myself another drink, and took it to bed with me (unlike Dave, a G and T doesn't answer back). I propped his pillows on top of mine, nestling down in the hope that some tipsy memories might send me off into sweet dreams. His smell drifted up from the pillowcase, and I imagined him lying alone in his lodgings, a sad smile on his face, thinking of me . . .

But I wasn't drunk enough. Before I could stop it, my imagination revealed the freckly back of some Irish girl lying asleep next to him.

And as the taste of the tonic turned chemical on my tongue, I realised. *Everything* since school has been shit. How I failed to notice for so long is a mystery, but then I've been busy marrying a bastard and having two of his kids.

I sat up in bed, trying to compare the good bits in my first sixteen years to the good bits in the last sixteen; it was so obvious. The sodding Youth Training Scheme, the endless nights on a fruitless quest for Mr Right, and the getting excited about getting engaged and getting married and then getting wise to the reality that all it means is more ironing, and having someone apart from my mother shouting at me.

As for the fulfilment of motherhood, it's a con. Sure, my two are the most beautiful children alive. But the other mums? OK, I had a few laughs in the antenatal group, though they were a dopey bunch compared to class 1G, too easily led for my liking. I used to enjoy a challenge. The only challenge that gets the new mums going is the race to finish knitting another pair of pink bootees. And now Kelly's started school, it's like salt in the wounds. She hangs on to me like a strip of Velcro in the mornings. I try to shoo her off, but she hates every minute of it.

You know those films, *Big* and *Freaky Friday*? That's my dream, to swap places, like Tom Hanks or Jodie Foster. Kelly would love to sit at home doing the dusting, watching daytime telly, eating biscuits and playing with Callum, and I'd give anything to be at school again, recruiting myself a little gang, kissing the boys and making them cry. I want to go back in time. And I bloody can't, and I bloody hate it.

At least, I didn't think I could. And now, you know, I reckon there might just be a way . . .

Smart Alec Productions, Beak Street, Soho, Central London

Jenny had known even before it started that this was going to be one of *those* meetings.

Alec hit pause on the remote control, then threw it across the table. A still frame of a bespectacled man with receding hair hovered on the widescreen TV at the end of the production company meeting room.

'What an idiot. Do you think he's actually got any old school friends who'd want to meet him ever again?' Alec sighed. 'Can you explain why this is so hard? Reunions are the new sex, aren't they? Everyone's at it, shuffling around to Spandau Ballet and eating Spangles. It's not rocket science to find me a single decent case we can follow, is it?'

Jenny bit her lip. 'Alec, we've got half a dozen reunions in the file—'

'Yes, but I'm not looking for dysfunctional retards with

issues. I want feel-good people. This isn't *Panorama*, you know.'

Better to let him finish when he was having one of his hissy fits – she'd learned that much in the last year at Smart Alec Productions.

'The clue' – he was now banging the file up and down on the desk to emphasise certain words – 'is in the commissioning document. It's *entertainment*. Go on, hazard a guess. What do you think that means we want the programme to be?'

He waited, but Jenny knew it was a rhetorical question. Annabel, the new researcher, had her mouth open to answer, and Jenny kicked her under the table.

'It means' – Alec had dropped the file on to the floor, and was speaking as if to an ill-disciplined child – 'that it should be *entertaining*!'

Annabel seemed to be blinking back tears.

Jenny took a deep breath. 'Alec, I know you're frustrated, but you're being a bit harsh. Annabel and I have been out every night meeting candidates. We've got one tonight, four over the weekend. But getting the right people takes time.'

Alec stared at her. 'Time, Jenny, is precisely what we don't have. If the BBC get their reunion show on air before us, it'll be my head on the block.' He paused before giving her a vindictive look. 'And yours, of course.'

There are times when I don't think I'll ever get out of the house. I thought kids got less dependent over time, but it's just not like that. Kelly acts as if I'm about to go on a year-long Space Shuttle mission instead of down to All Bar One.

'Don't go, Mummy. I want to read you a story.'

Well, *that's* tempting, isn't it? I know it's what you're meant to do as a supportive parent, and I do my duty once a day, make encouraging noises, but can't school send home a book that

4

isn't about kittens and bunnies and fairies? She's a much better reader than I was when I was six, but it's not exactly *EastEnders*.

Meanwhile, Callum's hanging on to my leg to stop me leaving. His fingers are covered in banana yogurt, so my one pair of decent glossy black tights is smeared with yellow stripes.

My mum's babysitting but she's no help.

'Poor little Callum,' she coos, and he reacts the way any toddler does to unexpected sympathy. He milks it without shame.

'Maaaaaaaaaaaaaaauuuuuuuuuuuuummmmmmmmmmmmy.' He starts quietly but builds up towards a high-pitched ending, which hurts my ears and makes me nearly lose my balance.

I somehow manage to escape from the house, and when I look back I can see Mum standing in the front window, giving me a dirty look. I can hear her tuts, despite the double-glazing. But after thirty-three years of practice, it's easy enough to ignore her disapproval.

Until now I haven't had time to worry about the meeting. But while I wait for the bus – I daren't drive because I need a drink or two to get through this – it finally hits me.

I can only remember feeling *this* nervous twice in my life.

First time was on my wedding day, because Dave did the traditional thing, had his stag do the night before, instead of months in advance like any sensible person, and I was convinced that when the big moment came for us to take our vows, he'd still be sleeping off his hangover, or be tied up in a mail sack on a sleeper train to Aberystwyth, courtesy of his 'fun-loving' mates. Now, of course, I do wonder occasionally whether the humiliation of being stood up at the altar would have been better than what's happened since, but there you go.

Second time was before I had Kelly, and that was partly fear of the pain, but mainly the fear that she'd be an ugly baby. Ugly people have a harder time in life, it's a fact. I'd waddled off the week before to see a girl from antenatal, and her bundle of joy looked like Mr Potatohead; not that she seemed to realise. Kelly's not quite what I'd expected in many ways, but she's been a looker ever since she emerged, a bit squashed, from my tattered nether regions.

So I guess the nausea I'm feeling now puts this meeting right up there with two of the most significant events of my life. Which I admit is ridiculous. Or rather, the boring Tracey Brown grown-up bit of me admits it's ridiculous.

But the girl who used to be Tracey Mortimer reckons this could be as big as the wedding and birth thing in the excitement stakes. Bigger even, because this is not about Dave in his tux, or Kelly in her Moses basket.

This is all about me.

I pay the bus driver, and the newspaper cutting flies out of my purse. My denim skirt feels too tight as I kneel to pick it up. I know the advert off by heart now, but it's nice to keep souvenirs of the stuff that changes the course of your life.

'*Dear reader,*' it says, '*are you itching to head back in time to those days when the worst thing you had to worry about was double maths? We could make it happen.*'

This sounds a bit like one of those scam cures for baldness or impotence, and I nearly didn't read on, but then there's nothing else in our local paper except letters about dog shit and corrupt local councillors so I kept going.

Then it says: '*We're making a programme for Channel 5 about school reunions, and if you think it would be fun to organise one, we'd like to hear from you. You supply the friends and the memories – we pay for the party!*'

Now you're talking.

'*If your reunion's under way then it's thanks, but no thanks – we want to be in at the beginning. So, if that trip down memory lane is still just a glint in your eye, get in touch with Jenny or Annabel at the address above!'*

I haven't thought about anything else for two weeks. And tonight I'm going to charm Jenny and Annabel, like I haven't charmed anyone since I set out to snare Gary Coombs in the first year.

Just hope I haven't lost my touch.

CHAPTER TWO

I'm running late but at least the girls will be waiting for me, and I won't be pestered for my phone number or, worse, asked by some random old bloke if I'm 'looking for business', like I was the last time I went to a boozer on my own. Though maybe these new places attract a better class of drinker. The girls in the shop reckon All Bar One has about as much atmosphere as a McDonald's, but I get so few nights out that this place feels like the hottest spot in town.

Well. OK. Maybe not *that* hot. It's almost empty. I reckon the researchers must be those two women over by the wall – they look too trendy to be from Bracewell, and one is irritatingly pretty. The other one's seen me and she's getting up.

I take a deep breath, reminding myself that I was the most popular girl in the school. That never goes away. *Does it?*

'Hi, you must be Tracey, I'm Jenny.' She's grinning away like my dental hygienist does before she starts a scale and polish.

'Let's get you a drink, then I'll introduce you to Annabel. She's already started on the red wine, but then these youngsters can't go five minutes without a drink, can they?'

Considering Jenny looks about twenty, this is hard to stomach, but I know from our phone conversations that she's about to hit thirty, and feeling paranoid about it. Either that, or her whingeing about age is part of an 'all sisters together' campaign

8

to get me onside. It's quite flattering that she's making so much effort. Can't remember the last time someone worked so hard.

I ask for a G and T, and Jenny suggests Bombay Sapphire Gin, which looks fabulous in the blue bottle, but is a huge disappointment when the girl pours it out because it's got no more colour than bog-standard Gordon's.

'Story of my life,' I tell her. 'This drink is a real fur-coat, no-knickers job,' and she laughs so enthusiastically that I nearly drop the glass.

It wasn't *that* funny.

We go to sit down, and Annabel starts jabbering on about the show. She's got a cut-glass accent and a cut-throat attitude to her work. I think she hopes she'll impress me by slagging off the other people they've interviewed for the programme, which just proves how immature she is.

Their desperation to become my new best friends is getting on my tits. All the most exciting relationships of my life have at least started with both of us playing hard to get. I want to misbehave. But I've got to fight that instinct, or I'll do what Mum's accused me of doing since I was old enough to talk. And cut off my nose to spite my face.

'Have you brought the pictures?' Jenny asks. I pull the photos out of my bag and lay them on the table.

When I got out the album to choose the best ones, I was amazed at just how awful we looked when we were eleven: I always thought I was a pretty child, but my looks obviously didn't kick in until after puberty. Parts of our body seem to be growing at different rates, and the effect is grim, from the outsize noses to the orang-utan arms hanging too far down our stunted little bodies.

'Fucking hell,' Annabel splutters as she picks up the group photo of class 1G in all its glory. 'I didn't realise you went to a special school!' Then she frowns, worried she's gone too far. But it just makes me smile: the first honest reaction I've seen.

I remember when the picture was taken, the week before Valentine's Day 1980. I was wondering if I might get a card from Gary. I already had my eye on him; he was the only decent-looking lad in my year, and so it stood to reason that he'd want to be with me, the best-looking girl in 1G.

Of course, it was only when he didn't show the slightest interest that I got seriously determined.

I guess I mustn't have noticed that I towered over him by a good four inches. Most of the boys didn't get tall till at least the second year.

Oh, and the uniform. Someone must have done scientific research on the colours, fabrics and designs most likely to stop kids fancying each other. The Crawley Park Comprehensive version involved a mint-green acrylic v-neck jumper, white polyester shirt, navy skirt and – the pièce de résistance – a canary-yellow tie. I would challenge anyone to come up with a less seductive outfit, though by the third year nothing would have stopped us copping off with each other.

In the picture, we're all wearing our ties the same way, the thick end rolled round and round and round so the knot's roughly the same size as a fist, with a tiny tail of fabric poking from the bottom.

'Not hard to spot you, Tracey,' says Jenny.

I'm in the middle – as usual – and though I look rougher than I ever realised at the time, at least I'm smiling, and my hair's not that different from how it is now, blonde and Rapunzel-like on my shoulders, and much prettier than most of the other kids' Brillo Pad hairdos. Well, in those days, the only shampoo most of us used was Vosene.

'So, talk us through your classmates, then?' Jenny's still bright as a sodding button, brimming with enthusiasm at

10

the prospect of hearing all about a bunch of bizarre-looking children she's never met.

I look down and even now, her face makes me feel empty inside. I point to the girl standing next to me in the photo, her jumper hanging off her, with fingers like single blades of straw poking from the scarecrow cuffs of her blouse. 'Louise Shrimpton.' Her mousy hair sticks out at right angles as though she's been doing a science experiment with static electricity. 'Shrimp. My best mate.'

Annabel has drawn a diagram on her notebook, with circles representing every child on my photo. She's marked my position with an X, and now she's writing Shrimp's name alongside the appropriate blob.

'She came from this huge family, she was the second youngest, and they were permanently broke. I mean, it's not like my mum was loaded, but compared to Shrimp, I felt like a millionaire.'

I look at the picture, and realise Shrimp is the only child in the class with black circles under her eyes. They didn't sleep much in her house; there was always someone screaming or laughing or wanting to play. Couldn't have been more different to ours, me and Mum always sending each other to Coventry.

'So, are you still in touch?'

'No. Shrimp died. She was run over.'

'Oh, God. When?' Jenny sounds genuinely shocked, as though for once she's not thinking about her TV programme.

'Second year, just after Halloween.'

Her parents saved up and bought her a second-hand bike for her birthday. Well, long term it'd save on the bus pass. But she got knocked off on her way home, in the dark. Kids wear cycle helmets these days, but back then it wasn't cool and I don't suppose the Shrimptons would have been able to afford one on top of the bike. Her older brother, Ricky, told me that when he saw her lying in hospital before they switched off the life-support machine, the crown of her head had been flattened, like a pumpkin lantern with the top left off.

But when I saw her in the coffin before the funeral, she just looked like Shrimp, minus the black circles. Though there was this sickly smell of vanilla, and when I copied what the adult mourners had done, and went to kiss her hair, I realised her face was thick with make-up. I think they'd even drawn her freckles back on, because there were more of them scattered across her bony nose than I remembered.

So one week Shrimp was mucking about with me, and the next there was just an empty chair alongside me in the class-room, and I thought I'd never get over it. We knew what the other one was thinking, we looked out for each other, and I was more in love with Shrimp than I have been with any bloke. Not in a lezzy way but, you know, she was my mate.

I reckon she knew that too, even after that last argument. We would have made it up. I know we would, the way we always did, if only . . .

Jenny and Annabel are shifting in their chairs, waiting for me to say something, so I look in the picture for my *second* best friend.

'Melody Tickell.' Until Shrimp died, me and Melody co-existed uncomfortably. Our class wasn't really big enough for two rival girl gangs, so it was natural that she filled the gap left by Louise – or tried to.

'She was my bridesmaid as well,' I say, and this seems to perk Jenny up.

'And that was in' – she looks at her notes – '1992, is that right?'

'Yes.' It's odd, having someone take an interest in me, after all this time. They must have a file on me, back at the office.

'Did anyone video it?' she asks, trying to sound casual,

12

though it's obvious from the phone conversations we've had that anything extra – photos, cards and, most importantly, film – could tip the balance in favour of *my* reunion being featured on the programme, rather than someone else's.

'Yes, it's brilliant stuff. Very early nineties. A lot of puffy silk.' I see Annabel add a couple of ticks to her diagram.

Melody and I always looked good together. We were total opposites, and men always liked that. There was me with my blue eyes, blonde hair and curves in the right places, and her with the French-style pointy cheekbones and pointy bobbed hair and pointy eyes, in matching shades of charcoal.

In the school photo she looks intense and studious, eye-balling the camera like it's a dare. But she was never all that bright, and the defiant act was a good way of covering up what was missing. The teachers always gave her the benefit of the doubt, thought she was capable of more than she achieved, that she just couldn't be arsed to put in the work. But if you'd spent as much time with her as I did, you'd realise that she didn't think about anything except how she looked to other people. Case in point: she was the first of our class to start smoking, to give herself the aura of being a tortured soul, whereas in fact the only thing that tortured Melody was figuring out what the lyrics meant in Madness songs.

'She'll be easy to get in touch with, anyway,' says Jenny, and she will; I know she still lives somewhere in Bracewell. I don't mention that I haven't seen her since my wedding. But that's my business.

'Who's the fatty?' Annabel asks me.

Poor Boris. She always meant well. 'Helen. Her nickname was Boris.'

They look at me curiously. 'It's a long story. Her surname's Morris, and someone in our class saw this film with Boris Karloff in it one day when they were pretending to be ill to get off going to school, and it rhymed with Morris, so that was that. You know how nicknames stick. But she never seemed to mind.'

Annabel writes this down. 'What about the boys?'

'OK. Well, that's Briggsy.' I point to the chubby bloke in the front row. He was my first snog, God help me, but we were both under the influence of Old Spice from an aerosol, sniffed through our jumpers. Someone in the fourth year had worked out that the gas inside could give you a high, and within days the local chemist's had had a run on body spray, courtesy of the local shoplifters.

I didn't get high, but I didn't resist Briggsy's determined tongue. I wanted to get the whole snogging business out of the way with someone who wouldn't tell tales if I wasn't any good.

'And then Gary was my first love . . .'

'This one?' Annabel is laughing. 'He looks so young.'

'Well, it was sixteen . . . no, seventeen years ago.' I keep forgetting it was my birthday last month. Dave forgot too. I didn't even get a card.

'Um, well, I hate to mention it, Tracey, but if this is you guys in the first year, then this was actually twenty-one years ago,' Jenny says, and I take a big swig of gin when I realise she's right. Maths was always my worst subject. 'So are you still in touch with him?'

'No.' There's an awkward pause as I struggle to say something that'll throw them off the scent. 'He wanted to be a policeman.' Though I think he buggered up his chances – with a bit of help from me.

'And this is your form tutor? Mrs Chang?'

I nod. Mrs Chang was as short as we were but unlike her, we still weren't fully grown. But the most striking thing about her in this picture isn't her height, it's her massive belly.

When we got to the birds and the bees session that first

summer, she was really massive, and it was hard to avoid the unpleasant conclusion that Mrs Chang, our *teacher*, who must have been at least *thirty*, had actually had sex within the previous six months.

'Yes, though she left at the end of the year.' I guess they'll love this story. 'We had our first sex education class with her, and she was trying to be open with us, so I asked her the question we all wanted answering. 'Miss, what's it like to have sex?'

Jenny and Annabel wait for the punch line.

'So she went a little pink, and she coughed to clear her throat, and she said, "Well, for da woman, it hurts a leetle at first, but then you get used to it. And after a while, you might even enjoy it."'

I stay deadpan, but they choke with laughter, and I join in, because I remember how shocked we were back then. Maybe the girls aren't that annoying after all.

Of course, if I really wanted to clinch the programme, I could tell them about Mr Carmichael, and his more proactive approach to sex education. But some things are better left in the past where they belong.

CHAPTER THREE

I'm having a *Casualty* day.

The best bit about watching *Casualty* is trying to predict what might kill off the characters this episode. There's a career woman skipping off to window-shop in her lunch-hour. Are her stiletto heels about to get trapped in the escalator, dragging her toned calves into the mechanism? Is that cheese and pickle sandwich going to trigger a life-or-death anaphylactic shock because some peanut dust ended up in the bread dough? Or – as she looks the right kind of age – maybe she's ignoring the stomach ache that is in fact a symptom of a potentially fatal ectopic pregnancy?

Well, today it feels as though Kelly, Callum and I are all TV characters, and everything we do could have grisly consequences. So Callum's plump chipolata fingers are groping around the kitchen, and I'm convinced they're about to close in around the blade of a sharp knife I've forgotten to put away, slicing them off.

Meanwhile, Kelly's wandering round with her shoelaces undone around her ankles because I haven't had time to tie them yet. I know kids are made of rubber, and more or less immune to falls, but maybe the random aches she's been moaning about this week aren't growing pains at all, but early symptoms of a rare bone-crumbling disease. So when she trips over, instead of grazing her knee, she'll fall to the floor with multiple fractures, and will have to spend a year of her life in a plaster-cast like a junior mummy.

My own hands feel independent of my body, as if they're about to do something I've got no control over. I move very slowly and purposefully, in case my hands pour too much boiling water into the coffee cup, and it runs down the sides like Niagara Falls, and scalds all three of us . . .

Then the bread gets stuck in the toaster and sets off the smoke alarm in the hall. When I return to the kitchen after resetting it, there's a stinking haze of carbon that makes me choke, and my hands grasp the butter knife to rescue the remaining bread from the still orange elements, and I see another vision of the near future: me leaping into the air in an electric shock, my body glowing Ready Brek-style, before I plunge to the floor and the kids can't rouse me, and then Kelly remembers from school that she should call 999, and an emergency crew arrives, and as they take me away on a stretcher, the kindly ambulance man gives Kelly a lolly to congratulate her for being such a brave girl.

I used to worry that I was going mad, but then I talked to some of the girls at the tumble-tots where I take Callum, and they said they felt pretty much the same: Paranoid Parents. My mum's cupboards contained Dettol and bleach – and there were no child locks, no specialist anti-bacterial cleaning sprays and foams and creams and impregnated cloths.

But there's no way out, because if you don't put everything they touch through a sixty-degree wash every other day, some-one'll probably report you to social services and you'll be left alone in your festering home, while the kids are handed over to more deserving parents.

Now there's a thought.

In a way, though, I find it reassuring that I worry so much. I see Mum looking at me sometimes as if I'm a monster for shouting at them. She doesn't think that I'm much of a mother, and she's probably right. Surely I shouldn't feel so frustrated? I know I love them more than Dave does; I feel it physically, in my stomach, if Callum falls over on the patio, or if I see tears in Kelly's eyes as she watches something sad about animals on TV. But I'm not sure I *like* my kids all the time. Especially not Kelly. Is it right to want to tell a six-year-old to pull herself together?

But at least I haven't failed Mum's ultimate test, and become a *single parent*. I think she should be quite proud of me, even though she's no idea of the sacrifices involved in staying married to Dave.

I check the kitchen clock, and realise I'm running out of time to get Kelly to school, and then get back before – fanfare – the film crew arrive.

I kind of knew I'd be chosen, but still, WOW! Today is stage one; they're going to record an interview, then film me playing with Callum, looking at the old photos again and talking about plans for a reunion. The party's scheduled for July because Channel 5 want to show it in September, so that only gives us three months to get in touch with everyone and organise it. But then again, my new chums Jenny and Annabel will be sorting most of it, so all I have to do is be the centre of attention . . .

At long last, a chance to do the thing I'm best at again.

'Kelly, Mrs Fellowes will be very cross if we're late.' Sometimes fear is the only way to get her out of the house, but when I've done their shoes and checked I've got the keys, locked up and then belted her in the back, put Callum in his baby seat, then double-checked all the locks – because it's a *Casualty* day – I catch a glimpse of her holding hands with her brother and biting her little cherub lips, and I wonder what she's done to deserve a mother like me. Not to mention a father like Dave.

Flat 2a, 422 Goldhawk Road, Shepherd's Bush, London

PC Gary Coombs nuzzled his girlfriend's neck, but she snaked away under his arms and towards the bathroom before he could start fondling her breasts.

'Gabby, don't be mean. I can't resist it when you're not wearing a bra. Gazza wants a cuddle.'

'Gazza'll be lucky to escape without a knee in the balls at this rate.'

'Oooh, you know how it turns me on when you get angry . . .'

He opened up his dressing gown to reveal a bulge in his counterfeit Calvin's. Gabby looked at his groin, shrugged and finished her tea in one swig. 'Much as I'd love to help you out,' she said, in a voice that suggested it was about as tempting as clearing the slimy hairball from the drainage tray of the shower, 'I have an urgent family case conference to attend to.'

'Awww, Gabby. This is pretty urgent, too.'

'Well, once I've done my teeth, it'll be all clear in the bathroom, so don't let me stop you. Just clean up after yourself, would you?'

He pouted at her back as she squeezed out a pea-sized blob of toothpaste, and then headed back into the kitchen, buzzing around as she finished loading the washer, adding powder and then setting it going. It was the biggest difference between men and women. Gary had never met a man who did anything else while they were brushing their teeth, while women couldn't bear to stand still.

'Ga–zzy,' she mumbled through the vibrating brush, 'you're such a – buzz – baby. And I don't understand how you can be randy – zzzzzzzzz – after a night shift anyway. Aren't you meant to be knackered?'

'All those women in uniform.'

'Yeah?' She spat the foam into the basin. 'Well, why can't you get *them* to give you a hand job before you get home, save you harassing me?'

'I did, love, but you know me. Insatiable.'

She pulled on her coat, the smart case-conference one, rather than the grubby one she wore for home visits, then moved right up close to the chair where he was sitting, pulled his dressing gown open, grabbed his hand and stuffed it up her sensible skirt, so he could tell she was wearing her lacy g-string. She gave him a brief, too brief, tongue-down-the-throat kiss, before turning round and running to the door.

'See you later, lover boy. And if you can drag yourself off the bloody Internet for a few minutes, that ironing is not going to do itself.'

He considered a last-minute leap to the door to stand in her way, but his legs had gone wobbly, so instead he just grinned as she blew him a final kiss.

Domestic bliss, he thought, as he pointed the remote at the telly and settled down to admire the showbiz reporter's legs on *Lorraine Live*.

I like my lounge, especially since I painted over the nasty peach sponging. Paint effects were the height of fashion when I was just married; it took me hours to get it right, working around Dave as he read the *News of the World* on the sofa. Now I've covered the peach with a more forgiving pale purple satin emulsion, Violet Sprig or Spring or something. With the light brown laminate flooring, the room looks a bit like a Scandinavian-themed makeover they did on *Changing Rooms*, and there's only the cream sofa to give me grief. But even that's not doing too badly, considering it was the first piece of furniture we bought as a couple, when we were too naïve to know that cream and kids didn't go. I've washed the covers more times than I can remember and it's only really the Ribena stain and the Biro that still show.

But the crew hate the whole room on sight.

'Oh, bugger,' says Jamie, the cameraman, who has nice brown eyes and a cute bum, but a mouth that curls down at the edges. He's my age, so I'm pretty surprised I fancy him – I've always tended to go for the older man.

'We're gonna need a couple more blondes and a redhead,' he shouts into the hall to Cliff, who told me he's the soundman. He has a kinder face than Jamie, but he whistles through his teeth when he comes in, shakes his head like a mechanic doing a twelve-thousand-mile service, then screams through the window to Frankie, who is the 'sparks'.

Frankie nods. He has the look of someone dropped on his head on to concrete at an early age. Nice muscly arms, though.

Jenny looks stressed. 'They're talking about their lights. I've never heard them ask for a brunette,' she says, stroking her own straight brown hair. They all troop back out to the van, where the men do a lot of pointing and shrugging, and I wonder if she's apologising for my bad taste.

Annabel's in the kitchen playing with Callum, but I can tell he's pretty suspicious of her, and she keeps her distance to avoid getting her designer jeans dirty. I can remember the days when I didn't know how to play with babies either, and frankly I'd rather be in her shoes than mine. Especially as hers are ultra-cool leather slip-on trainer-mules, and mine are reindeer slippers that my mum bought me last Christmas.

It turns out that it's not the decor they hate, but the enormous picture windows at either end of the living-cum-dining room. Light, it seems, is the enemy of camera crews, or at least uncontrolled light is. In an ideal world, Jenny tells me later, they'd do all their interviews in a bunker with a storeroom full of different lamps next door, because then they can play God.

We're on our third cup of coffee, but they're still not ready. Callum's getting fractious and so am I. I didn't feel nervous before, but the noise of the front door opening and shutting is starting to wind me up.

Then there's a knock at the kitchen door.

'Helloo?' says a male voice. A head appears. This, I presume, must be Alec, the producer. The girls have warned me that he's a bit of a shark, but – *hello* – I don't think I'm going to mind one bit.

Tall, sandy hair, fortyish but trying to look younger, with twinkly violet eyes that I'm *almost* sure aren't coloured contact lenses, and laughter lines that bunch up when he turns on full-beam charm, which he's doing to me now.

'Tracey! Lovely to meet you at last – I've seen your photo, of course, but it doesn't do you justice.' He shakes my hand and seems reluctant to let go. 'I feel like I know you so well already,' and he winks at me.

It's such a seamless routine that I know he's probably used it on a million women, but that doesn't make it any easier to resist. I catch the two girls exchanging glances. Well, their lives must be full of premieres and nightclub openings, but this is pretty much the most glamorous thing that's ever happened to me, so I don't see why I shouldn't enjoy it.

'If you'll excuse me just a second,' he says, as though he can't bear to tear himself away from the company of a dowdy thirty-something and her chocolate-coated toddler. 'Are they through here?' he asks Jenny, before disappearing through the connecting door.

I deliberately don't look at what they've done to my living

room, but I catch a peculiar blue glow from the corner of my eye.

'Boys!' I hear him shout. 'I'm so glad we've got you on board for this one. It'll be just like *Dream Weddings* all over again.'

'Except we're not in sodding Bermuda, we're in Bracewell New Town.'

'Yeah, but who needs the sun when you've got the best team in the business around you, hey, boys?' he gushes.

The 'boys' don't respond.

Alec pokes his cheeky-chappy head back round the door. 'Are you ready for us now, Tracey? Because we're ready for you.' And there's something wonderfully naughty in the way he says it.

CHAPTER FOUR

This filming business is more boring than I could ever have imagined. So, they've turned the living room upside down, blacked out the sunlight and the garden with a thick black cloth, and the stupid one, Frankie, is holding up what looks like a circular space blanket that reflects light on to my face and makes me squint. And there's no one to do my make-up. Alec flashes me this grin and says, 'You look fantastic as you are,' but I've got my suspicions that they want me to look dog-rough now, to achieve some kind of *Pretty Woman* transformation.

Middle-aged. When we did an essay in English once about what we thought we'd be doing after the millennium, I couldn't believe I'd ever get this old. But even though I've got the first wrinkles, I've got the sprogs, I've got the semi, I've got the boring part-time job in the shop, and I've got the face creams weighing down my bedside table, in my bones I'm the same as I always was. People don't change, do they? When it comes to the reunion, I'll bet you a tenner a time that Melody will still be a dopey manipulative bitch with come-to-bed eyes, Gary'll still be a pushover, Helen Morris will still be *larger than life* . . . Who else? Bodger Lewis will still be bad at maths and still have heavy metal hair, Suzanne Sharp will still be an insufferable swot with nasty red curls.

But am I still the one and only Tracey Mortimer? I try to

summon her up out of thin air, like Aladdin calling on the genie.

Yeah! I'm still Tracey and they'd better bloody believe it . . .

'Speed,' says Jamie for no apparent reason, and then Alec gives me another killer smile and says, 'So, to start with, Tracey, tell me what you're hoping to get from your school reunion?'

'Um,' I start, and realise my throat's gone dry because, much as I love attention, this is too much. Jamie, Cliff, Frankie, Alec, Annabel, Jenny and Callum are all staring. Then there's the camera, a long microphone coated with grey fake fur, and more lights than you get at Blackpool illuminations.

'Take your time, Tracey,' says Alec, but there's already irritation in his voice. I'm starting to go off him.

I had stage fright once, in the school play. When the auditions were announced at assembly, I decided that being in it was the *opposite* of cool, and went round telling everyone that only losers got involved. But then Shrimp found out that Pete from the fourth year was lined up to play Joseph. I changed my mind, and put the word out that actually unless you *were* in the school play, you were truly sad.

Of course, this triggered a last-minute auditioning frenzy.

I always had the power to set trends, and I loved watching the effect I could have as the word spread through school like ripples in a pond.

'I feel sorry for the others, Shrimp,' I said at lunch on the day of the auditions, as I finished off all the sultanas I'd put aside from the chicken curry, 'because it's so obvious that I'm going to get the best part.'

'That's not all you want to get, is it?' She nodded towards the dinner-hall entrance, where Pete, who was a prefect, was marshalling hungry kids with the natural authority that I'd recognised and admired from afar since our first week. Just along the table from us Melody and her friend Fran nudged each other. There was going to be competition. Of course, we weren't best mates then; it was Before Shrimp's Accident.

By the time we went in for afternoon registration, the word was out, and I kept hearing my name, as people whispered about who Mr Aaronovitch, the drama teacher, might pick for the show. The news fizzed around the room like Chinese whispers, as Mrs Chang struggled to get our attention.

'What is matter with you lot?' she snarled, then said, under her breath but we could all hear her, 'What additives did they put in your orange squash today?'

Everyone did *Joseph* in those days. Even *Grange Hill* put on the show that year. Actually, it's a rubbish play to do in a mixed school because all the parts are for boys, and camp boys at that, what with that bollocks about coloured cloaks and weird dreams. That's why it was such a smart move on Mr A's part to cast Pete as Joseph because he was the opposite of camp: he played rugby and was very hairy. OK, so his voice had broken, which meant he couldn't reach a lot of the notes in the solos without making funny gurgling noises, but no one was going to accuse him of being a pansy. And Mr A gave the part of the Pharaoh to an enormous black fifth-form girl called Karin, who had this bluesy voice that made everyone shiver, and he made sure three of Joseph's brothers were played by girls, and, in a final campaigning blow for equal opportunities, he invented a special part of a wife for Joseph at the end. Hardly the cutting edge of feminism, but it was better than nothing, and of course when I heard this, I decided I'd be Pete's missus, whatever it took.

'Right,' said Mr A, rubbing his eyes as if he couldn't believe the turnout to the first- and second-year auditions, 'cast members need to be brilliant in all three theatrical disciplines. Singing, dancing, acting.'

Shrimp nudged me; she'd heard me sing once in juniors, and she knew I was certainly no Sheena Easton. So I decided to nip to the toilet while he tested kids for that part, figuring that if I disappeared for a little while Mr A would assume I had actually done the singing already, and it just wasn't that memorable. Because they'd certainly remember if I *did* sing, and not for the right reasons.

So Shrimp waited until the singing had finished, then nipped back into the girls' toilets to fetch me. She always looked after me. I wish I'd done the same for her, when it mattered.

'Melody was quite good, I'm afraid,' she told me, as we headed back into the hall.

Mr A was beginning to look fed up at the time it was taking to get through all the wannabes, so he decided to combine the acting and the dancing. He counted the boys and the girls, and divided us up two girls to every boy.

'Right, you've all learned about Egypt, even the first years, so' – he was obviously thinking on his feet – 'um, when the music starts, I want the boys to pretend to be pharaohs, and the girls to be court dancers. And I want you to work on an improvisation where . . . let's see . . . the girls have to dance for a chance to become his wife.' I wonder if Mr A is now lurking on some kind of sex offenders' register, but at the time it seemed innocent. In Mr A's defence, he put us in groups according to our ages, and there was no way any boy of our age would want to touch any girl with a bargepole.

And I suppose it's nothing compared to what happened with Mr Carmichael later on.

I guess it was inevitable I'd end up competing with Melody for the attentions of a bemused second-year called Larry. I didn't know what sexy was, not properly, but I'd watched Pan's People, and so when the music teacher started playing some sort of slithery tune on the piano, I just moved my hips and tossed my hair – which was much better for that sort of thing than Melody's straight dark mop – and at the end I threw myself to the floor in front of the poor lad, who four years later became the first fifth-former in our school to come out as gay. I don't know if my little performance had something to do with it . . . But anyway, Mr A obviously preferred blondes, and so I got the part of Pete's lovely Egyptian wife, while Melody was a sheaf of corn. Ha ha.

I spent most of the rehearsals eyeing up Pete, who pretended not to notice, but I was undeterred. On the opening night, I went to town on my make-up, with brilliant blue and black eyes like Tutankhamun, and vivid lipstick, on top of a tan Pan-Stik base. That oily, earthy, baby powder scent still takes me right back; Boots does a foundation stick that smells exactly the same, and once, when I was feeling very old indeed, I bought one to remind me how it felt to be a kid, and I sat sniffing it and crying into my wine as I tried to get Callum to settle down for the night.

Anyway, I was convinced this seductive make-up – along with the midnight-blue cape Mrs Whitstable from home economics had made as my costume – would win over *my* Pete. Poor bugger. Although he was a prefect/rugby player/ fifteen-year-old pin-up, he seemed pretty shy with girls, and embarrassed at having this first-year mooning around after him.

I had loads of time to get nervous, because I wasn't due to appear until right at the end when Joseph comes back to Egypt. I started feeling queasy while he was croaking his way through 'Close Every Door to Me' and by the time he was singing about his dreams, I was considering doing a runner.

But it wasn't until he nipped out the back to prepare for the grand finale, and I saw him *snogging* one of his brothers – a girl from his class who was very pretty *and* had apparently been wearing a bra since junior school – that I finally realised that the last thing in the world I wanted to do was get on stage in front of all those people and say my lines.

I raced around looking for Shrimp, who was hovering in the background as a random Egyptian. I wanted to persuade her to take over from me. But then Pete, displaying a masterful streak that I cherished for years afterwards, dragged me on to the stage with the words, 'We're on now, you wally.'

Instead of walking elegantly at the side of my heroic Joseph, I tripped my way on to the stage. I'd found the hot yellow lights scary enough at dress rehearsal, but now they were much, much worse, because behind them were people, barely visible except for the whites of their eyes. All fixed on *me*.

'And Jacob came to Egypt,' the choir sang, as Daniel Grogan shuffled from the wings, wrinkles painted across his forehead and a grey woolly wig propped on the top of his number 2 cut.

Joseph and I walked towards Jacob, and a couple of serfs held a gold-painted cardboard chariot in front of us. This was one of the many moments where Mr A, dissatisfied with the lyrics of a musical that made millions all over the world for Rice and Lloyd Webber, had added some extra lines of his own.

'And Joseph brought his wife to meet the celebrating crowd,' his version went, and then it was my single line of the entire production: 'I know that my dear husband will make all of Egypt proud . . .' Mr A originally expected me to sing it, but once he'd heard my voice, gave me special dispensation to speak.

I opened my mouth. And nothing came out. There's a first time for everything, as my mum always says when she tells this story.

Everyone was looking at me. The audience, the cast, Pete, Mr A, the orchestra and the conductor. The conductor decided to give it another go, re-cued the orchestra and the choir, who

29

repeated the line about the celebrating crowd. This time I was determined.

'I . . .' No one could hear me, and Pete was whispering the words in my ear, trying to be helpful. I knew exactly what I should have been saying, but the words were stuck in my throat.

The conductor saw me trying and decided to give me one last chance.

'And Joseph brought his wife to meet the celebrating crowd,' they sang, willing me to get that last line before the rousing finale.

This time, it was going to be all right.

I opened my mouth again and from nowhere, clear and confident, came the memorable line: 'I know that my hear dustbin . . .' I looked at my *dear husband* and I saw myself as he saw me: a stupid kid who couldn't even get one line right.

'Bollocks to this,' I said.

There was a pause which seemed to last for ever, then all I could hear was Pete choking as he tried desperately to regain his composure to sing the final moving reprise of 'Any Dream Will Do'.

He failed, and all I can remember is my face getting hotter and hotter, and the music getting more and more jerky, as the conductor lost control of the orchestra in the most impressive display of collective hysteria ever seen at a Crawley Park school production.

I had detention for a fortnight for bringing the school into disrepute by swearing in front of parents, governors and the *Bracewell Bugle*. After that, Mr A begged me not to audition next year or any other year. Funnily enough, I didn't take much persuading . . .

'Shall we just stop the camera again for a second?' It's Jenny. I wonder how long I've been sitting here struck dumb, as the humiliation flooded back. Alec is waiting for me to say something good, but his encouraging smile is beginning to falter.

And then I remember something else: the hero-worship that lasted for weeks and weeks after the play was over. To have suffered stage fright, to have come through it and to have sparked this unforgettable moment in stage history, was suddenly the most brilliant thing I could have done. I think it was round about this time, December 1979, that the first year suddenly became *Tracey's year*.

They switch off the lamps, to stop the living room getting even hotter, and suddenly I feel totally different, back to normal. Better than normal, even. Back to being Tracey Mortimer, the girl who said bollocks in front of the head of the PTA.

'It's better without the lights,' I say. 'Could we do it without?'

'If we lose them,' Jamie says, 'we won't be able to see your face. Mind you, every cloud has a silver lining . . .'

'It's just that they're shining directly into my eyes.'

He grunts and Cliff, who has headphones clamped to his ears to monitor the sound levels, jumps up in shock, but then Jamie fiddles grumpily with the lights, and then the camera's rolling again.

'So,' says Alec, in the same voice I used when I was potty-training Kelly, 'Tracey, in your own time, what are you hoping to get out of your school reunion?'

And suddenly it's easy. This time, we don't stop until I've been talking for about an hour and filled two tapes, with Alec barely getting a word in edgeways.

I need chocolate now, so I go back into the kitchen to unwrap the KitKats I'd bought for the crew.

Jenny comes in. 'I think it'll look best in here, more natural.'

'It'd also save any more lighting trauma; there's barely room to swing a cat, never mind put up any lights,' Annabel says.

I think she's a bitch, behind all the fake niceness.

Jamie and Alec join us, and look suspiciously at the biscuits. I shrug. 'I'd have baked you a cake, but I'm not really very good in the kitchen.'

Alec shoots me a lightning-bright smile. 'Hey, but you're cooking on gas this morning. That interview was brilliant.'

I glow, despite the cheesiness of the line.

'Once you got round to it,' Jamie mumbles.

My glow fades a bit, but only a bit. Despite the chaos, it's brilliant having a full house. I can't remember the last time I had guests. Maybe I should learn to bake cakes after all.

'Yeah, this'd be a good location,' Alec says. 'We could set up the laptop here by the breakfast bar, and then maybe have little Connor—'

'Callum.'

'Yes, little Callum sitting alongside, eating his lunch or something. Nice cutaways.'

I give him a doubtful look. Another grown-up without a clue about children. 'I'm not sure I'd recommend filming him when he's eating. Can be a bit messy.'

'Hey, what's a few rusks on the keyboard between friends?'

Jamie tuts. 'Light's very orange in here. I'll have to use a couple of small lamps. Can you make yourselves scarce while I sort it?'

'Sure – why don't we have a bit of a dry run on the old computer?' Alec suggests, and I follow Jenny into the lounge.

She finds a socket, plugs in the machine and connects the modem to our phone line. 'Have you used computers much before, Tracey?'

I sit down in front of it. 'No, not really. Dave's got one for work, and Kelly's quite good, but I've never surfed the Web. It's for geeks, isn't it?'

'You'd be surprised. Why don't we have a trial run?' Jenny sits next to me, and points to a panel in the middle of the keyboard. 'This controls everything that goes on, using your fingers. So, if I want to go on the Web, I put the cursor – the arrow here – over the E, which stands for Internet Explorer, which is a Web browser, and double-click, and then—'

'Um – sorry, Jenny, but this is making less sense than double physics . . .'

Jenny frowns. 'You weren't kidding about being new to it, were you? Let me get online . . . Right, now we're connected, so let's get straight on the site that started the whole reunion craze. Friends Reunited – there you go, it's loading . . . we've set it up for you here. Bingo. Crawley Park Comp, year of leaving 1984 . . . recognise any names?'

CHAPTER FIVE

Bloody hell. Bloody, bloody hell. Names I'd forgotten I'd forgotten.

'Is my whole year group on here?'

Jenny says, 'No, only the people who've signed up to say they're interested in meeting old pals. Have a look round and then maybe you can e-mail a few old classmates while we're filming you.'

'I don't even have an e-mail address.' I feel very out of it. Never seen the point before, but looking at the screen, now I really want to learn. There was a mammoth number of kids in our year, the tail end of the baby boom. So this long list – there must be twenty-five or more on the screen – is only a tenth of the total, and some names I don't recognise. But there are a few I do.

Jenny says, 'If you see any with this symbol next to the name, that means there's more information about them.'

'I knew this one – Boris . . . um, Helen Morris. Remember – the fat one I showed you on the photos?'

She clicks on it, and up pops this little screen. I read it out loud: 'Hiya, Helen "Boris" Morris here, well I was Morris and now I'm Norris, ha ha, only one letter out, hardly had to change my signature. Married to Brian, I work in IT, quite senior actually, you'd never believe it, and we're expecting a new arrival in the summer, which means I've just given up work, and I'm pretty bored at home so would love to hear from any of the old gang, lots and lots of love, Boris!!'

'I just can't imagine roly-poly Boris as a high-powered executive. And in computers, too.'

Jenny nods. 'Yeah, most of the people who put their names on here early on have something to do with IT. Maybe they're more likely to be online. Or they're a bunch of lonely gits with no friends.'

I think about Boris, and reckon it might be the latter, but then again she is married and up the spout, and at school no bloke would look at her. Maybe people *do* change.

Jenny says, 'Due in the summer, eh? She might be fun to invite to the reunion.'

'Hmm.' I look down the list, and I half expect to see Shrimp's name there, then I tell myself off for being soft. I don't suppose you can log on to Friends Reunited from the afterlife . . .

GARY COOMBS

It leaps off the page and burns a hole in my eyes. 'Gary Coombs!'

Jenny grins. 'Yes, we saw that, when we checked it after our first chat.'

I'm dying to see what he's up to. 'Get his info up!'

'Oh, he's more reticent. No biog or anything. A lot of people don't put any details up on the site, they'll only accept e-mails, and then decide whether to reply. Do you fancy a go at e-mailing him?'

This is so strange. Is he single? Has he got kids? Did he ever get over me? What's he doing for a living? Where is he living?

Would he still fancy me?

Alec wanders in. 'I think we're ready for filming now.'

Back in the kitchen, I pull Callum into the high chair, bung the bib round his neck and heat up a jar of chunky lamb and veg korma, his favourite. It'll keep him quiet, though I know I'll pay the price at changing time. When the camera starts rolling, I load the food on to his plastic spoon, and pass it to him so he can get on with spreading warm orange gloop across every bit of exposed skin from the top of his downy head to the creases in his wrists. A few months ago, when I was feeling really fed up, I worked out in my head how many hot dinners I would end up serving by the time Kelly and Callum left home.

It didn't do a lot for my morale . . .

'Go on the site and talk to me while we film,' Alec says. 'So what are you up to?'

I turn to the screen. 'OK, well, I've just logged up to—'

'On to,' Jenny whispers.

'I've just logged *on* to this site, Friends Reunited, and I've never seen it before, and it shows all sorts of names I haven't even thought about since we left in 1984. Which is a scary amount of time.'

'Maaaaumm.' Callum's obviously still hungry, not surprising as he keeps missing his mouth with the spoon; he hasn't quite got the hang of feeding himself yet. I shovel a bit more sludgy food in his direction, and he gives me the wonky-toothed grin that makes me melt, and Alec has to whisper, 'Keep talking.'

'And, um. Well, I thought I'd try sending an e-mail, so here goes.' I try typing, even though it's been years since I had to do it. 'Sorry, fingers and thumbs. I was never the greatest at typing at secretarial college, and I don't have to use a keyboard at all in the stationery shop.'

'And who's it to?'

I fumble around, looking for the letter G. 'Sorry?'

'Who are you e-mailing?'

'Oh.' I feel myself blushing and I hope it doesn't show up on the film because I'd look a right tit. 'It's to my first ever boyfriend, Gary Coombs.'

Gary stared up at the TV, unable to believe that there was a woman with her boobs out on *Richard and Judy*. OK, it was something to do with breast self-examination, but they were nice and pert and frankly it didn't matter. He wasn't listening to the voiceover. The cameraman kept zooming in to her nipples.

He'd missed her getting undressed – damn – because he'd been busy on some of his favourite websites. He opened the history page on the browser and then started deleting the addresses from the morning's surfing, one by one, without looking away from the TV. It was one thing Gabby knowing he looked at smut sites – how many blokes, left on their own in the house, wouldn't take a peek? – but he didn't particularly want her to know which ones. They were all pretty innocent, really, but that kind of information was strictly between a man and his hard drive.

It wasn't something he was proud of, but what else was he meant to do when he was working night shifts and he couldn't sleep properly and all his mates with normal jobs were at work? That, and chat rooms, kept him sane.

Wilbur the cat – Gabby's cat, really – wandered along the coffee table sniffing at the row of seven dirty mugs, before stopping next to the glass, which had a couple of inches of water at the bottom. He stuck his head into the glass, ears folded back, so that his chin nearly reached the liquid, and then poked out his pink tongue as far as it would go, just breaking the surface of the water.

Actually, boob girl wasn't that cute. In one of the close-ups he could swear he could see a hair growing out of one nipple, and one breast was clearly bigger than the other. He definitely preferred Gabby.

'It's quite normal,' said the stony-faced expert, 'for the shape and size to be slightly different on either side. It's the same with our hands, or our feet.'

The computer beeped, and he looked down; he'd deleted all today's pages. Quick e-mail check, then a sarnie, then maybe bed; he was on shift again in another five hours.

Your dick as big as a cricket bat, one promised. Delete. No need of any help in that direction.

College girls in the showers, they don't know you're watching!!!!!!!!!!!! Could be worth a look later, although he was willing to bet that, number one, they hadn't been to college any time recently and, number two, they had a hunch that someone was watching because of the camera crew filming them.

Friends Reunited. You've got mail.

Cool. He'd had a couple through so far, no one he remembered that well, but when Gabby signed up he'd done the same, no harm in it. He clicked it open.

Gary
Remember me? I remember you . . .
Get in touch – if you dare.
Tracey Mortimer xxx

The cat had given up on the remaining water, and started competing with the laptop for Gary's attention.

'Fucking hell, Wilbur,' Gary said to the cat. 'What does that bitch want?'

The cat purred at the attention.

Gary reread the message then shrugged.

'If she thinks I'm running back to her, after all these years, she can fuck right off,' he told the cat, deleted the message, and went to find the least dirty of the unwashed mugs to make himself another cup of tea.

CHAPTER SIX

The secret of a lasting marriage is spending as little time as possible together, which is why Dave and I are still a couple.

Sadly, every now and then there's some kind of Irish bank holiday, and Dave's dad sends him and the other builders back to England. There's no excuse now it costs less to fly back than it does to take the train from here into London.

'Daddeeeeeeee,' Kelly's shouting at the top of her voice, while poor Callum doesn't seem to recognise the balding fat bloke in the bright pink fleece. Wish I could have a memory lapse too, then I could get away with shutting the door in his face.

'Hello, sexy,' he says to me. There's a faint Irish lilt softening his annoying nasal tones. Sadly, it's not the only souvenir he's brought me back from the Emerald Isle. Though at least the dose of Celtic crabs gave me an excuse not to sleep with him for a while. It's six months now, and I can't say I miss it.

Must have been like this in the war, when the soldiers came home on leave expecting an amazing welcome, and the women resented the way all their plans and routines had to be swept away so the men could muscle back in.

If only Dave was off to the front line . . . with a bit of luck he might come back in a box. It sounds harsh, but I've had to switch off all the feelings I had for him. Call it self-preservation. When I married Dave, I was full of dreams and hope and all the other stuff that's been drained from me over the years. Takes two to keep dreams alive in a houseful of potties and Milton fluid, and he's never been the dreaming sort. At least when he's not here, neither of us has to pretend.

He'll be home 'on leave' for an entire, almost unbearable, three days and then bugger off back to the front line of Dublin's property boom, where the biggest danger he faces is a pickled liver. Even then, he's always moaning about how expensive the booze is over there.

So Dave makes up for it when he gets home, straight down the pub with his mates, which would suit me fine if he didn't then come rolling back expecting a shag.

When he tries it on once too often, I sneak into Kelly's bedroom and sleep on the bottom bunk, soothed by the sound of her breathing. She's always annoyed when she wakes up next day because she says the bed belongs to Jolene, her imaginary friend. I don't know how to take that; I never needed imaginary friends when I was her age, I had more than enough real ones.

The only good thing about Dave's return home this time round is that the local paper wants a photo of my happy family for this article they're doing about the reunion and the programme. They can put it across two editions, the one that covers the scummy old Crawley Park estate, and the one for round here (which is the posher part of town).

'It might help drum up a few more ex-pupils. The guest list could do with a bit of a boost,' Jenny said when she rang me about the feature.

'Yes,' I agreed. 'I think the problem is that most of the kids I got on best with in the year aren't nerdy enough to be online.'

What's terrifying is that now I've got the loan of this laptop, I'm turning into a computer nerd myself. Though I'm disappointed, too. I'm surprised every time I log on, which is roughly once an hour, that I haven't got a full inbox. I've sent about twenty messages now through Friends Reunited, and I've had precisely two back. One was to this kid I vaguely remembered because Melody snogged him at a house party in the fourth year, and he e-mailed to say he didn't really remember me, but had I been Melody's mate, 'you know, the school bike?', which was spot-on, but not very charitable. He'd be interested in coming to a reunion, though, and if I wanted to pass on his name to the production company, he'd give them a quote to build a website just for the programme, because that's what he does for a living.

The only other person to reply is Helen Boris-Morris-Norris, who was sickly sweet in her e-mail. She'd been one of the first people to put her name down on the site and she was really chuffed that more ex-Crawley Parkers were joining up. She'd had about a dozen people contact her via the Web now, and it would be lovely to catch up on the good old days.

I don't get it. How come Boris has got all these e-mails, and I haven't? I reckon she's exaggerating, but, anyway, she said she'd put the word round about the reunion. She's feeling pretty isolated, because she's moved with her husband to a village ten miles from Bracewell, and he's away a lot, and she's had to give up work early because her blood pressure's been on the high side since she's been pregnant.

Just you wait, love, I wanted to e-mail back. You ain't seen nothing yet. Welcome to the glorious world of Mummy martyrdom.

The non-reply I'm most pissed off about is Gary's. Though I suppose I can't blame him.

'Some of the e-mail addresses on there might be out of date,' Jenny said, and she could be right, I suppose. The lack of info about him on the site means all I can do is fantasise about his life now.

Which I'm ashamed to admit I do rather a lot. Sometimes we're back at school, and he's much the same as he is on the photo I've got of us all on a day trip to Brighton in the fourth year, except his skin is clear. In reality, just as Gary's handsome jaw started emerging from the pretty-boy puppy fat, he was struck by acne. He was still the best-looking lad in the year, everyone knew that, but all those hormones erupted in red spots across his chin and cheeks. No one dared to call him pizza face, not with me as his girlfriend, but I did worry sometimes that when we were kissing, a pustule might explode, and bind us together a bit like those rubber suckers you get to stick hooks to the wall.

What with the acne and the mint-green uniforms, it's a mystery to me how any of us ever got to the snogging stage.

My fantasies now don't involve snogging. Instead, we're on the same trip to Brighton, but in this version we go down to the end of the pier and he gets down on one knee and proposes, and I agree, provided we can travel the world together. And then it all kind of goes fuzzy, like in a film, and we're sipping cocktails on Bondi beach, or another time we're on top of the Empire State Building, or he's buying me an engagement ring at Tiffany's.

No sex, no snogging, only the kind of soft-focus canoodling they used to put in the black and white photo-stories that made us crease up.

It's so different from my daydreams then. Me and Melody and the others, we were constantly wanting to get to the next stage of being grown up, and because it was what the teachers warned us about, we figured that next stage was fags and booze and sex. Mainly sex. Back in the eighties, before the average seven-year-old could look up everything from golden showers to bestiality on the Web, we were touchingly naïve, as well as insatiably curious. Sex was the final frontier. So we mocked the kids like Suzanne, who thought carefully about their options and even paid attention in careers lessons. We couldn't believe it when she let slip that she wanted to go to university but before that she was going to go travelling, to Australia and India.

It was like she'd stepped off another planet, and we never let her forget it. She kept quiet about her plans after that. We couldn't see why you'd bother to sit on a plane for days when we all knew the only down under worth exploring was located midway between the waist and the knees.

I guess now I've done enough shagging to realise that it doesn't make the earth move – all it does is take you on a one-way ticket to stirrups and the speculum, whether the end result is a baby or a nasty rash – suddenly that other Down Under seems unbearably appealing.

'I can't believe they're putting you on this programme,' Dave says, as the photographer tries to coax Callum into joining the charming family scene around the dining table.

'Why not?'

'Well, for a start, you'll bore everyone to death like you do me, with all your stupid stories about school.'

'I think you'll find it's my amusing anecdotes that made them choose me, actually. It's a bit more interesting than tales from the building site, you loser.'

I look at my miserable husband, and wonder yet again what Gary's doing now. He can't have joined the police, not after what he did. They won't take anyone with a record, will they? Maybe he's gone into car dealing or something. He always did have the gift of the gab.

I could have been living in a lovely detached house, nothing vulgar, maybe something Victorian, with a gorgeous BMW or a Merc in the drive. Except do Victorian houses have drives?

'. . . and when we meet the troll, he'll give us Cadbury's chocolate buttons.' Kelly is quite still, talking to the imaginary Jolene, who seems to be sitting in mid-air, somewhere to the left of my ear.

If I'd had Gary's kids, I bet I'd have had a boy first, and the photographer would probably be taking photos outside while Gary and our son . . . OK, what would suit the surname Coombs? God knows I used to play around writing our future children's names on my pencil case all the time in lessons. Jason, that sounds nice. So while Gary and Jason kicked a football around on our large decked garden, I'd be standing proudly next to them with a cafetiere full of fresh-brewed coffee. And at my side, there'd be an angelic little girl with gold ringlets, and a 'butter-wouldn't melt' smile the same as mine, offering the reporter and photographer cups of tea from an antique doll's tea set and learning to flirt.

I turn to the reporter. 'She's not normally any trouble. Kelly, stop chuntering.'

'I'm only talking to Jolene.'

'That's her little friend, you know, a made-up one. My mum's got all the old Dolly Parton LPs, so that's who we've got to thank.'

The reporter nods. I don't think he's listening. 'Can I just run through a few things with you for the article, then Derek'll take his snaps, and we'll leave you in peace?'

'Sure. What do you want to know?'

'Jenny from the TV company says you're planning the reunion for July, is that right? Seventeen years after you all left?'

'Uh-huh. That's right. We were the class of '84.'

'And how many people are you hoping will make it?'

'Well. There were getting on for two hundred and fifty in our year group, but it's obviously been a long time, so I'd be pleased if we got anything over a hundred and fifty.'

'Right. And are there any people you're hoping you might see that you've lost touch with completely?'

Who do I want to see, except Gary? The person I miss most is the real Tracey Mortimer, but she doesn't exist any more. Years of nappies, arguments and cashing-up in the stationery shop have made sure of that.

And of course, I miss Shrimp. The sound of her voice – I can still remember it now, surprisingly deep coming from such a skinny person, but always with a smile in every word, as though she was telling the punch line to the funniest joke ever. She's the one I long to share my adventures with. Of all the people I've called my friends over the years, she's the only one who'd dare to tell me what she thinks I should do about my kids, my marriage, my job. And she's the only one I'd bother to listen to. But even the Internet, and all the resources of Smart Alec Productions, would struggle with reincarnation.

'God, it's so hard. I'd like to see anyone from the days when 5G ruled the world! Tell them to get in touch with me – have you got the e-mail address?'

'Yep, the researcher sent it to me. And what about you' – the reporter checks his notes – 'uh, Dave? You're not worried Tracey might hit it off again with an old flame, childhood sweetheart?' He looks at us mischievously, his pen poised to jot down any good quotes in his notebook.

Dave turns to me, then back to face the journalist.

'I don't think anyone's going to meet Tracey now, and be sad they'd let her slip through their fingers, do you?'

And as the reporter and photographer exchange nervous

looks, unsure whether this is a joke, Dave helpfully tries to clear things up. 'But if they do, they're welcome. And please print *that* in your paper. Could be my lucky day.'

CHAPTER SEVEN

'Don't wanna get up,' Kelly says yet again, and it's one of those times when I almost sympathise with people who leave their children on church doorsteps. Only 'almost', of course, because otherwise I'd be a horrible parent and deserve the most terrible punishments, but I really wish it was acceptable to use a dummy to shut up a six-year-old. Come to think of it, if they sold husband-sized dummies too, I'd be over the moon.

'Kelly, there are a lot of things in life we don't want to do, but unfortunately we still have to do them.'

Holy shit, where did my mother appear from? Except I never moaned about going to school, my whingeing was always about homework or tidying my room or going to see her dad in the special hospital at Christmas, because he used to want to play peek-a-boo and that scared me because he was sixty-three.

Kelly's got worse since Dave went back to Ireland, so that's another thing I can blame on him. Except, for all his faults – and there are plenty – he doesn't carry the shyness gene any more than I do.

I feel so frustrated, because I don't know how to respond, and to be fair to Kelly, it doesn't look like a hell of a lot of fun for her either. At night she's lovely. I put her to bed and she does as she's told, and she makes the right kind of noises when I read a story, and kisses me nicely, and doesn't wet the bed.

But then overnight, she's transformed into a six-year-old

teenager. She's moody and surly, and everything's a battle. Getting her out of bed is the first skirmish – she insists she's ill or feels hot, and yet she's always a nice temperature, biscuity skin, not clammy or chilly. Her attempts to look poorly – half-closed eyes and fake-limp arms – are always betrayed by the colour in her cheeks.

Then I have to prise Bear from her, this disgusting toy that was once the colour of honey, and is now the colour of cow-pat. I occasionally manage to wash it, but only if she can sit and watch it going round and round the machine. She waves and sings Dolly Parton songs at Bear, as it bounces about in the foamy water, and if she doesn't see its face for more than about ten seconds, she panics, and we both sit on the floor holding our breath until the revolution of the drum propels its cracked plastic nose back towards the window.

It probably took scores of child slaves in the Far East less time to make her uniform than it does to cajole her into it, and that's not counting her shoes. She moves downstairs a step at a time, as though each one is a huge ordeal, and it's the same with every single spoon of her cereal. For a while, she tried deliberately spilling food on to her pinafore dress; I think she thought it would make her so late I wouldn't bother to take her to school at all. I lost my temper the first couple of times, which I'm not proud of, but it was so frustrating to have to clean her up as well as Callum. And then I had a brainwave, and stopped her in her tracks by making her wear a baby's bib. It was more than her pride could take.

'Not hungry.' That's the latest variation, and it's slightly more effective in raising my stress levels, because they say anorexia can affect the under-tens these days, and it's just a hunch, but I'd say Kelly has the right kind of stubborn nervous temperament to get herself into that sort of mess. I try to chase the thought away, in case thinking makes it happen, but it's too late.

We had an anorexic at school, Rachel Clark, and she was quite handy to have as a mate because she never spent her dinner money, and when word got back that she didn't buy any lunch, her mum would send her in with all sorts of goodies – Wagon Wheels, Dairylea triangles, those tiny packets of Sun-Maid raisins – and she was always desperate to offload them at break time.

Rachel: there's another possible guest, if she hasn't faded to nothing by now. I'm keeping a list on the fridge of people I suddenly remember, so Jenny and Annabel can have a go at tracing them. They've got this amazing computer program that means they can type in someone's name and it'll come up with their address or phone number, or all the people of that name in Britain, anyway.

I haven't asked them if they've looked up Gary yet. Half of me wants him to turn up at the reunion, sweep me off my feet. And half of me's too worried that I couldn't deal with the disappointment if he didn't live up to my expectations . . .

Smart Alec Productions, Beak Street, Soho, Central London

Jenny tried to stay calm. Maybe she was misreading Alec. After all, he hadn't said a word since she'd entered the meeting room.

Then again, he didn't need to. The man oozed malevolence from every pore. Annabel hovered with the tray of coffees, and the china clinked together because her hands seemed to be shaking.

'Put that fucking thing down before you drop it. You're in enough shit already without giving yourself first-degree burns.'

'Come on,' Jenny started, 'it's not that bad, we're starting to build up a good guest list and the agents for a couple of the bands have—'

'Not that bad?' Alec snorted so fiercely that she wouldn't have been surprised if flames had poured through his nostrils. Though Jenny thought that level of nasal aggression was high-risk behaviour for a guy with such a heavy coke habit. 'Not that bad?'

They waited.

'Not that bad, that we're now two months from this bloody reunion and a, we don't have a band to play, b, we don't have any human interest stories and c, the woman you assured me was the most popular girl in the school has so far failed to make contact with any of her enormous group of so-called best mates. Yeah, I suppose you're right really. At least we don't have to fix the hole in the ozone layer as well, or we really would be in trouble.'

Jenny sighed. 'I know it looks a lot to sort out on paper, but think about it another way. A month ago we didn't even have a reunion or a school to work on. The head teacher's said yes to us holding the party in the hall, we've got the registers from all the tutor groups in Tracey's year, she's great on camera and we've got loads of press interest. We can even play up the jeopardy of it in the show itself, the danger that she might be alone on her trip down Memory Lane.'

'It's not in the proposal.' Alec hated deviating from the carefully crafted commissioning document that had sold the idea to the channel in the first place.

'Sometimes things don't work like the proposal,' Jenny said gently. 'But that just makes things more fun. And Annabel has been checking out some other ideas.' She nudged Annabel.

'Yes, yeah. Um, for example. Well, why don't we take Tracey back into school? That'd make a nice sequence as she meets the new staff and the kids from 1G these days? There are a couple of teachers who remember her.'

Alec doodled on the side of the manila file, grinding his pen in zigzag patterns. But at least he hadn't interrupted them.

Jenny checked her notes. 'And I know you're worried we haven't heard back from Melody, but this other girl, Helen, was in the same class and she's very sweet and willing to do filming, plus she's pregnant, so that's human interest.'

Alec snorted, but less ferociously than before. 'We still need the band. We still need an old boyfriend.'

'Well, Annabel has had some encouraging noises from Madness, and you know that they're the ones we had in the original pitch to Channel 5. We might even get Suggs to be compère. And we think we've tracked down Gary. There are a few on the electoral register, but the most likely suspect is living in London, and we're going to write to him. So that's cool. And we had another idea.'

Alec buried his head in his hands, but then peered out between his fingers. 'Oh, God, am I ready for this?'

'Annabel and I thought, you know how in *Big Brother* they had those psychologists, that kind of made it look a bit more upmarket? So we thought, why don't we take Tracey to meet one, interview them herself and then she might have some amazing insight into the reasons behind school reunions and her own need to look back at the past, and even if she doesn't, we've got another sequence to pad out the film.'

Annabel was nodding enthusiastically. 'And you can bet BBC2 haven't thought of it!'

He looked at the two women and then up at the ceiling. 'OK. Whatever. But it's still down to you both to get it working. As the most experienced member of staff on this programme, I'm not taking the rap for cocking up the most straightforward commission Smart Alec Productions has ever had.'

Acton High Street, West London

Roger was bloody hard work compared to Gary's usual sidekick, but since Colin was nutted by a football thug, and was being lined up as a test case for mental injury by the over-ambitious Police Federation rep, Roger was as good as it was going to get.

'Oh, great,' Roger said as two Japanese women with dyed pink hair headed purposefully towards them, wielding a camera. 'I can't believe any tourists would stay on the Central line as far as Acton. I knew I should have combed my hair before I came out.'

'Come on, Rog, there are worse ordeals than posing with a couple of students.' One woman's nose was freshly pierced with a safety pin – they must have been to Camden Market. The other, who had matching black nails and lips, proffered her camera.

Gary stepped into position between the girls while Roger tried to work out which button to press. Pierced nose turned to Gary in irritation.

'No, no, with cuffs, with cuffs.'

Roger raised one eyebrow. 'You sure this isn't a set-up? Like *You've Been Framed*?'

Gary looked nervously at the tourists, then unbuttoned his jacket far enough to be able to flash the handcuffs. Pierced Nose lunged for them but he moved aside. 'No, you're not having them. It's this or nothing.' She moved back, and stood sulkily while Black Lips grinned for the camera.

As they walked off, waving, Gary shrugged. 'It's nice to keep the public happy, though, isn't it, Rog?'

Rog shrugged then looked mournfully up at the sky. 'Gonna rain soon. Just our sodding luck.'

Gary mumbled his agreement. This bobby on the beat stuff – sorry, high visibility community policing – was fine for about a month a year, in between the spring showers and the August heatwave. But May was unpredictable.

He racked his brains to think of something to talk about. He used to natter for hours with Colin about nothing in particular; they were as bad as old women, and even called each other old lady nicknames, Gladys and Coleen, but Coleen wasn't going to be back for at least a month, longer if the Fed bloke had his way.

Hobbies. Well, when did Gary have time for hobbies? Roger probably fished or train-spotted, but Gary struggled to think of his own prime non-work occupation. Drinking? That only counted as a pastime if you went for the fine wines option (hardly possible on a constable's wage, even with overtime) or the real ale option (not much better than angling). What about porn? That was the closest Gary got to a hobby, and he didn't want to risk telling Roger. Either he'd freak, or he'd divulge his own particular preferences. Horrible thought.

Indirectly, due to it being such a prime source of porn, the Web was also his hobby, but something told him Roger was a Luddite. There was precious little he could relate to when he watched *The Bill*, but they'd got grumpy Reg Hollis dead right: Roger would have been his twin separated at birth.

Then he thought of something anyone could relate to.

'Rog? Are you still in touch with anyone you went to school with?'

Roger thought it over as they trudged past the row of shops

and the baskets of past-their-best fruit and veg, sitting exposed to the pinching fingers of passing shoppers, and the poisonous fumes of passing lorries.

Roger seemed to be chewing: he reminded Gary of a cow in a field.

'No one.' Then he stopped, peered in through the window of a mini-mart, making everyone inside freeze as if they were playing grandmother's footsteps. 'Unless you count my missus.'

'Your wife? You were at school with your wife?'

'Only in the juniors. Went to a boys' school after that.'

'So was it love at first sight?'

'Wouldn't say it's love any time. She's a good sport, though. Doesn't moan like most women.'

Gary watched Roger as he carried on chewing the air. Mrs Roger was clearly a saint.

'Morning, Mr Mirchandani,' Gary said, nodding at the guy standing in the doorway of the newsagent's shop, who stood there most of the day, chain-smoking Marlboro Lights, most of his profit margin going up in smoke.

They walked a bit further, and it was clear Roger wasn't going to ask Gary the same question in return. So Gary decided to answer it anyway.

'You see, I've been thinking about some of the people I was at school with, lately.'

No response at all. But sometimes it still helped to say things out loud, especially stuff you weren't sure about, even if the other person wasn't listening.

'Well, one particular person, actually. My first girlfriend.'

Roger smiled knowingly.

'So. Yeah, you see, this girl. Tracey.' He found it hard not to say the word without spitting. 'Suddenly, out of the blue, this e-mail. Like it hadn't been seventeen years since she'd last been in touch, just "Hi, how are you?" Or something like that.'

Remember me? I remember you . . .
Get in touch – if you dare.

He'd tried to forget the message, but it kept popping up again in his head. Especially those last three words. *If you dare.* They taunted him when he was doing the washing-up, teased him when he was bored after the night shift, mocked him when Gabby told him to watch the speed limit.

Gabby would never get in a car with him ever again if she knew the truth.

God knows it had taken him long enough to get Tracey out of his system when they were sixteen, and it felt now as though she'd never gone at all, had just been lodging somewhere in his body, like a cold sore virus, waiting to reappear when he was at a low ebb.

'I mean, what made her do that? This is what I can't work out. I never could work her out. Women. But then it's not *all* women, is it, because my girlfriend, she's totally predictable. In a nice way.'

Roger stopped again. 'Lad,' he said, and Gary braced himself for what Rog obviously thought was going to be the wise counsel of a man of the world. 'Lad, if you haven't heard from her in seventeen years, and she's got under your skin like that again after all that time, I've only got one suggestion.'

'Yeah?'

'Move house before she comes looking for you.'

Millennium Child Campaign, Clapham Common, South-West London

Suzanne Marshall-Sharp clicked on to the one-week view on her PC organiser screen, then shook her salon-fresh red hair. A waft of expensive organic herbal conditioner drifted up from her curls, so she did it again. Yes, this was definitely a *good* hair day.

'Charlotte, we're going to have to cancel the Women's Institute. I don't like to let them down, but they're a captive audience, whereas the CBI . . . well, we're not going to get a platform like that again in a hurry, never mind right before Tony's keynote address on education.'

Just outside the window, a pigeon stopped on the ledge and peered in through the enormous warehouse windows.

'It's weird how you never see *baby* pigeons, isn't it?' Suzanne chewed her Cross fountain pen, then pulled off a Post-it note, and wrote 'Baby Pigeon'. 'I might use that in my speech. "Like baby pigeons, we want our young to be neither seen nor heard, until they can fend for themselves." It's quite a nice analogy.'

Charlotte scratched behind her left ear, as she always did when she was stressed. 'Sorry, can I just clarify? When you said *we're* going to have to cancel the WI, did you actually mean that I will have to call them and break the news?'

'Well, er, that is your job, Charlotte.'

'I know, but I hate turning people down, especially when there's hardly any notice for them to find anyone else.'

'OK, look, I'll call Floella, she loves those things, she might do it, for the cause. Don't suppose *she's* got an invite from the CBI.'

The three office phones rang suddenly, and the pigeon flapped away. Suzanne stared at the flashing light, then looked meaningfully at her PA, the unspoken 'it is your job, Charlotte', hanging in the air between them.

'Millennium Child Campaign, good morning!' Charlotte said brightly.

Suzanne smiled in satisfaction at the greeting; it had just the right combination of popular appeal and sincerity. Just like Princess Diana. Now she would have been the perfect patron.

Charlotte waved at her. 'Hello, Mrs Sharp. I think she's available, let me see if I can put you through.'

Suzanne felt her neck tighten as the extension on her desk started to purr. She took a deep breath.

'Hi, Mum. Bit busy right now. Sorting out a big speech.'

'Yeah, too busy to talk to me, I know. That's all right.' Mrs Sharp's London overspill vowels spilled out of the receiver. Suzanne had adopted a modified version of the accent, a hint that her background had more to offer than Roedean and Trinity College, without the ugly certainty of new town vowels. 'But I thought you'd be interested in something I spotted in the *Bugle*.'

Suzanne doubted anything her mother could tell her would be interesting, but she'd have to hear it some time. And at least being her own boss meant no one could tell her off for taking personal calls in 'work time'.

'It's Crawley Park. Your school.'

Well, yes, obviously, even my memory's not that short, thought Suzanne. Probably about to be closed down by a government hit squad, assuming the little buggers hadn't burned it down themselves.

'Not just your school, but your year, the ones who started in 1979.'

1979. The first year of Thatcher's reign. The year that, if you traced it back, probably started Suzanne on her journey, via 1G, college and psychologist training, to chief executive of the Millennium Child Campaign (supported by Cherie Booth QC).

'Hmm, what about them?'

'Well, they're having a reunion in July. And it's going to be on telly.'

Oh, God, any minute now she'll suggest I should go, Suzanne realised, and started inventing midsummer weddings and pagan rituals and dinner parties in Downing Street to cover all thirty-one days of the month.

'And I wouldn't even have called you but then I saw who was organising it.' Mrs Sharp paused, as if she knew the effect the two words would have. 'Tracey Mortimer.'

The room went a strange off-white. Time seemed to stop.

'Helloo? Are you there?'

Her hand went limp, and the receiver fell on to the desk. Charlotte looked up in alarm.

'Are you OK? Suzanne? You look as though you've seen a ghost.'

CHAPTER EIGHT

It always amazes me that teachers don't feature on those surveys of the public's most hated professions, along with dentists and insurance salesmen and tabloid reporters and politicians. People slag off dentists for being sadists, and the rest for being a bloody nuisance, but I think that to become a teacher means you have the desire to dominate and terrify small children, which is hardly healthy.

There are exceptions – the odd teacher who treats you as an equal, like Bob Carmichael. But generally, I think the profession stinks.

I'm hoping it doesn't show. Kelly's teacher Mrs Fellowes has summoned me to school, and I know the one thing guaranteed to bring out the worst in teachers is 'lack of respect'. What makes them think they deserve it automatically is a mystery to me.

Mind you, I can't deny that my heart leapt when Kelly gave me the note. The average mother would hate the idea that their little darling was causing enough trouble to merit a letter home, but for me, it's the first sign that she might be a chip off the old block after all.

I was always in trouble. I remember the feeling I used to have when I knew Mum was on her way home from yet another appointment with the head teacher: part dread, but also part excitement. I liked to be in trouble. It proved I'd never just be another no-hoper in a mint-green jumper.

But it can't have been easy for my mum. I can imagine the nudges from the two witches in the school office, the comments, 'You again, *Mrs* Mortimer?' and the whispers she was always meant to hear, as she waited outside the head's office. *'On her own, she is. And you know what they say about the lack of a father figure . . . that Tracey certainly needs a father's hand taken to her.'*

Most of the time when she arrived back, she'd just give me this look, as though she was completely confused by the idea that she could have played a part in creating the kind of kid the head teacher had just described. Maybe she told herself it was all from my dad's side. None of it was serious – fights in the sand pit, kiss-chase, playing silly tricks on people – but I denied it all. Much easier that way, and anyway half the things that Mum would repeat back to me in this weary voice I didn't even remember doing.

The only incident I remember in any detail was when I was about Kelly's age. Maybe I'd have been seven because it was June, and I'd have had my birthday in the March.

I'd been trying hard not to let on that I was upset while everyone around me made their Father's Day cards, pretending to myself that if I concentrated hard enough, I could make a card so special that Dad would actually appear. My fantasy dad, tall as a giant, with big hairy arms and a deep gruff voice that would only speak gently to me. He'd pull a box from behind his back and unravel a bow holding the lid on, letting me open it up to free the kitten inside.

My card had a cut-out of a man, a film star, and a box I'd painted in bright orange, and a kitten from the Victorian decoupage pictures the teacher had brought in. As a finishing touch, I was going to add blue glitter, like magic dust, to make it real.

Shirley Bishop, who thought she was a cut above because her mum was a dinner lady, nudged me, and nearly knocked over my glue pot.

'Dunno why you're making a card at all,' she said, loud enough for the whole table to hear. 'My mum says you don't even have a dad.'

'So do,' I snarled back, after a few seconds passed, and the shock wore off.

She'd seen it in my face, though. 'You so DON'T.'

I could feel my eyes stinging, and a tear dropped on to the box, smudging the orange lines. 'DO!' I shouted this time. It should have been a warning to her.

'Do-on't have a daddy,' she laughed back at me, sing-song provocation. 'Tracey's got no daddy, what do you have on Sunday? *No Father's Day?*'

I picked up the vial of blue glitter, carefully poured a small heap on to the glue trail I'd prepared around the edges of the card, and sprinkled off the excess on to the old newspapers below. And then I threw the rest of the tube's contents as hard as I could into Shirley Bishop's eyes. Her scream was the most satisfying thing I'd ever heard.

Mum was angry with me when the teacher told her, and she got angrier when I tried to explain. After she sent me to bed early, I could hear her crying downstairs, and then Granddad arrived, and brought me up toast. He understood. That was just before he went funny and they had to put him in the home.

That Christmas, Mum told me Dad would never be back because he had died in a car crash, along with the lady he'd gone to live with when I was a baby. I wasn't upset after that, because at least I never expected him to be there. And if anyone asked why I didn't have a father, I could just say he was dead, not that he'd left us.

But I always make Father's Day cards with the kids, even though Dave doesn't deserve one. I don't think they make them in class any more, not now half the kids come from one-parent families. They can say what they like about me at the school, and I bet they say plenty, but at least I've made sure my kids have two parents, despite the cost to me.

Some things don't change, though. Kelly's school smells of cabbage and disinfectant, and the brick walls are painted in shiny cream and khaki, and the floors are grey and slippery from millions of plimsolled footsteps. I admit I like the uniform here, the mole-coloured pinafore dress and the pale blue blouse with the round collar; she looks adorable in it, though I would have hated it at Kelly's age.

They've made an effort to brighten things up, with the obligatory drawings and projects, endless variations on the same themes: the Romans, mini-beasts (known in my day as insects) and Harry Potter. But the primary colours can't really disguise the fact that it's not fun, it's education, and they're two very different things.

I can see Mrs Fellowes through the glass panel in the door, and when I knock, it rattles in the frame. She smiles as she looks up, which surprises me, because I was expecting a hard stare.

'Hello, Mrs Brown, thank you for coming in,' she says and smiles again. She has tiny teeth; perhaps she was such a careful little girl that she never even lost her milk teeth.

'Do sit down.' She gestures towards the only other adult-sized chair in the room. From this distance I realise she must be much younger than she looks – no wrinkles on her make-up-free skin. All I can smell is sickly perfume, Lily of the Valley or Hyacinth, the sort of scent that you usually only smell combined with an acid top note of urine, in old people's homes.

'Now, what I want to talk to you about might be a bit of a shock to start with, so please realise that it's quite natural for you to feel upset, or even a little angry. But what we need to do is concentrate on what's in Kelly's best interests.'

Her face is all bunched up like a hamster's and I don't have a clue what she's talking about.

'Um, OK, yeah, well, that's what I want, obviously,' I say, then I wait.

'Kelly's a lovely little girl, really lovely,' and she pauses, as if I'm likely to disagree.

I notice that I feel very cold, even though it's a mild day and the monster-sized radiator along the classroom window is blazing.

'Very bright. And *very* hard-working.' And she smiles as though she is bestowing a huge compliment. But there's something about the way she's emphasising my daughter's goodness that isn't right.

'I wonder, has Kelly said anything to you at home about how she feels about school?'

It's never even occurred to me that she might. Can you really talk about that kind of thing to a six-year-old? We have so little in common that what we talk about is favourite colours and why she can't have a guinea pig.

'No. She's not a chatty child, but . . .' I rack my brains to find a comment that might show I do take some notice of my first-born child. 'She enjoys her reading, doesn't she?'

'Yes, she does. She's doing very well in the literacy hour.' Mrs Fellowes doesn't look as happy now. 'So you have no real concerns, then?' Her eyes narrow and it's clear she thinks I should be concerned. And something tells me this meeting has nothing to do with misbehaviour.

I shake my head and Mrs Fellowes takes a weary breath. 'Well, Mrs Brown, you see, I – not just me, actually, I've spoken to the playground supervisors and the head. So, *we* are rather concerned that . . . well, there's no easy way of saying this . . .'

SO JUST BLOODY SAY IT, I'm thinking.

'We think Kelly may have fallen victim to bullying.'

Kensington Roof Gardens, Central London

Suzanne read the menu of her favourite restaurant for the fifth time, and realised there was nothing there she wanted to eat. She threw it back on to the glass table.

Christian reached out to touch her hand, tickling the underside of her palm before she snatched it back.

'Christian, it's no use you trying to understand, because you won't.'

'Suz,' he said gently, 'I don't think that's very fair. You haven't even tried to tell me. All I know is that there's a school reunion and you're pissed off about it. So try explaining.'

She still couldn't quite believe that she was married to this perfect specimen of New Manhood, but this was the first time she'd ever felt a problem would be beyond him.

'It's not that I want to keep anything from you. But . . . OK, what's the worst memory you've got from school?' Suzanne sat back and waited, while he screwed up his adorable light hazel eyes, concentrating on the past. Of course, in Christian's case, school had been a much more recent experience.

'Well, um . . . I was pretty miserable when I first started boarding.'

There was always that, the suffering of the small boy sent away from his parents to a life of beatings and buggery. But it was a particular variety of upper-middle-class suffering so universal in Christian's contemporaries that it seemed more of a badge of honour than something to be ashamed of.

Suzanne shrugged, then gave in to his open face, and stretched both hands back across the table towards her husband. 'I'm not denigrating that, I think it's cruel and unnecessary and unforgivable—'

The waiter approached them. 'Order for me, Christian,' she said, and he selected comfort food, bruschetta and risotto and the waiter left them to it again.

She traced patterns on the glass with her finger, then looked out across the London skyline. She shivered. Maybe it was too early to sit outside. 'It's so hard. Bloody ridiculous as well. I've always talked for a living, haven't I? About exactly this kind of thing. It's probably why I even ended up doing the whole psychology degree and the public speaking and . . . oh, God.'

Christian was concentrating with every cell of his twenty-five-year-old body, willing her to explain, and himself to understand.

'I suppose what I'm saying is that actually, what I am now, it's mainly down to that fucking bitch.' Suzanne banged the table in frustration, then looked around her in embarrassment, suddenly aware of how loud her voice had become.

Christian smiled at her. 'Well, darling, in that case, I for one would love to meet Tracey Mortimer, and thank her very much indeed.'

'Bullying?' It makes no sense. Kelly, being bullied. She's six, for God's sake.

'Yes, I know it must come as a bit of a shock.'

It would be a shock if I actually believed Mrs Fellowes. But it's stupid to talk about kids of six being bullied, especially my Kelly.

'You've got it wrong. Kelly's fine. I'm the first to admit she's not the most outgoing kid, which is bizarre, because you can't shut me up, or her dad. But *bullying*?'

'Mrs Brown, I'm not talking about anything physical, so please don't worry about that. We're just concerned that Kelly is . . .' Mrs Fellowes is waving her hands around now, and it's almost making me laugh because she's flustering over something that's clearly complete rubbish.

'Is what?'

'Kelly's . . . different. Yes, she's quiet and there's nothing wrong with that – in itself. I – I mean, we are worried that maybe she doesn't really have the, how shall I put it, the social skills to make the most of school?'

Now this is getting surreal. First of all she's saying that her school is a kiddy war zone where infants go round threatening each other, and now she thinks Kelly's *backward*.

'What the hell is this about? Is this because I'm not in the bloody PTA?'

'Mrs Brown . . .' Every time she says my name I want to punch her, and I'm really not a violent person. But the way she drags it out, it's as though even speaking my name is too tiring. 'That's just silly. Now, we're sure that Kelly's at no risk, and we're introducing Circle Time into classes right across the school anyway, which gives all the children a chance to explore how they're feeling, so it could easily blow over. But I thought it was right to let you know, see if you might want to have a chat with Kelly. And depending on what she says, we might think about doing some . . . work with her.'

'Work?'

'The school has a close relationship with the Educational Psychology Service, and we do find that early intervention can prevent an awful lot of problems that might—'

'A psychiatrist? You think my daughter needs a shrink? You're off your head yourself.'

She gives me a long, long stare, then sighs and stands up. 'I don't think we're getting anywhere, Mrs Brown. It does seem this has come out of the blue.'

She rummages around in this enormous handbag she's got on her desk, and pulls out a leaflet. On the front there's a cartoon picture of various children, different skin colours, all grinning like maniacs. A big heading reads: '*Does your child need special help?*'

'Mrs Brown, why not take this away with you, and if you're interested in what you read, well, come back to me.'

I want to snatch the booklet and tear it up in front of her and stamp up and down on it, but I reckon she'd absolutely *love* it if I did that, so instead I tuck it away in my coat pocket.

She sighs again. 'We're only trying to help Kelly enjoy her time with us . . . and we do really need your co-operation to make that happen, Mrs Brown.'

I can't bring myself to reply to her, and it's a good job, because I think if I was capable of speech at this exact moment, what I'd say would not be very mature. It's all I can manage to get out of the door and not slam it so hard that the glass smashes out on to the floor.

'Good choice,' said Suzanne, as the rich risotto started to work soothing carbohydrate magic on her stressed nerves. 'Sorry to be so moody. I can't believe that just hearing her name has such an effect after all this time.'

'Kind of proves your case about the consequences of a crap time at school, though.'

'I did think I'd left it all behind but I suppose I never will. God, she was such a cow, but I don't think she had the . . . humanity to know what she was doing. Every single bloody day,

I hoped she wouldn't be there, that she'd be ill or move house or . . . I think I wanted her to die, actually. Or if she didn't, maybe I would.'

Christian leaned across the table to kiss her cheek. 'Poor Suz.'

'And I've met enough kids since who've had it so much worse, really unimaginable stuff, and it makes me doubt myself. If this still gets to me, even now, then perhaps we're wasting our time trying to help them.'

'That's so typical of you, Suz, thinking about other people at a time like this.'

They shared the smile of a couple utterly convinced that no one else was as lucky as they had been, in finding one another.

'Years of conditioning.'

'But maybe, Suz, maybe it's fate that it's happened now, so that you can finally put it behind you. Perhaps now that we're thinking about bringing our own little Suzes and Christians into the world . . . ?'

She played with the remaining clumps of risotto on her plate. 'I'm sorry, Christian. But all this makes it even less likely that now's the right time.' It was their one source of disharmony, and there was little sign of progress.

Christian pouted sadly. 'But, you said it yourself, at the inaugural charity dinner, in fact, we have to move on from our pasts, into our futures.'

Just occasionally, his naïveté failed to be utterly charming.

'I know. But that was before Tracey Mortimer came back into my life.' Then she stopped. A little of the steeliness she'd discovered since surviving school began to surge. 'Perhaps you're right, Christian. Perhaps this *is* fate. Perhaps this time I can make sure she won't get the upper hand . . .'

CHAPTER NINE

Today Boris is coming to tea. You'd think it was the royal family, the way Jenny and Annabel are behaving. And of course, they'll be recording the entire thing.

'She's really keen,' Jenny told me when she rang to fix a date, 'and we think it'll make a great sequence early on in the film.'

That's all they talk about, 'sequences' and 'structure', and I feel more and more like a performing seal. I always knew there was bound to be more to TV than you see on screen, but it's unbelievable the amount of acting they want me to do . . . I should be eligible for an Oscar at the end of all this.

'Could you try to look a bit more enthusiastic?' Annabel says, while Jamie films me buttering some rolls, and I wonder why she thinks making sandwiches should produce a state of ecstasy. She seems unimpressed by the idea that anyone should be 'just' a housewife, yet also seems to expect me to be as satisfied with my lot as a fifties domestic goddess. But Nigella Lawson I ain't.

Alec's busy in London doing whatever producers do – which according to the girls mainly involves *doing* illegal substances – so Jenny's in charge of filming today. I definitely get the impression they're disappointed in me. She's mooning around with the look of a parent who's invested a fortune in public schooling, only for her little cherub to end up working in an off-licence.

'I'm sure it's going to be fine,' she says all the time, in a voice that suggests the opposite. 'But we thought it would be nice to get you and Helen together, and Helen does seem to be in touch with a few more people.'

Which seems like a nice way of saying, where are all your mates? I must admit I thought it'd be easier than this, but the thing about people like Helen is that they're classic Christmas card senders. At school, she was big and pink, like Ermintrude from *The Magic Roundabout*, but very kind, and even in those days, sent cards to everyone, birthdays, Easter, any excuse, cheap Woolworths boxfuls, full of cheery insincere messages signed off with 'lots of love and kisses'. She even gave them to Suzanne, and most people wouldn't so much as speak to that silly cow, never mind give her cards.

I might even have had a few myself in the early years after we left. I think I forgot to return them, but most people would, out of politeness. So she's bound to have an address book crammed with school friends and a hundred other acquaintances from holidays or conferences.

But I need to remember that she would make a seriously boring TV programme – which is, of course, why they've picked me.

'Tracey, tell me what you remember about Helen?'

I know the routine by now; they like me to look at the camera, and natter on 'as though you're chatting to your best mate'. Except, I suddenly realised when Jenny said that, I haven't had a best mate since my wedding day. Me, Tracey Mortimer, the most popular girl in the whole of Crawley Park. How the hell did I let that happen?

'Helen?' I pause to butter another roll; there's a pile now that would feed a village of Kosovan refugees, but they've told me to keep spreading, for continuity's sake. 'Well, Helen was in 1G right from the start, like me. I hope she won't mind me saying this, but she stood out because she was quite . . . big.'

71

In other words, porky. But I don't want to sound like a complete bitch.

'We used to watch her at lunchtimes and she never seemed to eat more than we did, but there was no way she was just big-boned.' I add an extra layer of butter to the sandwiches.

'She was fat, but happy. You know the kind of girl. Everyone's agony aunt, someone to talk to, and maybe because she was big, she was no competition when it came to the lads, so she stayed out of the nastier arguments.'

I wonder how she ever found a bloke willing to delve around enough to impregnate her. Then I try to think nicer thoughts in case my bitchiness shows on camera.

'So did she have a nickname?' Jenny knows she did, of course, it's in the huge file she brings with her every time, but she always pretends not to when she's asking questions.

'Yup. Her nickname was Boris. Because her surname was Morris, and she looked a bit like Boris Karloff, the guy who played Frankenstein. Being eleven and a bunch of smart-arses, we made the connection. It made me laugh to see on the Web that she's gone and married a guy called Norris, so it still fits.'

Boris always seemed to take it quite well, but now I wonder if she hated it really. I only remember seeing her upset once, and that was in the weekly team-picking exercise in PE. It was winter so it must have been hockey. You know how it goes, the two sportiest girls get made team captains and they choose whoever they want on their side, and it's a game of brinkmanship, because naturally they go for the ones who play in the school teams first, and then for people like me and Melody, who couldn't give a shit, but have enough co-ordination to hit the ball if there's really no way of avoiding it. And then it gets to the last half dozen, the swots and the lard-arses, and you can see the captains working out tactics, normally a struggle for them because tactics require intelligence, and most of the really sporty ones were probably off doing a cross-country run when God was handing out brains. They did all their thinking with their feet.

Anyway, the implications were serious. Was a really hopeless four-eyed brain-box preferable to a team member who couldn't run without hyperventilating? If your attack was stronger than the other side's, could you afford to put Boris in goal in the hope that they'd never get as far as your end of the field, and if they did, then at least her bulk gave her a slightly higher chance of blocking the ball?

Well, this particular time, they'd chosen the swots first – maybe Suzanne bloody Sharp had managed some fluke contact with the ball the previous week – and Boris was the last girl standing.

Gillian Palmer looked defeated. 'So I guess I'm left with Boris. Go and get your pads on, Boris, I'll have you in goal.'

But instead of trudging off to get kitted out, Boris stood firm for a second, and I noticed that tears had started running down her face. They must have been icy on her cheeks, but she didn't even seem to have the will to wipe them away.

Gillian hadn't noticed, though. 'Oh, for goodness' sake, Boris, you're slow enough during the game, shift your fat bum into position, will you?'

One of Gillian's team-mates nudged her, but before she could do anything, Boris turned on her.

'Fuck off,' she sobbed, and Boris *never* swore. 'Fucking fuck off, Gillian. It's all very well for you, isn't it, with your place on the county team and your skinny legs, but you never think what it's like.' Snot was running from her nose, and the whites of her little piggy eyes had gone a violent pink colour. But she didn't seem so much upset as mad with rage. 'Well, I've bloody had enough of being a joke. I don't care if I get detention every night for ever, I'm never playing again and you can try and force me and I won't, I won't.'

It was *incredible*, and Miss Knowles, the PE teacher, who'd been messing about with equipment at the other end of the hockey pitch, was jogging over in our direction but before she reached us, Boris turned around and walked slowly towards the changing rooms. None of us went after her, and Boris never came out for team games again. I don't know if she got a note from her mum, but even the sadistic Miss Knowles didn't seem to want to argue, despite the fact that she normally wouldn't accept anything less than the amputation of both legs as an excuse for bunking off games. Not long afterwards, the PE department grudgingly introduced 'soft options' like trampoline and keep fit and badminton, which kept the sport princesses happy because they could play with themselves without having to bother with the rest of us.

Jenny's waiting for me to say something.

'Sorry, can you repeat the question?'

'Just, are you looking forward to meeting up again?'

'Yes, I think I am . . . Boris and I were never that close, but, yes, it'll be fun to catch up. Can't wait to see how she's changed . . .'

Jenny has outlined my suggested routine for answering the door when Boris arrives. She wants to capture both our reactions to the Big Moment on video, but she's only got one proper camera, which Jamie's using. So he'll film from outside Boris ringing the doorbell, but I have to wait for Jamie to move inside before I am allowed to answer the door. Or something like that.

'But don't feel you can't still be spontaneous,' says Jenny, after she's explained it.

The doorbell rings and Annabel skips past me. Callum's in his playpen, because it's the only way I can stop him diving face-first into all the food on the dining table. It's a frenzy of Mr Kipling's exceedingly good cakes, along with mountains of rolls filled with ham, cheese and egg mayo out of a tub. Then they brought orange squash, which is taking this whole nostalgia theme too far in my book. Gin and tonics would make for a more interesting afternoon, but then again Boris is pregnant, so I guess it would only be me drinking them. Not that I'd object.

Kelly's standing on my plastic stool, doing the washing-up. They wanted her to stay in her school uniform, because it's cute. She's cleaning the same bread board over and over again, pulling it out of the bowl every so often to check whether all the grease stains have gone. I'm not sure this perfectionist tendency is healthy in a six-year-old.

'Mummy, the water's going cold.'

Ever since that meeting at school, I can't help myself seeing signs that she's abnormal, and I'm really pissed off at Mrs Fellowes for making me so paranoid. A couple of days ago I even hid at the edge of the playground behind some of the other mums, and tried to watch her coming out, to see if anyone was bullying her. There was the usual stream of little girls running out with their mates, pretending not to hear their mums calling. And then the boys: there seemed to be more on their own, but they didn't look lonely, just absorbed in their own worlds as they kicked stray Coke cans, or completed world-saving missions on their Game Boys.

And way behind the straggling boys was Kelly. She kept her eyes down towards the tarmac until she was safely past the clusters of girls gathered at the classroom door. When her path was clear, she looked up, searching the crowd of mothers for me, her eyes wide with uncertainty.

I don't want to admit to this, but alongside the urge to rescue her, to grab her and take her somewhere where no one could ever hurt her again, there was something else, another emotion . . . I don't know how to describe it – no, that's wrong, I don't *want* to describe it. But I know the last time I felt it. Or the last person I felt it about. Suzanne Sharp.

It lasted only a fraction of a second, and then I found myself rushing forward through the ranks of pushchairs to hold my little girl before we both burst into tears. But mine were more about guilt.

I've tried to work out what it is that makes Kelly different, but I can't tell. With Suzanne it was obvious: ginger hair, glasses, an inability to catch or hit a ball, and the fact she was a total swot. She couldn't have been more of a target if someone had painted her Day-Glo orange and stuck a dartboard to her back. When I saw her, I tasted her fear and it made me restless. I never hit her – that would have been bullying – but it was impossible not to pick on her, just like it's impossible not to squeeze a spot, or run your tongue over a loose tooth repeatedly until the thread of gum gets thinner and thinner and eventually gives way . . .

But Kelly's pretty, she doesn't wear specs, and she's not been at school long enough to be branded a swot. I think the teachers are exaggerating. I've checked her clothes every day, and there are no rips, and when she was having her bath the other night, I looked closely and I couldn't see a single bruise. But it's making me jumpy. I even made her hold out her hands after school yesterday, pretending I was checking for dirt, but I was looking for red marks on her wrists from Chinese burns. I used to dish them out often enough in primary school. Not that they hurt *that* much, did they? I can't quite remember.

'You all right in here?' Jamie pokes his head round the door, his camera braced on his fantastic shoulders. He's wearing a short-sleeved navy T-shirt, and his arms are tanned and taut. He's incredibly cocky, but so gorgeous that it's hard to begrudge him the attention he gets. Even Kelly can't stop herself grinning at him, and Callum grins, man to man, when Jamie punches him gently on his chubby baby arm.

I nod, though actually I could do with someone to talk to, a bloke's opinion – blokes always tell it as it is – so I look a bit wistful, the expression I know men are intrigued by, and I wait. And he gives me a quizzical smile and then says, 'They're going to ring the bell again in a minute. So why don't I film you arranging the cakes on the plate, and then when you answer the door, I'll let you go in front of me, and then squeeze past you to get the two-shot. Yeah?'

So much for wistful. I sigh and then I take up my position, moving a fondant fancy a couple of inches to the left, and the doorbell rings . . .

And there she is. Helen Morris. Slimmer in the face, fatter round the midriff, but undoubtedly Boris.

'TRACEY!' she squeals, and my cynical core melts away as she seizes me with the enthusiasm I remember her showing for everything, from centre-spreads in *Smash Hits*, to the weekly serving of chocolate sponge pudding in the canteen.

She's gripping me so hard that I can hardly breathe, but where her distended stomach meets mine, I'm sure I can feel her baby's heels making contact with my belly button. And all of a sudden, I want to cry.

'Boris,' I manage, when she finally lets me go and we hold each other at arm's length, scanning each other's faces to see who has the most wrinkles, 'Boris, it's good to see you.'

And to my astonishment, I mean it.

CHAPTER TEN

The Forest Conference Centre, Croydon, London

'Good afternoon, ladies and gentlemen. Cast your mind back to being a child. What are your most powerful memories?'

Suzanne cast a long, meaningful look around the hall, making eye contact with as many members of the audience as possible. A hundred or so men and women, worthy types who'd not only volunteered to become school governors, but had also co-opted themselves on to membership of a national organisation guarding the morals and mental health of young people. Suzanne admired them, but secretly found them a little tedious at coffee break.

'Now I ask that question a lot, and I find the answers fall into two main categories. Put simply, the memories are either extraordinarily happy, or overwhelmingly miserable. Ring any bells?' A mild chuckle passed round the room.

'I don't propose to turn this afternoon into a Jerry Springer-style confessional, but I'm going to do something I've never done in public before. Tell you about *my* childhood.'

It was a pretty safe bet. Governors and Pastoral Education (GAPE) was a minor player, so there wouldn't be any press in the audience, but it was a good chance to try out the speech that had been fermenting in Suzanne's mind since the shock of finding out about the reunion. And if it went down well, there might be a repeat performance at a higher-profile gathering. Maybe even the CBI?

'Of course, in an ideal world, all psychologists, and, in fact, all children, would have a blissful time at school, a riot of fun and learning, so enjoyable that they can hardly bear to leave, and yet also the ideal launch pad for a life brimming with satisfaction and achievement.

'Well, it wasn't like that for me. And if I had to blame anyone – not that blame is in my professional repertoire – it would be a classmate I'll call Stacey.

'Stacey was the queen bee of our class. But she made every day of my life a misery. She never hit me – now and again one of her friends would take it too far, and push me around a bit, but there was no real physical abuse. No, this was the Chinese water torture version of bullying, the commonest and the most insidious.'

As usual, Suzanne had her key points printed neatly on to a handful of index cards. But she barely looked at them. This speech came from the heart.

'I'm not even sure if Trace— um, Stacey realised quite how bad it was, or that every morning I felt sick before I left for school, or that every evening when I shut the bedroom door behind me, I just wanted to stay there.'

It was strange how easy it was to talk about now, but then it had been the most humiliating experience: her digestive system churned so violently before she stepped into the form room that she was sure everyone could hear her stomach. She would tell herself over and over again before she fell asleep that *tomorrow* would be the day she'd stand up to Tracey, the day when life would become normal and she'd be off the hook and someone else would be in the firing line. She didn't really care who it was – not a very honourable instinct, but one shared by victims the world over.

'But I was lucky. Yes, it was a miserable five years, and, you know, you don't even get that for armed robbery these days.' The crowd laughed politely.

'But I moved on – found friendships and confidence and formed loving relationships, and now, a happy marriage. However, we know from our research at Millennium Child that many thousands of young people feel so profoundly damaged by their experiences that they find it impossible to contemplate trusting anyone in adult life.

'I was also lucky because despite the effect on my education – and there's no doubt that it was affected by my ending up too scared to raise my hand in class, or worrying if my marks went too high – I made it to college and into a career I love. Our research also shows that tens of thousands of adults have been left unemployed, and potentially unemployable, because they either refused to go to school due to bullying, or were so badly traumatised by their experiences that they learned virtually nothing.'

She had them now. Some of the audience were nodding in recognition; all were paying her complete attention.

'And I was lucky, more than anything else, because I survived – unlike more than a dozen schoolchildren in the last year alone, who took their own lives.'

Suzanne paused as it sank in. They knew the figures, but it was still shocking.

Had she ever considered suicide? She'd wanted it to stop, but going through the careful calculations working out how many pills, or how many storeys, or how much rope . . . she'd never gone that far. The thought made her shudder.

'Thankfully, most victims of bullying do find a way to leave their experiences behind. In a strange way, I think Stacey's responsible for me being here now. If it hadn't been for her endless taunts, I'd never have wondered what makes people tick and would probably have never thought of psychology. I certainly wouldn't have become involved in the fight to make childhood a safer time for all our kids. And I wouldn't have the opportunity, no, it's more than that, it's a privilege, to work with people like you to achieve that.

'So – I'd like to thank Stacey, and to suggest that it's not just the bullied but the *bullies* we need to help. I'll never know what drove her to behave as she did, but knowing what I know now about human behaviour, I don't suppose she was much happier than I was.'

Suzanne had wondered all over again, while she was writing the speech, what had turned Tracey into such a bitch. There was normally a reason. She remembered that Tracey's father wasn't around, but that was too convenient an excuse.

Hadn't the bullying got worse after that skinny Shrimp girl got run over, and Tracey joined forces with dopey Melody? Suzanne had counselled bullies, too, and sometimes their stories affected her as badly as the experiences of their victims. But with Tracey, she couldn't summon up any sympathy.

She paused again, building up to the grand finale.

'Fifteen years ago, bullying was seen as a fact of school life. All of us have a responsibility to change that attitude for ever. And I hope if I ever come across Stacey, whatever she's doing now, we could shake hands, and work together to make sure bullying is consigned to the history books, where it belongs.'

She looked down at the lectern and as the applause started, smiled back shyly at the warmth of their response.

The last bit wasn't strictly true. The only way she'd ever want to shake hands with Tracey bloody Mortimer would be if she knew in advance that the bitch was living in a B and B, had a job sexing chickens and had put on at least four stone. Sometimes forgiveness couldn't possibly match the appeal of sweet, straightforward revenge.

CHAPTER ELEVEN

This programme is like a full-time job, and it's not even as if I'm getting paid for it. As soon as one day's filming is out of the way, Jenny or Annabel are back on the phone with another bright idea and it's impossible to refuse them. They have the knack of talking anyone into anything.

Which is why I'm waiting for a cab to take me back to Crawley Park Comp for the first time since 1984. On the plus side, my sidekick for this latest trip down Memory Lane is the irresistible Jamie. After the false start over the fondant fancies, he's become noticeably less grumpy, and flirting with him definitely passes the time. I love the way he raises one beautifully bushy eyebrow at me whenever Annabel says something stupid – which is often.

Only Boris seemed unmoved by Jamie's magnificence, but then she was so excited about seeing me and catching up, that I think Brad Pitt and Ralph Fiennes would have been ignored as well.

'You're still so gorgeous,' she told me, as soon as she'd released me from her manic embrace. 'How have you done it, Trace? With two kids and everything and . . . oh, this is lovely.' She was skipping through the hall into the kitchen, with me, the crew and the girls sucked along in her wake like the debris from a hurricane. 'I would LOVE to have a kitchen like this and' – she stopped short as though someone had hit her across the face – 'and this has to be Kelly! She's ADORABLE!'

Kelly was still in the middle of her washing-up and the sudden arrival of this banshee – albeit a well-intentioned one – produced a look of sheer terror. Before she could even open her mouth to protest, Boris had thrown her dinner-lady arms around Kelly's waist, and was throwing air kisses around her in every direction.

'Look at her nose, and those baby-blue eyes. God, Trace, she's the spit of you, except I might even dare to say she's prettier. Aren't you, my pet?'

Kelly had gone so red in the face I couldn't tell whether she was about to have her first asthma attack, or was simply about to die from embarrassment. Making Kelly the centre of attention is just about the worst thing you can do to her. So I decided the only tactic was distraction, and hauled Callum from his playpen up to Boris's eye level. It's exactly the same technique I use in the supermarket when I'm trying to move the kids away from the breakables that they gravitate towards like magpies. Only in Tesco I use sweets as bait.

'Oh my word, the little man.' One second she was a human cocoon around my daughter, and a split second later she was all but licking Callum's face like a puppy. 'He's like a cherub and a miniature bouncer rolled into one. Can I take him home?'

Fortunately Callum's a tart like his dad, so he lapped it up.

'If my little one' – she patted her belly – 'is anything like as gorgeous as these two then I will be so thrilled I won't be able to speak for months.'

'I find that hard to believe,' I said, then instantly regretted sounding so bitchy in her presence.

She stopped, like Bambi caught in the headlights, but then her face rearranged itself into an even bigger beam. 'Oh, God, Trace, you're so right and it's such a relief that you haven't changed a bit. I'd have hated it if you'd gone all . . . soppy in your old age. Nasty is so much more fun!'

Then she stopped again, realising what she'd said, but instead of stuttering an apology, she clamped her hand to her mouth and began to giggle. It was so infectious that we all succumbed – first Callum, then Kelly and finally me – erupting into these uncontrollable spasms of laughter, only interrupted by gulping attempts to breathe.

It's only last week, but I really can't remember most of what we talked about, it was pure daft gossip. I just know that judging from the state of my stomach muscles afterwards, we didn't stop laughing until she left.

'Tracey? The taxi's here.' Jamie's got all his gear ready for the off in the hall.

I check my lipstick in the mirror. 'I'm ready!'

Jamie's told me to look wistful while he's filming me on the journey, so that's what I'm doing, but I've been checking myself out in the taxi mirror, and it's hard not to look plain dim.

Funny, I've hardly ever been back to school. It's only three miles away, but it's not on the route to anywhere I need to go. Unlike my primary school. Not that the Pines Junior and Infants is there any more, it's now a supermarket, so if they wanted to do a reunion there, we'd have to call the register in the in-store bakery, and sing 'All Things Bright and Beautiful' in the freezer section. I'd better not mention that, though, or Jenny and co would probably send me and Boris there so we can do exactly that.

From what I can see out of the open taxi window, Crawley Park hasn't changed. The property boom has bypassed this part of town, because even the most desperate first-time buyer knows that nowhere round *here* will ever be des res.

It's not just the litter and the smashed-up cars and the graffiti on the bus shelters. There's this gloom that hangs over the place: everything's the same colour, this mid-grey, even the little turfed embankments are grey; the grass has been worn away by kids pacing up and down like those polar bears you see on TV who've spent too long in a cage.

The driver takes a short cut through the estate where Shrimp used to live, and there are a couple of kids on the slightly larger than average strip of worn-away grass that she called the park. Bunking off. I did that myself a couple of times every term, but not for whole days, just when I couldn't face French or chemistry or whatever the most hated lesson was that term. The rest of the time, I wouldn't miss the chance to play up, do my thing, with the rest of 1G as my audience. Every hour mattered. I wonder if I knew even then that those really were the best years of my life.

The taxi slows to negotiate the chicanes the council must have put in to try to stop the joy-riders, and the kids on the grass spot me watching them.

'What chew fucking looking at?' the tall girl shouts at me; she's eleven or twelve. The other one gives me the finger. They look like the hollow-eyed kids in the video for *Another Brick in the Wall*.

'Little bastards,' the driver says, catching my eye in his mirror. 'It's like Beirut round here.'

I never saw it like that when I was growing up, but he's right. In my memories, it's only school that has any colour in it – the uniform and the wall displays and the bright strobe lights of the end-of-term discos – everywhere outside the gates is black and white. For all the crap he's put me through, at least Dave took me away from this grey, tarmacked world to the side of town where the grass really is . . . well, green instead of grey.

Because he was glamorous, Dave was. Or so I thought. A little of his dad's money went a long way when it came to convincing me that here at last was my route out. But there's a fine line between glamour and sleaze, and I was so blinded by his charm, I couldn't see the difference.

Mum did, but I never listened to her, until it was too late. I remember the exact moment when I realised she might be right. It happened on my wedding day, between taking my vows and throwing my bouquet. I've tried to wipe out the suspicions, by wiping out the person who put them there, but over time I've had to admit that Dave isn't what he pretended to be. Then again, neither am I. The funny thing is, I think Mum only saw Dave for what he was because she'd fallen for the same lines with my dad. Maybe we've got more in common than I want to admit . . .

There it is, in the distance, with all the architectural sophistication of a nuclear power station. Crawley Park Comp.

He's racing past, our driver, like he's worried we're about to get ambushed, so I can only just make out the local landmarks – the chip shop where we ate our lunches when we could afford to sneak out, and the newsagent next door where they sold us Slush Puppies so long as we only went in two at a time. The house with the proper front garden, where the couple had built little raised borders, and chosen a variety of jolly gnomes to nestle among the bedding plants. Even the worst lads in the year, the ones who were on probation by the third year, left that garden alone, and when someone did kidnap a fishing gnome, peer pressure forced them to put it back within the hour. We weren't all bad.

And these are the high metal gates we ran through the day after our last official assembly. I remember the feeling. We were grown-ups: we could do what we liked, we could earn a wage and buy what we liked and mess about and no teacher could stop us.

We were back the following day, more subdued, for the first of our CSEs. Actually, the teachers entered me for a couple of O-levels as well, but I kept that quiet. Being in the top set for anything was seriously uncool, and I managed to avoid it in almost every class. Except history. And that was more about the teacher than the subject . . .

We saw a lot more of those gates later, when we hung around school because we hadn't found jobs and didn't know whether we ever would, because we were Thatcher's generation, after all. We had nothing better to do than drift back towards the school we'd been so desperate to leave, and taunt the kids who were still there, who weren't free to do what they wanted.

The sign's changed.

Crawley Park College for Media and the Performing Arts.

And underneath, in smaller letters, it says 'a specialist school'.

What the hell's that about?

'Tracey, when the car pulls up, wait till I come round your side with the camera, so I can film you getting out,' Jamie says, and then tells the driver we'll probably have to reverse back on to the road and do it all again.

'Whatever, so long as the meter's running.'

By the main entrance, I can see a little reception committee of Alec, the girls and Cliff, who's travelled ahead with all the camera equipment. But I'm enough of a pro now not to wave or do anything to spoil the shot.

And there's another guy standing next to a white estate car covered in naff logos for Beautiful Berkshire FM. Its second distinguishing feature is the staggering erection sprouting from its roof. It's some kind of mast, but it looks obscene. Bob Carmichael always did accuse me of having a one-track mind.

Even though he was the one who sent me down that particular track . . .

We do the shot of me getting out, then Alec pulls Jamie aside to talk about the next part. The guy with the radio mast sidles up to me.

'Tracey?' he asks uncertainly, which is a bit dopey because if he's here to meet me, the fact I was the one being filmed must have been a giveaway.

'Yeah. And is that a mast on your car, or are you just pleased to see me?' OK, pretty feeble but I couldn't resist it.

The guy looks embarrassed. 'Hi, I'm from your local station. Could you spare a minute to do a live interview?'

I feel quite flattered really, this guy's here for *me*, when Alec strides over.

'I've already told you, mate, unless you want to hang around until we've finished then forget it.'

I don't know how I could have fancied Alec, even for five minutes. He's so rotten to this bloke that I instantly decide to do the interview.

'Wow, I listen to you all the time, what's that DJ in the mornings?' I say. It's not terribly convincing, and the reporter looks even more embarrassed.

'Um, well, we don't really play music, we're more of a speech station.'

'That's what I meant. I'm sure we've got a couple of minutes, haven't we, Alec?'

Alec returns my glowing smile with a snarl, but Jenny's been listening in.

'It might help with finding some more of Tracey's class,' she says, but Alec is already walking towards his car, a red sporty thing with wheels so wide they look as though they belong on a tractor. We watch him go, and I wonder if he's going to drive off in a huff, but instead the Verve starts blasting through his sunroof.

I turn to the reporter. 'Prepare for the best interview you've ever done!'

I send him off with a smile on his face – I give a *very* good interview – and now this is it, time for the tour. I'm standing on the steps that lead to reception, and despite the flashy new sign, it doesn't seem that different. All the schools round here have the same design, like wooden boxes stacked one on top of the other. It hasn't worn very well. The many coats of paint on the window frames seem to be all that's holding the building together.

Of course, we were never allowed to use the main entrance, that was strictly for staff and visitors, so it feels naughty to go back through those doors. I feel I should be taking the side entrance, into the humanities block for registration. I must have taken that route more than a thousand times.

I step into the hall and come face to face with a six-foot-high water feature, and a five-foot-high power-suited woman who is just as gushing. This must be Mrs Jacobs.

'Mrs Brown.' She thrusts a manicured hand towards me, and shakes mine with a fierceness that seems over the top. 'Welcome back.'

Standing next to her are two kids, a girl of about eleven and a tall Asian boy . . . well, he's not really a boy, he's far too tall and good-looking to be wearing that ridiculous mint-green jumper. Still, it's nice to see they've kept some of the traditions, however horrific. Oh, and the canary tie, knotted as tightly as a city banker's. Must be the fashion these days.

She nudges them and they introduce themselves. I've forgotten their names in an instant: too busy peering round the rest of the room, with its glass bricks and the marble reception desk that looks more like a bar. The water feature, I notice, is labelled the 'fount of wisdom'.

Our tour begins, led by the frighteningly self-assured Stepford Pupils. It's quite a convoy with me, Jamie, Cliff, Alec and Jenny following them. Annabel's been relegated to guarding the sports car. It's probably the only sensible judgement Alec's made all day.

I've been expecting some kind of flashback, like stepping into a time machine, but it's not happening. Sure, the sights and sounds and smells are what I expected, but they're not transporting me to 1979; it's as though there's this invisible barrier between then and now, and however much I want to, I can't cross over.

The boy is telling me that he decided to come to Crawley Park even though it involves a change of buses to get across town. He says it's worth it because of the facilities: the recording studio and the video editing suite and the full stage lighting rig, and it strikes me that some things have changed.

But then I need the loo, and nip into the ones that used to be closest to our form room, and I realise as my bum freezes when it makes contact with the cracked plastic seat that some things have stayed very much the same.

Finally we reach the first-floor corridor leading to our form room – not Mrs Chang's lab, which we left when she went on maternity leave, but Mr Carmichael's history classroom, our home from the second year till we left.

This is the room where I grew up.

As I approach the door, past a row of pegs that were never

used, because no one would be stupid enough to leave their valuables unsecured at Crawley Park, I'm almost expecting to see Bob Carmichael. He should be darting around at the front, firing questions off in his deep brown voice, and smiling so widely when a kid finally understands what he's getting at that you'd think he'd won the Pools.

Except, of course, I know it can't be him. If anyone should know that, it's me.

But this is still the closest I come to that 'back to the future' experience . . . because when I peer through the window, it's not Bob but Dick Phipps, who was already deputy head of humanities when I was here. Instead of the timelines, and the faded portraits of kings and queens on the walls, there are maps and pictures of rock formations. I wonder what he's done with his life in the seventeen years since we left him here. When he turns in response to the knock on the door, I know the answer. Nothing. His face looks exactly the same, except it's a couple of shades greyer.

He comes towards us, and makes an attempt at a smile, but there's no hiding the fact that as far as he's concerned, any reunion with me in this lifetime would be far too soon.

'Well, well, Miss *Mortimer* . . .'

He's been expecting me.

'Never thought I'd see you again . . . I don't imagine you've been anywhere near a school in recent years. Unless it's to deal with your no doubt numerous and excessively truculent off-spring.' He's always had this affected upper-class way of speaking, even though everybody at school knew he'd grown up by the canal on the Clematis Estate, the roughest part of the roughest side of town.

'Hello, Mr Phipps,' I say, intending to follow it up with some devastating put-down. But nothing comes. No sudden transformation back to the old me.

'Guess what, children. Young Miss Mortimer used to be a pupil here, and now she's brought a TV crew along with her; and why is that, Miss Mortimer? Because, perhaps, you run an international company, and they want to see how you came to be a successful entrepreneur from humble origins?'

'No,' I say quietly, feeling it's pointless to interrupt his flow.

'OK. So perhaps it's because you're a leading light in the arts world, and your experiences here at Crawley Park set you on your creative path. Let me guess . . . a modern artist in the mould of, I don't know, Tracey Emin?'

I know he knows I don't know who he means. I sigh. 'No.'

He is loving this so much, and I can't believe I've been stupid enough to let this happen. I want to tell him to fuck off, but even if it wasn't being filmed I wouldn't dare, and he knows it.

Surely Jenny and Annabel don't *know*?

'Well, you really do have me foxed on this one. Please, put me out of my misery. What incredible achievement merits your presence and that of your charming colleagues?' He's standing there, arms folded, with one hand resting curiously on his chin, like a bust of Shakespeare.

'It's a reunion. I'm having a reunion, and they're filming it.'

He nods. 'Ah . . . ah, and why you, Miss Mortimer?'

'I don't know. I suppose' – and he is going to love this even more – 'it's because I'm pretty average.' And I realise as I say it that that's exactly why they've picked me: Mrs bloody Average, two average kids, an average semi, and your average adulterous husband. I've never felt average is anything to be ashamed of, but now it's like I am standing in front of a high court judge looking down his nose at me, preparing to pass sentence.

'Average, Miss Mortimer?' He turns to his captive audience. 'Well, well. I must say, you *have* exceeded my expectations.'

And he smiles that sarcastic smile as I fight the urge to punch him, because we both know there's much, much more to his hatred of me than a few excuses over late homework.

CHAPTER TWELVE

I'm thinking of pulling out.

I know they'll be pissed off, but that's not my problem, and they seem to prefer Boris to me anyway, so I reckon they'll use her instead. The whole thing is a nightmare.

It's not just Phipps, though that didn't help. Afterwards, Jenny said, 'Oh, what rattled his cage? Did you play up in his class?' but I'm pretty sure they don't suspect anything more. And they said they're unlikely to use any of what he said, way too sarcastic for a feel-good show.

At least I know he's not going to let on, after all those years. Phipps and Bob have got way more to lose than me.

But it's more than that. I don't have the energy for this any more.

Dave's just buggered off again after one of his lost weekends in the pub, and we were talking about the programme – well, we never have what you could truly describe as 'conversations' but he cottoned on to the fact that I was feeling a bit grumpy about the whole thing, and he said something sensible. Always a shocker when that happens, though fortunately it's not very often.

'Sometimes,' he slurred at me, because it was after the pubs had shut, and I think he was trying to get in my good books for the usual bloody obvious reasons, 'it's best to leave the past where it is.'

'Oh, thanks for that,' I snapped back, out of habit and to stop him coming sniffing round me, but it's stuck in my head, and I think he might just be right.

Then there's Kelly. So much for all the flannel about *let's see what happens, these things usually blow over*, because last week I got this letter saying the school's made her an appointment with the educational psychologist.

Meet my daughter, the nutcase. With her dysfunctional, crap mother.

I don't know what to think, so I try not to think about it at all. But it feels all wrong to be messing about with this reunion rubbish when school is such a bloody nightmare for her. I feel I've failed her somehow.

And I hate to admit it, but what's scaring me more than any of the rest of it, is this: what if, after all this fuss, none of my *real* school friends even bother to turn up?

The single biggest factor keeping me onside with the programme is the thought of losing the TV company computer. It's my new best mate; in fact, I feel lonelier when Dave is around for the weekend and I can't log on because he takes the piss, than I do during the week when the kids are in bed and I can surf to my heart's content.

I wouldn't have believed that a computer could become so important, and I hate the fact it has, but I can't break the habit. Every time I go into the kitchen for a coffee or for a gin and tonic, it's winking at me on the breakfast bar.

Go on, Tracey, it's saying, *have another delve into cyberspace.*

Most of the time I give in. I always was weak-willed. It doesn't seem nerdy to me any more, even though a month ago I'd have dismissed the Web as the haunt of tragic no-hopers with no mates and nothing better to do.

Maybe I've joined them.

Time disappears when I'm on the Web. Seeing (1) in my inbox gives me a thrill like nothing else. At first, the e-mails were always from Jenny or Annabel, with news of the latest plans for filming. Now, it's mostly from Boris, but she's told me about these other sites where you sign up for e-mails, and I've got loads of them coming in now – the latest gossip on Brad and Jennifer, or details of fantastic holidays I could *book right now, online* . . . if only I had the money and didn't have Kelly and Callum to look after.

I was talking to Jenny about it, and she said, 'I can't stand spam, it's so intrusive.'

But I don't see it like that – every bit of gossip or suggestion about how to change your hairstyle or your sofa or your life is a bonus. I can't believe it's all free. I've got horoscopes coming in, two different ones, so I can pick and choose whether today is going to be a good one for staying at home or for going out to do the shopping.

I haven't dared log into any chat rooms yet, but I spend ages lurking, reading what other people have written. Women with too many lovers, women who want one but can't find one, women who want to rewire their bathrooms. You'd never need to feel lonely online, because you can eavesdrop on all these lives. Maybe one day I'll put mine up for inspection.

Though God knows why I'm being so shy online, when I've agreed to spread most of my life all over the TV this autumn.

Another reason to dump the whole idea.

Oh, and of course I had a look at porn. Late at night, after three drinks, I went to one of the search engine things and typed in sex, and had a surf around. It was like visiting a zoo where all the exhibits were bright pink. There's nothing attractive about people with their bits out.

Tonight my eyes are sore from surfing. Maybe I should e-mail Jenny about my second thoughts. Or maybe I should e-mail Boris first. She might look a bit daft, but there's more to her than fat ankles

While I'm deciding, I log on to my e-mail.

GARYANDGABBY

Who's that? I click on the e-mail.

Tracey
What a bolt from the blue. Sorry didn't come back to you straightway, been busy at work. I'm a copper now, would you have believed it. How about you?
So what's made you get in touch now?
G

Gary Coombs.

Gary bloody Coombs.

What took him so long, cheeky bugger?

How the hell did he get into the police, with his history?

Who is Gabby?

And does she know he's e-mailed me?

Maybe I do want to stay on the programme after all.

CHAPTER THIRTEEN

The Rusty Nail Fun Pub & Eating House, Brentford, Middlesex

Dick Phipps watched his old friend as he walked back from the bar. His bear-like frame sank an inch or so into the soggy patterned carpet as he headed back towards the booth. Bob Carmichael couldn't be unobtrusive if he tried.

'Sorry, Dick, it's not exactly going to win pub of the year, is it? But it was the only place I could think of where they don't know me.' Bob put the two pints down on the table.

'Well, we're not really here for the atmosphere.'

Bob peered around the room. 'You wouldn't bother coming here unless you were up to no good, would you? Though chance would be a fine thing these days.'

Dick smiled. 'So how is life at the top?' Neither of them wanted to start talking about the real reason they were there.

'Bloody over-rated, mate. Though the money's good. And the dinners. But you probably spotted that.' He patted his stomach, which protruded a little way through his linen shirt, but still appeared to be more muscle than blubber.

Both men laughed briefly, then Bob took a swig of his beer. 'So. No contact beyond the odd Christmas card for two decades and then it takes bloody Tracey to bring us face to face again. There's no escape from that one, is there?'

'You didn't even sound surprised when I rang you.'

Bob shook his head. 'No. I'm relieved, if anything. I always knew it'd come out somehow or other, and at least this way . . .'

Dick felt the old frustration come back. Bob had always been too bloody laid back, and look where it got him. 'It hasn't come out at all. And it needn't ever come out.'

'You don't actually believe that, do you, Dick? That we can keep it hidden? You don't know what it's like, they're crawling all over everybody for sleaze.'

'But you're not even an MP.'

'The way the papers see it, I'm even bigger prey than MPs, and I see their point. Unelected. Overpaid.'

'Over-sexed. Over here.' Dick grinned. 'Who'd have thought it, eh? You in and out of Number Ten. Hobnobbing with the rich and powerful. One of Tony's Cronies. So have you been to one of these parties, the ones you see the celebs at in the magazines?'

'One or two. They're not a lot more interesting than the PTA barn dances, to be honest, though the food's better.'

'Hey, it's quality stuff at Crawley Park too these days – garlic bread, nachos, hummus, the works. Now that we're a specialist school.' Dick still struggled to keep the contempt out of his voice: his beloved geography had taken a hammering for funding when media studies was invented as a subject.

'I bet Tracey loved that,' said Bob.

'Funnily enough, I didn't ask her. You amaze me, Bob. She nearly fucked your whole life up, and you still act as though it's a big joke.'

Bob shrugged. 'I never could get angry with Tracey, could I? You were angry enough for both of us.'

'I wanted to hit her when she came into my classroom last week. *Your* old classroom, it was—'

'Yes, and if it wasn't for Tracey, I might still be there.'

'Like me, you mean?'

'Dick, don't be daft, I don't mean it like that. Sometimes I wish I was still there – mainly when I'm sitting in a Joined-Up Thinking Symposium. Someone like Tracey would have cut them down to size in two minutes, but I have to sit there listening to them droning on and on . . . that's when I envy you.'

Dick had picked up a beer mat, and started peeling it apart. 'Well, we could reminisce like this for hours. It's not why we're both here, though, is it? I think you need to put a stop to this.'

Bob held out his hands, the gesture of surrender. 'No. I've worried about the press getting hold of it for so long that if it's finally coming, then I almost feel relieved.'

Dick felt sweat prickle under his arms, under his collar. 'Bob, be reasonable. What you – I mean, we – need to do is scare her off. It's not just you who stands to lose. Does she really want to look like a scrubber on national television? She definitely didn't like the idea of me sharing a few anecdotes with the TV crew.'

Bob sighed. 'I never got anywhere telling her what to do seventeen years ago, and I don't suppose it'd be any different now.' He wiped condensation off his beer glass. 'Does she look any different now?'

'I can't believe you even want to know that. She still looks like a scrubber. Just a much older one.'

'Dick, I know you think she was in the wrong, but I was the teacher, *she* was the pupil, remember? I was older and wiser.'

'Only chronologically speaking. She knew what was what.'

'Maybe. But so did I, and I knew what the consequences would be. Maybe it's time to give in gracefully.'

Dick cleared his throat. He'd hoped it wouldn't come to this but if he had to beg, then so be it. 'All right, if you don't care about yourself, what about the rest of us? How do you think it's going to look when the press are crawling all over the school? I don't think it's going to reflect well on any of us.'

Bob stared at his old boss. 'Oh, Dick, how disappointing. There I was thinking you had my welfare in mind, and the only thing that's worrying you is how it's going to affect *your* career.'

'That's not fair. It was me who made sure you had the option of resigning – you don't suppose you would have got where you are now with a sacking on your CV, do you?'

'I might not have lost *her*, though.'

Dick shook his head. 'After all this, you're still letting your John Thomas rule your head. Did you forget to grow up?'

'Maybe.' Bob frowned. 'I don't suppose you'll be wanting another drink, then?'

Dick downed the last of his beer. 'No thanks – *mate*.' He stood up. 'Fine. Go ahead, then. Destroy yourself. But do me a favour, and don't take the rest of us with you.'

Staff Room, Crawley Park College

'I don't know why any of you bother,' Dick snarled as half the staff room gathered around the school copy of the *Times Educational Supplement*. 'None of you is going anywhere, with this place on your CV. The only way out of Crawley Park is death.'

Carol Price, head of English, peered up from the paper. 'Shut up, you horrible old git. Did you get out of bed on the wrong side this morning?'

'I slept very well, thank you.' It was a lie. Tracey Mortimer had stalked his nightmares.

'Yeah, right. What makes you think we're looking at the jobs pages anyway?'

'Two things, Carol. One, who the hell reads that rag for the curriculum updates? And two, I can read upside down and the page you're all looking at is headed "*Vacancies*".'

Carol shrugged as the bell rang, and the paper was left abandoned on the leatherette chairs, along with Dick, blessed with a free first period for departmental admin.

Suddenly, the dry old *Times Ed* and its humanities section seemed strangely desirable.

He walked over to the kettle, and made himself another cup of coffee from the dregs of the catering-size drum of Golden Aroma or whatever unspeakable granules they'd got from the cash and carry.

It was all the usual stuff on the front page, as the nation's eleven-year-olds grappled with assessment tests, and their teachers moaned about exams stifling children's creativity.

Get used to it, Dick thought. Outside, a few remaining kids were heading for class, dawdling and play-fighting. Kids only need imagination for the important bits of school life, to invent excuses for late registration, late homework, late periods . . .

Page three, and the Inspector of Schools wants improved standards of literacy and numeracy in trainee teachers.

Don't we all? But someone's going to have to be cannon fodder for the comprehensives. Dick grinned at himself. Getting old was crap, but at least you could stop pretending to be cheerful, and embrace cynicism without embarrassment. And bloody hell, sometimes, it felt *so* good.

Page five: '*Broader sports curriculum "would reduce obesity"* '. Yeah, maybe, but then who could deny sadistic PE teachers the pleasure of laughing at the stragglers on the cross-country finishing line?

Page seven – who can be arsed with reading the even-numbered pages? – '*End bullying, pleads charity chief*'. Like how, he thought, and went to turn the page, but something about the picture, a young woman grasping her podium with a faraway expression, made him look again . . . '*The chairwoman of one of Britain's newest charities to promote juvenile mental health, the Millennium Child Campaign, made an impassioned plea to school governors to act to rid the education system of bullying.*

'*And Suzanne Marshall-Sharp confessed to her own personal agenda – having been bullied throughout secondary school, the former comprehensive pupil wanted to thank her own bully for giving her the motivation to succeed.*'

'Suzanne Marshall-Sharp.' He spoke the words out loud, trying to trigger a memory he knew was there.

'*Ms Marshall-Sharp, rumoured to be on the wish list for the government's new pastoral care working group, confided in delegates to the GAPE conference that her experiences of being bullied had given her a unique insight into the lives of the thousands of children her organisation represents.*'

Sharp. Sharp . . . He stared at the snappily dressed woman, gazing coyly from the photograph.

Suzanne Sharp. Thanking Tracey Mortimer, presumably.

How bizarre, that you could go years without thinking about any of your old pupils, especially not that bloody troublesome class of 1984, and then suddenly, there they all were.

Suzanne Sharp, a government adviser. Weird that Crawley Park should have produced two people who thought they had anything to tell the rest of the world about education. Suzanne, the original prig until the rest of the kids bullied it out of her, and Bob, immortalised in school gossip for being just that bit too dedicated to teacher-pupil interaction . . .

Dick went to turn over again. And then, with his hand holding page seven in the air, he had an idea.

Suzanne stared at the paper. 'God, Charlotte, trust the bloody *TES* to be in the audience. It's really buggered my plan to re-cycle that speech.'

Charlotte shrugged. 'No publicity's bad publicity.'

'I know, but the *TES* . . . The broadsheets won't want to report it when I trot it out again at the CBI if they know it's been printed already. What a waste of all that suffering, eh?'

The phone rang.

'I'm not talking to anyone but Number Ten.'

'Millennium Child Campaign? Yes, I'll just see if she's in, hold on.'

Suzanne whispered, 'Didn't you hear me? I hope it's Cherie at the very least.'

'No . . . but it's an original excuse. Guy called Richard Phipps?'

'Name rings a bell. Some tedious union person, I suppose. OK, bung him on, I can probably manage one more moron today.'

Charlotte punched in Suzanne's extension to transfer the call. 'Well, he says he used to teach you geography . . .'

Smart Alec Productions, Beak Street, Soho, Central London

Annabel put down the phone and wandered across to the viewing room, where Jenny was logging the videotapes from the filming at Crawley Park.

Jenny looked up from the TV. 'I really don't get this thing with Tracey and that teacher. Weird shit, the way he's laying into her after all that time . . . unusable, though. So, how's it going?'

'Bit of a result actually!' Annabel squeezed herself on to the table, which was piled a metre high with cassettes.

'Yeah?'

'Well, you know we've not been having much luck with the psychologist idea? I've just had a call from the boss of one of the country's big kids' psychology charities.'

Jenny shrugged. 'It's not really *child* psychology we want, is it? It's grown-ups and why they want to go back in time. Unless she's really brilliant, I can't see us being interested.'

'No, it's better than that. She does sound pretty good, actually, but this one has the best CV for our programme. Not only is she a psychology hotshot – she also went to school with Tracey!'

Jenny looked up from her notes. 'Ah . . . now that's different.'

'And she really, really wants to do the programme. Couldn't shut her up. I think it's what you'd call killing two birds with one stone!'

CHAPTER FOURTEEN

What do you wear for your six-year-old daughter's first appointment with her shrink?

I've dragged the dinky suits from the back of the wardrobe, the ones I wore when I worked in an office, before Kelly caused those snail trails on my belly. Despite the stretch marks, the little skirts and boxy jackets still fit, but they look so wrong: pastel colours and shoulder pads went out with the Tories. And they belong to someone flirty and fun, the kind of secretary I always pretended to be, the one who'd shag the boss in the Gents and still nip out at lunchtime to buy his wife a birthday present. I managed the mascara and the push-up bras, but I never shagged the boss. I believed in monogamy in those days, which didn't enhance my promotion prospects. And marrying at twenty-four didn't help either. After I had Kelly, it was thanks but no thanks, and the best I could get with my Pitman and my never-very-good typing was a job in the stationery shop. Dave said it was fine, which I should have taken as a warning sign. He's always had a soft spot for secretaries, and now I think he was knocking off other people's PAs in the site offices of his dad's firm within a year of our wedding.

The suits are out.

My usual collecting-Kelly-from-school gear – the tidy jeans and the pressed casual shirts that scream Racing Green – doesn't seem to reflect the seriousness of the occasion. But I don't have much between that and my hen night outfit, which last had an airing over a year ago when Martha from the shop took us out on her hen night at Careless Whispers in Slough. And though bias-cut red dresses have a lot to recommend them, I don't suppose they'd score highly with the psychiatrist.

Actually, she's not a psychiatrist, she's a psychologist, so it's not quite as bad as it seems – they don't tend to admit infants to mental hospitals for being a bit grumpy in the playground. But even so, the red dress isn't right.

A toned-down version of my regular Christmas ensemble seems the best bet: black skirt, my sexy black boots, plus a check shirt. Maybe a bit hot for late spring, but it's not slutty irresponsible trailer trash. It's also unthreatening – that's what people in authority prefer. Teachers, doctors, social workers, policemen . . .

Gary. It's not what I'd wear for a date with Gary.

Then it would definitely be the red dress. With the black bra peeping above the neckline – the lacy bra from Marks and Spencer's that snuck into my basket on Friday below the new pyjamas for Callum and the strawberry-patterned pants for Kelly. And I'd wear matching knickers. Or – even more daring – no knickers at all.

I've had sex on the brain since I got that e-mail. It's a sad indictment of my life that a few stray words (thirty-five, to be exact, I counted them when Boris told me that the art of e-mail flirtation is always to reply with fewer words than the other person used) from a guy I haven't seen for more than half my life have sent me into a hormonal frenzy.

But he's been misbehaving too. I bet this Gabby doesn't know he's been e-mailing, or how often. I know that he's off duty this morning. So while I'm taking Kelly to have her head examined, I could be at home exchanging ever shorter messages with a member of Her Majesty's Constabulary, and fantasising about the moment when we are reunited.

If we ever are. We're both avoiding everything contentious: his relationship, my kids, whether he's going to turn up in July, not to mention the events of June 1984. I'm learning that e-mail is perfect for staying away from things you don't want to think about.

Like getting older.

'Hello, Kelly, Mrs Brown! I'm Sandy Hunter.'

The woman in front of me can't be much older than twenty-one, and has this terrifyingly bright smile, like a Girl Guide leader. Any minute now, she'll say that this is going to be *so much fun.*

'Now I know you might be a bit nervous' – she's talking to Kelly, but what about me? I'm nervous too – 'but I promise I don't bite, and with a bit of luck, when we get to know each other, we might even have some fun!'

I feel my eyes both heading for my nose in a kind of cross-eyed, I don't believe this, piss-take expression, but of course there's no one to share my contempt. Kelly looks like all her Christmases have come at once. Someone to play with at least, even if her new playmate is being paid for it.

And suddenly, I hate myself so much. How can I think these things about my own daughter? She ought to have *me* to play with, except I'd rather spend my life sending e-mails to old flames and giving TV interviews to people who really couldn't give a shit.

Mother of the bloody year, that's me.

'Now, Kelly,' says the glowing Sandy Hunter, 'why do you think we're here?'

'Um.' Kelly stares at the carpet. 'Is it because I haven't got many friends?'

Oh, God.

Kelly's gone pink, and refuses to look at me. Sandy shoots me a glare, and I realise that the touchy-feely-smiley personality is a put-up job to fool the kids. I suspect we parents get an altogether rougher ride.

'And what do you think, Mrs Brown?'

It's such a shit question, and she knows it. 'I . . . I think . . . we're going to help Kelly feel happier about school, aren't we?' And I nudge Kelly gently with my elbow, and watch as she recoils slightly. And I see that bloody Sandy's seen it too.

'Yes. *We* are,' she says.

I should learn to keep my mouth shut. I thought I'd get my own back on St Sandy by asking her what exactly *she* thought we were aiming to do with Kelly, but she deflected it nicely, saying, 'That's up to Kelly, but we know it's going to be enjoyable.'

So now Kelly's playing a game, well, we all are, involving various rather creepy dolls that Sandy unpacked from her rucksack. They're the same size as Barbies but with bigger heads and no bosoms – childlike, I suppose. I have a horrible feeling that they might be anatomically correct under their brightly coloured cord trousers, and I start thinking about what else the dolls are used for, and the kind of things Sandy must deal with day to day.

It makes me sad, but it also makes me angry. How come the school is targeting me and my daughter, when there must be hundreds of horrific sexual or physical abuse cases to sort out?

My baby's just shy.

Isn't she?

Kelly is concentrating really hard on showing Sandy what happens at lunchtimes, and the doll that she's chosen to be her is skipping happily across the carpet.

'What about your friends?' asks Sandy, and I hold my breath.

Kelly concentrates even harder on the doll. Eventually she whispers, 'Jolene stays with me.'

Sandy looks at me hopefully. 'Jolene?'

I feel incredibly disloyal when I answer, 'It's her imaginary friend.'

'Oh . . . right. OK then, Kelly, I think that's it for today. But I have got some homework for you.' Sandy reaches into her bag, and pulls out a small notebook with coloured pages. 'Mrs Fellowes tells me you have lovely neat handwriting.'

Kelly beams.

'So I'd love you to write me a list before we meet again. A list of things that make you happy, and things that make you sad. Can be as long or as short as you want. And it's strictly your private book, no one else is allowed to look without your permission. OK?'

Kelly nods sagely. 'OK, Sandy.'

'OK, Mummy?'

I nod, though I don't exactly feel happy about it.

Kelly takes the notebook, excited at the prospect of showing off her spelling and neat hand-writing, and failing to realise that she's being manipulated.

'Right, and I'll see you in two weeks. Now get off back to your class, and I'll just have a word with your mummy. Bye, Kelly.'

We both wave as my little girl leaves the office, and when Sandy turns back to face me, the smile has faded. So has mine.

'Very clever,' I say. 'I suppose you're trying to uncover some kind of trauma at home so you can blame me for her being a bit shy.'

'This isn't about blame, Mrs Brown.' She sighs. 'But your daughter is obviously a troubled girl, and I'd have thought you'd be as keen as I am to find out why.'

110

She's got a point, but that just irritates me all the more. 'Of course I do. But isn't she too young for therapy? She'll make friends if she's left alone – it's natural.'

'I wish I could agree with you, Mrs Brown. I've seen too many children much older than Kelly who've never learned how to make friends, and they'd tell you there's nothing natural about it. But Kelly's young enough for us to work with and move on with . . . though I have to warn you, I will need your full co-operation.'

What can I do? I can hardly refuse, but there's something about this woman's manner that makes me want to throw her the v-sign, then run out of the door.

She delves around in her bag again. 'I've got a questionnaire here for you too, if you don't mind. And, yes, it does look at your home situation, your own attitudes and so on. Relationships between the most important adults in a child's life are bound to influence their behaviour, don't you think?'

Relationships? I'd hardly describe what goes on between Dave and me as a relationship. Maybe I'd be better off shagging someone else; at least it might cheer me up. And surely a miserable mother would also 'influence a child's behaviour'.

I thank her for the leaflet.

'No, no, thank *you* for coming, Mrs Brown. It's so important to have your support – after all, this is a partnership and we've all got Kelly's best interests at heart.'

111

Have you ever had that feeling of dread when someone says they've organised a something they 'just know' you're going to love?

Annabel called me last week, after I'd arrived back from my meeting with the appalling Sandy, and said, 'Book yourself a babysitter, Tracey, we've got a treat for you a week on Saturday. And I just know you're going to love it.'

For a start, anything involving filming is unlikely to be a spontaneous fun-filled night out. It was even more ominous when I asked her what I should wear, and she said, 'Oh, nothing special. We'll provide any extras you need.'

So now I'm wondering whether we're going ice-skating, or to one of those dry-ski slopes or a go-karting track, except I can't see what that's got to do with the programme.

Oh, I forgot, Boris is coming too.

So, now I think about it, that rules out anything too physical. She's still got two months to go, but she's clumsy enough at the best of times, and I can't see anyone being willing to insure *her* for dangerous pursuits.

At the back of my mind, I've been wondering if they might have tracked down another one of our classmates, and are doing something connected to it – perhaps a mini-reunion, to prepare us for the real thing. Jenny says they're worried about filling two half-hour programmes; the first one's meant to be the preparations, and the second one the party itself, but she reckons that despite all the time they've spent hanging round my house, and asking the same question over and over, they might be struggling to make episode one interesting enough.

The little demon that's now taken up residence in the penthouse in the back of my mind keeps saying, If they *are* taking us to meet someone, what if it's Gary?

I know it can't be, really, because I haven't told them about him getting in touch. I know I should have done, but this is one blast from the past I want on my own terms.

It's become even more of a fixation since meeting Kelly's shrink. I haven't filled in the questionnaire yet, but I've read it: how would you describe your relationship with your partner, if you have one? Is there anything about the relationship that might give your child concern/an unhealthy template for their future/a lifelong victim complex and need for therapy?

OK, I made the last bit up, but that's what it means. And of course, Dave and I are rubbish. No physical affection, constant sniping – on the rare occasions he's around – followed by loud arguments in the middle of the night, fuelled by his booze and my boredom.

It's so unfair. I've done it all by the book. Calmed down when I realised I wanted to get married, chose the right kind of bloke – easy-going, well-off, but not out of my league – and played the courtship game. Didn't live with him before marriage, traditional wedding, promised to obey as well as the other stuff, ignored the signs of trouble that might as well have been painted a hundred feet high, and kept working at being the loving partner. Then I waited until it seemed like the right kind of time to try for babies, kept myself pretty up to the first birth, between the babies and then afterwards until it became utterly fucking obvious that it made no difference, because as far as

Dave was concerned, the contract always included a clause allowing some discreet playing away.

Unless you were brought up round here, you wouldn't understand. Sure, we *know* about equality, but most of our mums worked not because they wanted careers, but because the cleaning and reception and waitressing jobs paid the bills. Especially if, like Mum, that was the only income.

And that's another reason feminism never appealed. I'd seen Mum coping without a bloke, and although we never talked about it, she made it clear hers was a second-best life. So I wanted the picture-perfect marriage, two point four children, cat, dog, goldfish, nice car, nice clothes, nice life – as much for her sake as mine. If you look at our family album, we have it all. But it ain't as pretty as it looks, not with a philandering husband, a lonely child and a gaping hole in my life I'm filling with daft memories and an obsession for the Internet.

So I've been thinking. Maybe it's time to start living.

And maybe that's where Gary comes in . . .

Flat 2a, 422 Goldhawk Road, Shepherd's Bush, London

'I think Mo's boyfriend is going to propose to her,' Gabby said, shutting one of her glossy magazines and throwing it at the coffee table.

Gary didn't even look up from the sports pages. 'Is that what you girls do on your nights out? Plot how to snare men over white wine, and then go back to someone's house to cast spells?'

'If we do, then they're not very effective spells, are they?'

He looked up at her. She didn't seem to be joking; in fact, she looked seriously pissed off. He dragged himself out of the chair to sit opposite her on the arm of the sofa. 'Aw, Gabs, how can you say that when I have invited you to share not only my life, but also my lovely home?'

They both surveyed the living room, its windows steamy from the rain, mugs stacked in the usual gravity-defying installation on the floor, Saturday papers carpeting the floor, an ironing board so much a part of the furniture that it was piled with bills and pizza flyers, a cat litter tray with suspicious sandy mounds humming gently by the sink, and the seventies relic of a TV throwing out the fuzzy sound of football results.

'Yeah. Thanks. Just a shame I never realised that moving to West London meant we were legally bound to live like *Steptoe and Son.*'

'Actually, Gabs, there *is* something I've been meaning to ask you. But . . . I dunno, maybe it's not the right time.'

'Well, you've started now.'

Gary took a showy deep breath. 'Gabs, will you . . . come to the pub quiz with me on Wednesday?'

'Oh, ha ha,' she said, throwing a cushion at him.

'Had you going, though, didn't I?'

'NO. And what makes you think I'd have you anyway?'

He stood up. 'Because I am irresistible.'

'I'd forgotten that. Saturday nights must be such a terrible ordeal for you . . . all those women desperate for a bit of uniform.'

'Well, I don't like to boast, but my rotas are published on the Internet, so my fans know when to have bitch fights and road traffic accidents . . .'

'In that case, I don't think you should keep your public waiting,' Gabby said, reaching for the phone. 'Now piss off and leave me alone to swap spells with Mo.'

*

Boris has arrived, almost incontinent with excitement.

'Ooh, Trace, what do you think it could be? Maybe a big meal somewhere posh?'

I laugh. 'Isn't your belly big enough already?'

'Nah – now I've got an excuse.'

'Anyway, what's that got to do with the programme? Unless it's one of those places in London where they sell spotted dick and custard served by women in suspender belts, who cane you if you don't clean your plate.' I look up at Jamie, who's setting up in the corner. 'It's not that, is it?'

'I'm saying nothing until Jenny gets here.'

'I don't care what it is,' Boris says, 'I haven't been out for weeks.'

'Your husband's almost as bad as mine for being away all the time.'

'The only difference is I miss mine,' she says, rubbing her bump. It hasn't taken her long to understand my domestic situation. 'But the more he works away now, the more time he can take off when the baby comes.'

'Men always say they'll be there afterwards. But they forget their promises the minute you've given birth, the same way women forget how much it hurts until they get pregnant again.'

'Brian won't do that.' She gives me an odd look. 'And I don't care how much it hurts. It'll be worth it.'

I'm shocked at how serious she's become, and as I rack my brains for something to say to clear the air the doorbell goes. Jenny rushes past me with two carrier bags.

'This is so cool,' she tells us. 'Right, Jamie-boy, get that camera rolling.'

He obliges, then says, 'Speed,' which I've now learned means 'Action'. We take our cue, and start rummaging in the bags.

The first things to emerge are two white shirts – not classy, tailored, posh, evening-out shirts, but cheap and nasty blouses with packaging creases warping the fabric. Another rummage produces a pair of fishnet tights each, and as I pull out a tie in a depressingly familiar canary yellow, a terrible conclusion is forming in my mind.

'God. We *are* going to one of these school dinner places, aren't we? I thought they were for pervy businessmen who miss being at public school.'

'Hang on,' Boris says, back to her normal self, as she pulls an envelope from her carrier bag. 'The tickets must be in here. Oooh, it's just like *Blind Date*.' The way she says it, you'd have thought being like *Blind Date* was a good thing.

I reach in for my envelope, and tear it open. ' "School Disco? A club night with all your favourite eighties tunes – only admitted if wearing school uniform"?' On the back, there's a Tube map.

We both look at Jenny, who grins back. 'Surprise!'

She's not joking. I haven't been to a London nightclub since I was twenty. And judging from the expression on Boris's face, that still makes me way more experienced than her.

I've never liked surprises.

Hammersmith Broadway, West London

Gary watched Roger as Roger watched the girls go by. It wasn't even dark yet, but the gaggles of females were already at the tottering stage, in their tiny skirts and ridiculous heels. Roger clicked his tongue sadly.

'If only I was ten . . . no, twenty years younger. Like you, in fact, Gary.'

'I'm past it, too, mate.'

The two policemen walked past the alkies and the dope-heads by the park. They were always there, and Gary had even given directions based on them: 'Turn left at the drunks, and the post office is up there on your right.'

'We're in such a hurry to be adults, and once we get there, we spend the rest of our lives regretting it,' said Roger.

Gary thought he probably preferred it before when he and Roger spent their shifts in silence, before Roger got comfortable with him and confided pearls of worldly wisdom. Endlessly.

Five women – one sporting the full hen-night uniform of L-plates, veil and last-chance sequinned boob tube – ran past them, turned back and wolf-whistled at Gary.

'What about that bird of yours? Has she stopped banging on about weddings yet?'

'She knows the score.'

'I bet she does. She knows she'll wear you down in the end. Oh, or get pregnant.'

Pregnant. Did women still do that, trick blokes into the full commitment thing with biological warfare? Maybe some did, but not Gabby. She was too . . . equal. And, thank Christ, too young to be paranoid yet about running out of time.

'What about the other one?'

'Other one?'

Roger smiled knowingly. 'No need to play dumb with me, mate. You remember. The one who got in touch from school?'

'Ah. Tracey.'

Tracey. Gary was kicking himself for e-mailing her back. He'd only done it . . . well, why had he done it? Oh, yes, that was it. He'd had a row with Gabby that day, and wanted to do something for himself. Sometimes he really was as immature as she said.

Then again, what harm did it do? Tracey existed alongside the other cyber-women on the Web, like Lolita ('from Russia with love') or Racquel ('bringing a taste of the Tropics to your laptop'). OK, so with Tracey he knew exactly where she was, and Bracewell didn't count as a faraway place. Not in geographical terms, anyway, though it was clear her life was now a million miles from his. However hard she tried to sound cool in her e-mails, the hints were there of a life – and a Tracey – so different from the old one that she might as well have been on the moon. She was trying to keep back the details she thought made her less appealing.

The fact that nothing could make Tracey less appealing had escaped her. But now and again something would slip between the lines: the fact she was married and had kids and then this business about the reunion. Though she'd been pretty forthcoming about that right away.

He couldn't pretend it didn't intrigue him, the idea of going back. He was sure he'd have done well compared to the others: the well-paid job, the long-haul holidays, the flat worth £120K (they didn't have to know it was next to a chippy, backing on to the Tube line). And Gabby was a catch, a cut above the average.

But it wouldn't be like that, if he went to the reunion. No exam to find out who'd scored top marks in life. It was Tracey's show – hadn't it always been? – and however superior he felt here, striding the streets like Blade Runner, it'd melt away the instant he walked into the hall, and came face to face with the only people who knew the truth.

That he had been dumped by Tracey.

In favour of a teacher.

'So?' said Roger, and Gary realised he'd been waiting for more details.

'I took your advice. I've got Tracey exactly where I want her.'

In the past.

CHAPTER SIXTEEN

The M4 is one of those roads that still seem romantic to me, despite the grime and the cones. The build-up starts with the planes and the signs for Heathrow. I always fancied working at an airport, not as a stewardess or anything, that's no more than glorified waitressing, but on the ground, escorting visiting celebrities, or rescuing lost kids.

Anything would be more glamorous than my life.

It's getting dark outside, and the lights under the planes make them look even closer than they are. Then the neon signs appear at the roadside, ads for Lucozade and courier companies, and the lanes narrow towards the flyover.

'We'll be there soon,' Jenny says. 'The club's in Hammersmith.'

I feel even more disappointed. At least if they're paying for us to go clubbing, it could be in the West End.

'Hammersmith?'

'It's pretty cool, these days,' she says. 'Nigella Lawson lives there.'

'Who?' says Boris.

I'm surprised Boris doesn't know this one. 'You know – the Domestic Goddess? The posh woman whose dad was a fat Tory?' But I can't see Nigella Lawson going to School Disco.

There are streetlamps over this bit of the motorway, and as the sodium flashes in and out of the car, I catch sight of me and

Boris in the car mirror. Not pretty. Boris comes off better: with that bump of hers, and her plump face, she could almost pass for a real pregnant schoolgirl. But as for me . . .

I just look like mutton dressed as lamb.

The queue is endless, but we're whisked in via the VIP entrance. The club PR people sweep us through a different way – apparently, when they've allowed filming before, crews have been swamped and followed like the Pied Piper.

'Weird,' Jenny says. 'That's exactly how kids behave in the playground when there's a camera around.'

Boris looks nervous, and I wonder if they've thought through the possible consequences of plunging a pregnant woman into what Jamie says is well known as a snog and beer orgy.

But the PR guy seems relaxed. 'We never get any trouble. Putting on a uniform makes everyone behave as if getting off their tits on snakebite – not that we sell it – is the most outrageous thing they can think of. So there're hardly any drugs.'

I guess he would say that, wouldn't he?

'You ready?' Jenny asks.

We nod, and with the reassuringly bulky presence of Jamie and Cliff behind us, we take our first steps into the arena.

The smells, sounds, thumping bass rhythms are standard club fare – the only difference is the view. But what a difference . . .

Below us is a mass of white shirts, more dazzling than a million Lycra outfits. It's like a giant vat of porridge which bubbles in time to the music. Steam rises off it, reeking of sweat and lager. Looks like I'm not the only one with the mutton-dressed-as-lamb problem. Pippi Longstocking plaits bob up and down next to balding heads.

And what music! It's naff and it's catchy, none of the dance music that forced me to accept the time had come to switch from One FM to Radio 2. New Romantics and one-hit wonders, it's wedding fare, without the Barry Manilow.

'Here are your drinks, ladies.' Jenny's been to the bar and brought an orange juice for Boris, and a cloudy pint of beer for me. 'So what do you think?'

I'm about to come out with a snide remark about how dodgy the whole thing is, but when I open my mouth all that comes out is 'Brilliant!' and Boris starts grinning as she drags me down towards the blob, to the opening chords of 'It's Raining Men'.

I'm on my third pint. I don't usually drink beer because it makes me gassier than a hot-air balloon, but G and T feels wrong for School Disco. So now I feel gassy and I need a pee every ten minutes, but I also feel rejuvenated. The music's fantastic . . .

Boris can't help herself either, she's screaming at the top of her voice: 'La, la, la, la, la, la, la, modern girl . . .'

The men aren't bad, actually, the uniform works wonders, which is slightly disturbing. But then all the girls look good too; there's something about the light in here, or the lack of it, that makes everyone look, if not teenaged, then at least younger than I guess they are in normal life.

Boris is banging her head up and down to the sound of Sheena Easton. And she's not even drinking . . .

Jenny and Jamie return; they've been off filming general crowd shots, in between buying me drinks. I suspect they want me to get pissed on camera. They do some close-ups of Boris, then turn to film me.

'So what do you reckon, Tracey?'

'This is really getting me in the mood,' I say. It feels like the kind of thing they want to hear. 'You can't help yourself with this kind of music. And it's like being sixteen again, or maybe younger. Feels very innocent here. Apparently people hardly even do drugs. Not that I know much about drugs, as a past-it housewife, but here, no one knows I'm a housewife. It's fun. And it's been a while since I've had some of that.'

Jenny nods the way she always does when she's happy with the way an interview's gone, and I notice her reaching back to pinch Jamie gently on the arm to show she's finished this bit.

The song switches to 'Girls Just Wanna Have Fun', and as I stand alongside a bopping Boris, a couple of girls come up and ask me why I'm being filmed.

'I'm doing a programme about school reunions,' I tell them.

'Wow! Wicked,' says one, who has impossibly straight blonde hair. 'Is this your first time here?'

'Yep. What about you guys?'

'God, no, we come every week. It's great for pulling,' she shouts above the communal singing.

The other one points at Boris's bump. 'Looks like your mate's already scored.'

'We love the music. It's so retro. Takes us right back to when we were at school and everything.'

Boris is slowing down a bit, but the girls are unstoppable.

'God, yeah. Though it's hard remembering, isn't it?' says the blonde one.

I like the fact we're all owning up to that nostalgia, that desperation to be young again. 'You're dead right. It'll be seventeen years this summer since I left. What about you two?'

They look at me oddly.

'Um. Well, um, two.'

Two?

The other one looks uncomfortable, almost guilty. 'Well, four if you don't count the sixth form . . .'

Suddenly, I feel like stringiest mutton again. But I guess that's kind of appropriate in this meat market.

'Tracey?'

I turn round to look at Boris, and she's stopped moving. In fact, she looks a bit sweaty.

'Tracey, I don't feel brilliant. Can we get some fresh air?'

I look around for Jenny and Jamie, but they're miles away – well, only the other side of the room, towards the Tuck Shop, but there must be a thousand people between us and them. I take Boris's arm, which feels quite clammy, and clutching my beer in the other, we head for the exit.

It's still warm outside, but at least we can kind of breathe out here.

'Is that any better?' I ask Boris, and I feel pretty stressed. Bloody stupid to take a pregnant woman to a nightclub anyway. I just hope it's all OK . . .

'Yeah, yes. Just a bit hot,' she says and she's looking less sick. 'But, what a laugh, eh? I'm coming back after the baby, I'll bring Brian.'

I think about putting her right, telling her that she won't go out for the first two years, but, hey, she'll find out soon enough. There's still a small queue of very pissed-looking blokes outside the club.

'Sold out, mate,' says a bouncer. 'It's just not going to happen tonight. You wanna get here a bit earlier next time. *And* you'll need a tie.'

There're half a dozen of them, and they look less friendly than the cute boys inside.

'Oh, go on,' says the bloke at the front of the queue, but it's obvious from the expression on the bouncer's broken-up face that he's not going to change his mind.

'I told you, boys. Move along, you might still make the last Tube.'

The leader, who's probably twenty-five or so, turns back to his mates, and there's this pause where it all seems calm, but *not*, you know. There's a whiff of something in the air. Carlsberg or testosterone or both.

And then, like a dance troupe, off they go, the blokes. Legs, arms, feet, fists punching, and loud mouths screeching and swearing, the sounds carrying through the summer air.

I grab Boris by the arm, and pull her away past the guys, back up towards where I think Hammersmith is. I'm not scared, though they're not messing around, these guys, and the bouncer's response is to slam shut the doors, leaving the men jostling and itching to fight, but with no obvious target. We're not a target, they want enemies their own size, but the risk of being in the crossfire is still serious. It's at this point that I realise that Boris pregnant is even more bovine than Boris at school. She's dangerously slow.

'Fucking let us in,' the men shout, stamping and threatening some of the other no-hopers behind them in the queue, who're too drunk to have the sense to move away.

I'm looking around us, hoping we are going the right way, and wondering what the hell we do next, two grown women dressed as schoolgirls, in the middle of the night, a long way from home.

Then – who says they're never there when you need them – I see two coppers ahead of us, and they're coming this way. I'm sure they're speeding up but I can't tell for sure if that's because they've worked out what's going on, so I drag Boris along and start to shout.

'Police,' I cry in their direction, trying to make sure the fighting blokes don't hear me. One of the policemen, a taller guy, breaks into a bit of a trot and behind him, one who looks older, steps up his pace.

'Over here,' I shout, 'there's a punch-up.'

The one lagging behind pulls out his radio, and the running one catches up with us, looking quickly at Boris and taking in her bump before anything else.

'Are you all right?' he says and there's something about the voice, I dunno, there's something, a softer accent than pure Cockney, that makes me look upwards – and fuck me . . .

'Gary?'

He stiffens, and when he's once-overed Boris for obvious injuries, his eyes come back to me and his face twists, and when he speaks he really doesn't sound all that pleased.

'Tracey. Tracey Mortimer. What the hell—' But before we can even begin to go back down Memory Lane, there's the crash of breaking glass, and my first ever lover runs past me, into danger.

CHAPTER SEVENTEEN

As reunions go, it didn't go well.

When the sounds of breaking glass (I wonder if they play Hazel O'Connor at School Disco) stopped, we headed back towards the club: I needed to see him. Reinforcements had arrived, and the guys who'd been fighting were handcuffed and restless.

Boris was so overwhelmed by dizziness that she didn't realise it was Gary, but how did I know it was him? His height? The little curls of hair on the back of his neck? And how did he know it was me?

I tried to catch his eye, while Boris went progressively greener. She was desperate to get home, while I was desperate for some kind of sign from Gary, something to give me hope. But he was absorbed in his work, which, once the fuss had died down, seemed to consist of striding about looking stern. I've never seen the appeal of S and M, but there was something very sexy about that macho air. I guess it was such a different side to the Gary I knew, who was permanently nice at school. Well, until the day he wasn't . . .

He looked at me just once before he melted away into the ranks of the other uniforms. I've been trying to remember every fragment of that look – and to work out what it meant.

He'd raised his eyebrows at me, I'm pretty sure of that. But why? An acknowledgement? A question? Or amusement that after all those years we ended up meeting like that?

Then his face turned harder, as though he was trying to look through me, to see . . . what? It wasn't a nice feeling. I felt exposed. And then just before he turned away, there was a softening – not a smile, I would certainly have remembered that and kept it as a screensaver in my brain, returning to it over and over. Finally his eyes narrowed as he made a decision.

But what decision?

It's Sunday afternoon, and I've lost count of the number of times I've logged on to my e-mail. Nothing. I could send one myself, but I have this feeling that I should wait for him to make the first move. I still think that somewhere in that short, sharp expression was the look of unfinished business. And I hope that means he will get in touch.

Mum thinks I've *still* got a hangover, so she's tutting around saying things to the kids like, 'Don't make any loud noises, your mummy's paying the price for her heavy night,' and then slamming the door behind me with full force.

I won't deny that my head aches a bit, beer always does that, but it's annoying to be cast as an irresponsible old soak when I behaved really well.

It's always been like that with Mum, though. At school, there were some girls who had amazing 'best mate' relationships with their mothers, and I'd love to have someone to talk to about the whole Gary business, but she knows so little about me that I know there's no point. I can't believe that we shared a house for two decades and all we've got to show for it is a common passion for Findus Crispy Pancakes.

Kelly's taking Mum's warning really seriously, tiptoeing nervously about, carrying the notebook the shrink gave her. She's getting obsessive about it, and every time I look round she's huddled in a chair, writing.

128

And I realise with a horrible jolt that Kelly and I are just as far apart as Mum and me, and that she's probably going to grow up thinking all the same things, that I don't understand her and she can't talk to me.

But I don't think there's a single thing I can do to change it. The glare from the computer screen is really savage every time I log on, but I can't stop myself.

One new message.

I clench my fists in frustration as the computer refuses to download my inbox, and shut it all down and go back online. But who is going to e-mail me on a Sunday unless it's . . . ?

It's Boris.

'Bugger!' I swear out loud and when I turn round I notice Kelly's scribbling something else in that sodding book.

Flat 2a, 422 Goldhawk Road, Shepherd's Bush, London

Gary staggered into the kitchen, rubbing his eyes.

'Any tea going?'

'Oh, the monster awakes. Kettle's just boiled, I'll make you one. So was it a hard night?'

He fell slowly backwards on to the sofa. 'Only the usual, being sworn at, spat at and generally abused. Plus a punch-up outside that School Disco place. Bunch of overgrown yobs dressed as schoolboys getting sulky because they weren't letting them in.' *Oh, and a momentary meeting with my first love on the Shepherd's Bush Road.* But Gary had already decided it was better to keep that part of the evening to himself.

Gabby handed the steaming mug over the top of the sofa. 'I fancy going there some time.'

'Really? You'd change your mind if you'd seen this bunch.'

'Yeah, but what about all those girls in uniform? Every bloke's fantasy, I'd have thought. Like being sixteen again.'

Gary shrugged. 'I don't have any desire to go back in time, thanks very much.' Not after last night. 'How was your night?'

'Just the usual spells and black magic. Couple of curses on Mo's supervisor in the adoption department. She's been getting a really hard time because of that court case, you know the one I told you about . . .'

She squeezed in next to him, and stroked his hand as she chatted on, her calm voice sing-songing with impersonations of her friends and their boyfriends and bosses. He loved the sound she made, but he wasn't taking in any of the words.

Tracey Mortimer was back like an old war wound, and just as hard to get rid of. On the Internet, she was harmless. In the flesh, it was something else.

She'd followed him back to the club. He felt her there before he saw her, and then he tried to sneak a glimpse without her noticing, but it was impossible, she was staring at him the whole time. He forgot how to walk, and felt instead that he was doing a bad impression of a policeman, striding around like a new plod in the drill yard at Hendon.

And when he did look, it was like looking into a tunnel with no end. He was paralysed. Maybe it was like this when you died, seeing your whole life flash before you. Except he didn't see his whole life, just Tracey's eyes, and the times he'd gazed into them, and all the things she'd been doing when they locked on his: messing about, flirting, confiding, kissing, fucking, taunting, teasing and, this time, asking him for something more, though he didn't know what.

He'd known all along it would be a mistake to see her. It was bloody awful the way those few minutes had churned everything up.

Did she look older? He thought maybe she had, tried to remember what impression he'd formed of her in the second or so before he realised who she was. But that told him nothing, because he'd been assessing what she was telling him about the punch-up, and so she was no more or less than a witness. Who happened to be in school uniform. Which happened to show she had good legs. Legs he recognised because, once upon a time, they'd been wrapped round his neck . . .

So where the fuck did this leave him?

'You're not listening, are you?' Gabby said, but she didn't sound pissed off.

'Sorry, love, I kind of am, just knackered, really.'

'Well, you can go back to bed because – as I was just telling you when you'd gone into your spaced-out mode – I'm going shopping with Dee. OK?'

She kissed him on the cheek, and went into the hall. He heard her zipping up her boots and throwing her keys into her handbag. 'See you later, Gaz.'

'Bye, Gabs.'

As the door shut, the computer suddenly seemed to grow to dominate the entire living room.

He'd had the big question in his head since he'd frog-marched those thugs away from the club to the cells. But he was no closer to answering it.

There was no harm, he supposed, in logging on to see if she'd e-mailed *him*. Then he could take his decision based on that.

At least Boris is OK. I've e-mailed her back saying I think it's bloody outrageous that they dragged her to a club in her condition, but she's so laid back about it, she says it doesn't matter, at least she's in one piece, and it's just a shame I couldn't stay longer because of her.

She's a sweetheart, Boris. She didn't even cross my mind for all those years, but now I realise what I've missed. I'd have thought it would have been Melody whose friendship would pass the test of time, but her behaviour on my wedding day put paid to that. And really, once you took away the shared bitching and the fact we were both decent-looking, what did we have in common?

Boris is the first friend I've had in years; embarrassing but true. I've always kidded myself I had mates: the girls at secretarial college and in my first office, then the ladies I work with in the shop, and the other mums from antenatal. But I hardly saw them, never rang them up for proper chats or arranged to go out. Now I think about it, there were coffee mornings and girls' nights out organised, that I'd hear about by accident, but I didn't want to spend time with those women anyway, so I didn't care that I wasn't invited.

But with Boris, well, there's something there, a connection; maybe it's just shared history, and the fact that we're doing the programme together, but I think there's more to it. I hope she feels the same way. It makes me feel nice.

I reply to Boris's latest message. She says the baby's having a manic afternoon, so I tell her that might mean it's a boy, because Callum moved loads more than Kelly did.

I send the message, and when the page reloads, there's the message.

From GARYANDGABBY, but there's no subject line. I click on it:

'ello, 'ello, 'ello . . . fancy bumping into you!

And that's it. One measly line. But it tells me all I need to know.

132

CHAPTER EIGHTEEN

I can tell it's going to be a big day when I wake up before Callum does.

Usually when I wake up in the morning, I feel this sense of vague doom, even before I remember the basic stuff like who I am, where I live, or whether I can afford a lie-in. The thought process goes something like this: I'm sad . . . I'm married . . . to who . . . ? to Dave . . . oh yeah, that's right . . . that's why I feel sad . . .

But this morning, I wake up to a buzzy feeling, and the clue comes when I open my eyes and see the clothes I've decided to wear already hanging on one of the handles of the built-in wardrobe. You can say a lot against Dave, and I do, but he's provided well for us. I have more cupboard space than any woman could wish for, with concealed lighting above the full-length mirrors that make me look quite glamorous on a good day.

And today, I hope, is going to be one of those good days.

I stretch my legs out to the very end of the bed – I love having the king-size to myself; it almost makes up for the lack of sex. I did enjoy sex when I was younger, but then I also enjoyed air hockey, and the opportunities and desire for both are rare. Callum was a big baby, so that didn't help on the libido front. Even Dave went off the idea eventually. Nowadays I think he finds the Moben fitted furniture catalogue a more enticing prospect in the bedroom. Except when he's pissed, of course, but then for men like Dave it's any port in a storm.

But in the last couple of months, I've noticed a gradual thawing in parts of my body I'd assumed were as chilly and out of reach as last summer's chicken wings at the bottom of the chest freezer. I suppose it's a reaction to being around decent-looking men for a change – Jamie, Alec and now Gary . . .

And the thought of Gary and his handcuffs is definitely speeding up the defrosting process.

I know I'm always disappearing into silly daydreams, but, for once, it's not just fantasy. It's actually going to happen.

After bumping into him like that, what had we got to lose? But after the disappointment of that first meeting, the stakes are so much higher to make the next time just right. And the next time is in approximately five hours' time.

I dress in my normal school clothes to deliver Kelly – we've got another psychology appointment due this week, which I'm dreading, but she's drawn little stars around the date on the family calendar in felt pen, so I guess she feels differently. Then I come back to begin the urgent restoration work . . .

I bought an anti-wrinkle avocado face-pack in the super-market yesterday, and I smooth it on before giving Callum a ridiculously early lunch. He's so intrigued by my newly green face that he reaches out with his fists to try to touch my nose and I have to reel backwards like a boxer. Then I drop him off next door, and retreat to the bedroom to complete the transformation.

I've chosen black linen trousers – it's sunny outside, but June's so unpredictable – and a slim-fitting beigey shirt that flatters my skin and my hair, even if I do say so myself; it can't look any worse than that stupid School Disco uniform, after all. And then make-up. I rarely bother with it these days but I'm going for the natural look, which takes twice as many lotions and potions as the unnatural look, but for a lunch date, I can hardly wear full warpaint.

By the time I've finished, I've probably erased a couple of years, but I'm not sure whether it's taken away the pleasant easy-going years at the end of my teens, or the shittier ones at the start of my marriage, when I realised Dave was never going to be able to make me happy, any more than I could do the same for him.

I wouldn't exactly describe myself as rejuvenated, but the effect isn't bad. Certainly it's good enough for lunchtime at the bloody Crown Hotel, where salesmen meet their bits on the side, and small-time manufacturing companies hold their annual dinner dances.

It wouldn't be my ideal choice of venue to meet my first love after seventeen years, but for some mysterious reason Gary actually wanted to come to Bracewell – and it saves me having to get a babysitter, because Maureen next door will always take Callum for a couple of hours. I didn't even think about getting Mum involved . . .

The disadvantage of the Crown is that it's tacky, it's old-fashioned and it smells. But the advantage is that no one I know would be seen dead there. All right, so we're just a couple of old, old friends meeting up, but I'm still married, and with Dave busy erecting things on the other side of the Irish Sea, it wouldn't take much to get the gossip going if anyone saw me with Gary.

I suppose if we enjoy today, then there's a chance that . . . that what? This is what I keep coming back to. What am I hoping for? He's got a girlfriend, I'm a housewife and mother; it's not as though this can go anywhere, is it? I've been trying hard to work out what I want from it, and I don't *think* I'm living in cloud-cuckoo-land, hoping to be carried off on a white charger, but if this is just a get-together with an old school friend, why have I been unable to think about anything else since last week?

Whatever the reason, I know one thing. Having a TV crew there is *not* going to help.

Which is why I haven't told them.

The Crown Pub, Station Road, Bracewell, Berkshire

Jamie walked into the storeroom. 'OK, that miniature camera's rigged up, and we've tested the undercover mikes as well.'

Alec and Jenny were glaring at each other in chilly silence. Jamie stopped, wishing he could walk out again. 'Sorry, didn't realise I was interrupting something.'

'No, don't mind us, Jamie. Jenny's just having another pop at me, aren't you, darling?'

'I can't actually believe you're going to go through with this, that's all!'

Alec shrugged. 'Yes, well, I've taken the decision, I'm the producer, and you're going to have to live with it.'

'I'm going to get a coffee,' she mumbled, leaving the store-room, which was crammed with monitors and tape machines as a temporary TV control centre.

'God, she's fucking hard work today,' said Alec.

'I kind of see her point, though, don't you? It could backfire really badly.'

'In which case, I'll take the rap, like I always do. Anyway that silly cow Tracey shouldn't have gone behind our backs, should she?'

Jamie made a non-committal noise and followed Jenny to the bar.

'There's nothing you can do when he's like that, Jen.'

'I can't fucking believe he's doing this. It's mad, the whole bloody programme could fall apart over it. Never mind the fact that it stinks. Morally.'

'Morally?'

'Well, I wouldn't expect *you* to understand that.' But she was smiling.

'It's a bit daft of Tracey, though. I mean, the company's spending a fortune on organising the reunion, so it's not on to keep stuff from you.'

'Maybe not. But I'm sure she'd have told us in her own time.'

'She knows you can read her e-mails, though?'

'She must have forgotten. And, of course, it wasn't *me* reading them that was the problem, was it? I would have kept my gob shut. Bloody Annabel has a lot to learn.'

The barman came over with her coffee. 'Going all right, is it? I used to love that Jeremy Beadle, *Game for a Laugh.*'

When he'd gone, Jamie said, 'Stroke of genius from Alec, though, this surveillance idea. Not to mention the cover story – the hotel have bought it totally. You've got to hand it to him.'

'Oh, yeah, he's brilliant at being a devious backstabbing cheat. But fooling the hotel's one thing. Dealing with Tracey when she finds out is going to be a totally different scenario.'

I considered taking a cab, but I can't get pissed because Kelly will need picking up from school in a few hours. I was tempted to take a swig of gin before I left the house – wouldn't even have needed the tonic to go with it – but the smell of alcohol on my breath wouldn't enhance the classy impression I'm trying to create.

I park the car near the town hall, and walk to the Crown. It's the only one of the pubs in town that we never went to when we were at school, because it was strictly for old farts. Everyone was an old fart when we were fourteen, of course, but it didn't stop us going into every other pub in the town.

And now I'm an old fart myself, way too old even to be thinking about sex. I catch sight of myself in a car window, and the shirt looks too tight, the trousers too dowdy, and the make-up not nearly thick enough.

What would the fourteen-year-old Tracey Mortimer make of Tracey Brown?

At first, she'd be horrified. Where's the house in *Homes and Gardens*, the Caribbean holidays, the designer clothes? Yes, the kids are there, she knew there'd be kids, but while Callum would have passed the test, Kelly would have been a serious disappointment. The teenaged Tracey wasn't particularly tolerant of anyone who didn't seize life by the bollocks.

So I'm not sure she'd think much of me, either. Boring life, boring husband, boring children, boring job . . .

But then again, the boring Mrs Brown isn't sitting on her arse waiting for it to get fatter. Sure, she's had a quiet period, falling in love, giving birth, falling out of love, but now something of the old Tracey is returning. How many other suburban mummies would talk a TV company into making two programmes about her? Who else would have the nerve to get back in touch with the guy whose heart she broke seventeen years ago? Never mind invite him out on a date . . .

It's like I've turned a corner – actually, I have turned a corner, the one that leads from the town hall to the street where the Crown is, but that's not what I mean. No, this is a change of direction that's long overdue. After six years in a daze of nappies and spinelessness, I'm having a Mortimer moment. It's about time, too.

138

Five to one.

Gary had been determined to be late, but he couldn't skulk around outside much longer. It was strange enough being back in Bracewell, without hanging about like one of the more obvious boys from the Drugs Squad.

He'd never been in the Crown, but once inside it was exactly what he'd expected: the swirly maze of a carpet, ridiculously gilded reception desk with an over-decorated receptionist behind it, a vague institutional smell of cabbage and boiled beef wafting from what, judging from the sounds of clinking cutlery, was the dining room on the right.

So that meant the bar must be to the left. Gary lowered his head to go through the doorway – built for a poorer nourished, shorter generation. The bar was dingy, and much busier than he'd expected, every table occupied. He couldn't see what attracted them. It couldn't be the atmosphere, because there wasn't any. He doubted it was the decor, with its horse brasses and tobacco-stained paintwork. And, he thought, as he approached the bar, it wasn't the welcoming bar staff or the range of real ales.

'Half a lager, please.'

The barman looked at him strangely, confirming Gary's suspicion that he looked like a bad undercover detective in his made-no-effort clothes. But that wasn't what was making him uneasy. What the hell was he doing here? A gentle amble down Memory Lane? Not when the present was so much better. Or maybe a twisted little look at the way things could have turned out, if he hadn't made a run for it . . .

But what if 'it' was still there, whatever it was that had driven him mad with hormones, and then nearly mad with grief?

What if, after seventeen years, he still hadn't got Tracey Mortimer out of his system?

'Sorry, mate,' he called out to the barman, who was bending over to reach a glass. 'Can you make that a pint?'

I wanted to do a last-minute make-up check in the Ladies, but I can't find them. The receptionist says they're through the bar, and as I step inside I spot Gary, and I back away behind the door frame to take it all in.

Still good-looking, no doubt about it, though there's a sulky look on his face that, if you didn't know him, you'd think was bad temper. But that's just his way of covering up uncertainty. He's always been like that.

It's *nice* to know he's feeling nervous. Another sure sign: he's clutching his pint with both hands like he's afraid of dropping it, and casting shifty little glances around the bar. It's surprisingly packed: maybe there's a convention of sprocket makers on in the function room.

Right. Shoulders back, head up, tits forward, lips forward. Advance.

'So, what's a nice guy like you doing in a shithole like this?' OK, cheap line, but kind of appropriate.

He turns, and I see it there, just before he pulls his face back together into a bland, Mr Plod expression, a flash of attraction that passes between us, and proves I've hung on to something from the old days.

'Waiting for someone,' he says and I can't tell whether he's playing the game or not. He looks at me like he's trying to work out the same. Then he flashes those enormous teeth of his in this odd smile. 'So can I buy you a drink until she turns up?'

I nod, and just when I'm looking round to see if I can spot an empty table, a smartly dressed woman at the best corner table stands up, sighing loudly and tutting at her watch. She continues sighing as she flounces past me and out of the bar, like an actor in a soap opera.

'Gin and tonic.' Well, one can't do me any harm. 'I'll just go and bag that free table for us, shall I?'

I watch him as he orders. He doesn't seem to have put on any weight; maybe running after criminals keeps him fit. The thought of him chasing around London like Dennis Waterman in *The Sweeney* makes me laugh, but also makes me feel quite flushed. There's a reproduction Coca-Cola mirror on the wall opposite me, and I do look slightly pink. Usually it takes a couple of gins to get me looking that perky these days.

He sits down opposite me. 'So.'

'So.' I want him to take the lead.

'What shall we toast?'

'School Discos?' We clink glasses. 'So did you bang them up? The guys from the punch-up?'

'Only the guy with the knife.'

'One of them had a knife? Bloody hell.' My big, brave, hunky hero.

'That's what it's like on the mean streets, Trace.'

Trace. He makes the 'a' really long, holding it in the back of his throat. It makes me tingle.

'So, do you like your job?' It's a lame question, but I can hardly ask about the things I really want to know. Do you fancy me? Do I look the same? Does your girlfriend know you're here?

'The pay's good, and we have a laugh when we're not being gobbed at.'

This is bloody hard. What did we talk about when we were fifteen? Not school, not gossip, not music. I suppose mainly we snogged, and messed about, postponing the moment when we were finally going to Do It. And now there's a whole list of things *not* to discuss, including most of the past, and all of the present: a husband, two kids, bucketloads of lost hope . . .

'Poacher turned gamekeeper, eh?'

141

'They nearly didn't take me because of what happened. Even though I was seriously provoked – don't you think?' He stares at me, and I find it impossible to hold his gaze.

'I . . . it was a long time ago. And London? Do you like living there?'

'It's expensive and it's dirty. But when I come back here, I don't regret getting out.' He drinks some beer. 'You weren't going to stick around in Bracewell, either, were you?'

He's needling me, and I think he's doing it deliberately. 'Things change, don't they? I got out of Crawley Park; that was far enough for me.'

He snorts. 'Right. I suppose we all had to scale down our plans for world domination.'

'I didn't get the grades to get on the world domination course.'

'Shame. You'd have thought old Carmichael could have put in a word for you. Personal reference, if you like.'

This isn't going the way I'd hoped. I laugh, but it's not funny. 'So, are you still in touch with anyone else?'

'I exchange Christmas cards with Briggsy. And one of the lads invited me to his wedding a few years back – do you remember Darren Bostock? But I couldn't see the point. I've got different mates now, in the Met. People I've got something in common with.'

'Yeah. Yeah, I know what you mean.' Only I don't know, do I, because if I had lots of those new mates, I'd hardly be organising a sodding reunion.

'What about you?'

'Well, Boris and I are pretty close.'

'I can't believe that was her, I didn't even notice, what with the punch-up to sort out. Say hi to her for me.'

'I will.'

What now? It's completely silent in the bar. Where's the

awful pub mood music to fill in the gaps? Everyone else is on their own, the businessman opposite with his head buried in paperwork, blocking the world out with his briefcase. The young girl reading an airport novel in the corner.

I try again. 'This place is like a morgue. I'm sure there are funkier places we could have met, but they'd probably turn me away at the door as too old.'

He looks me up and down. 'You look good.' But he says it with a complete lack of interest, as if he's talking about gloss paint or motor oil.

'I was worried you wouldn't recognise me.'

'What, not recognise my first lurve?' He smiles into space. 'I'd recognise you anywhere, Trace. And do you know why?'

I don't think I want to, but I think he's going to tell me anyway, so I shake my head, with a smile as false and brittle as an air hostess's.

'Because it's very hard to wipe out the face of the person who humiliated me in front of all my friends.'

Shit.

'Who chased and pursued and flirted until she got what she wanted, and then dumped me two weeks before the exams.'

It's my imagination, but it feels like the whole bloody bar is listening to what he's saying. I even catch the barman looking over, but he darts back under the counter.

'I've tried hard to forget, believe me, Trace. But then something will remind me. Maybe Gabby – that's my girlfriend by the way, gorgeous, she is – will switch on the radio and they're playing "True" by fucking Spandau Ballet, and I'll remember how it felt punching Bob sodding Carmichael in the face when what I really wanted to do was smash *your* face in.'

He's spitting the words at me now, though he hasn't raised his voice.

'Oh, don't worry, Trace. I'm not going to touch you.

Because this meeting is exactly what I needed to get you out of my system. You're just as small-town as I thought you'd be, and thank Christ you dumped me, because I can't think of anything much worse than being stuck here with you in Bracewell for the rest of my days.'

He stops and we both sit utterly still for I don't know how long. He looks even more surprised than I am at what he's just said.

I gulp and I feel stupid, humiliated and, I hate to admit it, tearful. But I'm not going to let him see that.

I down the last of my drink. 'I guess you won't be wanting an invite to the reunion then, Gary.' I stand up. 'Thanks for coming. Have a nice life.'

I head towards the opposite end of the bar to look for the loos before the bloody waterworks start. I feel so grateful when I see the Victorian sign for the Ladies as I battle against the unfamiliar vinegary sensation spreading from my throat to my nose, and then my eyes. I push my way through the door.

And walk straight into Jenny.

CHAPTER NINETEEN

The shock stops the tears in their tracks. It's such a ridiculous place for Jenny to be, like seeing an elephant on the North Pole.

'What are you doing here?' I ask.

She can't meet my eye.

'Oh. Um, working. What about you? You look very glamorous.'

'Thanks. What work?'

There's something wrong here. I've had a lifetime's ration of coincidence by bumping into Gary in London.

'Yeah, um, we're . . . sussing out where to stay for the reunion.'

We? Who else is here? I can't see them coming on a day trip to glorious Bracewell just to look at hotels.

I'm suddenly sure that she's here for one reason: to check what was going on with Gary. But how did she know we were meeting here in the first place? Unless. . .

'Have you been reading my e-mails?' Shit, I'd forgotten that she could get into my account. How could I have been so stupid?

'No!' But Jenny's a terrible liar, considering she works in television. I've had years of practice with Dave, so I can spot someone this crap a mile off. And I think she realises that because she says, 'Let's get a drink, shall we?'

*

145

'I can't see us using any of that shite in the show,' said Alec, as the technician spot-checked the recordings from the secret camera. There was barely space for them and all the equipment in the pub's storeroom. Not that Alec seemed to mind. Getting close enough to his researcher to see right down her cleavage was a small consolation prize for all the money she'd wasted.

Annabel looked upset. 'It might work,' but even she couldn't come up with a way.

'Mind you, interesting about this other pupil he mentioned. Bob. Sounds like a teenage love triangle. Maybe we could work something up around that. What have you got on him?'

Annabel flicked back through her notebook, shaking her head.

She was going to have to go, thought Alec. The cleavage wasn't even all that spectacular, close-up.

'Oh, for Christ's sake, Annabel, don't tell me she hasn't told you about him? Some researcher you are. And what's taking Jenny so long? You women spend half your lives in the toilets, don't you—'

'Now this is interesting . . .'

'That makes a change.'

Annabel ignored him. 'In my notes it says Bob Carmichael wasn't a pupil at all . . .' She paused for effect. 'He was her form tutor.'

One of the 'extras' drafted in from head office, a development producer called Steve, walked in from the bar, taking off his pin-striped jacket. 'Coast is clear now. How was it for you?'

'Dull as hell, mate. Except it seems our friend Tracey was a bit keener on teachers than she'd have had us believe. Bob Carmichael – I knew the name rang a bell.'

Steve said, 'I tell you why that is. Bob Carmichael is one of the government's advisers. School standards and all that. We interviewed him for a documentary on Channel 4 last year.'

'No, this one is Tracey's old teacher. Unless of course it's one and the same . . . Now that would be a story!' The men chuckled to each other.

'Alec?' Annabel tugged on his arm and pointed at the monitor, where the secret camera showed Tracey sitting back down again. With Jenny.

'Oh, bugger,' Alec said. 'This does *not* bode well.'

'You *have* been reading my bloody e-mails, haven't you?'

I'm as angry at myself as I am at Jenny. I can't even organise a secret tryst with an old lover without giving the game away *and* knowing she was somewhere nearby while I sat there, taking years of pent-up abuse from Gary . . .

At least Jenny has the decency to look a bit guilty. 'Ye-es. I'm sorry, Tracey. We weren't meaning to spy on you, but to start with we didn't know if you'd got the hang of the computer, so it was just a safety net. And then the next thing, you're in touch with Gary, and then didn't tell us, so we were worried you were keeping other things from us and . . .' She tails off.

I suppose I can understand why she's been logging in but I don't see why she had to follow me here. 'Well, there won't be a happy bloody reunion between me and Gary as it turns out so we've all been wasting our time.'

'Oh dear,' she says. 'Are you OK?' The way she's looking at me makes me wonder if she heard the whole saga. But then she can't have done, because she wasn't in the bar. The place is deserted now, which is weird too. It was packed ten minutes ago. I feel like I've gone into a topsy-turvy world where I'm paranoid about everything . . .

'It wasn't quite the jolly chat I'd been hoping for, but you win some, you lose some.' Actually, I feel like screaming the place down but I'm not going to tell her that.

'Maybe he'll come round,' she says. 'I suppose it's not always going to work as well as it has with you and Boris – Helen, I mean. Anyway, we do have some good news. Madness have agreed to play at the reunion! Isn't that ace?'

Yeah, ace. Funny how Jenny's slipping back into eighties-speak. But *Madness*? Even the fourteen-year-old Tracey would have had her reservations – excitement at the fact a real-life proper chart band was coming to Bracewell for *her* party, but irritation that it wasn't someone cool, like Joy Division or Morrissey . . .

And I can't get excited about a band when my whole past has just been hung out to dry. I want to shout at someone and, thinking about it, Jenny's the obvious person.

'I'm not even sure I want to go ahead with the bloody reunion if you're going to go behind my back.' She looks really nervous now, so I decide to rub it in. 'Anyway, what the hell did you turn up here for? If you wanted to eavesdrop, then you've missed the action, because he didn't hang around.'

'I'm sorry, Tracey.'

'Yeah, well. Whatever. I need to think about this whole bloody thing. I don't know if I want to carry on with the programme. I'll be in touch, but don't hold your breath.'

I stand up, and there's that shifty barman again, watching but trying not to look nosy. He dips down below the counter as soon as he sees that I've clocked him, so as I walk out, I lean right over.

'Sorry to interrupt your afternoon entertainment. Get a sodding video next time, instead!'

I storm out of the Crown, slamming the door behind me.

I know I've got to go home, but what I really want is to drive out of town to one of the old Roman roads, play a Black Sabbath tape, and put my foot down until I'm as far away as I can get.

I'm breathing heavily, and I can't work out what to do next, so I start walking back to the car. Emotions race through my system so fast that I can't even identify what most of them are. But the most powerful is anger, and it's not even fair to say it's directed against Jenny or even Gary.

It's myself I feel most angry with: for not changing the password on my e-mails, for arranging this stupid meeting, for shitting all over Gary in 1984, and, most of all, for having these unspecified, unacknowledged, unachievable hopes that one meeting with the man whose teenaged self I was once in love with could somehow change everything that's wrong with my life.

And then I see a car parked just along from mine: a red sports car with wheels so wide they look as though they belong on a tractor . . .

'God, I really need a drink now,' said Jenny. 'Vodka and fresh orange, please.'

'I suppose they don't always go according to plan, do they?' said the barman. 'Does that mean I won't be on telly now?'

'Probably not.' Jenny turned round as Alec and Jamie came into the bar. 'You owe me big-time for getting us out of that little hole.'

Jamie climbed under the table to start de-rigging, while Alec put his arm round Jenny. 'Yeah. Thanks – you did well. I really thought she'd worked the whole thing out when we saw you on the monitor with her. But she'll come round.'

'No, she fucking won't.'

They turned to see Tracey in the doorway. She walked across the bar to the table where Jamie was removing the microphone that was taped underneath.

'You as well, Jamie. I thought we *got on*.'

Alec started blustering. 'It's not what it looks like . . .'

'As the actress said to the bishop. I'm no TV expert, but I'd say this looks pretty much like you've been filming me without me knowing.'

Jenny looked away as Alec opened his mouth, but no sound came out.

'You can't even deny it. Bloody hell. What am I, to make you go to all this trouble? Some kind of gangland hitman?'

'Blimey, that was close—' Annabel said as she walked through from the storeroom, then stopped in her tracks.

Tracey stared at her. 'No show without Punch. Well, actually there'll be no show at all now.' She headed towards the exit for the second time in ten minutes. 'Oh, Alec, just a little tip from an amateur. If you're going to all the trouble of going undercover, then don't leave a note for the traffic warden on your dashboard saying you're filming with a TV crew in the hotel.'

CHAPTER TWENTY

Poor Boris. She had to listen to me on the phone for hours last night and now here I am cluttering up her lovely living room with more of the same.

'You should sue them.' Her voice is as soothing as the decor, all plumped-up cushions and cross-stitch wall hangings. Even Callum is sedated by it; he's sitting quietly on the floor stroking Pierrot, her Persian cat. 'It's invasion of privacy.'

'Yes, but I invited them to invade my privacy in the first place.'

'It's not the same,' she says, though I wonder if she's only humouring me, saying what I want to hear. 'As for Gary, well, he's obviously changed personality since he became a police-man. I always thought he was far too gentle – I mean . . .'

'Far too gentle for me, do you mean?' I ask, and that chubby hand goes to her mouth as it always does, and she blushes gratifyingly.

'Well, yes, but you're different now, too. You've mellowed.'

I wonder if she's right. I also wonder if it wasn't *me* that changed Gary for the worse. Or maybe I'm flattering myself to think losing my love could change someone's personality. Once upon a time I'd have been sure I could do that, but now . . .

'I don't feel very mellow at the moment. I feel I've cocked everything up.'

'It's the anticlimax. I'm sure there's a name for it and if there isn't, they'll probably invent one. How about Post Reunion Aftermath Tension?'

'PRAT? You're not bloody joking. I must be so stupid to think that one little meeting will sort out all my problems.'

She pats my hand. 'I know, petal. But you don't have *that* many problems when you think about it. You still look great, you've got a nice house, two healthy, happy children—'

'That'll be why Kelly's seeing a shrink then, because she's so happy? And you've forgotten my lovely husband. Oooh, and my wonderful career in the stationery shop. I can't believe I'm born sometimes.'

'Oh, Tracey,' she says softly, and with huge effort she pulls her front-loaded body forward, and puts her arms around me. 'Don't be sad.'

And it's been such a long time since anybody held me like that, expecting nothing back. I'm not even sure anyone ever has. Mum was too buttoned up for spontaneous affection, and with Dave, hugs were only ever a kind of foreplay.

I start crying and it feels as though I'll never stop . . .

Department for Education, London SW1

Suzanne watched as a man in a green sweatshirt worked his way through the jungle of plants in reception. He followed the same routine with each one, stroking the leaves gently, then stepping back like an artist surveying the landscape. Discoloured leaves were removed, and tablet or two of food placed just under the soil before watering. With a final flourish, the man leaned in towards the plant and patted its bark or stem, as if to say, goodbye, see you next week.

Suzanne pulled out her palmtop, selected her ideas file and scribbled in 'plant man – nurturing – dedication'. She'd always kept notes like these, either electronically, in notebooks or, back in the bad old Crawley Park days, in pink lockable diaries. In the last few years it had started to pay off, as the observations could be used for speeches or in the articles she was asked to write for professional journals and, recently, the occasional Sunday supplement.

The woman behind the reception desk looked up. 'Are you *still* waiting?' she said, as if Suzanne were deliberately cluttering up her personal space.

'Suzanne?'

She turned. 'Mr Carmichael.'

He smiled. 'I think I'll be happy with Bob, now. Unless that makes you feel uncomfortable. Bit like calling your parents by their first name, I guess.'

'I'll try it. *Bob.*'

'Righto. I've had enough of the office, shall we go to a coffee shop round the corner?'

She nodded, and as they walked, Suzanne stole glances at him. Once her favourite teacher, then a terrible disappointment, then an object of snatched gossip in between revision periods and O-level exams – and now, more bizarre than all of those, a potential colleague.

He didn't look that different: the hair was lighter and the suit darker, and the cut of both clearly more expensive. She knew most of his pubescent female pupils had thought he was tasty, but she'd been a late developer, and it was only now that she could see it – the strong profile, and the eyes that looked more inviting with age, in the annoying way that men's features often did. In the old days, she didn't admire him for his looks, but for his intelligence. And his integrity. What a joke.

They arrived in the coffee bar, an Italian place with hissing espresso machines, steamy windows and a guy behind the bar who smiled at Bob and eyed Suzanne with unconcealed curiosity.

'Double espresso for Signor Carmichael, and . . . ?'

'Cappuccino, please,' she said, before taking a seat by the window. He followed her.

'This is proving to be a year of reunions,' said Bob.

'So you already know? About Tracey?'

'Yes.' He smiled at her. 'I didn't think you'd got in touch after all this time to talk about education policy. Though we can do that, if you like.'

She felt herself blushing. 'Maybe another time.'

'I must say, though, I liked the sound of your speech. The one about Tracey. Something of an indictment of Crawley Park. And me, I suppose. Though you seem to have made the best of it. You look great, and that charity of yours is terrific.'

Suzanne gulped. 'I was very disappointed in you. For going off with Tracey. I mean, it never would have occurred to me to fancy a teacher, but when she ended up with you, it was like . . . I thought you had more taste.' She stopped. She'd said too much.

Bob's eyes seemed to narrow in amusement. 'I think there was more to Tracey than maybe most people could see. Sure, she was a pain in the arse if she wasn't the centre of attention, but all the stuff with you and with her . . . I honestly don't think any of us realised it was as bad for you as you said in that speech.'

'Perhaps not. Anyway, Dick Phipps called me and said you didn't want to stop her doing it. Aren't you worried?'

'No. He's scared of the scandal coming out, and making him look bad for letting me resign, but I'm not that worried. She was over the age of consent, it was hardly the pinnacle of my career, but at least it wasn't illegal – and the rules were different in those days.'

'All the same, with your job and your profile . . .'

'OK, ideally I wouldn't want it dragged out again, but if Tracey has a reason for doing this, then that's her decision. So what about you? Will you be going?'

'I don't know. I rang the TV company, and they're quite keen to have me as the programme's resident psychologist, which could raise the profile of Millennium Child. But then that speech could be a problem. If someone finds that, and puts two and two together, things could get messy.'

'You're sure you don't want things to get messy?' He was still canny.

'No,' she lied. The truth was she didn't know what she wanted yet. 'The charity's the big thing for me now. Yes, I'd like to raise the profile of what we're doing, but not if it leaves behind a nasty taste in everyone's mouth.'

'Sometimes it is better to leave things as they are.' He sounded sad.

Suzanne studied his face. 'Dick said he thought you wanted to see her again. That surprised him.'

'Poor Dick. He never did understand deep feelings. That's why he taught geography, I suppose.' He chuckled at his feeble joke. 'Of course, my subject was about learning from the past. Which is why I won't be going even though, yes, if I'm honest, I would like to see her again. I know it seems daft, but despite all the unpleasantness, Tracey isn't someone you can forget.'

'No,' Suzanne agreed.

'But I'm not going to gatecrash her party. I'll find it hard to resist watching the programme, though.'

'I bet.'

He looked at his watch. 'I ought to go. But if you *do* want to get involved in the citizenship group, the one you arranged this meeting about' – Suzanne blushed slightly – 'then I'm sure you could make a valuable contribution.'

'Thanks . . . though it smacks a bit of the old school tie, doesn't it?'

'Well, if Eton and Harrow can abuse their positions, why shouldn't Crawley Park Comp do the same?'

'Yes. You're right.' Suzanne stood up. 'I'd better head back to the office. Thanks for meeting me. And I'll think about the working party.'

'Thanks. You should be proud of yourself, you know. You're doing an important job.' He reached over to touch her hands, and then glanced at her wedding ring. 'And your husband's a lucky man, as well. See you again, perhaps, Suzanne . . .'

The sun was warm when she left the café, so Suzanne decided to walk back to her office. She needed to think.

It was almost too easy. All she had to do was go through her contacts list, identify a likely journalist and tip them off. No one would find out it was her – after all, the whole school had known about the affair at the time. She didn't much like reporters, but they were scrupulous about protecting their sources.

She caught sight of herself in a shop window. Surely she was too grown-up to want revenge. But then again, hadn't she had to fight for ten years to lose the persecution complex? The conviction that from the instant she stepped into a room, until the moment she left, she was a target; and the certainty that every giggle, nudge or whisper was directed at her? The fear that everything she did – from the way she brushed her hair, to the way she held her pen – might trigger a whole new campaign of mockery.

She'd spent five years in the shadow of Tracey Mortimer, and it had taken nearly twice as long to *unlearn* the lessons of Crawley Park. The only thing that had kept her going through those agonising classes and lonely break times was fantasising about how she could get her own back. Mostly it involved a large pair of scissors (for cutting off all that wavy blonde hair) or a millionaire boyfriend (to take her to the school disco, and strike Tracey, Melody and the rest of their cronies dumb with jealousy).

But she'd never imagined that the perfect opportunity would arise now, of all times, when she was happier than she'd ever been. What was it they said about revenge being better served cold?

When I stop crying, I'm exhausted. I'd forgotten how knackering wailing can be.

Then, after I'm sure the tears have finished, we decide to change my life.

Boris says the way to start is to make a list, so that's what we're doing. She swears by them, and now I'm looking, I see them everywhere in her house: by the phone, in the kitchen, next to the huge arrangement of flowers that she tells me Brian sends her every Wednesday, to make up for being away. She shows me one she's got programmed into one of those electronic organiser things she carries in her handbag, and even on there her lists are subdivided into work, friends and family, and household.

'I don't know where I'd find the time,' I say, and then I get this pang because there's no longer any reason for me to spend hours on the Internet, composing pithy e-mails to Gary, so I will need something else to occupy me.

'Think of my system as the A-level of lists,' she says. 'We'll work our way up to it. Remember, I've been doing this more or less since I left school. It's sooo lovely when you can tick things off!' She goes rummaging in the drawers of this huge dresser in the dining room, and pulls out a padded notebook featuring pictures of hedgehogs in bathing costumes at the seaside.

'Since when have you been a branch of WH Smith?'

'You can't make lists without paper!' she says, and it strikes me that this isn't just pregnancy-related hoarding. Boris has been nest-building all her life. 'Right then – what shall we call this list?'

'Crap things about Tracey?'

'No, let's call it "Wish List". Things you'd like to change.'

'Being married – I wish I wasn't.'

'Well, we can always sort that out if you *really* don't want to be, but it's a big decision. Life change begins with the tiniest things.'

Am I miserable enough to want a divorce? I suppose what I want is a straight swap for the current husband. I'll trade you my good-looking, cocky, middle-aged wide-boy for a good dad, someone sweet and funny and, above all, faithful.

Dream on, Tracey, you've never gone for that type anyway. And if I divorced Dave, I'd probably just lose the house while he got away scot-free. Oh, and I couldn't bear the knowing looks from Kelly's bloody psychologist.

'I'd like Kelly to be happier.'

We both look at Callum, who is chattering happily into the pretend mobile phone he takes everywhere with him.

'Well, at least he's proof it's nothing *you*'ve done,' Boris says.

Maybe she's right, but it feels too easy to take responsibility only for the kid who's turned out right, and to let myself off the hook for the one with the problems.

'What else do you want to sort out? Work?'

'I don't really care about the job. It's only eight hours a week, anyway, and I was never going to be a career woman, was I?'

She smiles at me. 'It's not all it's cracked up to be, believe me.'

'So why did you and Brian wait this long for the baby?'

'Things don't always turn out as you expect them, Tracey,' she says, and I wait for her to explain. But she doesn't. 'OK, let's leave work for now; we can get you the chief exec's job at Boots once we've sorted the other stuff. What about the whole reunion thing?'

'Oh, don't. I had another message on the mobile this morning from Jenny, grovelling like mad. But they're wasting their time.'

She raises an eyebrow. 'I hope you don't mind me saying this, Tracey, but I think you've been looking for an excuse. Not that this isn't a bloody good one.'

That's another thing I suddenly remember about Boris. Behind that sugar-pink fairy-godmother face, she lets nothing pass her by. It makes me feel uncomfortable. I know she could easily throw me off my high horse.

'I don't know why you say that.'

'Just a hunch. I suppose I think that you liked the idea in theory, but it's not turned out to be what you had in mind. You can't recreate the past.'

'I wasn't really trying. I thought it would be fun . . .'

'Yes, I know. But it's not that easy to go back in time. Anyway, if you're definitely not doing it, they're going to have a job on their hands letting everyone down. How many people are due to be coming?'

I can't bring myself to tell her that the last time Jenny talked about it, she had fewer than a dozen confirmed. So much for the Good Old Days. 'I don't think it'll be too much of a problem getting the word round.'

'How many?' And the expression on her face shows she's going to keep going until she gets an answer.

'Er. Ten.' I feel really stupid.

'Right.' She looks at me sympathetically. 'Is that another reason why you've been so down about the whole thing?'

I shrug. 'It doesn't really matter now, anyway.'

'Let's forget the programme for a minute. If you could have a reunion no one's filming, just for the sake of it, who would be there?'

'You, obviously.'

She grins. 'Goes without saying. And . . . Melody?'

'No bloody way.'

She doesn't ask anything, even though I can see she's dying to know why. 'Gary?'

I hesitate.

'I'll take that as a yes. Bob?'

I laugh, despite myself. 'Gary *and* Bob? We wouldn't need any fireworks, would we?'

'Is there anyone else?'

There is, of course, but how can I say it without looking strange?

Boris waits. Then she says, 'Fantasy reunion. You know, whatever you want, never mind if it's possible or not. Dream a little.'

I feel the back of my throat go tight. 'OK, if you really want to know. Shrimp.'

She doesn't look surprised, just sad. 'Do you miss her?'

And I'm only in tears again, a one-woman bloody sprinkler system, but I can't seem to find the tap to switch it off. She holds me again.

'Yeah. Even now, how fucking stupid is that?'

'It's not stupid.'

'I want to say sorry.'

'For what, honey?'

160

'For killing her.'

She pulls back to look at me. 'But you didn't kill her. A car killed her.'

'I said the worst things. The worst things. And Ricky, you know, her brother, he blames me and he's right, because if I hadn't had this huge row with her, said horrible things, she might have been concentrating harder, she might not have been hit and then she'd be my friend and her kids would play with mine and even if they didn't it wouldn't matter because at least she'd be alive and—'

'Tracey.' She sounds stern now. 'Stop it. You can't know what might have been. You can't. It gets you nowhere.' She's stroking my hair now. Mum used to do that, when I was very small. 'Shrimp died because sometimes people die before they should. Not because of anything you or me or anyone did.'

She's got tears in her eyes now, and I know she's trying so hard, and I want to believe her, but I can't. So I pretend.

'I know,' I say.

'We need more tea,' she tells me, and she disappears into the kitchen, while I try to stop myself crying by thinking about anything but Shrimp. It works, up to a point. I've been doing it for twenty years, after all. When she comes back, she seems calmer too.

'The thing is, Tracey,' she says, 'I think that now the TV company have cocked up so badly, they owe you. But they still *need* you to do this programme, and I think they'll do pretty much anything to keep you on board. Which puts you in a very strong position.'

'I've got too much to think about at the moment.' It's a crap excuse.

'Maybe you have. But then again, maybe you could use them

to give yourself a break. A holiday, say? I reckon they'd pay for that if it meant you'd stay with the programme; it's still cheaper than them starting over with someone else. And it stops you going to the papers.'

'You think I should blackmail them?'

She giggles, but behind the girly innocence I catch a glimpse of the tough businesswoman she's turned into. 'That's not a very nice word. But I think we could make it work to your advantage. And I was quite looking forward to the reunion, whether there're ten of us or a hundred.'

'I'm just not sure I've got the energy.' And maybe it's all the crying, but I do feel completely worn down.

'You could let me . . . negotiate on your behalf. I'm really bored at home waiting for junior to make an appearance.'

I'm torn between wanting to chuck the whole bloody thing in, and wondering whether she can really make it all right.

'Go on, Tracey. Give me, what, a few days? If I haven't sorted out something that makes you happy by, let's say, next Monday, then we can just forget the whole thing. You've got nothing to lose, have you, not really?'

She's smiling again, like it all makes perfect sense and I'd be a spoilsport to deprive her of her fun.

'Next Monday?' How can I refuse? 'All right.'

She rubs her hands together, then reaches out to shake mine. 'Oh, brilliant! Tracey, you definitely won't regret it. I think we should toast it.'

I follow her through to her kitchen, where she starts the kind of proper tea-making ritual I thought you only found in Japan. Watching her is so soothing.

'Is that your phone?' she says, above the hiss of the water in the kettle.

'Probably Jenny again – I'll put her straight on to my agent, shall I?' I shout through, as I retrieve the mobile from the depths of my handbag. 'Hello, Tracey speaking.'

'Mrs Brown? It's Mrs Fellowes from school. I've been trying to get you at home. It's Kelly. Now please don't panic, but I'm afraid there's been an accident.'

CHAPTER TWENTY-ONE

There's only one thing worse than finding out your six-year-old daughter's had an accident.

Finding out it wasn't an accident at all.

Boris drives me and Callum to the hospital, because I can barely speak, never mind steer. On the phone Mrs Fellowes told me not to worry, but that's like telling a baby not to cry, or an injured pet not to bite through its stitches. Boris lives half an hour away, but drives like a maniac through the country lanes.

And when I get to casualty, the nurse rushes me through, and I'm terrified that I won't be brave enough to cope with whatever it is I'm about to see, and then she moves back the cubicle partition and there's Kelly – sitting up on the bed, with a cut and a big bump and bruises blooming on her face as I watch, but otherwise apparently still in one, rather pale and tearful, piece. In an instant, I run through the same checks I did when they gave her to me in the delivery room: two eyes, two ears, one nose, ten fingers, ten toes (or at least, feet in undamaged patent leather shoes).

'Mummy, my head hurts,' she says, and then I'm off *again*, sobbing uncontrollably, while poor Callum looks on, completely unused to seeing me showing any emotion except irritation.

After a while, I hear a cough – one of those 'I'm making my presence felt' coughs rather than 'I'm in hospital because I have a bad case of TB' coughs – and look round to see the school secretary.

'Hello, Mrs Brown,' she says, and she sounds really nervous. 'Now, the doctor's checked Kiely over—'

'Kelly!' I shout back at her. 'Her name's Kelly.'

'So sorry, yes, but anyway, the doctor's checked Kelly, and they think they can discharge her, she's had a bump on the head, but they think concussion's unlikely, but they want to have a word with you, and tell you what to watch out for, but they think it's best to take her home and keep an eye on her there.' Finally she stops talking long enough to breathe.

I'm relieved, but then most of that I could see for myself.

'What happened, Kelly, love?'

'Mrs Brown, shall we talk about that outside?'

'Kelly?' I reach out to hold her little hand, which is grubby with dirt and dried blood, and damp from tears. She grasps her hand back, then starts crying again.

I turn to the school secretary. 'What happened?'

'What did Mrs Fellowes tell you on the phone?'

'Just that there'd been an accident. Then I came straight here.'

She nods several times, as though she's thinking something over.

'Right. Right . . . well, it's really quite early to say exactly what happened, obviously it was in the playground, and—'

'But, roughly?'

'OK. Well, roughly. Well, it looks as though what might have happened is that Kelly had her accident when, well, when two of the other little girls from her class got behind her in the queue for the slide.'

It's not making any sense. 'Kelly? Tell me what happened, love.' But she just looks even more small and scared, like she

165

does when she comes out of school alone, and can't see me or Callum waiting for her.

And then it dawns on me.

'These little girls . . . this wasn't an accident at all, was it?' I can feel this anger like nothing I've ever felt before, starting somewhere in my chest and spreading in waves like nausea through my body.

'As I say, Mrs Brown, I think it's a little early to say, but Mrs Fellowes has stayed behind at school to see if we can get to the bottom of this as quickly as we can.'

'Well, *you* might need a full-blown bloody inquiry but it's quite obvious to *me* what's going on. My daughter has been attacked and injured by *bullies*, because your precious school can't even keep a bunch of infants under control.'

She won't look at me, and is shifting uncomfortably from side to side. The rational part of me – yes, there is one, though it's buried very deep – is pleading her case, saying it's not her fault, there are others to blame. But the scary earth mother lioness part of me, that I didn't even realise existed until now, is having none of it.

'Get out. If you can't protect my child, then you've no place here with me and my daughter.'

She opens her mouth to placate me, but I rush at her. I'm not going to thump her, but she obviously doesn't realise that, because she backs out of the cubicle without even looking behind her.

I'd forgotten about Boris, but even her tranquillising qualities aren't enough to stop these awful feelings of rage and something else . . . Guilt, yes, it's guilt.

'Boris. We'll be fine now. We'll get a cab home. I think we need a bit of time . . .' and she understands, and leaves the cubicle without a word.

166

All I can do is turn towards Kelly and, tentatively, place my arms around her, and, like Boris did with me an hour ago, hold her until she stops crying.

Bracewell General Hospital, Berkshire

Boris raced through the hospital corridors using her bump like a battering ram, sending patients and staff scattering in her wake. She was on a mission.

She broke the speed limit all the way home, but knew from experience that a whispered 'I'm in a terrible hurry,' and a coy glance down at her belly would persuade most policemen not to give her a ticket.

Pierrot the cat was waiting at the window when she pulled into the drive, and meowed at her silently behind the double-glazing. He wasn't going to like the new arrival any more than he liked the bell on his collar.

'Hello, baby,' she said, as he greeted her with a flourish of the tail and a rub around her waterlogged ankles. She smiled as she encountered the solid lump that stopped her taking off her boots. 'And hello, other baby.'

Boris grabbed a packet of cookies from her biscuit stash, and took them upstairs to her office. Well, it was more of a cubby-hole really, but painted a fresh yellow to stop it feeling cramped. Shelves ran from floor to ceiling, loaded with books on computer theory and business financing, with one solitary row of classic novels, and a superstitiously small section on pregnancy and birth. Opposite her desk, there were carefully organised box files of paper and envelopes, plus two of the plywood boxes of mini-drawers IKEA sells by the pallet-load, which Boris had hand-painted to match the surroundings, and then filled with paper-clips, printer ribbons and sticky labels.

She switched on the computer, and picked up the phone. 'I'd like two numbers please. Yep, the first is for Gary Coombs, London – I think it's West London . . . You don't? Oh, OK. Right, the second's for Crawley Park Comprehensive – sorry, College . . . Thanks, that's brill—' Boris stopped, as she realised she was no longer talking to a human.

She opened her hedgehog notebook and began to type Tracey's Wish List into a file on her main computer. 'What do you think, Pierrot? I reckon we should rename this one, to reflect the urgency of the situation.'

She took a cookie from the packet, and crunched purposefully for a minute. Then she highlighted 'Tracey's Wish List' on the screen, deleted it, and in its place typed 'Reinventing Tracey'.

I'm glad Boris didn't insist on staying, because her sweetness would only make me feel even worse. All it does is show me how inadequate I am as a mother, to let this happen to my child.

Questions keep popping into my head – and I wish I could stop them but they come back again and again like those cockroaches that infest tower blocks.

Why Kelly? Why not someone else's daughter, the child of a junkie teenager, maybe, or the offspring of a shy weirdo, like Suzanne Sharp?

And it's worse than that. Because the question I keep asking myself and I want to ask her, except she's too young to understand, is: why the hell didn't she stand up for herself?

The white-haired nurse gives me a photocopied sheet about the symptoms of concussion. 'We don't think she'll have any after-effects, though. It really wasn't a very serious fall, but just keep an eye on her.' She smiles at Kelly, and strokes her hair.

'You'll soon be right as rain, won't you, my angel? Back to normal.'

Normal? I have to shut my mouth before a hollow laugh escapes. I don't know what normal is any more.

I take Kelly's hand, strap Callum into his pushchair, and head back through the chaos of the waiting room.

The cab driver grins at us, this blonde family straight out of a mail order catalogue. 'Been in the wars, then, love?'

Kelly darts out of sight into the back of the car. 'No need to be shy,' he says, looking more annoyed than amused, and I wonder if her whole life's going to be like this, avoiding attention.

He doesn't say anything else all the way home.

Tracey Mortimer, aged fourteen, would have hated the idea that she might end up 'normal'.

But right now, I'd do anything to achieve exactly that.

The mobile phone rang, and Boris checked who it was, then waited four rings before answering it.

'Hi,' she barked, as though she had far better things to do than eat the rest of the chocolate chip cookies.

'Helen, hello, it's Jenny.' Her tone was already apologetic. Boris sensed victory before she'd stated her demands.

'Jenny.' She left a long, painful gap in the conversation, as though she were not even convinced she should be talking to anyone from Smart Alec Productions. 'I've been with Tracey.'

'Yes. I feel terrible, Helen. I don't care what happens but I do want you to know that I argued against what Alec did. I think it was terrible, and I really don't blame Tracey for being angry.'

'You're still working on the programme, though?'

A pause. 'Yes, touché. Not that we've got a programme any more, not without Tracey. I know you're her friend, and I totally respect that. But do you think there's any way she'll come round?'

It was going to be really easy, Boris realised, and she felt ever so slightly disappointed. She'd geared herself up for a proper fight. Though there was still Tracey's marriage, job and children to sort out, not to mention the small matter of getting more than a dozen people to the reunion. 'I don't think she'll change her mind without a lot of . . . input. It all depends on how far you're prepared to go to convince her you're not out to get her.'

'But she might change her mind?' She sounded so desperate that Boris almost felt sympathetic. Then Jenny spoke again, this time much more quietly, so it was nearly a whisper. 'Between you and me, I don't think there's *anything* Alec wouldn't do to get Tracey back on board.'

There was only one cookie left now, and Boris sucked at it like it was a rusk, humming gently so Jenny would know she was still on the end of the line.

'Well, first of all, I think that the whole business has made Tracey very stressed. Her daughter's been taken to hospital today.'

'Shit. Is Kelly OK?'

'Yes, just a playground accident, cuts and bruises. But it's the last straw for Tracey, so even to get her into a position where she can make a decision about the programme, I think she needs a break . . .' Boris left it for Jenny to fill in the gap.

'I think I see what you're saying. There's this health spa I know that might help restore her . . . um . . . equilibrium. And I'm sure it'd be much more fun if she didn't go on her own.'

'That could be just what we – she needs, provided, of course, that a film crew don't come along for the ride.'

'There aren't many places to hide a secret camera in the sauna, Helen. Tell you what, I'll have a word with Alec, see how the budget's looking and then I'll come back to you. And, thanks . . .'

Boris put down the phone and clicked on the file marked 'Reinventing Tracey'. She typed in a summary of the phone call, and placed an electronic tick in the box alongside it.

One down, four problems to go, she thought. Not bad for an afternoon's work.

Time for another packet of biscuits.

CHAPTER TWENTY-TWO

I'd hoped for a Caribbean beach holiday, but Boris says long-haul is overrated, and a weekend at this health farm costs about the same as Barbados, and there are no kids there, and no Rastas hanging round the beaches offering you the chance to 'ride the big bamboo'. I feel guilty about the no kids rule, and curious about the bamboo . . . since Dave can in no sense be described as having a big bamboo (think Twiglet at best). But Boris – who had her honeymoon in Barbados – says all the attention gets boring.

'You don't even have to say yes to going back to the pro-gramme,' she says when she picks me up in her shocking-pink Mini Cooper. 'Though if you do, we can go back to the negotiating table and see what other bonuses we can arrange! It's a win-win situation.'

She makes me laugh when she uses phrases like that – it's probably the only sign that she's grown up since school, and done all the shoulder-padded businesswoman stuff. It's hard to take her seriously, with her little-girl's voice, though maybe that's her secret. She certainly got the TV people eating out of her hand.

I feel bad leaving Kelly, but Dave is back this weekend and Sandy the psychologist says one of the top items on Kelly's 'things that make me happy' list is 'playing with Daddy'. It's a kick in the teeth, but, if I'm honest, not much of a surprise. It's the same with divorced couples, isn't it? Mum is Mrs Angry, who makes you tidy your bedroom while Dad's the fun one who takes you to the zoo or McDonald's.

Or in my own case, Dad was the one who was never there, so my fantasies about how much more fun he'd be than my weary mother were undiluted by reality.

After Kelly's 'accident', I was really dreading the second appointment with Sandy. Half of me wanted to shout and scream and threaten to sue her and the school for being unable to protect Kelly, and half of me thought I should be the one under attack for messing up her life. But it was Sandy who rang me the day after we came back from hospital.

'Mrs Brown, the school have told me what's happened, and I wanted to suggest coming round to your home before Kelly goes back, so we can try to come up with some strategies for her and for you.'

How could I refuse? But as I put the phone down, I wondered if she had a hidden agenda: to gather more ammunition for labelling me a bad parent. Too much disinfectant, or too few room-fragrancing sprays? A garden too tidy for proper playing, or a hazard-filled bathroom without the right kind of children's toothbrushes?

But in the end, Kelly was too busy showing off the Barbie buggy my mum had bought her for being a brave girl at the hospital for Sandy to notice very much at all. Even the cup of tea I made went un-drunk; maybe she was too appalled by the hygiene conditions in my kitchen to risk it.

'Mrs Brown, what I'd like to do is maybe spend a little bit of time with Kelly, going through the work she's been doing, and then get back together in thirty minutes so we can all chat about going back to school?'

I wondered if I'd be allowed to go back myself, if I asked her very nicely.

They trooped upstairs to Kelly's room, leaving me feeling a complete spare part. When they came back down again they seemed to be best mates, and it's daft but while Sandy was explaining how we needed to work together, especially at play-times, so Kelly could feel safe and make friends, all I could think about was what was so special about bloody Sandy, how come my daughter could giggle and play happily with her but not with me?

And then I realised I was jealous, and it seemed an even bigger sign of my inadequacy that I should be jealous of the woman who has come in to help Kelly overcome the problems I've probably caused in the first place.

'Kelly and I have been chatting about how she's going to work with me and Mrs Fellowes to see which children in her class might be nice new friends. And then we're going to try some drama so we can practise being less shy.'

'That sounds good,' was all I could muster.

'And I'm really impressed with the work Kelly's done in her book. I think you're quite enjoying your homework, aren't you?'

Kelly smiled shyly, and I reached out. 'Let's have a look then,' but she flinched and moved away.

'Remember, we did decide that Kelly's book should be private, Mrs Brown. Though of course if she wants to share parts of it with you, then she will.'

Private? She's six, what does she need to keep private? It'll be different when she's fourteen, and full of sinful secrets. But now? When I looked at Kelly, she wore a guilty expression, and I knew that there must be plenty in her notes that wasn't favourable to me.

I laughed, tried to make light of it. 'Oh, I wonder what kind of terrible secrets you've got in there. Go on, girls, tell me what you've been writing down.'

Sandy said, 'Well, I think we can tell Mummy that it makes you happy playing with the school guinea pigs.'

'Russell and Flo,' agreed Kelly, and I wondered if this was a sophisticated plot to make me procure some pets, and then loathed myself even more for being suspicious of the poor kid's motives.

'Yes, Russell and Flo. We often find, incidentally, Mrs Brown, that giving a child like Kelly direct caring responsibility for an animal such as a guinea pig or a rabbit can have a very positive effect on self-esteem. But obviously, that's something for you and your husband to discuss. What does he think about the situation at school?'

'He's obviously very concerned and we're going to talk about it when he's back from Ireland at the weekend.'

She nodded with intense sincerity. 'Yes, Kelly's explained that he's not around as much as you'd like.'

He's around quite often enough for my liking, I almost snapped back, but Sandy hadn't finished.

'I think it can be difficult for children to understand why one parent might be absent some of the time, so it's very important to explain it in such a way that they realise it's not *their* fault . . . especially when, like with Kelly and your husband, there's such a strong bond.'

I raised my eyebrows – I couldn't help it.

She nodded again. 'Yes, that's one of the really positive things to come out of our little chat upstairs. Of course, I wouldn't want to suggest that your daughter's mental health should be weighed against the financial necessity of the arrangement, because obviously it's none of my business, but I do think it's something we could build on, the relationship between father and daughter.' Then, after a pause, she added, 'And, of course, your own relationship with Kelly.'

Oh, of course. Mothers have the worst of both bloody

worlds, don't they? All the responsibility, all the guilt, none of the credit.

'So the next stage will be for Kelly to return to school, and we're going to have a special class meeting about it. Mrs Fellowes and I will do some work on improving the supportive aspects of the other pupils' behaviour. We're going to put in place some Circle Time exercises. I don't know if you've heard of the approach, but it can be incredibly effective in a situation like this—'

'Hang on a minute. That's all very nice, circles and triangles and whatever other shapes you fancy, but the most important thing is that the kids who did this are taught a lesson. For all the problems Kelly might have, they must be pretty disturbed to be violent at this age. You have to nip these things in the bud.'

She looked at me warily. 'I do agree that problems of this nature must absolutely not be allowed to drift. And I can assure you that the work we'll be doing has been proved through the research to be the most effective way forward. It's a holistic approach.'

'But the kids who pushed Kelly—'

'We don't know for sure they pushed her.'

'It's what she says, isn't it?'

'Ye-es, but there were no adult witnesses, and the rough and tumble of the playground does occasionally lead to the odd problem. I'm sure you remember from your own childhood—'

'So, are you saying the brats aren't going to be punished?'

She sighed. 'I understand your need for retribution, but we're trying to focus on what's in Kelly's best interests, and, at this stage, if we can rebuild relationships in her class, then the prospects are much better. Wouldn't you agree?'

No, I wouldn't, but it was obvious there wasn't any point in telling *her* that. Schools are dictatorships, and there's no point fighting the system.

So next Tuesday, Kelly goes back to school, and they're going to sort her out by sitting the kids down in a great big circle and making them tell each other how they feel. I try to imagine how we'd have reacted at my school. I reckon if we'd heard some wimp of a kid saying how miserable they were at being teased, we'd have started looking forward to having another go at dinner time.

Nothing like this, though. For one thing, these are *little* girls. There has to be something wrong with them to make them behave like this so young, trouble at home, all that jazz. And second, it was never serious with us, was it? We were just having a laugh. Shrimp was my best mate, but she could also stand up for what she thought – she *always* told me if she thought I'd gone too far, and then I'd back off. I was never cruel . . .

Though I don't remember Melody ever telling me to stop. She was more likely to egg me on.

Maybe I'll ask Boris about it over the weekend. I wave goodbye to my little nuclear family, ignoring Dave's panicked, hard-done-by expression, and load my suitcase on to the back seat of the Mini – there's no room in her minuscule boot because she's got this mammoth Samsonite jammed inside. God knows what she's got in there. I thought health farms were places where you wandered round in a bathrobe and slippers, kind of like a cross between heaven and a maternity ward.

I haven't left the kids for a whole night since . . . well, it's been more than a year, and the last time was because the hen party I went to was in glamorous Slough, where all the trains stopped at midnight, and I kipped on the hen's sofa. The kids came out of it better than I did – I haven't been invited out with the girls since, something about me making bitchy comments about the groom after a few too many Bacardi Breezers.

But the kids loved the sleepover with their nan, and this time they're even more excited by the novelty of undivided attention from their dad. I suspect that'll change when they realise his idea of childcare is to put them to bed early and send them back without a backwards glance if they dare to creep downstairs and interrupt his beer-fuelled viewing of *Soccer Special*.

Look on the bright side, Tracey. Tonight could be the night they both get the spring vomiting bug. I'd love to see Dave dealing with that.

The journey takes about an hour, leaving behind the well-made roads and the rows of houses exactly like mine. Now we're on dirt tracks and even Boris is slowing down in case a wilful tractor is thundering towards us round that blind bend.

And then there it is: not a tractor, but a grey, Gothic building with turrets and enormous wooden entrance doors, and an apparently endless line-up of small men who race out as we arrive, to park Boris's car and relieve us of our luggage – and, presumably, our emotional baggage too.

The reception area is wood-panelled and cosy, heated to subtropical levels, with a platter of pineapple, mango and a strange white spotted fruit I don't even recognise alongside the guest book.

'This is going to be good,' says Boris as we check in. 'Last spa I went to was lovely outside, but inside the swimming pool ceiling was damp, and the walls were covered with yucky brown stains. And you had to *pay* to rent a dressing gown. The cheek. Dressing gowns are the uniform at health farms, yet they wanted to charge for them!'

The receptionist smiles soothingly, and reaches below the counter, emerging with bathrobes so fluffy that we can barely see over the top of them when we take them in our arms. 'Well, these are on the house. Terry will show you to your room – and you'll find your treatment schedule laid out on your beds. I know you're going to enjoy your stay with us.'

It's cheesy here, but its top-notch cheesy. Our room is larger than the whole ground floor of my house, and we have a double bed each, facing a widescreen telly, with a fridge instead of a bedside table either side. I can't resist looking inside.

'Bloody hell, Boris, I thought health farms were alcohol-free.' There's a full-size bottle of champagne in mine, alongside some fresh juices and mini-bottles of spirits. I guess there must be the same in hers, and since she's pre-natally challenged, I can see myself having an interesting evening.

'Depends on the place. Wintersham House is more about pampering, though you can go for the diet detox option. But we're getting the Wintersham Full Monty – unlimited food, booze, treatments. We must write a thank-you letter to Uncle Alec.'

'Never mind him. It's you that deserves one. Well done for sorting it, Boris, this must be costing them a bomb.'

'Yep. And I reckon they'll have had to call in a load of favours to get this suite and *these* treatments at such short notice.' She picks up the timetable on her bed. 'There's a three-month waiting list for this two-person Thai massage.'

'Two person – what, we get done at once?'

She laughs. 'Er, no. It means you get two people giving you their undivided attention for two hours. I challenge you to remember your name, never mind what you're stressed about, after that.'

I've been in a sauna before, down at the health centre after a session of step aerobics that I'd been press-ganged into by one of the girls from the shop. The class was more pointless than physics, and afterwards we sat there, our towels on top of the wooden slats, waiting for things to warm up, but there was so much through traffic that it never got properly hot. Then someone poured some water on the coals and the steam sizzled so much that it made my nose hurt. This was meant to be relaxing?

But here there's a steam room as well, and it's wonderful. I feel like a Roman or Greek goddess – whichever one it was that went for mosaic tiles in a big way. Anyway, there are thousands of tiles covering these stone beds, circled around an ornate fountain, with steam rising from pools of water in ceramic bowls below. It's scented – at the moment the fragrance is rose otto, which the assistant says is fine for pregnant women. In the ceiling there are twinkling fairy lights in different colours.

'Usually, steam rooms are like plastic pods,' Boris says, who knows about these things. 'Like being in the Tube with extremely sweaty people. But this . . .'

I've had my head massage, followed by the two-person session, which made me feel very self-conscious at first. But pretty soon all my worries about it being a kind of posh-person's threesome disappeared with the rhythm of it. Dave, funnily enough, has never really seen the benefits of massage, unless it's me massaging his dick, of course.

Boris has had a manicure, which has transformed her chubby little fingers into pink talons, and a pedicure – the beauty therapist had to use a mirror to show her how it looks. But Boris is one of those women who really suits being pregnant – the bump doesn't look glued on, like it did with me, but simply adds to the overall cuddly effect. She'd hate me for even thinking it, but in her yellow swimsuit she's a dead ringer for Laa-Laa from the *Teletubbies*.

'So, is Brian excited about the baby?' I'm very curious about Brian, who I haven't met, and who doesn't seem to have made any mark on their girly home.

'Hmm,' she says. 'Yeah. It's what he's always wanted. A little boy . . . or a girl, though I think he'd prefer a boy. We don't like to talk about it too much, though. Superstitious, you know.'

'You're on the home straight now.'

'Maybe . . . a lot can happen in six weeks, though, Tracey.' And she strokes the bump.

I wonder about my two, and hope Dave is behaving himself. But then I know he'll call my mum the moment he runs into the slightest hitch. And she'll be round there like a shot, sympathising with him, because he's been abandoned. After all, how can any woman just leave her children for a whole weekend? Never mind that at least one of the children wouldn't care if Mummy was never seen again.

'Anyway, we've got something else to think about before my baby, haven't we?'

I know she means the reunion, and it's a subject I've been avoiding even though it's the whole reason I'm here. 'Do you think I'm going to have to do it, now they've paid for this?'

She shakes her head. 'No way. Think of this as a bribe to stop you going to the papers about their dirty tricks. But it might be worth reconsidering . . .'

'Really?' If I never see them again, it'd be too soon.

'If you think back to when we first got together, you were so excited about it, Trace. I think that if I can give you a hand here and there, just with the arrangements, it could still be brilliant. I love parties.'

'It won't be brilliant if no one shows up. Anyway, I don't think I've got the energy and what little I have got I should be focusing on sorting out Kelly.'

'Forget the hassle of it for now. Just think about how you'd like it to be; in your fantasies, imagine being there, the belle of the ball. I bet we can talk them into giving you a fantastic designer outfit – something *really* expensive.'

It's impossible to resist thinking about what I'd wear if

money was no object, and I was going to be centre stage . . . something long, slinky and clingy, perhaps, with a split from ankle to thigh: my legs are still my best feature.

'And we quite liked School Disco, didn't we, apart from my funny turn? Well, it could be just like that . . .'

'Except for the fact that it'll be just you and me dancing round our handbags.' I come back down to earth with a hell of a thud.

'It's early days. Anyway, if they'll pay me to organise it all, then I guarantee a full house. After all, who can turn me down?'

Through the steam, I see her determined expression, and I feel that resistance is futile.

'I suppose there's no harm in trying. But if you haven't managed at least, I dunno, fifty people by a week beforehand? Then I want a get-out clause.'

'Of course,' she says, and winks at me. But I realise I've just proved her point about no one ever turning Boris down. And it makes me feel strangely reassured.

CHAPTER TWENTY-THREE

So, Boris the fairy godmother waved her magic wand, and out of nowhere appeared one hundred and twenty ex-Crawley Park pupils, who say they wouldn't miss the reunion for the world. She also conjured up a designer promising to take the best of eighties style to create my dream outfit, *and* a production team who can't do enough to keep me happy.

A month ago I wouldn't have thought any of it could really happen, and what she's achieved is amazing. The bandwagon is rolling merrily. But it still doesn't feel like enough.

Trouble is, I can't imagine what would be enough. If I could, I'm pretty sure Boris '*Jim'll Fix It*' Norris could fix it for me. She seems to have a way of working out what has to be done, then doing it, before anyone else has even noticed that anything's the matter. Though shouldn't she be using her special powers for the UN or animals in danger of extinction, rather than ungrateful old Tracey?

Maybe this is what it was like for the man who invented the nuclear bomb? There he was, messing about doing random bits of physics, thinking it was all theoretical, and bang, he splits the atom, someone gets to hear about it, and before he can say Enola Gay, they've blown up several million Japanese people and triggered the international arms race.

I don't want to sound melodramatic, but I keep wondering if the reunion will be *my* Hiroshima. Before all this, I was toddling along, not happy exactly, but not viciously unhappy either, waiting for *something*. The kids to grow up a bit, perhaps, and make me laugh by bringing home unsuitable blokes and slutty girls. The household bills to get smaller so we could afford to go on holiday abroad, instead of to the West Country. Maybe I was even waiting for Dave to do what I'd always known he was going to do, and decide that rather than bother with all the effort involved in bits on the side, he might as well run off with a younger woman.

But the reunion's made me think, and once you start thinking you can't stop. I dunno about Pandora's box, but Tracey's box is full of all these memories I thought were one thing – carefree, funny, joyful – but when I take them out and look at them properly, they're not what they seem at all.

It's like when people take their relics to the *Antiques Roadshow* thinking they'll be worth a mint. So they prepare those shocked expressions and a speech for the moment when they get the valuation: 'Dear me, I should insure it for *how* much, goodness, I had no idea, but of course, I won't part with it.'

But instead the expert gives them a strange look and says, 'Well, yes, I know it *looks* like a van Gogh, but actually if you examine it under a magnifying glass, you'll see that the leaves on these sunflowers have in fact been airbrushed, and an airbrush is one of the tools that poor Vincent didn't have at his disposal.'

And they try to control the grimace of acute disappointment before the camera zooms in, but it was there long enough for everyone to see it.

And then the expert says, 'But I'm sure you wouldn't have wanted to sell it anyway,' and they feel obliged to respond, 'Oh, you're so right, how could we do without something that gives us so much pleasure.'

And my memories don't stand up to any kind of proper

examination, either. The bits I thought were funny have warped over time, so when I think back to them, I can almost hear us cheering as someone else is crying. Taking the piss out of people like Suzanne Sharp no longer seems harmless. Maybe it's because of Kelly.

That seems to be the one thing Boris can't fix. And I can't get into my daughter's head . . . even though I've tried.

I have a terrible confession to make. I read her book.

I can't quite believe I did it, and I know it makes me just about the world's biggest scumbag. I could pretend that I was cleaning up and came across it open at a page, but it's not true. I waited until Callum was having his nap in the afternoon, and I went and searched for it. There's no way I would have stumbled on the book, because it was hidden beneath her collection of Beanie Babies.

'*Things that make me happy*' had been written in copperplate by Sandy, and beneath it, in Kelly's own uneven writing, was a list:

Playing with Daddy
Jolene
Barbie buggy
Russel and Flo (ginny pigs)
Choklut rice crispie cakes we made at nanas
Weakends

I turned the page, and there, below Sandy's second heading, '*Things that make me unhappy*', were:

Dinner time at shcool
Felling lonely
Carotts
Callum wen he is crying two mutch

Waspps
Zoey and Cahtherine and Emmily espeshully at dinner time
Peeple hoo are horrible too animuls

I didn't even matter enough to be on either list.

I turned the page and found a kind of diary. It was obviously something Sandy had suggested after the playground incident, and Kelly began by writing another one of those neat headings.

Going to Hopsital
*I went to hopsital becos Emmily tripped me up in the play-
grownd and I hit my head and it hurt and then the sekreterry
took me to the hopsital and Mummy was there and she
lookd upset and Callum and my face went a funny colur all
blue and swelld up and then I had days of school which was
verry nise.*

Underneath, she's drawn a little picture of her face, adding a black eye with felt-tip pen. On the opposite page, there's another heading:

Going back to shcool
*I donnt wont to go back too shcool but Mummy and Daddy and
sandy and evrywun says I haff to and I think its unfair becos they
donnt go and they donnt haff Emmily and Cahtherine and Zoey
beeing horrible*
*   Today I went too school and everwun was nise but then
Cahtherine sed I hadunt orta tell tales any morr and it skared
me but I think I will tell sandy becos she will be nise and help me
get morr freinds.*

I turn over and there's only one more heading.

Making new freinds

*I haff been making new freinds at school theres Sasha who is nise
but her freinnd Rosie is not as nise to me and I think she is jellus
and today I saw her tolking too Zoey and it skared me agen becos
what if they gang up on me and then we had sercle time we sit in
a big sercle and we all haff to say wot we are feelling and I sed I
like haffing Sasha and Rosie as my new freinnds and Mrs Felloos
smiled a lot and sed that's nise evrywun we are all freinnds in
our class but its not true reely but evrywun sed oh yes we are all
verry happy and I think I am kind of happy now but also wot if
Rosie is horrible it will be the same as it wos beforr and then I
donnt wont to go ever ever agen*

And underneath that, in different pen, though of course
there's no way of telling when she wrote it, the shortest sentence
yet.

I hate Rosie and I donnt never wont to go back

There. Now I knew for sure. Motherhood was the hardest
thing I've ever done. I was prepared for the shit-shovelling, and
for the vomit, and the sleepless nights. But what nobody could
ever have prepared me for was the powerlessness. I sat on her
bed with the notebook in my hands, and I couldn't decide
whether to cry or to go down to that bloody school, find Rosie
(or Zoe, or Catherine, or Emily) and give them a taste of their
own medicine.

*

Tesco Car Park, Brook Green, West London

Boris limbo-ed her way from under the steering wheel, and out of the car door. She was terrified that one day the baby would grow a single extra millimetre while she was driving, and trap her so the only way she could get out would be by calling in the fire brigade to cut off the roof. It was almost as scary as the ridiculously tiny ladies' loos cubicles you got in shops, which she'd found stressful enough before she was pregnant, and now made her feel like an elephant in a phone box.

Hammersmith looked different by day. She'd driven round the roundabout where the Apollo was, past the club where they'd gone to School Disco, and, as Gary had suggested, she parked in Tesco. Maybe she could do her shopping on the way back. Though she was getting very tired these days, so after a hefty lunch she'd probably be fit for nothing except a nap in the car before heading home again.

An elderly man smiled benevolently at Boris and her bump, as she ignored the signs saying the car park was for customers only, and turned down the alleyway that would take her to the restaurant. *Turn left at the end, then the road veers two hundred degrees north, and it's the second building, ten yards along.* Typical policeman. He could probably have told her the exact number of paces, or the OS grid reference.

The maître d' opened the door for her as she approached. Lovely! The restaurant was all blond wood, and chrome buckets of fresh gerbera flowers, with purple-painted screens enclosing each pair of leather banquettes. Soft classical music played in the background, and there was a strong smell of garlic and fresh-baked bread. It was exactly her kind of place, but she was surprised that it was Gary's sort of place, too. Still, people changed.

'The reservation's in the name of Coombs,' she said as the maître d' took her coat.

'Excellent, your husband's already here. Can't keep you and the little one waiting, huh?'

He showed her to their table, and Gary stood up, a filled-out version of the unformed fifth-year lad she remembered, with better manners. Police training obviously had its advantages. He stepped out from the table and kissed her on both cheeks. *Very* London.

'Hey, Boris, haven't you grown!' he said, smirking. The maître d' gave them an odd look, and handed them the menus before retreating.

'He thinks we're married,' Boris explained.

'Well, you are, aren't you?'

'And what about you, Mr Coombs, are you a confirmed bachelor?'

'I don't think Gabby would call me that.'

Boris grinned. 'And how long have you and . . . Gabby been an item?'

'Eighteen months or so. We met when we went on a raid to snatch some kid from a crack house – she's a social worker, you see.'

'Very right on. And is she the one?'

Gary shrugged. 'No such thing. Not as far as I'm concerned. But she's all right. Decent company. Sharp.'

'And does she feel as . . . non-committal?'

'Nah. No offence, Boris, but she's a woman. And I haven't met one that thinks like blokes do, that can take it or leave it, not since—' And he stopped mid-sentence.

'Since Tracey? That was what you were going to say, wasn't it?'

He shrugged again. That was one thing that city living and the Met hadn't got rid of, Boris thought, the nonchalant gesture that professed he didn't care, but told the world that he really, really did.

'Yeah. She's what you're here to talk about, isn't it? I mean, it's great to see you, but you didn't ask to meet me just to go over old times?'

Boris giggled. 'You're right, of course, Gary. But slow down. We haven't even ordered our lunch yet.'

Eggstra-Special Café, Clapham Junction, South London

Suzanne was regretting her choice of journalist. She'd called Andrew Grey because of his reputation as a remarkably civilised Rottweiler who always protected his sources. But like most attack dogs, patience wasn't his strong point.

'I still don't see why you want me to give up a whole Saturday without giving me a hint of what it's all about.'

'I'm sorry. I just can't. Not yet. But I promise July twenty-first will be worth waiting for.'

It was their third meeting and she still didn't feel she could trust him. Maybe the surroundings didn't help: the greasy spoon added to the seedy atmosphere of their chats, and she knew she'd never be seen there by anyone she knew, but the ambiance didn't exactly enhance the feeling of mutual respect. She felt like an extra in *Lock, Stock and Two Smoking Barrels*.

'I'll be missing a wedding,' he said sulkily.

'Well, if you can't spare the time, there are a couple of other journalists I could talk to. No hard feelings on either side . . .'

'I'm not saying that. But it'll be someone big enough to make a splash?'

'Andrew, I wouldn't lead you up the garden path. I've got my reputation to think of.'

'Except you want to stay anonymous.'

'But *you'd* know. I'm sure you'd find a way of getting word round that I wasn't to be trusted, even if you didn't say why. I'm not that naïve.'

'I'm not sure the interest hasn't gone out of education stories, anyway,' he said, stubbing out his cigarette with an affected flourish. He really wasn't an attractive man, for all the labels and men's grooming products he clearly used.

'This is *not* an education story. This is a scandal,' said Suzanne. 'Sex, politics and history people have tried to keep hidden. Blockbuster movies have been made around less than this.'

'Sex, eh?'

'Yes, sex. But you've already pushed me too far, Andrew. Just wait your turn; in two weeks' time you'll have the exclusive and you'll wonder why you ever doubted me.'

'And what about you, Suzanne?' His eyes narrowed, closing off the only mildly attractive part of an otherwise featureless face. 'What are you getting out of giving me this great scoop?'

'I don't think it's any of your business,' she snapped back.

It was quite simple, she thought, as she left the café. One word covered it.

Revenge.

Boris and Gary both ordered mushroom and marsala soup as a starter, followed by the duck for him and the salmon for her. She chose a poppy-seed roll, he picked one flavoured with Mediterranean herbs.

'It beats chips and gravy in the Crawley Park canteen,' Boris said, dipping her bread in the little dish of oil on the beech table.

'Don't know if it does, you know. Just more expensive.'

Boris gave him a sly smile. 'If you're so keen on the good old days, you ought to come to the reunion.'

Shrug. 'Can't see Tracey wanting me there. Not after the row at the Crown.'

Boris looked at him carefully. 'I wasn't there.'

'I bet she told you, though.'

'I'd like to hear your version.'

'Are you sure you're not really a secret agent, Boris? You have that determination about you.'

A waitress appeared, carrying two wide white bowls of steaming chestnut-brown soup. In the centre of each, a carefully placed dollop of thick cream, and a single, perfect wild mushroom.

'I'm completely sure. Are *you* sure you haven't picked up tips on avoiding questions from your criminal acquaintances, Gary?'

'Fair point.' He took a spoonful of soup and moaned gently with pleasure.

'You're still saying that's no better than the school canteen?'

He studied the dish. 'I don't know what happened, Boris, I really don't. I suppose I'd thought I might tick her off a bit; it was humiliating the way she did it. You've got to admit it.'

'Hmm. But it was also seventeen years ago.'

'I know. I never thought about her, you know.'

Boris looked at him. 'Are you sure about that?'

'Well, hardly ever . . . OK. Now and then. But only, I dunno, if I was having a row with Gabby or something, getting angry, and then, I'd think back to the angriest I've been, and, well, you know when that would have been.'

Boris nodded. She knew.

'But you know, I've moved on. It's good, my life. And when I got that e-mail, I was intrigued, but nothing else.'

'Why did you e-mail her back, then?'

He laughed. 'Stupid, stupid thing to do. It was after I fell out with Gabby over the washing-up. I suppose I just wanted to prove I wasn't . . .' He waved his spoon around, struggling for the right word.

'Hen-pecked?'

Another shrug. 'I never expected to see her. Not that night, not ever. But when I did, it seemed like . . . fate? I dunno. I hate that horoscope bollocks, so does Gabby. I mean, that's one of the things I lo— I like about her. She's sensible, you know, more like a bloke than some daft girl. No offence.'

'None taken. But you're a true Scorpio, Gary. With a temper to go with it.'

'Like I say, I really don't believe in any of that shit, but to bump into her like that, there had to be a reason for it, didn't there?'

'Go on.'

'I didn't plan to have a go at her. But seeing her – it was like the Bob business happened yesterday. She didn't look any different. None of us does, do we? You don't, except for the bump.'

'Do you think we'll feel the same when we're sixty – that we still look sixteen?'

'Probably. But she really does look the same, and we were sitting there and . . .' Shrug. 'Something just snapped. All the stuff I wanted to say back when it happened, but didn't have the guts to, it came out, and she just sat there, and I felt so much better having got it out of my system. I caught the train back and this huge weight had been lifted.'

'She didn't feel the same, funnily enough.'

'No. No, I don't suppose she did. If it's any consolation, that feeling didn't last. When I thought about it, it seemed like a pretty shit thing to do. But I couldn't help myself.'

They sat in silence, until the waitress took away their empty bowls.

'Do you want to know what I think, Gary?'

Shrug, but with a smile this time. 'Not necessarily, but I'm sure you're going to tell me anyway.'

The waitress returned with their main courses, plates piled high with fish and fowl, plus side plates of potato dauphinoise, green beans and honeyed carrots.

Boris loaded her fork with crumbly salmon and fresh salsa. She took a bite. 'Yummy. I think the reason you had such a go at Tracey is that you haven't got over her yet. Oh, do stop shrugging, Gary, it's driving me mad; how does your girlfriend put up with it?'

He went to shrug and stopped midway.

'And I think you're going to find it almost impossible to move on until you and Tracey have made your peace.'

'I don't think—'

'Well, I do. And between you and me, things aren't going too well for Tracey at the moment. You know she's got a little girl, Kelly?'

'She didn't mention her kids directly,' said Gary, and they both considered the implications of this. 'Though I kind of guessed.'

'Well, she's got a daughter, and a baby boy. But Kelly's nothing like Tracey – dear little thing, but so shy.'

'Tracey's daughter, shy?'

'I know. But it's worse than that. I was with her when she got a call to the hospital – some bullies had pushed the poor kid over, and she'd hit her head.'

'Shit.'

'She's OK. But she's six years old.'

194

'Bloody hell.' He shook his head. 'We weren't like that, were we, Boris?'

'I hope not. Tracey's having a tough time, though. I worry about her. I know she always seemed hard, but I think it's a defence mechanism. And she's worried about the reunion too, what it'll say about her if no one comes. I've got a long list of people now, but they're not the people that were important to her.' Boris paused. He didn't interrupt, which had to be a good sign. 'At least think about it.'

'You don't give up, do you, Boris?'

'No,' she said, not looking even slightly guilty.

'I've only got one question,' said Gary. 'If you want the people there that were important to Tracey, then shouldn't you be inviting Carmichael?'

CHAPTER TWENTY-FOUR

It's reaching the point of no return. Well, OK, if I'm honest, that probably happened a month ago, when I took the aromatherapy-scented bribe from Smart Alec Productions. I've tried to hang on to the illusion of freedom, but, like a tiger at Whipsnade, I don't have a way out that wouldn't involve major bloodshed. Today is the last bit of filming before the reunion proper on the 21st. This afternoon I get to see this mad eighties fashion creation that I'll be wearing at the party, but before that there's an interview with a psychologist about why in God's name anyone would organise a reunion.

I'm buggered if I know.

I've avoided seeing Annabel and Alec and Jamie since the whole secret filming business, and I'm nervous about meeting them again. Annabel because she's irritating and now I don't care about the programme, I will be very tempted to tell her to shut the fuck up. It's the same but worse with Alec – he's an odious tosser and I'd love to tell him so. But he's got the power to make me look a complete hag in the finished programme if I get on the wrong side of him. I know, I've seen how they edit *Big Brother*. So I have to bite my tongue until the programme's gone out. After that, I'm going to give him both barrels.

But it's different with Jamie and Jenny. I feel so disappointed. I thought they were above all that. I wasn't exactly great mates with Jenny, but she seemed a decent human being, and I felt the same about Jamie. Sorry, that's not strictly true. The difference with Jamie was that I thought he seemed a decent human being. *And* I wanted to rip his clothes off. Trouble is, with my warped taste in men, now that I know he's a scumbag I'll probably have an even harder job keeping my hands to myself.

Department for Education, London SW1

Bob Carmichael turned the invitation over in his hands. Despite all the dangerous things he'd done during his early midlife crisis, just holding the invitation felt like the riskiest activity he'd undertaken in years. More dangerous than jumping out of planes and hang-gliding and water-skiing and pot-holing and the other pointless macho ways he'd found of filling his weekends.

His Post Tracey Phase. Strange how she'd hit him harder than any woman before or since. Not that there'd been very many women.

He was still attractive. He saw it in their faces, a momentary contraction of the muscles around the eyes as they clocked him and decided that he wasn't bad at all, considering his age. He'd even overheard his research assistant, Heather, choose him over three younger men in the team when they were playing 'Fantasy Fucks', a game invented by the girls in the Joined-Up Thinking Unit. They spent their fag breaks deciding who was untouchable, who was passable and who was fanciable. He'd been quite chuffed to be near the top of their wish list.

But he couldn't go to the reunion, of course. He'd thought it through quite carefully, trying to work out whether to ring the TV company for an invitation, and decided that no, he was past his dangerous phase, and this reunion was on a par with free-running in a hurricane. Sure, if the whole thing came out, it came out and, just as he'd told Phipps, he'd been ready for that to happen for seventeen years. But there was no sense actively encouraging the premature end to his career. He'd get the chance to see what Tracey was like now when the programme came out and, really, that was the only reason he'd have wanted to go, to spy on her from the sidelines and wonder . . .

Dirty sad old git that he was.

But then an invitation arrived anyway. He had no idea who'd sent it. The envelope had been handwritten, and was marked personal, so for once his nosy PA hadn't opened it first.

And all there was inside was the ticket. No note, no letter of explanation, just this small card, embossed like a wedding invite, with the date, time and address of the Crawley Park Comp Reunion, 'sponsored by Channel 5'.

Was it sent by the TV company? Dick Phipps's idea of a joke?

Or was it Tracey? He liked this idea the best, though he couldn't explain it without some mental gymnastics. Perhaps Tracey had somehow seen his picture in the paper and cut it out and then agonised over whether to invite him. Though he had to admit he couldn't imagine Tracey buying the kind of newspaper that printed his photograph. He'd never made it into the *News of the World*, though maybe she'd seen him in the line-up next to Cherie Blair that they printed in the *Daily Express* . . .

Anyhow, it hardly mattered who sent it. Because he couldn't go.

His hand hovered above the bin. But instead of throwing the invitation away, Bob opened the top drawer of his desk, and tucked it under the £20 he had put aside for the odd random taxi home.

No harm in keeping it as a souvenir.

Jenny gives me a lift to the interview. She's a little nervous when I answer the door, and then overcompensates by gushing about the 'perfect' person they've found for me to interview, and the perfect location. I don't try all that hard to suppress the sneer that creeps on to my face.

I have a near-permanent sneer on my face these days; when I get up it's there, and when I go to bed I feel as though I have to wipe it off with my bumper pot of Nivea. My mum used to threaten me with the wind changing, and that seems to have actually happened.

Jenny gets the message, and we don't talk much on the way. The pretence that we're girly friends and *isn't this filming the best fun ever*, has been dropped since what Boris now calls the Crown Affair. So Jenny drives carefully, and I feel like a kid being ferried to the dentist or the piano teacher. I know there's no way round it, and it probably won't be that bad when I get there, but that doesn't mean I'm going to enjoy it.

'You've read the briefing notes?' Jenny sent me a mammoth e-mail full of questions to ask the psychologist.

'I waded through them, yes, but I don't know if I'll remember them all.'

'I'm sure Alec'll prompt you if you don't,' she says. We've turned off the motorway, and into the outskirts of some nondescript town.

'Is he being a pain in the arse as usual?'

'He's my boss, you can't expect me to comment.' But then Jenny gives me a sideways look. 'Yes. It's funny, but early on, me and Annabel were convinced you'd fancy him. He can be a bit of a smooth talker.'

Was that only three months ago? 'Yes, but he can also be a bit of a wanker.'

She grins at me then opens her mouth as if she's going to say something, but seems to change her mind.

'What were you going to say?'

She shakes her head. 'It's nothing . . .'

'Go on.'

'I don't suppose I should tell you this, really, because it makes me look like I'm dobbing everyone else in it. But it's important that you know I really didn't want to do what we did at the pub. I argued with Alec for days beforehand, I thought it was a shit thing to do. But, he's my boss, you know; at the end of the day what he says goes. I am really sorry we did it.'

I do believe her, but it doesn't make much difference now. 'Yeah, well. I suppose it's not your fault.'

'Alec's learned his lesson, though. The thought of the whole programme being off, all that filming down the pan, was a pretty effective ethics lesson.'

So I've been a positive influence on that ratbag's moral development. What an achievement.

'And Boris is coming along later?' Jenny says after a while.

'Yeah, another antenatal this morning. But she'll be at the fitting.'

'You two seem thick as thieves these days. It's lovely that you still have so much in common after all these years.'

Except we never had much in common in the old days. After Shrimp, I never bothered to make *real* friends.

Jenny steers into an industrial estate, which is not what I'm expecting at all. I'd been imagining an empty classroom, or a Victorian schoolhouse or something. But we pull up alongside Alec's bloody car next to a low-rise prefab.

'Exciting location,' I say and Jenny just grins at me.

We walk in through a side door, and as my eyes adjust to the light, I feel as though I've drunk an *Alice in Wonderland* potion, and shrunk to two-thirds of my normal size. I'm surrounded by enormous gun-metal-grey lockers and PE benches and doors where the handles are level with my chest. It's like being eleven again.

'Isn't it brilliant?' Jenny says. 'It's all the leftovers from the education exhibit at the Millennium Dome; they built everything big so adults would feel child-sized – even the school bell.'

She points up to one of those bright red metal bells that splits your ears when it goes off. And as my eyes drop to ground level, I see something that is even more effective in taking me back: a distant figure, with long red hair, talking to Alec, gesticulating wildly.

'A surprise for you, Tracey,' Jenny says, touching me on the elbow to propel me forward. 'The psychologist we've told you about also happens to be your old classmate, Suzanne.'

And the red-haired figure steps from the shadow and holds out her hand to shake mine.

'Tracey. I can't believe how long it's been.' She smiles. But it's not a real smile, and I can see she's clocking me as much as I'm clocking her. It makes me feel very, *very* uncomfortable.

While they're setting up the lights for the interview, Suzanne – who now has a double-barrelled name because she found someone desperate enough to marry her – offers titbits about her life, and I do the same. We're unnaturally polite to each other. The first time I have ever been polite to Suzanne Sharp.

'You look great,' I say, and she does, actually. We used to tease her for being skinny, but now she's admirably slim, and her hair is a statement, rather than an affliction, though Christ knows how much mousse she needs to control those curls. But the compliment seems to make her even more suspicious, as if I'm about to follow it up with a killer insult.

'Thank you. You haven't changed a bit,' she says, and I'm sure that's not a good thing as far as she's concerned.

'And you're a psychologist?' I feel like the Queen, asking questions to pass the time, without caring about the answer.

'Yes. I've done direct work with children, and now I run a charity.' She looks at me warily, eyes hooded. It's years since I've seen the silly cow but that hangdog face is so familiar it makes my fingers twitch.

'Really?'

'Yes. I help children who have been bullied,' she says, and gives me a significant look. And then I realise why her defensive expression rings so many bells.

It's the same one I see on Kelly's face every time I wave her off in the playground.

'We're ready for you both now.' Alec is grinning enthusiastically but there's tension in his smile. He looks worried that I might flip any minute. Serves him right.

Jenny sits us down in orange plastic chairs like the ones at primary school, but made large enough to accommodate adult bums. 'So, you'll start with some general stuff about memories and how those are key to people's identities, then move on to how that changes when people actually have a reunion.'

I can't see the point myself, but Jenny says that since all the reality TV backlash, they're trying to make it feel that there's more to the programme than entertainment. I don't even think it's going to be that entertaining anyway.

'Speed,' says Jamie, and his voice still sends little electric pulses through my body. Damn.

'Um. Right. Are people's memories of school usually good?'

Suzanne looks pretty startled at the question, which is odd, because I get the impression she's much more experienced with the media than I am.

She shakes her head slightly as though she's arguing with herself. Then she speaks. 'I think the idea that school days are the happiest of your life is responsible for a great deal of *unhappiness.* As soon as we walk out of the school gates, and we literally put those days behind us, we put on the rose-tinted specs and forget all the petty rules and restrictions, the lack of power, the terrible pressure to conform. And instead, we invent for ourselves this strange mixture of memories that are more about children's books and magazine articles than our own experiences. A lot of us are in denial about our pasts.'

Rightio. It wasn't exactly what I was expecting, and judging from the silence that follows, it wasn't what anyone else was expecting either. I'm trying to find a way of replying, when Alec says, 'Suzanne, um, that's great and everything, very interesting indeed . . . but I wonder if we could be a little bit more . . . upbeat?'

She stares at him. 'You'd like me to dumb down, would you?'

He flinches, but then smiles in a way that's clearly meant to make women melt. 'If that's how you see it, then, yes. We can get the message across about things not always being sweetness and light, but I happen to think we can do it more subtly.' He turns to me. 'Tracey, why don't you start with why grown adults might want to dress as schoolgirls, like at School Disco?'

It's twenty minutes before Alec shouts, 'Cut,' and Suzanne's done a much jollier interview, all about reclaiming lost youth and comparing your wrinkles.

'So are you coming to the reunion?' I ask her.

'I think so, yes. If I can bring my husband.' She sounds incredibly smug when she says the word 'husband', as though she's landed the lottery jackpot.

'Mine's coming,' I say, keeping up. 'And my kids, for the early part at least.' That's trumped her, as she obviously hasn't got any.

'Lovely,' she says, and for the first time there's a real interest there. 'How old are they?'

'Kelly's six going on to seven, and Callum's nearly twenty months.'

'Oh, so you're almost finished with the really messy bit, then? I love them when they start talking to you properly. And the kids we work with, they tend to be pretty bright, and you can make such a massive difference in such a short time; it's great, seeing them blossom.'

'Really?' Her enthusiasm surprises me. 'But surely there's not much you can do with these kids, is there? I mean, if they're shy, then they're shy; if they're not popular, that's the end of it.'

Her face hardens again. 'It's not that simple, Tracey, though I'm not surprised that *you* see it that way, I suppose. Change is always possible. I've found that out myself because I've been able to turn my life around in adulthood. Fortunately, now, there's much more effort going into trying to intervene earlier, so children don't have to endure what I went through.'

'I didn't mean—'

'I think I know what you meant, Tracey.' She starts walking away. 'I'll see you next week.' She doesn't sound as though it's something she's looking forward to.

She certainly seems changed from school, though sadly she hasn't lost the priggish, superior tone. But I don't care about that. I *do* care that she mentioned working with bullied kids, and now I'm wondering if she might have some advice. Though I'm not sure I could bear the smugness that would probably unleash . . .

'That went well,' says Jenny, bouncing over. 'Alec's very pleased. Now, if you're ready, I'm your taxi to the dress fitting. Think of me as your fairy godmother.'

CHAPTER TWENTY-FIVE

Jenny deposits me outside the dressmaker's, and it's not very promising. I was expecting a flash boutique in Bond Street, like the ones I read about in magazines on the rare occasions I get time to get my hair cut in a salon.

But the 'designer' they've commissioned to make my reunion outfit is based in a suburban wedding shop. When they told me to send in my measurements because she was too busy to meet me, I'd imagined she was making couture numbers for 'It' girls. Instead, it seems she probably had a backlog of frou-frou bridal gowns to finish.

Bella's is the last shop on a run-down terrace, past an old-fashioned ironmonger's, and one of those nasty bakeries where the nearest they get to baking is pumping air-filled cream into ready-made doughnuts.

Predictably, Boris is already in the café. Eating one of those cream-filled doughnuts.

'How did you get on?' we shriek simultaneously, as I rush up to the plastic table where she's nursing a cup of tea and a sandwich made from finest neon-orange Cheddar cheese.

'You first,' she says, and I notice she looks pretty worn out. Not surprising, at her stage, though. Jenny disappears to get the coffees.

'It was *Suzanne Sharp*,' I say. 'She's only gone and trained as a psychologist. Bizarre. She was really odd with me, too.'

'In what way? And what does she look like now?'

'OK, actually. Expensive clothes, and she'd had something done to de-fuzz her hair. And she was narky, you know the way she always was. Superior. Anyway, you'll see for yourself at the reunion. What about you? How was the hospital?'

'Oh, you know. Boring. They want to keep an eye on my blood pressure, I'm probably just a bit too porky.'

She grins at me, but high blood pressure's not great, is it? Even I remember that from the baby manuals. 'When are they seeing you again?'

'They just want me to go to the nurse every day or so.'

'Every day? Boris, that sounds bad.'

'No . . . it's just something they want to monitor.'

'But that—'

'It's not going to help to talk about it,' she snaps. 'Sorry. I'm stressed enough without discussing it, that's all.'

Jenny comes back with the drinks in two chipped mugs. 'Jamie and the boys are in the workshop already, setting up the camera. So, you looking forward to seeing your outfit?'

I look at Boris, but her face is calm again, the tension's passed. 'Judging from the window display, it's going to be fluffy. And I don't really do fluffy.'

'Bella comes highly recommended,' Jenny says. 'You can't always judge a book by its cover, you know.'

'If I don't like it, I'm not wearing it on TV. That's non-negotiable.'

'Maybe it's stone-washed denim,' Boris says suddenly. 'I always wanted a stone-washed denim jacket.'

'Er, I hope not. I don't want to look like a retired member of Bananarama.'

'White was very popular, wasn't it?' Jenny says. 'And no, that's not a hint. We haven't given her any brief: just your vital statistics and your photo. Then we let her loose.'

'But you did tell her I wanted to look sexy as hell, I hope?'

Boris is in a world of her own. 'Maybe there'll be a ra-ra skirt. I did have one of those, it was pink. With polka dots . . .'

I smile at the memory. 'What were we like? I had pink pedal-pushers.'

'The eighties look is the big thing this summer, apparently,' says Jenny. 'So whatever Bella's done, you'll be the height of fashion.'

'How's the rest of the party planning going?' Boris asks her. She's finally handed over the reins to the TV people, as she's been getting tired and her husband insisted it was time to put her feet up. Judging from the dark patches under her eyes, it's a good job too.

'Bit like organising a wedding – not that I ever have, but it's just as worrying. Though of course you made it easier by doing such a fantastic job on the guest list.'

'Nothing to it.'

I feel a bit left out. 'Just hope I recognise some of the people at *my* reunion . . .'

'Don't worry,' says Boris, with a wink that makes me sure she's got something else up her sleeve. 'You will.'

The electronic door chime plays 'Here Comes the Bride' and through the window I can see a small woman rushing into the shop from the back. She's got Goth-black cropped hair, and she's wearing a tight cerise satin bodice with a pair of black jeans. Not at all what I was expecting.

'Tracey!' she says. 'I recognise you from your picture. Come on up.'

We walk through the showroom, which is painted sugar pink and has a chaise-longue by one wall. A little girl's dream – but Bella looks more like the wicked witch.

The door at the end leads up narrow stairs. This is much

more her: the walls are painted crimson, and framed prints of designs from *My Fair Lady* hang all the way up.

'It's been brilliant to let my imagination run riot for once,' she says. 'Much more fun than all those blancmange frocks.'

I follow her into the room on the left of the staircase, and shut my eyes until they're accustomed to the bright lights the crews have already set up. 'I hope you haven't gone overboard.'

'Oh, don't worry. I think you'll like it.'

Behind me, Boris is breathing heavily. She just about squeezes into the room, leaving Jenny hovering on the landing.

I peer around for clues. It's cluttered and chaotic, with fabric and shoes strewn all over the floor. It's also a bit of a fire hazard, with huge lit pillar candles balancing on magazines and pattern books, and a couple of those headless tailor's dummies, both covered with sheets. I guess this must be my outfit, but the cotton shrouds aren't giving anything away. On one of the walls there's a noticeboard crammed with photos and newspaper cuttings and even an album cover. Kim Wilde's backcombed halo dominates the image.

'Is that a clue?' I say, racking my brains to remember what she used to wear. There's a glimpse of a striped T-shirt at the bottom of the cover, and it rings a few bells. And wasn't there some jacket with enormous lapels?

'ARE YOU RUNNING?' Jenny shouts from the hall. 'Just pick up actuality, Jamie.'

I catch Jamie's eye and before I remember I'm meant to be annoyed with him, we share a look of irritation. 'Yeah, I'm running,' he says.

Bella smiles at me. In this light, I can see her face is heavily lined, and she must be at least fifty. I hope I can get away with those clothes when I'm fifty . . .

'I must admit that Kim Wilde wasn't my immediate thought

when it came to designing for you but then I noticed that the two of you do actually have very similar bone structure . . .'

And as she's talking I remember that Gary once told me I reminded him of her, back in the days when he bothered to pay me compliments.

Boris says, 'She presents gardening programmes now, you know. I saw her on one of those daytime shows the other day. Very nice. Down-to-earth.'

Bella nods. 'Yes, well, the inspiration for your design, Tracey, came from the way she looked fifteen years ago. It's a bit of a cheat, really.'

She tiptoes over the debris to the covered dummies. 'I actually copied a dress from one of her album covers. Naughty, I know, but it was so perfect. And then, to jazz it up a bit, I took a bit of inspiration from Adam Ant. I think he was a fashion student once, wasn't he? Anyway, my dear, I do hope you like them. Would you like to do the honours?'

She places the corner of the sheet from the first dummy in my hand and pats me on the shoulder. 'Go on.'

I pull, and the sheet drops to the floor, revealing an ornate dandy highwayman's jacket, with epaulettes and gold buttons. It's over the top, dressing-up-box stuff, but also completely gorgeous. 'Do I have to wear the stripe across me nose as well?'

'It's not compulsory. Do you like it?'

'Definitely . . . can I try it on?'

She lifts the jacket off, and when I put my arms into it and shake my way into it, Boris laughs. 'I love it, Tracey, you look so funky.' And when I look at myself in the cheval mirror, I have to admit it fits well, even over my T-shirt and jeans.

Bella fusses around me. 'I might take a quarter of an inch off the arms . . .' Then she stands behind the other dummy. 'But if you want to be the centre of attention, I think it's *this* that's going to achieve the desired effect . . .' She pulls off the second sheet.

'Wow,' says Boris.

It's a knee-length sleeveless black leather dress, close-fitting, cut off at sharp angles by the arms to make a feature of my shoulders. It's certainly sexy, and I have a vague memory of Kim Wilde wearing the same thing, standing on a rubbish-strewn building site. I reach forward to touch the leather, which is baby's bottom soft.

Then she turns the mannequin round, and I remember what was really show-stopping about that dress: apart from three shoestring leather straps holding it together, the whole back from neck to lower waist is exposed. It's stunning.

'Better book myself a few sun beds before next week, if I'm going to carry this one off,' I say to Boris.

She grins back. 'There aren't many girls of our advanced age who could pull that off, but I think you're the exception.'

And my inner Tracey Mortimer is smiling a wicked smile.

CHAPTER TWENTY-SIX

It's the Day Before.

I'm sitting at the kitchen table smoking a cigarette. Another thing I haven't done since the day of my wedding. I only ever learned to smoke because it was cool, and never really enjoyed it. But just occasionally a nicotine hit is the only thing that will do to distract you from your fate.

At least I don't need to worry about the dress. I'm lucky because I lose weight when I'm stressed, otherwise eating might be a problem tomorrow. I think Bella poured years of frustration at being forced to create chiffon fantasies into making my outfit. By the time she'd fiddled about at the fitting, pulling the seams even tighter, I was worried all that stretched leather would make me look too much like a baby seal. Instead, when she turned the mirror towards me, I was visual Viagra. Even Jamie looked impressed.

Though since then I've been almost too nervous to speak and that really doesn't suit me. Dave arrived home last night to be at my side for the reunion, highly irritated at having to be here when the rest of the lads had a big piss-up planned, but then he saw the dress, and now keeps stroking it and trying to talk me into modelling it for him. Men are so bloody predictable.

Take stockings and suspenders. I tried them once, when I was sixteen. I went to Marks and Spencer, and bought black stockings patterned with little dots that I now realise made me look like I was suffering from a skin disease, and a white lacy suspender belt. I felt uncomfortable and ridiculous, but Gary could hardly contain himself. And he was *my* age . . . I can understand it with the dirty older man (and yes, it wasn't long before I tried the same trick on Bob, to the same effect) since they've been reared on black and white pin-ups of forties starlets. But why would my age group, used to full frontals and money shots, react the same way? Is it something instinctive? Could you parade up and down in a suspender belt in front of an Amazonian hill tribe, and get the same reaction?

I used to waste an awful lot of time and energy trying to understand men, but I gave up on my wedding day which was also the last day I wore stockings. Maybe Callum will give me an insight into the male psyche when he's older, but by then it'll be too late for me.

Is it already too late for me? For all of this? I'm definitely struggling to see the point of the forthcoming festivities. The list of people I'd actually like to see after all these years is shorter than the skirts Melody used to wear. Gary's off the list, been there, done that, and it was hardly a roaring success. Maybe it'd be fun to see Briggsy, but he was always a waste of space without Gary. Suzanne I never wanted to see in the first place. I have a horrible feeling that Melody will be on the guest list. I did ask Boris not to invite her, but Annabel or Jenny will have added her name for sure: they want to get my wedding video into the programme somehow.

I can be grown up, can't I? She didn't manage to split Dave and me up, and she doesn't have to know how miserable we are. Plus, I bet all that sunbathing and smoking will have taken its toll on her skin. Yeah, Melody, bring it on!

And what about Bob? Where is he now? He's probably aged less than me and Boris because he was older to begin with. I'd like to see Bob. He was always a gentleman to me, whatever people said. The first guy to make me feel like a woman instead of a girl . . . But maybe I'm better off with my memories.

The only person I would really love to see is poor Shrimp.

I can hear Kelly upstairs, running up and down the landing. She's brightened up so much since school broke up on Wednesday – a different child, almost. I just wish I could stop worrying about her being lonely, stop scanning the swings and the street for potential friends for her like a deranged match-maker. Loneliness sucks. I've only realised recently how much. *She* seems happy enough in her own little world, it's me that's unhappy about it. But it can't be much fun, really, and all you need is *one* good friend . . .

Which is exactly what I've been looking for ever since Shrimp. Someone to watch my back, while I watch hers. A second chance at being there when it matters. Whatever happens tomorrow, the most important person there will be Boris.

My old, new friend.

Department for Education, London SW1

'What about you, Bob? You up for a party?'

'Eh?' Bob Carmichael peered up from the report he was proof-reading. *Building Bridges, a school-based approach to community relations.* Yet another government publication that would use up a few thousand trees, and sit unread in tens of thousands of staff pigeon-holes. At least it was another entry on his bibliography.

'I was asking what you're planning to do to celebrate finishing that sodding report?' Heather, his research assistant, had already had a few at lunchtime, while he'd been checking the final draft. 'You should come out with us later on, we're going to a party in Fulham – probably going on into Saturday night, too.'

She was quite serious with her invitation: after all, he was one of her chosen 'Fantasy Fucks'. But he didn't think her twenty-something friends would appreciate his presence. 'I think I'll go home and open a nice bottle of red I've had waiting for exactly this kind of occasion.'

'Boring or what? Don't you ever let your hair down?' But Heather didn't wait for an answer, and moved to the next office to round up more party animals.

Bob grinned to himself. If only you knew. He read on: 'the importance of the partnership approach, have been accepted by all parties in the multi-agency pilot study'. How had they missed that? He crossed out 'have' with the pencil, which snapped under the pressure, so he reached into his drawer for another one. And spotted the invitation.

He hadn't forgotten it, not exactly. Ruled it out, obviously, but he knew it was there, felt its dangerous glow whenever he looked at the desk. Bob imagined Tracey making preparations, with her girlfriends gathered around, starting a marathon of buffing and shaving and painting and conditioning.

Dick and the rest had never understood her, never seen past the cloud of Impulse and the stream of smart-arse abuse she gave every teacher . . . but Tracey was brighter than a class full of insufferable Suzanne Sharps. She had a natural spark – much more appealing than a trained, fixed intellectual brain – that he'd never seen in anyone else.

Not to mention the sweetest grin, when you caught her dropping her guard.

But Tracey Mortimer could never have worked. Wrong age, wrong lifetime, wrong part of town.

Fucking hell, Bob thought, he'd been thirty, it wasn't *West Side Story*, star-crossed lovers at the mercy of society's disapproval. He was old enough to know better even before it started, or, once it had begun, old enough to take control, to end it or to take the punishment if Tracey was worth more than his career and his reputation. Surely he'd owed her that.

OK, so she dumped him before he had the chance to whisk her away to a better life, but he might still have been able to pull it off if he hadn't been a coward.

He pulled out another pencil, and slammed the drawer shut. But even as he scribbled 'has' in the margin instead of 'have', he knew the carefully chosen bottles of wine in his cellar wouldn't be able to compete with the invitation burning a hole in his desk.

Millennium Child Campaign, Clapham Common, South-West London

'Has Christian even visited a state school before?' Charlotte asked.

Suzanne tried to gauge from her secretary's face if she was being sarcastic, but the sun was reflecting off the silver café table, and so she couldn't see properly. 'I don't think he has, no.'

'So he'll be seeing your humble origins!' Now she definitely sounded as though she were taking the piss.

'It's not where you start, it's where you finish, Charlotte. Corny, but true. If anything, it'll just prove to him that I was made of better stuff than all the other hopeless cases there.'

'And what about the bitch you did your speech about? Will she be there?'

Suzanne sipped her prosecco, which had gone unpleasantly

warm and flat in the glass. Only Christian knew who 'Stacey' really was, thank God.

'I'm not quite sure, but that's all water under the bridge. You can't let your past rule your present.' Suzanne hoped she sounded convincing. Because she hadn't yet convinced herself.

Flat 2a, 422 Goldhawk Road, Shepherd's Bush, London

'I've told you, Gary, I'm not coming. I see enough dysfunctional families during the week, without spending time with your dysfunctional friends from school. No way.'

They were sitting on what the estate agents lovingly called their 'outside space'. It was actually a tiny area of flat asphalt roof overlooking a traffic-clogged main road. The potted herbs had withered from the heat and pollution, but Gary and Gabby still insisted on having their Friday night Budweisers alfresco.

'I don't even want to go myself, but I promised Boris I would.'

'Can't believe any grown woman would still let people call her Boris.'

'You'll love Boris. Everyone does.'

'No, I won't, because I won't be meeting her.'

Gary stared at the bus below, spewing blue smoke from its exhaust. *Convenient for public transport.* What was he doing in London, anyway? He decided to try a change of tack. 'You know my first love is going to be there.'

She stopped picking the dead bits out of the mint plant. 'What, the legendary Tracey? You saying I should be worried?'

'Well, I'm happy enough as I am, but she can be seriously determined when she puts her mind to it.'

'If she's a threat after all these years, then you're not really a great loss, are you, petal?'

God, she was cool. It was what he loved about her, but his ego still longed for her to demonstrate a touch of jealousy. Just to prove he wasn't disposable. 'It's not that. It's more . . . well, I want to show you off, don't I? Show the rejects of Crawley Park that one of us at least got the girl and got the hell out of there!'

She was trying not to smile at the compliment. 'School reunions, eh? It's got nothing to do with reliving old memories. It's all about settling old scores.'

'So will you help me settle this one?'

'I'll think about it . . . in the morning. If you get the drinks in tonight!'

I'm helping Kelly choose her outfit, when Dave bellows up the stairs, 'Boris is on the phone.'

I wasn't expecting to hear from her till later, because I know she's been back at the surgery for her check-up, this time with the legendary Brian. He arrived back in England last night, and is confined to barracks while they wait for the Big Day. I'm looking forward to meeting this paragon of manhood.

'Hi, Boris, how ya doing?'

'Not good, Trace,' she says and in those three words I hear so many things. The hiss of a mobile and the labouring of a car engine and the grind of hot rush-hour traffic. But most of all the *tininess* of her voice. She sounds more like a little girl than she ever did when she actually was a little girl.

'What?'

The wait for the answer is the longest I can remember. 'Brian's driving me into the hospital now. My blood pressure's off the scale. I don't know . . .'

And then she starts to cry, single sobs at first and then big growling sentences of crying that I can't make sense of. In the background, Brian is telling her to calm down, it can't help her blood pressure to get all upset.

'Boris, listen. I'll come down to the hospital. Dave'll just have to babysit. You're going to be in the right place, they can monitor you and the little one and the rest of the pregnancy's gone fine, so there's no reason at all that once they've got you in there, everything shouldn't go according to plan.'

I gulp as I realise that there's no way she's going to be at the reunion with me. I know it's selfish, but all I can think about is that I am going to be totally, completely, utterly alone for a party that I no longer even want.

My reassurances don't seem to have helped Boris either. She sounds like a wounded seal, and I only catch the odd word. 'But . . . baby . . . before . . . can't come . . . want you there . . . no good . . .'

'Boris, breathe deeply for a minute then you can tell me what you're worried about.' But the tears are still coming, and I wonder if the phone will stop working under the deluge.

There's a rustling and then a male voice. 'Tracey, it's Brian. Sorry we haven't met yet. You can't come to the hospital, I'm afraid. That's what Helen's trying to say. They're probably going to induce the baby.'

'Induce it? Can't they wait?'

There's silence and it sounds like the phone's gone dead until I hear a horn blaring and Brian shouts, 'Fucking wanker. Not you, Tracey. The thing is . . . Helen hasn't told you, has she, but you see it's happened before. And last time . . . The thing is, last time, our son . . . our son was called Harry, and he didn't make it.'

There's a pause as this sinks in, and then Brian speaks, his voice thick: 'I can't drive and talk, sorry, Tracey. We don't need a road accident on top of everything else. I'll call you as soon as there's any news.'

And I just catch another heartbreaking sob from Boris before the line really does go dead.

CHAPTER TWENTY-SEVEN

I haven't slept much, and it shows. My eyes are red, my skin is dry and on my cheek you can see the creases from the pillow. I'm sure this never used to happen when I was younger. But then, when I was younger, I never worried about anyone except myself.

Poor Boris. I tried ringing the hospital, but they're not giving anything away, and her mobile's switched off. And what would I say if I did get through? I thought we were close friends, yet she couldn't even tell me she'd lost a baby. Some mate I am. I've learned nothing from what happened with Shrimp.

Nothing at all.

'Mummy?' Kelly's hovering at the door. 'You excited?'

I summon a smile from somewhere, and she comes and joins me on the bed, giving me a kiss. 'Ugh, Mummy, you smell funny.'

I lick my hand and sniff it; I read in a magazine that it's the best way to test your own breath, and sure enough, it smells as sour as a cat's bottom. I suppose I always thought that motherhood would make me too wise to want to drink myself into a stupor before going to bed without brushing my teeth. Silly Mummy.

'So do you, Kelly!' I tell her, but she knows I'm messing, and starts giggling. The school summer holidays have turned her back into a child I still don't understand, but can at least recognise as my own.

I let her pull me out of bed, and then I follow her slowly down the stairs. The hangover's not as bad as I'd feared, but I still don't have a clue how I'm going to make it through breakfast, never mind the whole reunion.

Downstairs, Dave is feeding Callum cereal using the aeroplane trick, 'coming into land, open wide . . .' which never works when I do it, but right now seems to be achieving remarkable results on the plate-clearing front. Just for a moment I wonder whether I might occasionally judge my husband a little too harshly.

'You decided to get into the reliving your youth stuff a bit early last night. Paying for it now, though?' Amazing how quickly he can extract himself from my good books.

'Make me a coffee, will you?'

'What did your last servant die—'

'I've asked you to make me a coffee once – *once* – in nine bloody years of marriage. Is it too much to ask?'

Kelly covers her ears and Dave sighs, pulling her to him. 'What's got into Mummy?' he says brightly, then murmurs, 'Too many bloody gin and tonics, that's what got into Mummy.'

He gives me my coffee, after much more clattering of crockery and cutlery, but it's thin and rancid-smelling, with most of the granules stuck to the side of the mug, spreading in the steam like bacteria under a microscope.

I look at the clock. I'm running out of time to get ready before the cab comes to take me to Crawley Park for a photo call.

I hold my nose and drink the coffee, trying to suck the caffeine into my system like a drug.

It's going to be a long day.

Fortunately for the taxi driver, I'm getting changed at school, so he's spared the sight of too much of my flesh in daylight. In the space of three-quarters of an hour, I've managed to shower, shave my legs and underarms, put on some body lotion, drag my jeans over the slimy residue, and then throw all the gels and serums and sprays I can find into a Tesco carrier bag to bring with me.

'What are you doing going into school on a Saturday?' he asks me, catching my eye in his mirror as I rummage around in the bag of tricks, pulling out concealer and that French stuff that looks like egg white and tightens up your skin. It's got its work cut out with me.

'It's a reunion.'

'Oh, I thought maybe you was a teacher. So – how long's it been?'

I think about asking him to guess, but when I see myself in the mirror I decide that the way I look this morning, I wouldn't like the answer. 'Seventeen years.' No wonder I look so old.

'Bet it'll feel like yesterday when you're there, though.'

Will it? Maybe when the others are there, it'll take me back. Because right now it feels a lot longer than seventeen years.

I use the chrome back of my hairbrush as a mirror to work out which bits of my face are crying out for concealer, though it occurs to me that it might be quicker to apply it all over. The roads are pretty quiet this morning, less traffic than I'd expected, and I think of Boris and Brian going through the jams to get to the hospital last night.

'Could we do a bit of a diversion before we go to school?'

He looks a bit doubtful. 'It's on account.'

'Yeah, they'll never notice. But I'll make up the difference in cost, if it takes too long to get back.'

*

They've done a *Changing Rooms* makeover on the hospital reception since I had Callum, so now it's all glass bricks and soothing water colours. But once I've followed my nose back to Rosebud Ward it's just as horrible as ever, reeking of disinfectant, with the radiators on full blast, even though it's a hot July day. A zombified pregnant woman nearly walks into me, pulling her drip along behind her like a wilful Great Dane.

I stick my head round the bay where they used to put the women who were confined to bed for the duration. But there's no one there. So I walk towards the reception desk, where a tired-looking midwife is hitching up her trousers to scratch her ankle.

'I'm looking for my frien— sister.' If she's that ill, there's no way I'll be allowed anywhere near her unless I'm a blood relative. 'Boris . . . Helen Morris. Um. Norris.'

She gives me a funny look, the same one she probably gives to women who come in and can't decide if they're having contractions or not. 'And you're sure she's your sister?'

I nod, and I guess I look the part – frazzled and surviving on no sleep, exactly the right attitude for a dutiful sister in the midst of a crisis.

'She's in Lily Room,' she says, pointing down the corridor.

Of course: a private room. Brian's never there, but at least he's earning enough to keep their grief ring-fenced from the common people.

'Don't stay too long,' she shouts after me.

I can't hear any wailing or arguing through the crack in the door. I knock gently but don't wait.

Boris is on a monitor, and when I walk in she moves her head extremely slowly, as though she's scared of breaking something inside her if she reacts too fast.

'Tracey,' she says quietly, and I flatter myself that she sounds pleased that it's me.

223

At the window, there's a tall man, silhouetted against the sunlight. He turns round. Brian. Nice-looking, bit bashed about – I'd guess he was a rugby player who stopped before he got a second cauliflower ear. Bit too 'casual sportswear' for my liking, but he's not looking very crisp now. I guess he's been at the hospital all night.

I lean in to kiss Boris's cheek, and squeeze her shoulder through the cotton nightie. Then I reach across her bump to shake Brian's hand.

'I wish we weren't meeting here,' I say. He looks through me. 'What's the latest?'

Boris nods at him to explain. She looks as though even talking might be a dangerous waste of what little energy she's got left.

He sits down and stares sadly at Boris's belly. 'We're expecting the consultant any time. He's got to decide whether to induce or do a caesarean.'

'So the baby's definitely got to come out now? At least it won't be very premature.' Last night I dragged out one of my old pregnancy books, and looked up high blood pressure. The index referred me to dire warnings about pre-eclampsia, which was one of those words they mouthed grimly at antenatal classes, the way actors do with *Macbeth*. As if even to say it could bring disaster.

'I wanted to give birth *properly*,' Boris whispers. 'I've got the TENS machine and spare batteries and everything.'

'Well, I don't care so long as the baby is born alive,' Brian says, and then bites his tongue at how harsh it sounds, reaching across to kiss her cheek, muttering, 'Sorry.' Looks like foot-in-mouth disease is one thing Boris has in common with her husband.

'You're in the right place,' I say, resorting to cliché.

'We were last time, too.'

224

None of us can think of anything more to say. I wish I hadn't come – Lily Room already feels like a funeral parlour.

I wave vaguely at the window. 'My taxi . . .'

They both nod at me, and Boris smiles. 'I wish I was coming with you, Tracey. Can't believe I'm not going to be there.'

'Nor can I.' I feel the sudden pressure of tears behind my eyes, but I won't cry. 'At least you'll be able to watch the video!' It's a very feeble attempt to be cheerful, but Boris still tries to smile, to make *me* feel better, which makes me feel even worse.

'I'll be thinking about you.' I place my hand on her belly as gently as I can, and I'm surprised at how hot it feels. 'And about you, too, Baby . . . I'm looking forward to meeting you.'

I don't think Brian even notices I'm leaving the room.

The taxi driver is happily watching the total on his meter mount up when I get back to the car.

I clamber in, and jam myself into the corner as far as I can so it's hard for him to see me in the mirror. A few tears have snuck out of my eyes, and my nose has gone red with the effort of holding the rest in. I smear on even more concealer. I've used most of a stick on my face, and the rest seems to have collected under my nails.

'Any more unscheduled stops?' he asks hopefully.

'No, thanks.' I sniff. I try to stare at cars, road signs, anything I can see out of the window that has no emotional significance whatsoever. But the signs point to the maternity unit, and the car in front has a 'baby on board' sticker in its window. So I fix my eyes on the back of the passenger seat, with its torn leatherette upholstery and fabric head rest.

I concentrate on individual threads of cotton until they all swim in and out of focus, and I feel slightly sick. Maybe I even fall into some kind of trance, because it's only when the driver pulls on the handbrake that I realise we're there.

He pulls up just inside the school gates and my handwriting is blurry when I sign the account. When I get out, the car park's busier than it would be on a school day, but instead of Minis and Clios and Fiestas and other teachers' cars, the space is taken up by Volvos and Saabs, a couple of big lorries and a generator. There's even a catering van.

The only person I can see is a teenager wearing a fluorescent bib marked 'Marshal'. He's hovering at the end of the car park, smoking like an amateur.

He sees me, and tries to hide the cigarette behind his back. It's depressing to think he sees me as an authority figure.

'Don't worry, I don't want to interrupt your fag break,' I say, and wink at him.

His face relaxes and he takes a long drag, which makes his face colour. I'm much happier now I realise he's trying to impress me.

'I'm here for the reunion.'

'You press? You're a bit early.'

'Er, no. It's actually *my* reunion. I'm Tracey. I was a pupil here, oooh, seventeen years ago – we used to smoke by the bins at the back of the canteen in my day.'

He frowns at me, and I think he's struggling with the concept of anyone being daring enough to smoke seventeen years ago, i.e. before he was even born.

I give up – I get better conversation from Callum. 'I'll go and see how they're getting on with setting things up.'

I walk round the other side of the hall, where the windows are, and it's as if I've stepped on to a Hollywood film set. People are striding around with supreme self-importance, carrying the tools of the trade – clipboards, cables, clipboards, lights, clipboards, loudspeakers. Oh, and did I mention the clipboards?

It's at this point that my stomach starts to feel like a washing machine on spin cycle. All this here because of little old me.

Well, little old me, and the need for Alec's grubby production company to squeeze money out of Channel 5.

I want to run away but my legs are refusing to co-operate. So I stand like a statue at the edge of the action, and everything slows down, the rushing figures I don't recognise are going blurry and an echoing voice seems to be calling out from somewhere else: 'Tracey . . . Tracey . . .'

I think I'm going to be sick.

'Feeling any better?' Jenny asks me. We're in the staff room, which has been relabelled the green room, and has a new keypad lock on the door to make sure no pupils, press or even guests get to raid the secret supplies of booze. I've been told the code, which proves they see me as part of the production team now. Though I bet I'm the only one here not being paid. Even the smoking marshal will be getting cash in hand.

'Yeah. I had a really bad night because of Boris—'

'What about her?'

Oh shit. 'You haven't heard? She's been admitted to the general and they think they're going to induce her, because of her high blood pressure.'

'God. How awful. I'd better tell Alec.'

'I'm sure he'll be very concerned – about how it affects his precious programme.'

She looks as though she's going to argue back, but then she shrugs. 'Yeah. You're probably right. But we do need to get you back to looking human, and the good news is our floor manager is also a dab hand with a make-up sponge. So she's the next step in your preparations for ordeal by journalists . . .'

CHAPTER TWENTY-EIGHT

I don't think I'm up to a press conference. Brenda, the floor manager, whose abilities with a make-up brush have not been exaggerated, used to go out with a journalist.

'They're bastards. Think Alec times ten,' she says, as she blends foundation around my albino-rabbit pink eyes. She's had to remove all the stuff I'd smeared on in the taxi and begin again. Her own make-up is so perfect that I have no idea how old she is.

'They can't be that awful. Surely?' Up till now I haven't had a chance to worry about it, which is a good thing, but then again I haven't had time to prepare for it, which is a bad thing.

'They are. The men are bad, but the women are definitely the worst – they suck up to you and pretend to be your friend, and then stab you in the back.'

'I guess things didn't work out with the boyfriend, then?'

She snorts at me. 'I learned the hard way.'

By the time she's finished my face, I look like I've been on a long relaxing holiday, but my insides are churning more violently than before. Brenda takes me to the classroom where we're doing the press conference. Annabel is waiting for me, with ten noisy children.

'Surprise,' she says.

It's that all right. They're about twelve, and dressed in school uniform even though it's Saturday *and* the holidays. 'Meet the kids from the current class 1G. We thought it'd be fun to get some of them in for the photographs.'

Fun for who? We all eye each other suspiciously. The kids are much better-looking than we were, less smudged and warped. The girls are well groomed, I'm sure a couple of them are wearing lipstick, and even the boys look clean. They're already flirting with each other, and sending signals as blatant as any you'd see in a nightclub. It makes me want to run home and wrap Kelly up tight, to stop her growing up, like when the Chinese used to bind their daughters' feet.

'So who is your form tutor, then?' I ask them, not knowing what else to talk about.

'Miss Nicholls,' says one of the girls with lipstick. 'She's a frigid bitch.' Everyone laughs at this.

'Oh. Well, that's teachers for you. At least if they don't have sex, they won't breed more teachers.'

I think I've gone too far, and the kids look from me to the cocky girl, waiting for a response.

She's weighing it up and after a bloody long wait, she finally grants me a sly smirk. 'Yeah, right,' she says, and I know I'm in the gang.

Annabel walks towards the door. 'I'll leave you *children* to it then,' she says, making it clear she's including me in that. 'We're expecting the journalists in about ten minutes, so I'll bring them up in one big group.'

Now that I'm officially cool, the kids all talk at once, telling me about their friends and their pets and their siblings and their favourite bands, and they're not nearly as grown up as they're pretending to be. Bless 'em. It's nice to let it wash over me, the trivia of life before puberty hits like a juggernaut. And meanwhile I try to second-guess what these reporters will ask me.

What would I ask myself? With my insider knowledge of

229

what makes me tick, what would be the worst questions they could come up with to throw me off course?

When was the last time you had sex?

Not really an obvious question at a school reunion, but it would certainly throw me. Though maybe it's not really that embarrassing that me and Dave no longer bother to do it after nine years; it's probably worse that I'm not sure I even miss it.

Whatever happened to your first love?

Even that's not impossible, is it? He's a policeman living with his girlfriend in London.

And is he coming tonight?

'No, I think he's working a night shift . . . yes, it is a shame, but then again, I don't think we'd have much in common any more. People change, don't they? What if he had a horrible beer gut now?'

I almost convince myself.

What's the secret of an enduring friendship?

I keep thinking about Shrimp, and about Boris, and it makes me feel sick. What's the right answer to a question like that? Something that makes me sound wise and balanced and mature, instead of the way I feel, which is shallow and clueless and lonely.

'The secret of enduring friendship is to know that people change, but to hang on to the things that made you friends in the first place.'

I think that sounds good. I almost come across like someone you'd want as your friend.

School Road, Bracewell, Berkshire

Suzanne Marshall-Sharp slumped as far down as she could in the car seat and, not for the first time, wondered whether she

230

was doing the right thing. 'I'd better get away before anyone sees my car. Guests aren't meant to come here till the evening. But I'll tell you the rest when you come to my mother's later.'

Andrew pouted. 'You really are making a meal out of this. Why can't you just tell me now what the bloody story is?'

She looked at him and realised that she didn't regret what she was doing, but she truly regretted her choice of journalist. He was such a whinger.

'Because it has to be this way.'

'I don't see why. And I really don't like being led on a wild-goose chase. I should be at a wedding this afternoon.'

Suzanne sighed. Within twelve hours, Andrew would have served his purpose, and she would never have to have anything more to do with him. Best that way, so that no one could ever make the connection with her.

'Ring me,' she said, and opened the passenger door to let him out. 'I'll see you later on.'

The cloak and dagger stuff was a good distraction from the reality of what she was doing. She'd even kept it from Christian, who never disapproved of anything she did. She was thirty-three, with years of professional compassion behind her. Wasn't it time to bury the hatchet? Suzanne still felt unsettled by her thirst for revenge. But she had to admit she also felt a little excited.

She watched Andrew trudge over to his own car – freelance journalism must pay well, his BMW was newer than hers – get in and then drive through the school gates.

Somewhere inside that building, Tracey Mortimer was about to meet Andrew. And with it, her nemesis.

Did she deserve what she was about to get? Suzanne felt a moment of regret, but then a memory flashed through her brain. It had haunted her for so long, and as it played out yet again, she knew that she was doing the right thing.

It had taken the thirteen-year-old Suzanne Sharp ten days to believe Gary Coombs could possibly fancy her. And ten years to get over the fact he didn't.

The note had looked genuine enough.

Will you come to the Easter Disco with me?
Gary

He'd slipped the piece of paper into her maths exercise book as it was handed back along the rows of desks. She hadn't actually seen him do it, but when she went to check the mark she'd been given for her algebra homework, the note fluttered to the floor like a feather. She read it while she was leaning down beside her desk, and by the time she surfaced again, her face was as red as her hair.

Suzanne had never dared to fancy any boy, because she was sure no boy could fancy her back. And even if they did, they'd never dare admit it. It would be utterly uncool to want to go out with the class swot. But as she absorbed the content of the note, repeating each word to herself, she wondered . . . If there was *anyone* with enough credibility to get away with dating her, it was Gary. So handsome and so smooth that he could do as he pleased. The image of the two of them as a couple formed in her head, despite her best efforts to stop it, and within seconds she saw a nicer future, one where the class bullies would never dream of having a go at her, when she was Gary's girlfriend.

She accidentally caught his eye once during the lesson, and he blushed. It made sense. Maths was the best time to send the note. It was her weakest subject, and his strongest, and the only one where Tracey and her cronies didn't rule the roost, because they were in the bottom set. Suzanne knew Tracey had her eye on Gary, and she'd assumed he felt the same way, but what if he really wanted someone more . . . intelligent? It happened in the movies, didn't it, where the school hunk fell for the clever girl who was then revealed to be a stunner.

OK. She could only think of *one* movie where that happened – *Grease* – but, bloody hell, she identified with the bit where Olivia Newton-John peered into that paddling pool and sang her teen heart out.

The hardest thing about school was having no one to talk to, and the note reinforced her isolation: she couldn't ask anyone whether it might be true. So she tried to interrogate it herself, to read between the lines (there were only two lines, after all) to see if it was truth or dare.

Her first step was to check the handwriting to see if the note had actually been written by Gary. At least that was easy. Mr Phipps always kept his pile of marking stacked in alphabetical order, so she brushed against his desk to knock them over. Gary's book was near the top when she gathered them up again.

Yep, it was definitely his writing – angular, heavy-handed.

Back home, she couldn't concentrate on her homework. Not even English, her favourite subject. The possibility of going to the disco with Gary kept distracting her. To start with, it was unreal, like the idea of going to the disco with Sting or Martin Kemp. But, as she worked out the details – what she would wear, what he would wear, how they would get to the disco, and, most exciting, the reactions when they finally arrived – the picture in her mind became ever clearer. And sharper. And suddenly, terrifyingly attainable.

Three days later, Suzanne did something she hadn't done since primary school. Initiated a conversation with someone in her class. OK, so it was only Boris, but it was still a breakthrough.

She cornered her at break time. 'Helen?' she said, and Boris didn't turn round, because no one ever called her Helen any more. Suzanne tried again. 'Boris?'

'Hmm?' Boris looked startled that Suzanne had spoken, but not hostile.

'Just wondering if you wanted to share some cake with me? It was Mum's birthday yesterday, so she's put chocolate cake in my packed lunch, but I'll never manage it on my own.' It wasn't true, of course. Actually, she'd bought the cake from the shop, guessing that it was the best way to attract the attention of the fattest – and least vindictive – girl in 3G.

Boris thought it over. 'Has it got butter cream?'

'Yes. And icing.'

'OK, then.'

At lunchtime, they headed to the back of the field. They hadn't discussed it, but Suzanne knew Boris would appreciate being as far away as possible, in case anyone saw them together. Maybe all that would change when she was going out with Gary. It would be nice to have friends.

Suzanne had cut the cake into several odd-shaped pieces, to disguise the fact that it was shop-bought. But she realised immediately that it didn't matter to Boris, who was wide-eyed at the sheer quantity.

'Tuck in – I don't even like chocolate,' Suzanne lied. Then she watched in awe as Boris polished off half the cake without speaking, licking the sugary filling from her fingers as purposefully as a kitten. When she was finished, Boris looked up and grinned.

'Boris? What would you do, um . . . ? I mean, if you thought that maybe . . . ?' It was an awful struggle to know where to start, so finally Suzanne rummaged around in her bag, pulled out the note, and handed it over.

Boris unravelled it and looked even more impressed than she

had at the cake. 'Have you stolen this from one of the other girls?'

It wasn't what Suzanne had hoped to hear. 'No . . . no, he slipped it into my exercise book in maths.'

'Wow!'

'You don't think it could be a practical joke, do you, Helen?'

Boris thought about it for a second, then reached over to pick up another piece of cake. She finished it before she spoke again. 'Prob'bly not, but there's only one way to find out. Write one back.'

It took Suzanne all weekend to write it. She bought a couple of teenage magazines with what was left of her pocket money after paying for the cake. They had an agony column in both mags and though the problems weren't quite the same, the message for dealing with boys was always the same: play it cool, and make him wait (she hadn't dared to think ever before about being in a position where she'd have to make any boy wait, but for the first time it began to seem like a possibility, however distant).

On Monday, she tried to catch his eye in maths, but he ignored her. Embarrassed? Annoyed because she hadn't even replied? On Tuesday, she did the same, and this time he blushed, as he had the week before. It gave her courage.

On Wednesday, she offered to hand out the exercise books, and slipped her own note into Gary's book. It was written on a piece of pink paper, folded in half so no one else would see it poking out of the cardboard cover. She'd practised her writing, tearing the many previous versions into confetti-sized pieces so her mum wouldn't be able to decipher the message. In any case, all it said was, 'Yes, I'll come, from Suzie'. In a daring moment, she added 'xx' after her name.

She liked the idea of being Suzie, it sounded better alongside Gary's name, and it also sounded like someone else, the person she wanted to be. Suzie wouldn't get top marks; in fact, Suzie might sometimes be so busy going out and having fun that her homework would be *late*. And Suzie wouldn't even care.

She had to lean back in her seat to see his reaction. He opened the book, saw the pink paper, then shut the book immediately, checking that no one else was watching. Suzanne looked away, and when she felt brave enough to turn round again, she knew she'd made a mistake. He was frowning, and when he realised she was facing him, he shrugged, asking silently what she meant. All she could do was wait for something to happen. She had a bad feeling about it.

It didn't take long. On Thursday, when Suzanne walked into Mr Carmichael's room for registration, everyone was waiting for her. Boris looked nervous, Gary looked embarrassed. And Tracey looked triumphant. In her hand was a piece of pink paper.

'Well, well, well, Suzanne. I think we need a little chat about *my* boyfriend . . .'

Annabel returns eventually with the journalists: five blokes and a girl. The girl is from the local rag, there's a youngish man from the evening paper in Reading, a nerdy-looking radio reporter, and two photographers dragging huge canvas bags behind them, trying to outdo each other with the lengths of their lenses. And then there's this shifty guy, better dressed than the rest. Andrew is a freelance 'all the way from London', Annabel says, and it's clear she's only interested in what he thinks. Though I do get the impression she's disappointed at the turnout.

'Let's do the Q and A first, before Tracey poses for pictures with the pupils. If that's OK with you all?' Annabel says, but she's only looking at Andrew.

He goes up to one of the photographers – the one with the

biggest lens – and says, 'Dunno who I'm going to flog this to, yet, but would you shoot a roll for me too? Can't guarantee anything, but it might be worth your while.'

The guy shrugs, but takes Andrew's card. 'All right then.'

The radio guy sets up his tape recorder, and the kids look bored.

'So who's firing the first question, then?' asks Annabel.

'Tracey, what's been the biggest surprise of the preparation for your reunion so far?' The radio reporter puts on a trans-atlantic DJ voice, but it's so different from the way he looks – like a train-spotter – that I have to work hard not to laugh.

Where would I start, if I was going to answer truthfully? The fact that I seem to be the only person who enjoyed school? The fact that my first boyfriend still hates me with a vengeance after seventeen years? Or maybe the fact that I've forgotten what it's like to have a friend?

'It's probably not what you'd think, but the biggest surprise has been how much hard work it is making a television pro-gramme. Endless filming appointments, a compulsory trip to a health farm to make me look more glamorous, my own designer-made dress for tonight . . . It's been exhausting. So if anyone's thinking of signing up for something similar – in the words of the *Grange Hill* anti-drugs campaigns – JUST SAY NO!'

They grin. I know I'm going to be what Annabel calls 'good copy'.

The questions don't get much tougher. The girl from the weekly waffles on about the improvements to the school's results, and wants to know whether I'm surprised that Crawley Park is now a media college. The bloke from the evening paper is talking about old friends and what's happened to them, and I talk a bit about Boris running her own company, but try not to think about what's happening to her right now . . .

Andrew's the least talkative, which seems odd as he works for the nationals. After we do the photographs – which involve me posing with today's class 1G – he's still hanging around looking shifty. Annabel looks concerned. 'Have you got what you wanted, Andrew?'

'Not yet,' he says, but flashes a smile. 'I thought I'd come back later, soak up the atmosphere. I'm more likely to be able to sell it as a feature that way.'

'Well, strictly speaking, we're not letting any journalists come back for the reunion itself – we don't want to do ourselves out of publicity when the programme goes out.'

Andrew shakes his head. 'Oh, I shan't reveal who gets off with whom. My main outlet is the *Guardian* features pages. Social trends, that's my take on it.'

'Let me have a word with Alec about it.' I bet slimy Andrew gets his way. There's something about him that doesn't ring true, but then I remember what Brenda said, and I guess looking dodgy is an occupational hazard for journalists.

'Delighted to meet you, Tracey,' he says, kissing my cheek. 'Maybe we can catch up again later on.'

Hope not. 'Yes, that'll be great.'

I'm getting good at saying the opposite of what I really mean.

I ring the hospital.

'Hello, I'm Helen Norris's sister – I was in earlier?'

It's a different nurse, but she seems to accept this. 'Right.'

'I wondered if there was any news about whether she's being induced?'

'Hang on a tick . . .' The phone clunks as she puts it down. After a couple of minutes she comes back. 'Mrs Norris has gone to theatre. The doctor thought that would be better than her having to go through labour like the last time.'

'No! Do you mean the baby's . . . ?' I can't say it.

'Look, I'm afraid I can't tell you any more at the moment. I'm sure her husband will call you when there's any news.'

'But, can't you tell me—'

'I'm sorry,' she says firmly. 'You're going to have to wait. There's really nothing you can do. Nothing any of us can do.'

CHAPTER TWENTY-NINE

I'm queuing at the catering van, for food I don't really want. But I know I need to 'keep my strength up' for the coming ordeal.

They dish up a dry veggie burger when I reach the counter, which isn't very Hollywood, but then this *is* Channel 5, and I'm hardly Gwyneth Paltrow. And I don't suppose I'd have a better appetite if they were serving sushi prepared on the bellies of virgins, or whatever it is that celebs demand.

It's a stunning day, temperatures as high as I remember in the summer of '76, when the tar melted under our Clarks sandals and we had standpipes because there wasn't enough water. My jeans are sticking to my legs, and despite the sun, the layer of sweat on my thighs makes me shiver. I'm in a bad way.

I look for somewhere quiet, and find one of the benches facing the back of the playing field, where we used to sit and watch the lads playing football. We'd cram on as many people as we could, which was fine for me because I was always in the middle, but the girls at the end would be perched on one buttock each, trying to keep their balance. And when one of the boys scored between the goalposts marked by two green jumpers, we'd all leap up, and they'd be toppled off like the losers in a game of musical chairs.

I force down the burger and after a while my stomach feels less empty, so I have to conclude that it wasn't just raw emotion about poor Boris making me feel quite so grim. It was also hunger. I really am a shallow bitch.

It feels decadent to have the whole bench to myself, and eventually I can't resist lying along it full-length, like a tramp. I close my eyes and imagine I'm not on my own. Boris should be next to me, of course, and Shrimp and Melody and Gary . . .

But why would he be here instead of on the pitch? I invent a convenient twisted ankle. Or maybe a groin strain. By the fifth year we were certainly busy enough below the waist for him to suffer one of those.

He's got his arm around me, and is playing with my hair, twisting it round, and watching it spring back. On my other side is Shrimp, taller and less skeletal than the last time I saw her. Not to mention one hundred per cent more alive. She's stretching out her ankle-socked legs to try to catch the sun, but it's like trying to brown a jacket potato in a microwave.

Boris is next to her, a healthy pink colour compared to Shrimp's yellow skin, plump meaty legs alongside Shrimp's skinny calves. But they're both grinning. And on the other side of Gary is Melody. No surprises there; that girl always gravitates to the men, never mind that they're dating – or even marrying – her best mate. Though with Shrimp and Boris here, is she really my best mate? It always was a friendship of convenience.

'It's been too long,' Shrimp says, and it makes me jump.

'Bloody right,' says Melody. She's the only one who looks her age, a fan of crow's feet around her eyes, and the puckered proof of twenty years' chain-smoking around her mouth. The rosebud lips are starved of colour, and the rest of her skin is grey on the cheeks, mottled with pink thread veins around the chin and nose.

She budges herself a bit closer to Gary, even though there's plenty of room. But he's still transfixed by my hair, and doesn't seem to notice she's there.

Boris isn't pregnant any more. 'So what are you up to these days, Melody?'

Melody curls her lip. 'Shelf-stacking.' She sounds defensive and defiant.

Ye-es!!!!

'It's not easy affording three kids on my own, and the child support don't seem to get very far with chasing their dads.' She has this sour look about her that I don't remember from the old days.

Boris leans across to pat her on the hand. 'Still, they must bring you so much pleasure. What about you, Shrimp? Any kids yet?'

Shrimp shakes her head. 'No, don't forget we always had a houseful at home. I'm a traveller. Been all over. Grape-picking in South Africa, bar work in Sydney, conservation in the Amazon jungle. I don't get back very often. You're lucky to get me here. Bet none of you ever thought I'd end up a free spirit!'

'It's exactly what I hoped you'd end up being,' I tell her, sitting up and putting my arm around her skinny shoulders.

I suppose my kids will do the same, backpack their way into adulthood. I'm jealous. But well done to Shrimp for escaping the brat-race.

'And Gary's a copper in London,' Boris tells the others, who start laughing.

'I know,' he says, joining in. 'I suppose I've got Trace to thank – or to blame, really. I could have ended up patrolling this estate for the rest of my life, if it hadn't been for what happened . . .'

He tails off, but he's still smiling at me.

'It's funny how things turn out,' he says, and kisses me on the cheek. I want to turn my head so our lips meet, but it seems wrong to force things.

242

'Feels odd being back,' Boris says. 'On our own, I mean. It's too quiet.'

Melody says, 'I see hundreds of the little buggers every day. I only live over there,' and she points to the other side of the field, where the old estate houses are packed together like beach huts. 'I remember what it's like to be fifteen, which none of you seem to. It wasn't that great. What's happened to you, Gary? Don't you remember what she did?'

Gary looks at me, and I known damn well he remembers, but he's been trying really hard to keep things light-hearted. She's a bitch.

'Fuck off, Melody. You're in no position to slag me off anyway. Not after the way you behaved on my wedding day, you jealous cow. Dave might be a bit of a lad, but he was marrying me, not you and you just couldn't hack that.'

Boris turns on her. 'Melody, what did you do?'

Melody shrugs. 'Tried to warn her what she'd let herself in for, that's all. She threatened to have me thrown out.'

'You were lucky I didn't rip your head off. And everyone understood why I did it. No one believed you.' *No one except my mother.*

Shrimp holds up her tiny hands. 'This isn't what we're here for, is it, girls? It's water under the bridge.'

She's right, and I'm surprised at how easy it is to let the resentment go, especially as Melody's life is obviously so much grimmer than mine. No wonder she had to resort to making up stuff. I brush the past aside with a flick of my hair.

We sit peering at the estate that we've all escaped. Well, all but Melody. Along from the older houses is a cluster of better homes, more *Brookside* than prefab, with proper cars parked in driveways, instead of the old wrecks everyone had our way, the ones made mainly of fibreglass filler. Maybe even Crawley Park is pulling itself out of the gutter.

I catch sight of another figure out of the corner of my eye, and turn my head slowly. I already know who it is from his height, and the way he's stooping to try to conceal his size.

He's aged, too, but less than Melody. Seventeen years is less cruel when you're going from thirty to forty-seven, than from sixteen to thirty-three . . .

'Tracey,' he says. And when I look around me, I realise that the others have gone, disappeared into thin air. And I'm on my own with Mr Carmichael. Not, of course, for the first time.

Afterwards, when it came out, people who didn't know me thought it must have been Bob who'd done all the running. The sophisticated teacher seducing the vulnerable schoolgirl. But that's so far from the truth.

I'd defy most blokes to resist the campaign I mounted for Mr Carmichael. Not because I'm gorgeous – sure, I was pretty but aren't teachers trained to resist pretty sixteen-year-olds? – but because I was determined.

It had started as a joke – a competition between Melody and me to see which of us could make a teacher blush. We each chose our prey, and set about being as provocative and flirty as we could. My victim was one of the PE teachers, but Melody chose Bob, and he stayed immune, however much she tossed her hair and thrust forward her chest and crossed her legs. But by Day Two, I found myself feeling jealous. It was completely out of the blue. First of all I was angry I hadn't chosen him, and then I started to feel protective towards him; I wanted to tell him that Melody was only playing games.

But he resisted all her ploys, and that tipped the balance for me. I *had* to have his attention, to prove I was better than Melody. There are plenty of good excuses to spend time alone with your teacher when you're in your final year – especially if you've never been academic, but suddenly experience a change of heart about learning. Teachers love that – the idea that they're inspiring you, making a difference.

But I wasn't really as cynical as I sound. I think I'd always seen something in Bob that was missing from my life. He was popular: Kids respected him because he respected them. And while I'd always fancied Gary in a straightforward physical way, with Bob it was the first time I'd found a man's mind as attractive as his body. Probably the last time, too, thinking about it.

I set the pace. I hung around after school to talk about how unhappy I was at home, how I felt I'd wasted my education, how I felt frustrated by my friends and their lack of aspiration. And if in the beginning some of that was exaggerated to appeal to him, the basic emotions were genuine enough. I did feel lost; I did hate living with my mother; I did feel that spending my time with Melody was a frightening premonition of where my life was headed; and I did worry about what would happen once I was out there in the Real World where, even then, I sensed my pole position on the Crawley Park circuit would count for nothing.

I first kissed him on the Monday, the night after my mum threatened to throw me out because she found the Pill in my bedside drawer.

It was after school, we were sitting close together, going through my options: would the social help me get somewhere of my own? Could I sign on the dole before I left school?

I knew it was just another one of Mum's threats, and it would blow over once I'd been humble enough, but Bob didn't, and he was so concerned that it felt very natural to lean forward, to do what I'd wanted to do all along. He started to respond, and then pulled away. He actually looked quite hurt. Until then, perhaps he hadn't realised that I wanted more than advice.

He tried to ignore me after that, and I let it happen. But after about a week, I hovered around at the end of class.

'Can I talk to you, sir?'

'Not here,' he said. 'Daisy's, at five?'

And Daisy's at five it was, for four nights, one after the other, right at the back where no one could see us, but with my history essay book open on the table, just in case. He drank black coffee. I had Coke floats. I know he struggled with his conscience. But I was sixteen. I was legal. And very, very determined.

He never really stood a chance.

CHAPTER THIRTY

'Are you really here?'

He looks at me, pinches himself. 'Ow. Well, that hurt. So, I suppose I must be.'

Oh, that voice.

For a second, I consider explaining that I'd been daydreaming about the old gang, that it had seemed so real, but I decide that will only make me sound crazier.

'I didn't invite you, you know.'

He doesn't look surprised. 'No? I'm disappointed. May I join you?' he says, pointing at the bench. I don't reply, and he sits down where Melody was. There's a gap between us big enough to seat Boris.

'I wonder who did invite me. Dick Phipps has been in touch about it, he wanted me to talk you out of it. And then I had a visit from Suzanne Sharp—'

'God, really? I saw her too, last week. The TV company made me interview her about the psychology of school reunions. It must be her. What's she up to?'

'An attempt to cause trouble, perhaps? Which is partly why I've come now instead of later. Though I can't really say why I've come at all.'

I hear some of the words he's choosing, as he always does, with precision. But I'm mainly listening to the sounds he's making, the voice that was always like crème brûlée in a world of Angel Delight. Dense and creamy compared to the thin, common way everyone else spoke, including me.

'Have you come to see me?' It sounds vain, but why else would it be?

He raises his eyebrows. 'Yes. But why now? It wouldn't have been that difficult to find you, Tracey.'

Did I mention that nothing was ever straightforward for Bob? That no emotion or reaction or sneeze or cough, and certainly no orgasm, could escape his analysis. I'm surprised he hasn't outgrown it, like kids who finally learn to stop asking 'why' because, more often than not, there's no answer.

He looks me up and down, slowly and carefully, as though he's taking in a painting. He never hurried anything – including making love. Of course, that couldn't have been more of a contrast to Gary and my mates; we tore around like we were trying to beat some kind of imminent life deadline.

'I'm glad I've come, though. It's wonderful to see you.' He doesn't try to touch me. Maybe he's lost interest in sex; it happens when men hit middle age, doesn't it? But something about him, his confidence, his bearing, makes me pretty sure that's not happened to him.

'It's a shock . . .' I start, not knowing where I'm going. What's the etiquette for conversation with a man who lost his job because of your relationship?

He puts his finger to his lips. 'Don't say anything, Tracey. I didn't want to upset you. I suppose it was fairly selfish, to turn up and expect a warm welcome.'

'I'd have thought I'd have been the last person you'd want to see again.'

'What happened was my fault, Tracey. You were my pupil, it's against the rules and it's morally wrong.' He speaks evenly, no hint of anger. I can't imagine how many hours he must have devoted to thinking about our affair. 'Though I don't regret it. Do you?'

His eyes are a surprisingly bright blue, like Paul Newman's. When I look into them, I remember the moment I stopped seeing him as a teacher, and started weighing him up as a potential lover. Back when I had some power over men.

'No, I don't. Though I think it's a bit insulting to take all the blame. I had a part in where we ended up, didn't I?'

I realise I want to kiss him. It's a shock. What's worse is that I'm convinced he knows it. He always could see through me. While poor Gary never knew what I was plotting, Bob could scan me like an X-ray machine, all the way through to my soul. He was pretty much the only person who thought I *had* a soul. With him, I felt naked, and I loved it.

'All the same, it was my responsibility, Tracey.'

There were six other Traceys in my year; it was a common name, in every way. There are millions of us, born somewhere between the moon landings and Donny Osmond's first album. But Bob spoke it as though my name might have inspired Shakespeare to write one of his finer sonnets. And hearing him say it again now is hypnotic.

I try to shake myself out of it. I'm over-tired; just a minute ago I was daydreaming about my dead best friend.

'So, are you married now, Bob?'

He shakes his head, neither sad nor happy. 'No. I was with someone until last year, but she wanted children. I'm sure you can imagine that I wouldn't take a decision like that lightly. And you, Tracey?' He nods at the wedding ring. 'How long have you been married?'

'Nine years.' I try to say this as neutrally as possible, but I still hear sourness creeping into my voice. 'I didn't think so hard about kids. I've got a daughter who will be seven in August. And a son who'll be two in September.'

'Perfect. One of each. I can imagine you with a son. And your husband?'

What about him? Is he worthy? Definitely not. Is he what you wanted? Ditto. Would you rather it was someone else, like the person sitting next to you?

'Dave. He's a builder. Works away a lot.'

There are conversations going on between us that can't be heard, like dog whistles that are beyond the range of human ears.

'And do you work?'

'Part-time, two half-days, in a stationery supplier's shop. Gets me out of the house, but it's not a career. But I was never really cut out for one of those.'

'I never understood how someone so attractive and confident could have such low expectations, Tracey. I wish that at least I could have told you that there was more out there for you.' Now he does look sad.

'If it's any consolation, I think I might finally be growing up. Even though it's taken me seventeen years . . .'

'I think the benefits of growing up have been exaggerated over the years. And you've got kids. That makes you more of a grown-up than me, Tracey.'

'Yup, I'm a Stepford wife. Bet you're glad we never stayed the course . . .'

For the first time, he reaches across to me, and touches me gently on the cheek. When he takes his fingers away, my face feels hot. 'You have no idea.'

But he hasn't denied feeling relieved. Then again he said he didn't regret the relationship. But maybe he's being kind.

I have to stop this pointless agonising. 'So, what do you do, Bob? I worried about it. About how what we did would affect your career.'

He looks at me suspiciously, but then starts to chuckle and

then I find myself joining in. I don't have the faintest idea what it is we're both laughing about, but it's unstoppable, Every time I look at his face I start again.

When we finally get our breath back, we sit in silence for a while, and no matter how hard I try to banish the image from my mind, the flushed camaraderie reminds me how we both used to look after sex. And when I finally trust myself to look him in the eye again, I have this strong feeling that he is thinking the same thing.

'So what's the joke?' I ask him eventually.

'Oh, God, Tracey. It's going to sound so feeble now. The joke is that if it wasn't for you, I'd probably still be here, waiting for Dick Phipps to retire and give me the chance to apply for head of humanities. But I'm actually better off than I could ever have imagined: I work shorter hours, and I don't have to go anywhere near a classroom.'

Another person whose life I've changed for the better. How weird is that? Suzanne, Gary and now Bob. I seem to have done for people's careers what Carol Smillie did for their bathrooms. While my life remains resolutely avocado.

'So what is it you do, exactly?'

'I work for the government. I have an office near Westminster, and I advise them on how to get people talking to each other, how to get schools working the way they want them to. I state the obvious, for a fat salary.'

How come everyone else has made it, and I'm sitting here with a grotty husband, two un-designer children, and a life that struggles even to reach the pinnacles of being mundane?

'Good for you,' I say. I don't really mean it.

'None of it's that satisfying. And I hate the publicity – I used to worry about them finding out. About us, you know . . .'

'I'm surprised you risked coming.'

'Tracey,' he says, staring very deliberately into my eyes. 'I've wanted to come and find you since I left. I really have. And if they find out now, then I wouldn't be ashamed. But I don't want you dragged through the mud, which is why I'm leaving now, before anyone makes the connection.'

Do I believe him? I suppose the fact he came must prove I meant *something* to him; unless he's just another middle-aged man revisiting old conquests.

'Yes, probably best for you to get back to the metropolis. Before the tedium starts rubbing off on you.' He looks hurt, so I say, 'Joke!' Even though it's not.

He gets up from the bench, and I want to stop him. For good. But before I can, he turns.

'Tracey, it's not too late. I was only slightly younger than you when I escaped. I mean, I didn't want to at the time. But without you, there was nothing left for me.' He stops, embarrassed. 'Anyway, that's the past. But you always had more balls than me, didn't you?' He punches me on the arm, trying to be light-hearted.

'Yeah, I guess. See you around,' I say, knowing I won't.

He hesitates, then pulls out his wallet. 'This seems very formal, but if you want to get in touch, if I can give you any help, whatever, anything, here's my card.' It's classy parchment paper, embossed with 'Robert Carmichael, Senior Educational Consultant'. He scribbles a mobile number on the back.

'I mean it,' he says and leans across to kiss me on the cheek, and I wonder if this is any more real than when Gary did this in my imagination a few minutes ago . . . but this time I do what I wanted to do then, and turn my head slightly so his lips brush against mine. It's as awkward and as thrilling as it was in 1984, and it's over as quickly.

'Whoops,' I say, as if it were an accident.

He looks at me, then leans forward again, planting a tiny kiss on my nose, as an indulgent grandfather might to his first granddaughter.

'You've got my number,' Bob says, then walks steadily back towards the school.

I follow him, at a distance of a few paces. We cross the playground, where people are striding along purposefully with their bloody clipboards. Alec is shouting at a girl holding a pile of T-shirts. As we head towards the car park, I spot Andrew the reporter standing next to a BMW, talking into a mobile. Next to it is an old MG, and I know instantly it must belong to Bob – he was always one for classic cars.

I watch Bob as he goes. He has to squeeze right past Andrew to open the door, interrupting the reporter's phone call. But instead of moving out of the way, Andrew stares at him.

He keeps watching as Bob reverses out of the parking space and drives through the school gates. And the look on Andrew's face – as if he's just worked out something that's been puzzling him for a while – makes me wonder if he's *really* only here to write a feature about nostalgia.

CHAPTER THIRTY-ONE

Alec is having a temper tantrum because they've cocked up with the T-shirts he'd ordered.

He'd wanted a hundred with 'TRACEY SAYS REUNITE' across the front and back, like the Katherine Hamnett ones from the eighties. But instead, they read 'TRACEY SAYS RELAX', which seems better to me, but he's a control freak, so nearly right is not nearly good enough.

'Someone ought to take his Diet Coke away,' I tell Jenny.

She laughs. 'It's not the diet kind of coke that's the problem. Ignore him.'

There's plenty around to distract us. The crew for Madness are running sound checks, and there's a nice rhythm in the way they work that's soothing to watch. They get things done without talking to each other.

It's time to get changed into my dress, and when I take off my jeans, Bob's card is in the pocket. I stare at it, put it into my handbag for safe-keeping. I can't believe how churned up I feel, his words ricocheting round my head: 'It's not too late.'

I know that's rubbish. I mean, it is too late for me. What would I do if I wanted to escape: leave the kids in Dave's incapable hands, while I follow Dick Whittington's path to London? Live in a penthouse apartment with Bob, go to restaurants that cost more for lunch than I spend on a month's supermarket shopping, and hang around at cocktail parties discussing the single currency and illegal immigration with Cherie Blair?

But the Mortimer streak has never been strong on logic. And the old Tracey wants to know why. Why can't I be living a better life? Why have the girls' magazines promising fun and glamour been replaced by the women's glossies promising can't-fail sponge recipes and the elimination of germs? Why Suzanne, why Gary, why Bob and why *not* me?

But then there's Boris. Life hasn't been fair to her, even though she deserves it more than me. Right now, a surgeon's probably cutting her open, taking away what she wants most of all. Sure, she's got the money and the house and she's got the husband, who I'm pretty sure from one meeting is too dull – and too loyal – to shag around the way Dave does. But it's nothing for her, without a little Boris or Brian to live out her dreams for her.

And when it comes to fairness, what about poor Shrimp?

So instead of envying Gary and Suzanne, maybe the question I should be asking is why Shrimp, why Boris, why *not* me?

M4 Westbound, Berkshire

'Bet you were a right goody-two-shoes at school,' said Gabby.

'Just shows how little you know me,' Gary said, hitting the indicator and moving into the fast lane.

'Don't tell me, you were actually a rebel without a cause, terrifying the residents of Bracewell with your gang warfare? Can't see it somehow.'

'Let's just say I haven't always been on the right side of the law.'

'You're not saying you once stole a pencil sharpener from the newsagent, are you? Or – hang on – maybe you wrote rude remarks about one of the teachers in the boys' toilets.'

'You're just so funny, aren't you?'

'Go on, Gary, tell me. I like the idea of you being a wild child,' she said, moving her hand across to his knee and up his thigh. 'It's so sexy . . .'

'You keep your hands to yourself, madam. There's nothing sexy about a conviction for dangerous driving.'

'You see, you're too bloody sensible. I can't believe you've ever done anything illegal.'

'Not even . . . I dunno. Twocking?'

'Hot-wiring a car? I don't think so. You can't even wire a plug.' She laughed, but Gary didn't. He kept his eyes straight ahead. 'Gary? You are joking, right?'

'And what if I'm not? Does that make me so much cooler all of a sudden?'

'Well, if you want an honest answer, then yes. It makes you seem more . . . rounded, as a person.'

'Cheers. So by your logic, if I'd been done for GBH I would have been chat show material? Grow up, Gabby.'

'Don't have a sense of humour failure. It's just with you being in the Met, I assumed you'd been part of the establishment all your life.'

Gary groaned but said nothing.

'Come on, Gary. I'm not taking the piss. Plus, you know, as a social worker it'd be cool for me to have an ex-con as a boyfriend. Go down well with the homies, eh?'

He steered the car carefully back into the middle lane. 'I wasn't convicted, actually. Sorry if that disappoints you.'

'You're going to have to tell me the details now, mate.'

'What's it worth?'

Gabby moved her hand back up his leg. 'Are we talking sexual favours?'

'Might be.'

'I'll give you a blow job at the hotel . . .'

Gary sighed. 'OK, you win.'

'You drive such a hard bargain, Gary. Go on, then, spill.'

'I thought we were waiting till the hotel.'

It was Gabby's turn to groan.

'Sorry. OK. I took a car, I drove it around the estate, pretty slowly, got caught, got taken in for questioning, got a few thumps from my dad, disappointed looks from my mum, and then a few days worrying about what was going to happen. And then, I got cautioned.'

'Is that it?'

'Sorry, but yeah. That's it.'

'How old were you?'

'Sixteen. Which was also handy, because the Met were willing to overlook a little youthful misdemeanour.'

'Did the owner see it like that?'

'Actually he was pretty determined the police shouldn't press charges.'

'You knew him, then?'

For the first time, Gary looked embarrassed. 'Yeah, as it happens. The car was my form teacher's.'

Bracewell Comprehensive School, Berkshire, 1984

Melody Tickell never could keep a secret, and when her so-called best mate Tracey refused to give her the lowdown on the night of passion at Mr Carmichael's house, it was only a matter of time before she got her own back.

But how? If there was one thing Melody liked more than sex,

it was attention, and the best place to get maximum attention was surely morning assembly. So she waited until Bob, as head of year, was explaining the arrangements for the O-level revision sessions, before whispering in Gary's ear, 'You wanna know why Tracey doesn't fancy you no more?'

Gary ignored her. He could be so superior, sometimes, which pissed her off. She tried again. 'I said, don't you wanna know why Tracey's gone off you?'

Gary looked confused. 'Eh? Gone off me? What are you on about?'

Melody was losing patience. 'It's because . . .' she started, and this time her voice was loud enough for everyone in the front two rows to hear, 'she's fucking HIM.' And she pointed towards the stage.

In the few seconds that followed, big things changed. Tracey realised her best friend was definitely not to be trusted. Bob realised his teaching career was over. And Gary realised that nice guys came last.

No more Mr Nice Guy.

He leapt up on to the stage, and the shame on his teacher's face told him all he needed to know. Gary broke his nose with a single punch. It took at least ten seconds for the shocked silence to end, and the hysteria to kick off. Even the head teacher came out to find out what was happening and stood, dumbstruck, as a senior member of the history department tried to stem the flow of blood from his nose. Gary ran from the school hall, found the red Triumph Herald in the car park, and finally put into practice the hot-wiring skills his older brother had been trying to pass down for the last three years.

He did three circuits of the estate, and then, in front of most of the fifth year, he drove Mr Carmichael's Triumph slowly, but surely, into the school gates.

18 Marigold Mews, Bracewell, Berkshire

Suzanne watched from behind the net curtain as Andrew walked up the path to her mother's front door. Bees buzzed around the red and white geraniums stuffed into a dozen hanging baskets. When he rang the doorbell, it played 'Home, Sweet Home'.

'Andrew. You're late. I thought you'd be champing at the bit to find out what this is all about.' She showed him into the front room, which was obviously only ever used for visitors. It was as quiet as a library and smelled of Pledge furniture polish.

'I've been doing some digging of my own. It's Bob Carmichael, isn't it? Your classmate was shagging him.'

It was almost a relief that he'd guessed, rather than Suzanne having to spell it out. It felt less tacky somehow. She nodded. 'You're not as stupid as you look.'

'He was there, you know.'

She looked surprised. 'Bob? What, this afternoon?'

'Why, had you planned for him to turn up later and be on camera, too? You're a bit of a snide bitch on the side, aren't you?'

'No, I didn't—'

'Oh, don't worry, I mean it as a term of endearment. This is a good story, like you promised. And I'll deliver my side of the bargain. No one will make the connection with you.' He sat down in the carver chair at the head of the table. 'And you're sure no one else is on to this?'

Suzanne sat next to him, her chair creaking. 'How could they know? It was all hushed up at school, lots of rumours but nothing concrete. Only a few of us knew, for sure, because we talked to the police.'

'It gets better.'

She glared at him. 'Don't get too excited. There was nothing against him, she wasn't under-age when it started, or if she was, they couldn't prove it. And she was hardly a virgin by the time he got in there.'

'Bob Carmichael, though, eh? We've never managed to get anything on him before this.'

'Yes, well. Congratulations on your powers of deduction. You won't be wanting tea, will you? Better get back to London so you can write your piece?'

'Anyone would think you're trying to get rid of me.'

'We had our deal, and I don't really want you here, Andrew.'

He relaxed back into the seat. 'My, my, we're not very friendly now, are we? What did she do to you, Suzanne? Or was it him? What made you want revenge so badly? Because you're right-on, aren't you? You've staked out the moral high ground, with your charity, but this isn't what I'd expected.'

'I'm not interested in your clever-dick analysis, Andrew. You've got your story. Now I'd like you to leave.'

He raised his arms behind his back, yawned, then stretched out like a cat. 'Yeah, sure. You've got your reasons. People always do, or I wouldn't be in business, would I?'

Suzanne stood up, folded her arms in front of her chest, then immediately unfolded them when she saw in the mantel mirror how much she looked like her mother. Andrew got up and walked past her, out of the front door, his feet crunching ominously in the gravel.

'See you later,' he said, grinning.

'What do you mean?'

'I need to get both sides of the story. One of the first things they taught me at journalism college. And, as I know exactly where Tracey is going to be later on, it would be silly to waste the opportunity to strike while the iron's hot.'

'But you don't have to do it tonight. I mean, you promised—'

'To keep you out of it? I will. But I've got to check it all out, and you shouldn't be surprised if it gets messy. I mean, that's what you wanted, surely?'

He waved at her, then headed back to his BMW, leaving Suzanne standing in the doorway, wondering what she'd started.

CHAPTER THIRTY-TWO

'You know the routine, Trace,' says Cliff, sticking his hand
down my bra without ceremony. 'Sad, isn't it? This might be
the last time we're ever this close.'

'Oh, shame,' I say. I don't think I'm going to miss having
Cliff groping around in my cleavage.

'This radio mike's got a switch,' he says, clipping the microphone just under the neck of my leather dress. 'If you remember
to flick it off, we won't have to listen to you going for a pee.'

Attaching the transmitter to my expensive designer outfit is
more difficult, so Cliff sticks it to the small of my back using
that extra thick black masking tape they carry round for these
occasions. And, presumably, for impromptu bondage sessions.
Cliff looks like the type. Though Jamie definitely wouldn't need
to tie me up . . .

My bloody hormones. Is this a last surge before the meno-
pause or something?

Alec comes into the dressing room: the same dressing room
where I fought thirty other kids for space by the mirror to apply
my Egyptian kohl when I played Joseph's trophy wife.

'Can't you do better than that?' he says, pointing at the
transmitter. It does makes my back look slightly deformed, but
there's nowhere else for it to go.

'Where else are we meant to put it?' Jamie says. 'No,

seriously, Alec, I bow to your superior brain and salary. Tell me where to stick it, and I will.'

Jenny and I wait for Alec to reply. He opens and shuts his mouth like a fish, but nothing comes out. For once, he's been shown up for what he is. Someone who likes dishing it out, but can't take it himself.

Eventually, Alec points at the Adam Ant jacket hanging on a chair. 'Just make sure she wears that most of the time,' he says to Jenny before he struts out. He doesn't even bother to talk to me any more.

'Who's she, the cat's mother?' I say. No one replies.

This is the worst time when you're throwing a party: the wait to see if anyone's turning up. This time, of course, it's even more of a nightmare, because I've had no control of the guest list or the music or the venue. And yet I'm supposed to be part of the entertainment. That's why they chose me to do the bloody show. But I don't feel in any mood to put on a song and dance act.

'I bet you're nervous,' Jenny says.

'Yes,' I say softly. 'I suppose I am.'

'Mummy!'

I turn round and see my family. Funny, I hardly ever think of them that way, we seem so disjointed, but right now that little gathering makes me feel grounded. Kelly's wearing one of the 'Tracey Says Relax' T-shirts, even though it's so big that it trails round her ankles. 'You look lovely, Mummy.'

Brenda's given me another going-over with the foundation, thick enough to grace Barbara Cartland, and I do look like a nicer, slightly artificial version of myself, as though I were an actress taking the role of Tracey Mortimer. I think that's the way I have to look at it tonight: I'm going on stage, playing a part, in return for the dress and the party and all the other things I thought I wanted so much.

Dave's wearing a Mod-style suit with a skinny tie, and he's

eyeing me up, like he must eye up the Dublin girls after a night on the beer. He's still a catch, of sorts. Rich enough to buy all the drinks, good-looking enough to make arm-candy, and confident enough to suggest that sex would be better than the average fumble. His technique wouldn't disappoint, either, I'll grant him that.

'Scrub up well, you do, Tracey,' he says, as though this is a compliment.

Only Callum is holding back. 'Come here, Cal,' I say, and he recoils as though I've hit him. 'It's Mummy, come on, love, nothing to be scared of,' and I crouch down, reaching out my hand. He turns his face away, but recognises my leg and races forward to grab it. I hope he's not going to turn into a shy kid. Don't know how I'd cope with two like Kelly.

'It looks amazing out there,' Dave says. 'Like a proper gig. Racks of big lights and everything.' I think he's trying to be nice. But he's as much of a kid as Callum, and I can't help but think of Bob. A proper man.

'Yeah. I'm sure they'll let you bang on the drums, too, if you ask them nicely.' I smile.

'People should start arriving soon,' Annabel says.

In under half an hour, in fact. It's 6.34 p.m. Who are the people she's talking about? I've got no idea who's coming, except Andrew the journalist. If only Boris was here, I could ask her for some clues.

If only Boris was here.

'Time to get out there,' Jenny says. 'The longer you sit worrying, the worse it's going to get. The only way to deal with nerves is to face them head-on.'

I know she's right. So, with Jamie behind us, I lead my brood out into the arena, like a Bracewell version of the Von Trapp Family Singers . . .

I've been in the dressing room for a good hour, and even in that time the transformation in the hall is enough to make me blink. They've turned the space into a *real* disco. Dave was right about the lights – they've taken the lamps that were already there for school productions and added dozens more, mounted on tall scaffolding towers. There are pools of coloured light falling on the stage, on to shifting areas of the floor, and then a whole set of screens at the opposite end of the hall which are lit from within.

As we step in the centre of the empty parquet dance floor, the speakers buzz, as though we've triggered an invisible switch, and I recognise the first notes of the first song . . . I look at Dave and realise he does, too.

Kelly clamps her hands to her ears. 'Mummy, it's too loud, it's too loud.'

'Don't be daft, Kelly,' Dave shouts over the top of the opening rhythms, and she looks at him, shocked at the uncharacteristic knock-back. 'So, Tracey, wanna dance?'

And to the astonishment of our children, who I hate to admit have probably never seen us embrace, we start circling round each other to the sound of Cyndi Lauper.

Girls just wanna have fun . . .

Dave grabs me by the waist and we dance and something about the way the music is pounding from the speakers fills my head and my body and I can't help myself . . .

Just wanna . . .

I head back towards the old days and the old feelings. The sensations from the beat and the light and even, I'm surprised to notice, from my husband's fingers pressing against my flesh through the leather dress, are making it real . . .

The DJ mixes from Cyndi into 'Feels like Heaven'. Dave and I pull apart, both of us flushed and embarrassed. We're grown-ups – we've created the two kids who're watching us suspiciously from the edge of the hall – and yet a couple of minutes of teenage fondling have deprived us of the power of speech.

'Look, Mummy,' Kelly calls above the music, pointing towards the screens at the end of the hall.

The blank white spaces have been replaced by projected images, which keep changing, and it takes me a moment to realise that it's pictures of us: of me, and Gary, and Boris, and the others. When I go and stand next to the screen, the photos are bigger than life-size, and slightly fuzzy. Just like the memories.

'That's your mummy,' Dave says, lifting Callum up so he can touch my foot-long nose. 'Isn't she pretty?'

I'm drawn towards the pictures, looking for something in my teenage face. What made me so certain that life was mine for the taking? It wasn't innocence. I'd sussed out how the world worked well before I arrived at Crawley Park. And it wasn't confidence, because I've still some of that left . . .

Maybe Tracey Mortimer just felt safe in the knowledge that whatever happened she could take control, exactly as she had taken control of class 1G.

There are pictures there I don't recognise – Boris must have asked the guests for spares.

There's Shrimp and me on the ferry to Calais, flaunting our daring 'flick combs' that we thought were as cool as banned flick knives – though of course when you pressed the switch, it revealed you were in possession of nothing more than a styling device.

Oh, and there are half a dozen girls, me and Melody in the centre, doing the can-can – we must be in the third year then, judging from the haircuts.

And then one of me and Gary on the bench at the back of the playing field – the same bench where I sat a few hours ago – seconds away from a snog . . .

'I hope he's not coming, whoever he is,' Dave says. 'Might have to deck him for getting there first.'

All this Memory Lane stuff is obviously turning me into a big softy, because I don't feel angry with him. I feel sorry for him.

'I don't think there's any danger of him coming, Dave. So you'll have no reason to defend my honour!'

Jenny appears from the car park. 'Hope you like what we've done. The one of you and Gary is priceless.'

'I wasn't bad, was I?'

She shakes her head. 'Don't go all maudlin on us already; you're not bad now, either. Have you seen the way the sound guys are ogling you in that dress? It's nothing to do with age, Tracey, you've either got it or you ain't – and you've definitely got it.'

Did I say before that I'm starting to remember why I liked Jenny?

'Anyway, I didn't come in here *just* to boost your ego. Your first guests are arriving.'

It's real, now, no more kidding myself that this is just a family party on a slightly bigger scale. I follow her out into the car park, and I'm aware of Jamie and Cliff right behind me, ready to film. The sunlight is a shock, and it takes my eyes a while to adjust to the row of people – five, no, four, standing just outside the doors.

Jenny sees this, and buys me some time. 'Now then, not all of this lot were actually in your year, so you're excused if you don't remember all of them.'

The man furthest away from me immediately makes me uneasy. He's more familiar than the others, but I can't work out why. Just occasionally, you see someone you recognise, and even though you can't remember who they are, you feel an overwhelming emotion associated with them – whether it's laughter or misery or humiliation.

With him, I feel guilt.

'OK, you guys, looks like you're going to have to give Tracey a clue.'

The first one steps forward. A plump guy, dressed for the occasion in a frilly New Romantic shirt (at least I hope that's why he's wearing it), with a hint of a receding hairline. 'Tracey – it's Bodger – from your maths set? Remember?'

Oh yes, Bodger Lewis, the guy who never got anything right. He hasn't changed that much. Maths was my worst subject, and so it was only in that set that I ever came into contact with the real low-life of Crawley Park. The people destined for the production line at the custard cream factory.

'And this is my missus, Angela,' he says, proudly dragging forward a girl with long mousy hair. 'You wouldn't have known her, she was still at primary when we left. Bit of a looker, eh?'

'Hi,' I say. They look well-suited, anyway: neither has any obvious signs of a personality.

The next girl in line doesn't look familiar, either. 'Tracey, well done for getting this going – it's brilliant. Maybe we should do a quick song from *Joseph* while we're at it, do you think?' She seems slightly irritated that I don't rush forward to hug her, but I've just realised who the last guy is, and the blood is rushing to my head. 'I'm Kathy, I was a sheaf of corn, along with Melody. Great laugh, eh? I gave them some photos to use as well, of the performance.'

'Lovely,' I say. The last bloke waits his turn. I take in his height and his thin legs in the drainpipe trousers and the cliff edges that form his cheekbones.

'And I'm—'

'I know who you are,' I say quietly. 'You're Ricky. You're Shrimp's brother.'

CHAPTER THIRTY-THREE

Classroom 2J, Humanities Block, Bracewell Comp (1980)

I hate Shrimp. I hate her bike. I hate the way she reckons she's better than me now she's got it, when everyone knows she's poorer and she lives in a smelly house and she needs me to make anyone even want to talk to her or be her friend. But she's acting like *I'm* the sad one.

It's only because she's got all those brothers and sisters; Mum says Shrimp's mum and dad breed like rabbits, and someone should make him have an operation to stop them having any more. Mum never wanted another baby after me, she says. Sometimes I think that's a good thing, perhaps it's because she thinks I'm the best; how could she get a nicer daughter than me? And sometimes I wonder if I'm horrible and that's why she didn't want any more. Actually, she says that herself sometimes when she gets angry.

Not that she could have any more anyway, because Dad left her when I was a few months old. She says sometimes that that's my fault, too, though she always apologises, and tells me it's definitely not my fault he died.

'Tracey Mortimer, are you with us, or are you with the Woolwich?' That wanker Dick Phipps thinks he's so funny, but he doesn't know that we all call him Larry Grayson because he lives at home with his mother, so we all know he's *that way inclined*, as my mum would say.

'Yes, sir.'

'Well, that's excellent, Miss Mortimer. So perhaps you'd like to take us through the differences between sedimentary and igneous rock?'

Can't see the point of geography. Maps are useful, but who cares about rocks? Most of school is pointless, except home ec. Last week we made a mixed grill, and some of the boys didn't even know how to do *that*, and their sausages were so burned that they looked like turds. You couldn't have eaten them, so I nicked some from Suzanne Sharp for Gary and Briggsy to eat, and she knew it was me but she didn't dare tell.

'Not sure, sir.'

'Would anyone care to enlighten Miss Mortimer?'

Oh, and there she goes, Suzanne Sharp shoving her hand in the air. She's even more annoying this year because she's got a bra, nothing to put in it, though, it's a double A; we hid it in the changing rooms, under the showers, and she had to go without it all day because it was too wet to wear.

But my mum won't get me a bra. Cow. And I'll need one soon.

Don't suppose Shrimp will ever need one. Her mum's got no tits, and neither has her sister Debbie, who's fifteen.

Shrimp's sitting next to me and I want to give her that look we always give each other when Suzanne is talking in lessons: we raise our eyebrows, cross our eyes in a mad squint, flare our nostrils and curl up our lips. It's harder than it sounds.

But Shrimp and me aren't speaking, and that even rules out taking the piss out of Spazzy Suzanne.

It'll blow over, but she's being really stubborn this time. It started at morning break because I wanted to sit round the back of the playing field, where Gary was, but she said it was boring and I said she was boring and she said I was obsessed with lads and didn't care what she wanted and if I was that bothered, then maybe Gary should be my best mate, not her.

Or something like that.

And I said – I didn't really mean it – that he'd be a better best mate than her, because at least he's not a skinny cow, and too poor to be any fun.

I said it because I knew it would hurt her feelings. I get like that sometimes; I know exactly what's going to upset people the most, and I even quite like it when they react. But then afterwards I feel really, really bad. Not when I do it to Suzanne or the teachers – they know they're winding me up, and they could stop if they wanted – but with my friends and Mum, I feel mean.

It's said now, anyway, and she's obviously in a right mood because she lasted not even looking at me all through French; and then, dinner time, I had to hang about with Melody and the others instead so I didn't look like a saddo, and she just sat there very quietly on her own eating her chips and gravy (she always eats that, it must get so boring but it is very cheap) and then she went to the *library* till the bell rang.

And then there was registration and maths, and now it's double geography, then home time. Usually we walk out together to where the road splits, but I'm pretty sure she's going to keep up the bad mood until tomorrow, try to make me feel guilty.

Well, she can suit herself. She'll come running back tomorrow. We're best mates. She's just never going to find anyone else who makes her laugh like I do.

'Hello, Tracey,' Ricky says.

Still the spit of her, despite his shirt and tie. It's like coming face to face with what Shrimp might have been if she'd had the chance to grow up. After all, she never grew her hair, and Ricky's as slight as she ever was, with the same fair hair and slightly uneven features.

'Bodger, Kathy? Shall I show you where the cloakroom is?' Jenny comes to my rescue, yet again, and I wonder how much she knows. They follow her, and Ricky and I face each other, awkward, alone.

'Why have you come?' I ask eventually, though I already know. He wants to see me squirm, to go over it again, all the reasons why it's my fault. But he doesn't know that there's no need – that I remember every word he said the last time. At Shrimp's funeral.

He starts walking, and I walk alongside and then I remember the crew behind me. I turn to Jamie, look straight at him. 'Give me a bit of space, guys, please?'

To my surprise, Jamie nods, and holds back. Maybe he still feels bad about Gary and the Crown Affair.

Ricky and I walk until we reach the playground. I wonder if Shrimp would have been quite this tall. He's almost six feet, and if anyone ever deserved the label, 'lanky streak of piss', it's him. He's got a wedding ring on one spaghetti finger, and I can see the top of a tattoo above his collar. It looks like a name: his wife? His kids?

'Boris invited me.'

Boris. Images of surgeons and knives and blood and blue babies drift back into my head and I shake it, as though that'll send them away, like it does water from your ears when you've been swimming. All it does is remind me that last night's hangover still hasn't gone.

'She invited lots of people,' I say and nod back towards the car park, which is starting to fill up. 'It still doesn't explain why you've come.'

'Because Boris thought I . . . that there are things that oughta be said.'

'I think you said it all before.'

It had all been going fine, Shrimp's funeral. Well, as fine as it can be when it's the funeral of a twelve-year-old girl knocked off her bike as she cycled home from school. And when that girl was your best friend, who you thought would live for ever, just like you, and when you know that the last words you spoke to her were 'I don't want you as my best mate, anyway, you're ugly, skinny, and you've never got any money, anyway. So we can't have any fun because you're TOO POOR!'

It's bad enough carrying that around with you while you wait for the news, and hope that there's something the hospital can do, and then it sinks in that there's going to be no miracle recovery.

But then you go to her house before the funeral, and you see her, or rather, her body in the coffin, and despite your fears she looks more peaceful than she ever did when she was alive, because she was always fidgeting, Shrimp was, as though she knew she had only a limited amount of time.

And the funeral's grim, and there're loads of tears, but it's comforting somehow, all the ritual. Incense, altar boys, more crying. And then they take you back to their house for the wake, and it's wrong to be there without Shrimp, and the aunts and the cousins are talking to me about how lovely it is to have a best friend, and how brave of me to come, but time will heal, there'll be other best friends, though you'll never forget Louise . . . *Louise who? She was Shrimp.*

And then Ricky appears and starts pointing. 'What are you doing here? It's YOUR bloody fault, they said at school that you and her had another row that day, and she was always careful on her bike, and you should have seen her with her head caved in, she wasn't Lou any more, even before they switched her machine off and it's YOUR bloody fault and you should know that and bloody live with it for the whole of the rest of your life and even then it won't be long enough because it's YOUR bloody fault she's dead.'

'Tracey?'

Ricky is looking at me.

'You can't make me feel any worse than I did then. All those photos of me and Shrimp, they make me feel bad all over again. So if that's what you wanted to know—'

He puts his hands up to stop me. 'You're wrong, Tracey. I wanted to say sorry to you.'

'What?'

'It was nobody's bloody fault, Tracey.'

'You don't mean that. We both know that if I hadn't—'

'She always did used to go on about how no one could get a bloody word in edgeways with you, Tracey Mortimer.'

I look at him, trying to work out why he's smiling. 'Eh?'

'Tracey, we were kids. Kids say stuff they don't mean. Especially when they're upset.'

I nod. That's what got poor Shrimp killed – me saying things I didn't mean. What did they say in the war? *Careless talk costs lives.*

He smiles again. 'It's easier to blame someone. Especially when you're young.' Ricky seems to be struggling, but I bite my lip to stop myself butting in. 'I did think it was your fault, for . . . I don't know, maybe a couple of months. But like Dad kept telling me, over and over, it was a bloody accident.'

I stare at his lips, watching them form the words I suppose I've always wanted to hear, but unable to believe it's Ricky Shrimpton saying them.

'And he was right, Tracey. Lou died in an accident. Maybe she was in a mood because you'd had a row. But then again, she might have been daydreaming about what she was having for tea, or what Top Forty single to buy.'

'Don't Stand So Close To Me'. That's the single she was

274

going to buy with her birthday money from her grandparents. We'd been talking about it all week.

'You move on, Tracey. OK, I feel crap every time I remember that I haven't thought about her for a few days. Don't bring her back, though.'

'No,' is all I can say.

'When Boris came to see me, I was gobsmacked that you were still thinking it was your bloody fault. It's been twenty bloody years.'

And despite the make-up I can feel weighing down my skin, I start to cry, and Ricky leans in and hugs me so tight I can feel his ribs through his shirt. He even smells like Shrimp: milky and yeasty, like a house with a baby in it.

'I came for Lou's sake, Tracey, I came to tell you that it wasn't your bloody fault. And that she'd be well pissed off that you're still thinking it was. And that she'd say what I'm gonna say: live your life for her, as well as you.'

This crying business is starting to become a habit, but, for the first time, it makes me feel better.

CHAPTER THIRTY-FOUR

Ricky doesn't want to stick around. He's got to meet his wife down the pub and she went to Bracewell High School, our deadly rival, so she wouldn't be seen dead here, even now.

But I think that's an excuse. Really it's because staying here is too much of a reminder of what Shrimp should have been.

First Bob, now Ricky. I won't have any guests, the rate I keep sending them away.

As I head back towards the hall, I'm surprised that Jamie and Cliff are still there, facing me, but after what happened at the Crown, surely they wouldn't have been filming me at a distance while that was happening. Would they?

I walk right into Briggsy.

'Tracey Mortimer!' he says, as though he's surprised to see me. Dopey bastard, it is my reunion, after all.

'Gavin Briggs!' We perform a stage hug. 'I could say you haven't changed a bit, but you're way fatter and way, way uglier.'

'Yeah, and you're still an old dog.'

We've always talked to each other like this. It's a sign of affection.

I lead him through to the bar area they've set up in reception – a distinct improvement over the usual displays of dodgy pottery by fourteen-year-olds.

'All the booze is on me. Or the TV company, really. Free bar till nine.'

'In that case, Trace, can I buy you a drink?'

I feel slightly sick at the thought, but maybe it's the best thing to calm my nerves. I ask for a G and T and Briggsy gets a bottle of Bud.

'So,' I say, as we walk back into the hall, which now has about a dozen people in there, a few of whom I vaguely recognise. They're playing 'Oh What a Night', which isn't very eighties. All the guests are clinging to the wall like houseflies. The free bar should fix that before long . . .

'So,' he says. I was lying before about him looking different. He looks the same as he always did, though the stubble on his face suggests he finally does have a real need to shave every day. Even in the fifth year, his chin had only the slightest hint of bum-fluff, however hard he tried to coax the bristles with razors he nicked from Superdrug.

He was a slow developer, bless him, Robin to Gary's Batman. It works that way, doesn't it? A good-looking girl to pull in the opposite sex, and then a nice or clever or funny one to keep them there. When I first met Dave, he had a sidekick called Trev who cracked jokes all the time. And before that, I already knew, aged eleven, that Shrimp would be perfect as my side-kick. Perhaps that's why Melody and me were never as good together. We were always competing, and maybe to be friends, one person has to be top dog.

'It's been a darned long time, Briggsy, but it's good to have you back. What are you up to these days?'

'Engineering foreman.' He looks proud, and I guess he should be.

'Foreman, eh? I thought you'd never work again once the YTS stopped paying your wages.'

'Yeah, well. I heard that the only reason you kept your job was cos you nobbed the boss every payday.'

'Found anyone desperate enough to nob *you*, yet?'

He holds up his ring finger. 'Yeah, and she married me too.'

'I'm surprised they let you go dating at the school for the blind, mate.'

'And which guy did you snare?'

'He's . . .' I look around but I can't see him anywhere. Which is annoying, because from a distance, with the light behind him, he looks like a good choice of husband. 'Here somewhere, but he must have taken the kids to the loo, or something.'

'Kids, too? You don't scrub up too bad, considering . . .'

It's the nearest to a compliment he's ever given me, and makes me feel all warm inside, and a bit embarrassed. 'You don't mean it?'

'Yeah, I do. Though I always preferred the younger model myself . . .' And then he tails off.

'What?'

'Um . . . well, looks like Gary does, too . . .'

And I turn round, and there's Gary and this stunning woman. Five ten tall, easy, and she's not even wearing heels. Gabby.

Gary sees me too, and shuffles forward, with gorgeous Gabby trailing behind. Finally, when he's close enough to me to talk, but still out of punching range, he says, 'Hi. Hope you don't mind me coming. Boris said it wouldn't be the same without the old gang.'

*

Lower Playing Field, Bracewell College

Annabel cornered Dave and the kids on the grassy bank near the cricket nets. The light was fading, so it was only Kelly's T-shirt that made them visible.

'Hello, you three, wondered where you'd got to. I was looking for Tracey.'

'Haven't seen her,' said Dave, without looking round. He held a pint in one hand and a cigarette in the other. 'If you find her, tell her it's her turn to watch the kids.'

'OK,' Annabel said, vowing yet again never to have children. Men were so lazy. 'By the way, have you ever met Suzanne, she was in Tracey's class? And this is her husband, Christian.'

Dave finally turned to see a couple hovering behind Annabel. 'Nice to meet you,' he mumbled unconvincingly. 'I'm Dave, Tracey's house husband.'

Christian laughed loudly, like a privately educated donkey. Shame. Annabel quite fancied him when he kept his mouth shut. 'Excellent. I'm Suzanne's toyboy, but one day, I might get promotion to be her house husband!'

'I don't think Dave's serious, darling,' said Suzanne, walking over to where the children were playing with grass. 'Are you Kelly? I used to know your mummy when she was a little girl. I'm Suzanne.'

Kelly gave her a suspicious look.

'Don't bother with her, she's very awkward with strangers,' Dave said. 'You'll get more out of Callum and he can't even talk properly yet.'

Suzanne ignored him. 'That's a pretty daisy chain, Kelly. Would you show me how to make one?'

'Ah, well, if Suzanne can't get anything out of her, no one can,' said Christian. 'Bit of a speciality of hers. She runs a charity for children with problems, bullying and what not. Though when we get round to it, ours will be supremely well adjusted, won't they, darling?'

Dave shrugged. 'Tracey and me aren't exactly backward at coming forward, but it hasn't stopped Kelly being like this. We've even had a shrink in to talk to her, but she still won't say boo to a goose.'

'Oh, for God's sake!' Suzanne turned on him. 'It's hardly surprising she's like that if you talk about her as though she isn't here. Hasn't it occurred to you that some children are just quieter than others? It's not a crime.'

'Temper, temper,' Dave said. 'Not setting a very good example yourself, are you?'

Terrific, thought Annabel. Why did all the drama in this programme have to happen off camera?

Suzanne tossed her hair in irritation. 'I know it's not easy being a parent, but Kelly needs your support.'

'No. She needs to toughen up a bit. Or she'll always be miserable.'

'Maybe I could talk to her . . .'

Christian leaned across to touch her arm. 'Always on duty, eh, darling? We're at a party, let's leave it for now.'

'No, fine,' Dave said. 'I'd love to see what you can do in ten minutes when we've been bringing her up for nearly seven years; and while you're at it, why don't you take Callum too? Then I can go and get pissed. When you've finished, you'll probably find me propping up the bar. Which is all you think the likes of us are fit for, isn't it?'

And before any of them could answer, he marched back towards the school building.

I don't know where to look.

Gabby's entered into the spirit of the reunion with a tiny pleated skirt, which skims the very top of her cellulite-free

280

thighs, and a tight white shirt tied Britney-style at her waist, revealing a belly-button ring, which is the only bulge on her otherwise flat stomach. Her blouse also shows off her cleavage – her breasts are smaller than mine, but she hasn't got a bra on and they still bob happily along without any help. Mine rest on the bottom of my ribcage, unless I enlist the help of underwires.

'So what do you do, Gabby?' I ask her on our way back from the bar. She's drinking fizzy water because she's driving.

'I'm a social worker – child protection.'

Bloody hell, a do-gooder as well as a supermodel lookalike. *Haven't* you done well, Gary?

'That must be stressful.' Gabby the Perfect Girlfriend makes me feel better and worse at the same time. Better because there wouldn't have been much I could have done to tempt him away from this goddess. Worse because . . . well, I used to be the one who could get any man she chose. And I chose Dave.

'Well, yeah, but I'm an adrenalin junkie, and it has its fringe benefits.' She looks over her shoulder at Gary. 'Like the hunky policemen we get to meet . . .'

'Right . . .' Gary and Briggsy catch us up as we enter the school hall. Now they're playing 'Venus'. The playground version of the lyrics goes round my head: *I'm your penis, I'm your bra-a, your desire!*

I'm about to sing it to Gabby, but then I do a quick sum in my mind, work out she was barely walking when the song came out, and decide not to bother.

'Shit, is that Nigel?' Briggsy says, pointing to a bulky guy strutting his stuff in one of the spotlights. He goes running across the dance floor to join in. That's what we are now, eh? Embarrassing middle-aged parents trying to look cool at the PTA disco. Not that my mum ever turned up to those things; the best thing about having a single mother was that she never dragged me to that kind of event.

Gabby runs after him, and I'm relieved to see that she dances almost as badly as Nigel and Briggsy. The goddess has a flaw. But she's also sensitive – I realise that she's probably left Gary and me alone on purpose. Say what you like about do-gooders, but they've got hearts of gold.

'Thanks for coming.'

'No, well, no . . . thank Boris. She talked me into it.'

Boris to the rescue again. 'Gary, I know it's a bit late, but I owe you an apology. For what happened.'

He looks down at me, and shrugs. I can't believe he's a bloody policeman; to me he's no different from the wet-behind-the-ears sixteen-year-old who was genuinely shocked the first time I suggested giving him a blow job. Not for long, mind you. They learn fast not to look a gift horse in the mouth.

He watches the lads on the dance floor, then shrugs again. 'It's OK. I was upset, yeah, course I was. And . . . what I said and everything, when we met in the pub. It wasn't on. Should have said it there and then, when we were sixteen, not bottle it up. My mum always said bottling stuff up is stupid. Sorry.'

He leans over and kisses me on the cheek. And it's weird, but I realise that, as far as Gary's concerned, that is that. Seventeen years of heartache and agonising and envy and bitterness, not to mention a touch of joy-riding. All *finito*.

The song finishes, and the others return, casting slightly nervous glances at us, then relaxing when they see we're grinning.

'Things are really hotting up here at the great Crawley Park reunion,' says the DJ. 'It's not long to wait now till the highlight of the night – hang on to your baggy trousers because in less than half an hour, it'll be absolute . . . MADNESS!'

There's a loud cheer, and I realise how many guests are actually here: seventy, maybe even eighty. The group around me keeps growing, people are coming up and chatting. Steve

282

the plumber, Shazza the midwife, Colin the security guard, Rachel the aerobics instructor, Darren the postman . . .

It's fun, all these faces from the past popping up and repeating the same false compliments – you haven't changed a bit, it's brilliant what you've done to get this sorted, you can't have had two kids and still look that good – so that by the end you're almost believing it.

And then someone appears to shatter the whole bloody thing. Dave the builder.

But where the fuck are our kids?

'What have you done with the kids?' I scream at Dave.

'Oh, you're all right, Trace,' he slurs, and I want to hit him for being pissed so early. 'They're in good hands. Better hands than ours, according to your mate. I've left them with the perfect parents – Christian and Suzanne.'

'Suzanne?'

He takes a swig of lager. 'You were at school with her. Stuck-up bitch with ginger hair. Reckons we've messed up with Kelly, so I thought I'd let her have a go.'

Suzanne Sharp.

Sod bloody Madness. I've got a score to settle.

CHAPTER THIRTY-FIVE

'There,' Suzanne said, winding the daisy chain three times around Kelly's neck. 'That looks really pretty.' She rummaged around in her Anya Hindmarch flowerpot handbag for a mirror. 'Look . . .'

The sun was nearly gone, and it had left a pink midsummer haze, turning everything mellow. Suzanne could see Christian tickling Callum's feet with a blade of grass, and could hear them both laughing. She was sitting with her legs stretched out on the earth, which was radiating heat like an oven with an open door. But she knew the whole thing was unreal.

Christian didn't know any better. He thought that this tickling and giggling and messing around was what parenthood was about. But he worked in banking – admittedly with a bunch of grown-up children – where everyone acted as though Thatcher were still in Number Ten and pin-stripes were cool.

'It's nice,' said Kelly.

This was the reality. Kids brought issues of their own. Kelly was a bag of nerves, and knew already what a disappointment she was to her parents, and yet had no way of knowing how to change.

Suzanne had worked with enough of them to know *that* look. At Kelly's age you could still reach them. Once they hit their teens, the dead eyes gave it away. She'd seen the same flat expression on the faces of prisoners of war on newsreel footage.

'So apart from making daisy chains, what do you like doing, Kelly?'

Kelly rolled her eyes. 'Trying to remember . . . I wrote it all down, for Sandy. She's my cyker . . . cykergist. At school. You know.'

'Psychologist?'

'Yes, Sandy made me write it all down. If I had it here I'd show you.' She looked lost.

'It doesn't really matter, Kelly. Let me see, when I was the same age as you, I used to like . . . reading. Do you like reading?'

'Yes. A bit. Mummy doesn't like me reading all the time, though.'

Suzanne sniffed. 'No, I can imagine that. And I always loved animals. Ponies and rabbits, especially.'

Kelly smiled as if she'd discovered a kindred spirit. 'Guinea pigs. I love them. They're all . . . roly poly. More gentler than rabbits. The rabbits at school growl sometimes.'

'And what about dancing? Do you like dancing, Kelly?'

'On my own, in my room. Not where people can see. Makes me feel silly.'

'No one can see here, though. We could have a dance here.'

Kelly looked doubtful. 'There's no music.'

'We could sing some, make our own. It'd be fun.'

'Fun.' It was clearly an alien word to Kelly. In some ways, the kids who threw dolls or wooden bricks or even plastic chairs at you were easier to deal with than the ones who quietly accepted their friendless fate.

Suzanne stood up, shook the grass from her skirt, and held out a hand to Kelly. No six-year-old child was a lost cause.

Even when her mother was Tracey Mortimer.

I don't know what I'm going to say to bloody Suzanne when I find her. I've left Dave chatting with his new best mates, Briggsy

285

and Gary. A couple of jokes and a couple of burps was all it took for them to believe he was a decent bloke. Just wait till he tries to pull Gabby. Then they'll realise what he's *really* like.

I'm prowling the school site when I run into Jenny and the crew – they've been keeping their distance, which impresses me.

'How's it going?' I ask Jenny.

'Yeah, fine,' she says. 'You all seem to be getting on better.'

'Suppose so. There's a lot of water under the bridge.'

'And nice of Gary to apologise like that,' she says, and when I stare at her, she adds, 'Oh, don't worry, we won't be using it.'

The fucking radio mike. No wonder they haven't been stalking my every move – it's just as good for them to stand back and film from a distance as I bare my soul and settle old scores, because perfect sound is being transmitted back to their camera. I can't even slag them off this time – it's not as if they sneaked it on to me when I wasn't looking.

'Right,' I say.

'Actually, can we do a little catch-up interview now?' Jenny says, and Jamie turns the camera on me. 'So is it turning out the way you expected?'

I know what to say by now, and from somewhere I dredge up a 'ring of confidence' smile. 'Yeah, it's amazing . . . I was worried that maybe I wouldn't recognise people, or wouldn't have anything to say to them. But it must be that shared experience that means we all still have so much in common. And it's gonna get better later because of course this is the first time I've seen most of us legally drunk!'

'I believe it's also the first time you've seen your first boyfriend since you left school,' she says, winking at me.

'It's sooo weird,' I say, remembering not to answer yes or no, as per my instructions. 'Gary was my heart-throb all the way through school, and he hasn't changed one bit. Still drop-dead gorgeous, I could definitely still fall for him. But he's got a girlfriend, and I'm married, of course, so there's no danger of history repeating itself. It's great to see him, though. Might see if I can grab him for a slow dance later on . . .'

Jenny nods. 'Thanks, Tracey.'

'Would you do me a favour for a few minutes? I'm going to nip off to find the kids, and it'd be nice to be properly on my own just for a bit, without the camera. Is that OK?'

'Sure,' she says. 'Must get a bit tedious, and we could do with a break; give me a shout when you're back. And make sure you're not too long, Madness are on soon.'

They head for the bar, and I switch off the mike, then I walk towards the playing fields. I can hear Callum laughing hysterically and when I look over, he's chasing a lanky guy around. That must be Christian. Nicer-looking than Suzanne deserves, and young too. As I watch them, he pretends to trip over and Callum leaps on him, pummelling little fists on the guy's chest.

A little further away, I suddenly see Kelly's profile skipping along the horizon, followed by Suzanne. They're moving quite fast, and as I approach them, I realise they're singing.

'*What's new, pussycat?*'

'Woah, Woah . . .'

It's one of Kelly's favourite songs. Mum loves Tom Jones, and every time we go round there, Kelly demands to hear it. But it's unusual to see her bopping, her oversized T-shirt flying up and down as she jumps about like Tigger.

Suzanne sees me first; she must have sensed I was there, and she stops moving. But Kelly carries on leaping about and singing – the same chorus over and over because she can't remember the verse – until I'm close enough to whisper her name.

'Kelly.'

She looks up and stops dead. Her shoulders slump and she

blushes, as though she's embarrassed that I've caught her doing something she shouldn't.

'Hello, Tracey,' Suzanne says, and I can't see the expression on her face. She reaches out to hold my daughter's hand. 'Kelly and I have been having our own disco.' Kelly grins at her.

I don't know why, but this makes me feel even angrier. Who the hell does she think she is, playing with *my* daughter? Maybe she thinks she needs to tell me how it's done, how to be a mother.

'Kelly, go and play with Callum,' I say, pointing back to where her brother is.

She squints at me, then lets go of Suzanne's hand, and trudges off.

'Your husband didn't seem to mind, Tracey.'

He wouldn't, would he? 'I mind. I don't want to leave my child with just anybody.'

'I am trained in working with . . .' she starts, but I'm frowning so hard that she stops again. 'No harm done, anyway.'

She begins to walk off in the same direction. 'Hang on,' I shout. 'I want to know what the hell you think you were playing at, inviting Bob Carmichael.'

She stops. 'I . . . I don't know what you mean,' she says, without turning round to face me.

'Yeah, right. He turned up, and I certainly didn't invite him.' I walk in front of her, so I can see her face. She's got that irritating look that always used to make me mad at school – martyred and superior at the same time.

'Tracey, I can't think where you got the idea that I would invite anyone to *your* reunion. What's it got to do with me?'

'Good question. I've been wondering that ever since he said you'd been to see him.'

'Oh. Well, I wanted to talk to him about this citizenship working party he's involved in. It's an area I'm very interested in developing.' But even she doesn't look as though she believes what she's saying.

'Don't talk shit, Suzanne. I know we didn't see eye to eye at school, but I can't see what you're trying to achieve by messing with my life. And you fucked up anyway; if you wanted to embarrass me, or make things awkward, well, it hasn't worked, because Bob's been and gone. I think you should do the same, don't you? I've never wanted you around before, and I don't now.'

She stares back at me. 'You really don't scare me any more, Tracey, however loud you shout. I didn't ask Bob Carmichael, but I don't actually care whether you believe me or not.' Then she starts walking towards me. 'You're right, I did go to meet him, I can't explain why, but when I heard about the reunion, it brought back a lot of stuff I'd tried to forget. You made more or less every day here a bloody misery—'

'Don't talk shit, Suzanne, you knew—'

'No, you listen to me for once,' she says. She's not even shouting. The only sign that she's losing it is that her accent's slipping back into how it sounded when we were all at school, rather than the artificial 'posh' voice she used when we were filming the interview for the programme. 'I felt sick every day before school and it was because of you. Because you're an ignorant, callous bitch. I dare say you haven't even thought about any of that since we left, but it's stayed with me, all right. I've talked to lots of bullies over the last few years, and most of them are the same as you – stupid people with no interest in anybody else, except if there's something in it for them. All the shit you put me through, it was just a power game, wasn't it? A way of proving you were in charge, and sod what effect it had on me, or anyone else.'

She pauses for breath, and I wonder if I should say something. But what? She's exaggerating. Bloody drama queen. Sure, there were moments when I couldn't resist showing her up, but she deserved it, everyone agreed with me. She was such an easy target, but that was her choice. I can't believe she's been agonising about it for seventeen years. It's bloody tragic, but it's not down to me. She's the weirdo.

Isn't she?

'Well, Suzanne, this is very interesting, but I'd better get back to my party.'

'Oh no, you don't,' she says, and she runs in front of me, trying to block my path. 'I haven't finished.' She's close enough now to lower her voice to a whisper. 'I fought to get over it, to get back some of the self-respect you systematically took away from me over *five* years. When I heard about the reunion, I couldn't work out what to do. It brought it all back to the surface, and I was scared that it might just make me feel like shit all over again.

'But now I've got Christian.' She nods over to where Kelly and Callum and her husband are messing about. 'And friends, and a good job, and a life, and I thought I'd risk it. And do you know, it's been the best thing I could have done. Do you want to know why?'

I open my mouth to tell her I don't, thanks all the same, but she keeps going.

'Because I look at you now, and I realise you're nothing. Sure, you were queen bee for a few years, ruling a bunch of kids who knew no better. But the minute we walked through those gates for the last time, you lost your crown, and while the rest of us got on with our lives, you were stuck here, weren't you, in your head? Stuck in the days when Tracey ruled the world.

'Well, guess what? She doesn't any more, and if you thought this whole reunion was going to give you another crack at things, you're so wrong. Because we're not here to celebrate. Oh no. Everyone in that hall came to see how badly you fucked up your life. And didn't you do us proud? A no-hoper husband who couldn't get shot of your kids soon enough so he could get pissed. No friends that I can see. And a daughter who looks as terrified of you as I was. And why's that? Because she's got a bit of sensitivity, some intelligence, a bit of imagination? Oh, well, I'm sure you'll manage to bully it out of her before too long, Tracey. Then, one day, she might be just like you. Isn't that something to look forward to?'

This time she waits for my response, but I don't know what to say. Of course, the warped cow is wrong. About me, about the reunion, about Kelly. She has to be wrong. Tracey Mortimer was fun to be around, a laugh a minute, a catch. The situation with Kelly is completely different. Those girls are picking on someone who can't defend herself. My daughter's not even seven, for Christ's sake.

Suzanne was big and old and daft enough to look after herself, wasn't she?

Wasn't she?

What I really want to do to Suzanne now – slap her and pinch her and pull her hair – is not going to win me this argument.

'Speechless, eh?' And she grins. 'That really is a first.'

I wonder if I should remind her of my stage fright in *Joseph*, but I don't get the chance.

'You know, I hoped that at the end of this I'd be able to feel sorry for you, because pity is a wonderful revenge. But I don't. For all the pleasure of seeing you for what you really are, I also feel very sad. Because I'm about to walk away from your screwed-up life.

'But you can't. And neither can your children.'

291

I watch her walk back to her perfect husband and my imperfect kids. She lifts Kelly up, and says something that makes her laugh, then leans over to kiss Christian.

Maybe they'll decide I'm such a bad parent that they'll wander off into the sunset with my two, and give them a posh upbringing. Take Kelly to junior yoga, and Callum to toddler pottery, feed them polenta and sun-dried tomatoes, send them to private school.

And then what would I do?

Leave Dave, for a start. He's an OK dad, but an utterly useless husband, and if I wasn't tied to him by their genes, I'd be off. *Where?* that's the harder question. Would I have the guts to join Bob in London? To start over with a man just old enough to be my father, and probably repeat the whole kids thing, but this time have a Chloe and a Sam, as well as the money to give them the benefits of a proper middle-class childhood?

It's all cloud-cuckoo-land.

I can hear Kelly laughing, and it hurts. I wonder if Suzanne sees every giggle as proof that she's right after all, that my daughter prefers a woman she's never met before to me. That I am the terrible mother she thinks I am.

Part of me wants to go and seize Kelly and Callum back, drag them off to the green room, and force them to play nicely with

Annabel's sister, who's been drafted in as babysitter for the night. But I can't spoil one of Kelly's rare moments of fun. For all Suzanne's insufferable smugness, she seems to have a way with my daughter . . .

And anyway, I don't want the kids to be around when I talk to Dave.

I start to head back, keeping my distance, and pulling my Adam Ant jacket back around me. Now the sun's gone, it feels quite cold. Or maybe I'm shivering because I can see my future.

I've lost sight of Suzanne and 'her' Perfect Family by now, there's no one outside the hall, and I can hear someone speaking rather than music on the loudspeakers. I speed up.

'. . . it's typical Tracey that she's never around when you want her. But it's also typical Tracey that she can gather together such an amazing bunch of people for a reunion.'

I peer in through the doors, and realise it's Briggsy on stage, loving the attention. I want to jump up beside him, tell them it's not me who sorted this out, it's Boris, and we should all go to the hospital now and stand outside, chanting messages of support to show how much she's loved. Because that's what she needs right now.

'And it doesn't stop with the memories, because now, to take us all back to the time when we were pulling hair and eating dirt, we're going one step beyond – with MADNESS!'

There's a split-second pause when nothing happens, and then everything goes *mental*. Lights, drums and the cheering of a free booze-fuelled crowd who're determined to make as much racket as a Wembley stadium full of fans. I feel a rush of excitement pass through my body as they play the opening notes to 'Baggy Trousers'. Then I think of the kids, and start panicking: where has Suzanne taken them? All this noise must be terrifying, especially for Callum.

As well as the lights on stage, there are spotlights streaking

293

their way across the people in the hall, and I scan the room for them and Suzanne and Christian. And for Dave. But I can't see any of them. Part of me wants to rush to the front of the stage, to relish the moment, to reach out to Suggs and the nutty boys who are here because of me. Maybe I could climb up with them, and take Gary with me, and pretend, just for a minute, that we're still teenagers and there's everything to play for and nothing can go wrong.

But my head is starting to fill with horror stories: Callum running away from the music straight into the path of a car, or Kelly scared by the masses of people, walking out of the school gates into the clutches of a passing paedophile . . .

Where the bloody hell is Dave?

Staff & Visitors' Car Park, Bracewell College
(sixth-formers park on street, please, clamping in operation)

'It's a bit loud for you two in there,' said Suzanne. 'Christian, are you sure you can't see Dave – he's not in the bar, is he?'

'No. And I've been back to look for Tracey but she's not on the playing field any more.'

Callum had run out of steam, and decided to lie flat out on the concrete. He was already snoring softly.

'Oh, God, I'd better put them in the car.' Suzanne found the keys in her bag and clicked the alarm. 'Let's settle you two down in the car, Kelly, while we wait for Mummy to come for you both. OK?'

'OK.' Kelly clambered into the back seat, and stuck her thumb in her mouth. Suzanne and Christian took one end each of Callum, and lifted him into the front, without him waking up. Once they'd covered him with the dog blanket, a seatbelt fastened loosely over the top, they closed the door and sat down on the bonnet together, exhausted.

'So why did you send Kelly back to me?' Christian asked. 'Having some girl talk with Tracey?'

'Not quite. I had things I'd wanted to say to Tracey for seventeen years, and it seemed like a good opportunity.'

'And do you feel any better for getting it off your chest?'

Suzanne sighed. 'Not as good as I'd hoped. I mean, yeah, it was nice to do the talking for a change – she didn't get a word in edgeways. But it was a bit like kicking someone when they're already down. If you look at the two of us, who's come out of it better?'

'But you've put some ghosts to rest?'

'I suppose so. I feel more sorry for these two than anything,' she said, tapping gently on the car window.

'You can't help everyone, Suz. Sometimes you've got to walk away. And once we've found their dad – God help them – I think we should leave, go back to London and you can put Crawley Park and Tracey Mortimer and the whole inferiority complex thing behind you.'

'I don't know that it's going to be that easy.'

Christian leaned across and planted a kiss on her lips. 'I can think of one way to make a new start. To have our own.'

'Ye-es . . .' Suzanne said, meaning 'no'. 'Let's talk about it when we get home.'

I feel slightly unsteady on my feet – a combination of the heels and the gin. But I can't go slowly when there's so much at stake. I've calmed myself down a little bit about the kids; Suzanne might be an appalling stuck-up bitch, but she obviously knows about children. I just hope Kelly doesn't start talking about anger management and conflict resolution when I get her back.

My first job is to deal with Dave, ask him what the hell he's doing abandoning the kids. I bet he's already too pissed to be in charge of a packet of fags, never mind two children. All right, *I* know there are alternative arrangements: I asked Mum to come and pick them up at nine thirty, but I deliberately didn't tell him that. Thought it was about time he took some responsibility. Huh.

He's not in the bar, which was the most likely location. So I head out the other side of the school, towards the terrapins, which were decrepit enough in my day, but now look as though they're held together by chewing gum. The least fashionable subjects were always shunted off into the mobile classrooms, like smelly relatives hidden in the granny flat. In our day it was maths and German. I jump up to look through the grimy windows, and see scruffy posters Blu-Tacked to the walls. 'Grape varieties of the Rhineland', says one. 'German composers through history', reads another. I'm sure that one was up there back when *we* were struggling with our verb endings.

Beyond the terrapins is the science block, with the dining room, gym and changing rooms in the basement: food, chemicals and sweaty socks, all in one building.

It's really the last area where there's anywhere to skulk, though I don't know how he'd know that. By the bins was our equivalent of the bike sheds; they moved the bike sheds halfway through my time here, as an anti-smoking and anti-snogging measure. It was a bit stinkier behind the bins, but when the men came to empty them, we could hide in the little porch where the PE teachers stored metal cages of outdoor sports kit.

I had my first kiss there, the Old Spice aerosol-induced one with Briggsy. Actually, it was Melody's idea. Not the deodorant, but the snogging. And before any of us knew what was going on, she was diving on top of Gary, making strange humming noises. Not to be outdone, Briggsy pressed his face hard on to mine, as though I were a pane of glass, and he was playing that game where you squash your lips against it so you look hideous to anyone on the other side of the window. His teeth ground into my jaw, and then a hard tongue tried to force itself between my lips, and I was so shocked, that I let it in. Once inside, it circled inside my mouth like a washing-up brush trying to reach every corner of a saucepan.

We were twelve. I didn't ever think I'd forgive Melody for that. It should have been me and Gary sharing our first kiss – although it was some consolation when we finally lost our virginity together a few years later. Shrimp would never have done that. She knew the rules of best-friendship.

I can still hear pounding from the hall; it's hard to identify the song, but judging by the whooping that's accompanying it, a good time is being had by all. I walk past the bin store. Nothing.

Maybe the bastard's gone home. Conveniently forgotten about being a dad, and caught a taxi. But then I look at my watch, and it's not nine o'clock yet. Can't imagine Dave leaving before the free drinks run out. My feet are killing me in these shoes, so I sit on the steps upwind of the last bin, and massage them. Through a process of elimination, I realise the band's playing 'House of Fun'. How appropriate. Everything – sex, smoking, all the grown-up things – was more fun when we were too young to do them. Before it all became a chore.

'Shhh . . .'

It's a woman's voice, followed by giggling. Coming from the porch area. There's something about it that's familiar but . . . I drag myself to my feet, and I hear my knees cracking so loudly I'm convinced whoever's hiding must hear them too. I tiptoe along the path that's been worn away by generations of kids taking the same route from the bins to the safe haven of the PE porch. Nice to know some traditions are still upheld at Crawley Park College for Media and the Performing Arts.

It's a couple. Obviously deciding to go for the full reunion experience, complete with groping and the risk of discovery. I was never terribly excited about the idea of being discovered during sex when I was a teenager, but I suppose it was such a constant risk that there was no novelty value attached. It's only when we get middle-aged that we need new ways to get the horn.

The man has his back to me, and the girls face is hidden, but I see enough – dark hair, white shirts, pale skin – for the pieces of a kaleidoscope to click together and form an image so vivid, so painful and so unmistakable that I want to vomit.

Dave.

And Melody.

CHAPTER THIRTY-SEVEN

On my wedding day, I could easily have killed her. Right now, I wish I had.

It's not on, is it? I'd paid all that money to make her look great – the hairdresser, the make-up girl, the slinky bridesmaid's dress. I even let her give a best woman's speech, 'because it's not fair that the best man gets the attention and I just get to sit there with my mouth shut looking pretty'.

And she repaid me with three minutes of 'funny' stories about my wild past, and a load of unsubtle hints about Dave's own bad behaviour.

'It's always good when a groom takes preparations for a wedding as seriously as Dave Brown has,' she began, 'but I never realised that extended to checking out the chief brides-maid's underwear . . .'

Everyone laughed nervously. And as it got worse – Dave was like a dairy cream chocolate éclair, apparently, 'naughty but nice, and more than a mouthful' – I sat there, trying to smile, but wanting to run away from my own wedding. I'd been married for two hours and twenty minutes, and there was my best friend telling the world that my husband was, at best, a flirt. At worst . . .

'How could you do that to us, Melody?' I hissed at her, after everyone had finished the wedding breakfast and left the room to gossip about the speech in the garden. It was just me, her, plus my mum pretending to pack pieces of leftover wedding cake in tin foil. 'You made it sound like Dave tried it on with you.'

She looked at me steadily. 'You've always thought you're the cleverer one of the two of us, haven't you, Tracey? But you're not as smart as you think.'

'Meaning?'

'Well, what do *you* think?'

My mum came over then. 'You should clear off, Melody, before you get yourself into trouble.'

Melody ignored her. 'I tried to warn you what he was like at the hen night.'

I tried to remember what she'd said – I'd been very drunk at the hen night. Nothing came back to me. 'And what is he like?'

She shrugged, then lifted one of her ringlets away from her neck, to reveal a love bite. 'I told you. Naughty but nice.'

'That's it,' said my mother. 'We all know what you're like, Melody. Half of Bracewell could have been responsible for that. Now, you can either leave at once, or I will get Tracey's uncle to throw you out.'

And that was that. One less bridesmaid, but a lot more whispering. I asked Dave when we got back to the hotel that night if there was any reason why she'd say those things.

'She's just jealous of what you've got, Tracey,' he said, pointing towards his groin. 'What girl wouldn't be?' And then we had sex again.

A couple of years ago, I found out that they can use computers to remove unwanted relatives or friends from your favourite photographs, and I considered having it done, because some of my nicest pictures have got *her* on them. Kelly loves swooning over the images of my day as a fairy-tale princess, and seeing Melody there riles me.

In the end, though, I decided it was a waste of money. I'd

already done it, mentally. So when I looked at the photos, she was still there, but only in the way a headstone is there, in the background of the churchyard. Kelly picked up on it too, bless her, only asked me about the lady in the sky-blue dress once before she realised it made me uncomfortable.

But now I know, don't I? She was telling the truth, and I was the fool. She already had what I had – Dave's supposedly perfect body, the one he said always caused second glances in the communal showers at the football club – but without the long-term commitment or the sock-washing.

And it wouldn't surprise me if they've kept each other on the side for years. I bet they've laughed at me, at my stupidity, at the reunion. I can almost hear it.

Fuck, maybe they were her crabs he gave me. Talk about *something borrowed . . .*

As I run back to the hall, I look down and realise my feet are bare, and one of them is bleeding. I'm still holding on to my strappy shoes. Madness are playing 'My Girl's Mad at Me'.

Andrew stood at the back of the school hall, trying to spot Tracey. He'd had a hectic afternoon checking things out, and he still didn't have all the information he wanted, but it wouldn't take much to make her confirm the story. He'd deliberately left it a while before coming to the party, because there was a fair chance she'd be pissed by now.

But she was proving irritatingly elusive. One person he'd asked had assured him you wouldn't be able to miss her in her leather dress and embellished jacket. 'Hot,' the bloke had said.

Photos from the night itself would be good. He might be able to get stills from the TV company. He was pretty certain they'd run with the idea that all publicity was good publicity when it came to boosting viewing figures, and so the kind of

301

publicity he was about to guarantee for Tracey and her reunion could only be a gift.

It wasn't his kind of story, normally. He'd left the grimy door-stepping behind him when he left the provinces for London to pursue serious journalism, but this was a scoop that had everything – sex, politics, power – and it was bound to bring him big bucks. Which was a good job because the exhaust on the car was about to fall off, and the parts for BMWs didn't come cheap.

No, she definitely wasn't here. He walked back through the bar, which was almost empty. A handwritten sign pinned to the front of the beer pumps explained why: 'Sorry, all drinks after 9 p.m. to be paid for'. Loads of people in pretend school uniform, but no tarty blonde in a leather number. Married, two kids, part-time job in an office supplies shop: she really was so average it was untrue. Except for shagging the teacher. Maybe even that passed for normal at Crawley Park.

Through the doors from reception, Andrew could see Suzanne standing by her car, talking to a guy who must be her husband. That was the story that *really* interested him: what had she got against Tracey that would make her want to stitch up her classmate so badly? He'd never push it, of course; when it came to protecting his sources, he'd be as good as his word.

He bought himself a mineral water, and stood in the doorway. Perhaps Suzanne would know where she was.

Andrew walked towards their car. 'Hello,' he said, and Suzanne turned and gave him a venomous stare.

'Sorry to bother you both, but I'm looking for Mrs Brown. For Tracey? And I can't seem to find her. I wonder if you've seen her.'

The fair-haired man smiled politely. 'Snap! We're trying to find her too, but she seems to have disappeared off the planet. We've got two sleepy kids in here who want their mummy,' he said, pointing into the car. Suzanne pursed her lips.

'Oh, right . . .' Andrew said, peering through the window. A chunky toddler was out cold in the front, a trail of dribble snaking down his chin. In the back, a girl looked back at him through saucer eyes. So she's left her kids with strangers, too. Another nice line for the story. 'Bless 'em. What's she like, abandoning her babies? Naughty Tracey . . .'

My foot has really started to hurt now, even though I put my shoes back on. I must have trodden in a fragment of glass as I made a run for it. But I can feel my heel slipping about in the blood that's collected in the sole, and it'll probably soak through the leather and be ruined. I'll have to keep the shoe as a souvenir of the night my marriage died. Very fitting.

I thought they might at least try to come after me, but there are no cries of my name, no footsteps behind me, no 'wait, I can explain', just the creak of my own heels as I trudge back. My head's clearer now, my sore foot has sobered me up, and I've called Mum to ask if she can come straight away to pick up the kids. All I've got to do is find Suzanne.

I've got to time it carefully, so my mother doesn't have time to interrogate me, or demand that I leave *right now, young lady*. I wouldn't put it past her, and I can't risk it.

Because I'm getting out. Fuck the reunion, fuck the TV programme, especially fuck Dave (go on, Melody, you're welcome to him and his wandering genitals). I'm walking out of those bloody gates again but this time I'm not looking back.

Which is all very well, except I don't have a clue where I'm going.

'Is that her?' Christian said. 'She appears to be limping.'

Suzanne looked up. 'Thank God for that. I was starting to think we'd have to call social services.' She turned to Andrew. 'Do you mind leaving us alone to sort this out please?' she snarled.

'Darling . . .' Christian frowned. 'Sorry, she's not normally this rude. It's been a long day, you know, and I think—'

'Shut up,' Suzanne said. 'We don't owe him an apology.'

'What, you know him?' He glanced from his wife to the stranger, and back again. Neither said anything. 'Oh, hell's bells, what is going on?' The only thing he could be sure of was that the faltering figure drifting towards them was definitely Tracey. 'Yoo-hoo . . . Over here,' he shouted, desperate for an explanation.

When I reach the car park, I see Suzanne's dopey husband, and then Suzanne, the two of them huddled around a car. They don't seem to be panicking, so the kids must be with them.

There's a third guy, and as I approach I realise it's that reporter. How bloody cosy. Suzanne's got the most unbelievable nerve – first, she tries to set me up by inviting Bob, then she gives me the mother of all going-overs at my party and now she's chatting away to some bloke who is probably even now plotting to put me on the front pages.

Unless it was her who tipped him off in the first place . . .

'Tracey,' says her husband. He has the most annoying accent. 'We haven't met properly, I'm Christian. Are you all right? You seem to have hurt your foot.'

'It's fine,' I say, and I look into the car. Kelly and Callum are asleep.

He smiles. 'The kids suddenly became rather tired, and we couldn't find your husband, so we brought them here away from the noise. Are you *sure* you're OK? It looks as though you're bleeding.' He turns to Suzanne, who is much quieter than she was on the playing field. 'Because Suzanne's a qualified first-aider, aren't you, darling?'

'I've had enough help from your wife for one day.'

'Really?' he says, and the sarcasm's escaped him completely. 'That's my Suz. She was telling me about Kelly's problems, but I'm sure it'll blow—'

'That's not what I mean. I'm talking about the help with publicity.'

Andrew glances at her for just long enough to tell me it's true.

But Christian blunders on. 'Darling?'

'Oh, hasn't she introduced you to her partner in crime?'

'Tracey, I don't know what you're talking about,' she says, in such a patronising voice I want to slap her. But now is not the time.

'Yeah, right. Of course you don't.'

Andrew steps forward. 'Mrs Brown, I was just asking your guests here if they knew where you were, because I was keen to have a private word . . .'

'You had your chance at the press conference.'

'This is rather more personal . . .'

'Well, I'm sure it's not so personal you can't talk to me here, in front of one of my oldest friends.' Poor Christian now has the same expression as Stan Laurel, and I half expect him to scratch his chin.

'Mrs Brown, I really think—'

'I'm afraid I can't neglect my guests, so this is your one chance.'

Andrew sighs, takes a deep breath and says, 'OK. Suit yourself. I'm following up a story about you and Bob Carmichael, the government adviser. I understand he used to be a teacher

305

here, and that you had a relationship while you were a pupil. I wanted to give you the chance to put your side of things . . .'

Now Christian's mouth is hanging open, and Suzanne tries to look surprised.

'I think you're barking up the wrong tree,' I say, and turn to go.

'I've got evidence, Mrs Brown. So whatever you say, I'm afraid the story is likely to be published. But you were very young, and I don't think it'll reflect badly on you, especially if you're willing to talk to me.'

The penny's dropping with Christian, too. 'Suz?' he says. 'Darling, did you know about this? Or about him?' He nods towards Andrew.

'Don't be ridiculous,' she snaps.

I turn on her. 'You admitted to me yourself that you met Bob last month. Unless you're going to deny that now?'

'No, I—'

'Suzanne?' Christian says, using her full name like a parent telling off a naughty child.

'And I suppose it's a coincidence that you're chatting to this scumbag journalist?'

She stares at me.

'It doesn't matter,' I say. 'You can stuff your stupid story, print it, what do I care? It was seventeen years ago.'

Andrew waits for a second, then reaches in his pocket, and pulls out a business card. 'I'd advise you to think about this more carefully when you're a bit calmer. All my numbers are on here. But don't leave it too long.' And he walks off, leaving the three of us in silence.

I suddenly feel overwhelmingly tired.

'Tracey.' Christian says my name, and despite the annoying accent, he sounds worried. 'What an awful thing to happen.

I'm sure Suzanne's got nothing to do with this, but, honestly, if there's anything we can do . . .'

'Actually, there is. I need some space to think, but my mum's on her way to pick up the kids. To save waking them up twice, would you mind waiting for her and telling her I'm fine, but I had something to do? She's due any minute, in a beige Mini Metro, Y-reg?'

Suzanne leaps in. 'Of course. No problem. We'll make sure they're fine.' If I needed more proof she's guilty, this is it. But it doesn't matter any more.

I blow kisses at my sleeping children, and hobble slowly out into the night.

CHAPTER THIRTY-EIGHT

Once I've made my grand gesture, I don't have a clue what to do next, so I hide in the bushes to make sure everything's all right when Mum arrives. Even at this distance, I can see that she's angry. She's all smiles with Suzanne, but her body language is screaming, 'How could Tracey be so irresponsible, dumping the kids like this?' It doesn't help that she's right.

When she accelerates off, sending aggressive puffs of smoke out of the car's knackered exhaust, I crawl out of the undergrowth. Still no sign of Dave. The kids could have been on their way to a sweatshop for all he cares. Bastard.

I still don't know what to do so I limp to the late-night shop, and buy tissues for my foot and a packet of fags.

'You been at this reunion?' asks the guy behind the counter, pointing at my Adam Ant jacket. 'We had a bloke in here earlier, a journalist, nosing around about the girl who organised it. She was shagging her teacher, he reckoned.'

'Really?' He's been snooping around bloody everywhere.

'Yeah. Couldn't tell him anything. Only been here three months. Four-sixty, please, love.'

The fag is disgusting – I only ever smoked to look good – but it buys me thinking time. When I say I don't have a clue what to do next, that's not strictly true. I know exactly what I *want* to do next, and I'm trying to work out some convincing reasons why I shouldn't.

What I want to do next is call Bob. Apart from anything else, he does need to know that this bastard Andrew is on to him. But that's not the real reason.

I also want to call him, just because I want to call him. Because through all the grimness of today, the Gary-Shrimp-Suzanne-Dave-Melody moments, there's only been one thing that's kept me going. And that's the knowledge that what I'd had with Bob, however sordid it seemed to everyone else, was real.

Boris would understand. But that's the other thing. There've been whole stretches of this evening when I haven't specifically thought about her, even though I've had this constant sense that something is missing. But what can I do? I'm not wanted there, any more than I am by my own husband and kids, or by the hundred-plus 'friends' in that school hall who came for the free booze and the free band, but partied away quite happily without me there.

Maybe Suzanne had a point. Maybe no one ever *wanted* to be my friend. They just didn't want to risk being my enemy.

I pull out Bob's card, and examine it under the streetlamp. It's the loops that make up my mind. On the back, he's written 'mobile' followed by the number, and the 'b' and the 'l' are both topped by curly loops, and it reminds me of the only love letters I've ever had, each one on the thickest, creamiest paper, crammed into parchment envelopes, addressed to Tracey in fountain pen, with a final flourish on the 'y'.

I key his number into my phone, but have to smoke another fag before I finally press send.

It rings four times, enough to make me think again, but as I'm about to cut it off, he answers. 'Hello.' His voice sounds flat, and I hear traffic in the background.

'Bob,' I say. And then I'm tongue-tied.

'Tracey?' He says my name as though he can't quite believe it. 'What – where are you? What's happened?'

'Nothing . . . everything. I don't know.' *Pull yourself together*, Tracey, for Christ's sake. 'They know. A reporter, he turned up at the reunion, and he knows about us. He wanted me to talk about it, but I didn't, but he says he's going to publish anyway, and it's going to ruin your life, and—'

'Tracey, shhh . . . Listen, where are you?'

'Outside school, I've done a runner. And I'm leaving Dave. I found him with Melody, I think it's been going on all the time we've been married. Before, even.'

'Hold on, Tracey—'

'And then there's Boris, I need to know what's happened to Boris. I've been so selfish, and she's lost her baby and I've been too busy obsessing about myself even to make sure or go to the hospital but then I bet she wouldn't want to see me, anyway. Oh, Bob, I'm such a bitch. They all think so, even bloody Suzanne, and they all blame me for messing up my kids, and they're right, you know.' I'm on the edge of tears and I look down at the pavement, and see the blood crusted along the side of my shoes, and that does it. 'Oh, and I've cut my foot open.'

There's a pause, and then he says, 'Have you got any money?'

'Yes,' I whimper, hating myself for being a pathetic cry-baby.

'Take a cab to the hospital. Is Boris at the general?'

'Yes.'

'Right, get yourself to casualty, and I'll meet you there. We can get you patched up and then we'll see if we can find out what's happened to her.'

'But I can't . . . what about the TV crew?'

'Sod the TV crew. This is your life we're talking about, not someone else's light entertainment. You've had a shock. They'll understand.'

I can't see Alec understanding, but somehow that doesn't

make me any keener to go back to the party. 'But you're in London . . .' I bite my lip in the pause that follows. Please argue back. Please look after me. Please take control.

'No . . . no, I'm not, actually, not tonight. I decided to book myself into a hotel, Marshall House? I can be at the hospital in twenty minutes.' It's his turn to sound lost, as the implications of the hotel booking hang in the digital signal passing between our phones. 'A treat to myself, really, it's not like I was expecting that anything would happen, you know, with you . . . anyway, ring a cab and I'll see you in A and E. OK?'

'OK,' I say, relieved to be told what to do. Maybe that's where I went wrong after Crawley Park – playing the field, trying to make my own decisions – when all I really wanted was a replacement for Mr Carmichael. Or maybe even a replacement for my non-existent dad.

I've started to think like a shrink. It's that bloody Suzanne's fault. I really do need to pull myself together.

In the cab I start worrying that my stupid outfit will be horribly embarrassing once I get to casualty, but it's such bedlam that the girl on reception doesn't even seem to notice.

'Description of injuries?'

'I've cut my foot on some glass.'

She raises her eyebrows. 'How badly?'

'Well, it keeps starting to bleed again. I think it might need stitches.'

'Your decision, of course,' she says, as though she wouldn't trust me to decide on a lipstick colour, never mind anything health-related, 'but you couldn't have chosen a worse time to come into casualty with a minor injury. It'll be a long wait.' She nods in the direction of the waiting room behind me, where the patients are uglier and rowdier than the ones on *Casualty*.

'I'll try my luck.'

I find the ladies' toilets, and try to lift my foot into the basin to clean it up a bit. But the leather dress isn't designed for high kicks, so I have to hitch up the skirt part around my waist. I wash away the dried blood, and I'm surprised at how deep the cut looks. It begins to bleed again, and I wedge a pile of green paper towels into the front of my shoe and limp back out.

I realise how hungry I am. Life-changing trauma can make you peckish. But after the taxi, I don't have any change for the vending machine. I pick up a pile of magazines, and flick through them, just reading the ridiculous headlines. '*My aunt is my gay lover*'. '*DIY plastic surgery: I gave myself a facelift*'. And even – this one made me laugh out loud, an achievement under the circumstances – '*My husband's other woman is a Dalek*'. There's a picture of a middle-aged couple, sitting down to breakfast, alongside a life-size model Dalek.

But it's not much weirder than my life. I could fill an entire magazine on my own. Page 2, my daughter's bullying hell. Page 3, my husband shagged my bridesmaid. Pages 4–5, lessons in love from my form teacher. And on the back page, the problem page letters: how I discovered I was the school bully. How my life has been one big sham. How I failed my friend in her hour of need.

'Tracey.' He looks dishevelled and worried, and older than he did six hours earlier.

I realise in a single moment that he won't be going back to his hotel room alone. I feel better when I know this – my foot still hurts, as do all the crap things in my life – but at least I know I don't have to go home tonight. And that I can put off thinking about the things I don't want to face.

But then I come over all shy, worried he can read my mind. 'Hi.'

He sits down on the plastic chair next to me, and the whole row shakes slightly. 'How's the foot?'

'It's sore, but I don't think it's going to fall off. It's just everything else happening that's made me overreact.'

He puts his hand over mine, and I'm relieved that they're still young man's hands, warm and firm. 'I don't think any of it's an overreaction. But we can sort it out.' He taps my knee. 'Let's have a look, then.'

I take off my shoe and hold up my foot. The bleeding's stopped again.

'Not nice, but I think on balance you might be more at risk of dying from a hospital superbug if we hang around here for ever. How about we go and see what we can find out about Helen?'

Without me having to ask, he stands up and lets me lean on him. We tell the receptionist to take my name off the list, then head for the lifts.

'I've never been to a maternity ward before,' he says, and I wonder what he's done with the last seventeen years. Sure, he's got the flash job and the flash lifestyle, but is that all there is? Expense accounts are nice enough, but what's the point of posh hotels if you're on your own?

'Don't worry, they keep the fannies under wraps,' I tell him, and I feel the old Tracey returning, momentarily. But as we step out of the lift, she disappears again. I nudge him towards the desk. 'Will you ask? I can't bear to know . . .'

I can't even bear to stand near enough to hear the midwife say the words. Through the window, I try to locate Crawley Park in the distance, but there are too many different orange lights out there, too many people getting on with their Saturday nights, trying to forget the life and death stuff that's staring us in the face on Rosebud Ward.

'Tracey . . .'

I turn around slowly, but when I finally face him, he's smiling. Insensitive bastard. I know he's trying to help, but . . .

313

'Tracey, Boris is asleep. But if they can find Brian, we might be able to take a peep at the baby.'

Baby?

'Tracey? If that's what you want?'

I walk up to the desk, to ask the midwife, in case Bob's misunderstood.

'Could you tell me what's happened with Mrs Norris?'

She lets out a low moan. 'I've told your husband already. She's tired after the caesarean but we're monitoring her, and everything seems fine. And the baby's small, but she's fine, too.'

Another nurse comes back and says Brian's asleep as well. But we should ring in the morning and see about popping in then.

Back in the lift, Bob and I don't know what to say to each other. He leads me out of reception, to the car park. When we reach the car, I stand on one leg like a stork, folding my injured foot up behind me. I don't know where to put myself.

'So . . . can I offer you a lift?'

I smile. 'I hear there are some nice hotels around here?'

CHAPTER THIRTY-NINE

From a distance, the hotel looks like a wedding cake. But inside, Marshall House is very masculine, all mahogany and chrome, with a strong smell of furniture polish.

The night porter lets us in. He takes in my jacket and my lack of luggage, and gives Bob a man-to-man glance, avoiding my eye entirely.

'Sleep well,' he tells us, handing over a key mounted on a Bible-sized wedge of wood.

The journey from the hospital has been short on conversation. Bob even switched on a CD to fill the awkward gap, but it was Bob Dylan, and as he wailed about rolling stones, it just made me question what I was doing.

We take the lift to the second floor, even though my foot hardly hurts now any more. He opens the door, switches on the lights, then gestures for me to go in ahead of him. Always the gentleman.

It's not just a room, it's a suite. The hallway widens out to become a lounge, and the room is lit by a mad modern chandelier, with tiny ultra-bright bulbs on the end of a dozen tangled wires. Underneath, there's a huge leather sofa, a big TV and a thick creamy sheepskin rug on the wooden floor. To the right, there's an archway, and I peep through to see an enormous bed, one of the French ones shaped like a boat, and it looks like it's been carved from a single chunk of oak. On top, there are half a dozen pillows and a huge duvet, covered in crisp white cotton, plumped up with fresh air and feathers.

I turn away. There's just something about it that's too scary, too horizontal, too *bed-like*, for me to feel comfortable with it. So much for big, brave Tracey Mortimer, who'd always fantasised about fucking in a posh hotel.

Bob puts his hand on my arm. 'I'm more than happy to sleep on the sofa.' I shake my head. 'No . . . no. If anyone's going to do that, it'll be me. You must have paid a fortune for this suite. I'm not tired, anyway. Though I am hungry.'

'That's something I think I can help with.' He walks across to the TV, and just behind it there's a mini American retro fridge. He opens it, and empties slabs of chocolate and fruit on to the floor. 'Can I get you a drink?'

'God, yes.' I grab one of the bars, perch myself on the arm of the sofa, and break off small pieces of dark chocolate, though what I really want to do is cram the whole lot into my mouth at once. I take off my shoes, and when I let my feet rest on the floor, it's warm. It makes me smile, and he notices as he comes over with a gin and tonic. He didn't even have to ask.

'They've installed some kind of Swedish heating in all the floors – the attention to detail is amazing.' Then he grins, looks embarrassed. 'How middle-aged am I, Tracey? Mind you, the power shower *is* incredible . . . And I promise this isn't part of a seduction routine, but if you do want to change and have a bath or whatever, there's a spare one of those huge bathrobes I'm told women love.'

'You saying I smell?'

'No, of course not, I—' and he stops when he realises I'm winding him up.

A bath would send me to sleep, and that's not what I want to do until I've worked out exactly *where* I'm sleeping – but a shower sounds good.

The bathroom is as uncompromising as the rest of the suite, and the lack of a shower curtain throws me. There *is* a bath, but it's tucked behind the door, and is clearly not the main event. The room itself is the size of my lounge, and is coated floor to ceiling with mosaic tiles in different shades of blue; the floor slopes away to a drainage hole, and along the walls are a variety of nozzles but I've no idea which one is the shower.

Apparently I'm not the first guest to be confused, because by the door there's a chrome plate engraved with the words 'guidance on using the wet room is available from reception'. Which makes me laugh – has anyone ever had the guts to ring down and admit they don't know how to work the shower?

I strip off, laying my dress and underwear to the side of the marble basin. It's impossible to avoid seeing myself in the mirrors running alongside it. Actually, it's not as bad as it could be. Or maybe the lights and the mirror are designed to give that impression, to make you feel as glossy as the room itself.

What do I look like to him? The last time he saw my body I was sixteen – tits pointing to heaven, cellulite-free skin, and a heartbreakingly flat stomach. And now? I turn slowly in front of the mirror, and my skin still looks soft, only the very top of my thighs resemble orange peel. My stomach's rounder, but not fat.

It's the bits you can't see in the mirror that have changed the most – and no one but Dave has seen me there since I was all stretched and torn by childbirth. I wonder sometimes whether men talk about what women are like *down there*, the way drunk women talk about dicks. I shudder and move on.

My breasts are bigger than the last time he saw me, but they've not yet travelled as far as my waist. And I like my back, and the way my hair skims my shoulders and sways with me as I move. I suppose it all depends on whether Bob fancied me for myself, or fancied me because I was sixteen. And if I believe it's the latter, then what am I doing in a hotel room with him?

317

I step into the shower area. Tucked inside are a series of buttons – this really is a boy's toys bathroom. I press the largest one; there's a low roar and then torrents of water launch themselves out of the nozzles in the ceiling and the walls. I turn the big central dial towards the red indicator, and I cover my body with designer soap from the built-in shelf, and play around with the different buttons – one increases the pressure so it's like standing under a waterfall, and another one makes jets burst out of different nozzles in orgasmic spurts; steam is filling the bathroom, and I don't ever want to leave.

I don't know how long I stay in there, but by the time I force myself to switch the shower off, I feel as if I've just swum in a lake, or run through a forest – alive, invigorated, cleaner than I've ever been. And in the mirror, my face is flushed and my hair hangs together in a horsetail, darkened by the water. I unhook the huge bathrobe, which has been warming on the towel rail, and when I lose myself in the thick white towelling, I feel as innocent as a newborn.

'Better?' Bob asks as I walk back into the suite. He is sitting on the sofa, reading a magazine. Or pretending to – I get the impression he's as nervous as I am. There's jazz coming from the CD player.

'Much.' I sit beside him, and it feels strange being naked under the robe. I drain the glass, and the kick of the gin and tonic warms my near-empty stomach. 'Shall we go to bed?'

'Are you sure?'

'No . . .' I say, and his face falls. 'But I feel like taking a risk.' I take his hand and we walk through to the gigantic bed.

I'd never fucked in a bed before Bob. When you grow up, you forget that teenaged sex is all snatched knee-tremblers in the back of friends' cars – if you're lucky enough to have friends old and rich enough – or sessions on the sofa when you're

318

babysitting for well-meaning neighbours. Mum would never let Gary in my bedroom, and he had to share his room with his brother. It's a miracle we ever found enough privacy to lose our virginity together.

But a bed was different. Grown-up. Scary. A bed was almost more frightening than the idea of sleeping with my teacher. Melody covered for me, pretending I was round hers playing records. It was a calculated risk. Once I'd told her, I knew she'd love the fact she had the juiciest piece of gossip in the history of Crawley Park, and I also knew there was a risk attached. But I felt like I had no option because I needed to find an alibi within twenty-four hours. Bob finally gave in at teatime on Friday and asked me round. At seven o'clock on Saturday, I went to the bus stop where he picked me up. I don't think he wanted to give himself time to change his mind.

Bob lived in the old part of town, in a small terraced house – they're pricey now, but no one wanted to live in them then; they wanted draught-free homes with upstairs bathrooms.

He bought a Chinese takeaway on the journey to his place, and I wanted to eat it from the cartons on our laps, but he insisted on serving it properly, on plates. He'd lit a candle in the middle of the old dining table, and put jazz on his record player. I still don't actually like jazz, but it always makes me feel grown-up.

I don't know who was more nervous – I suspect it might have been him. He treated me like a 'real' date, complimenting me on my hair and my clothes (a new pink top from Chelsea Girl, which showed far too much cleavage), topping up my glass with white wine, but insisting I drink exactly twice as much water, to stop me feeling drunk, or hung over the next day.

The next day. There was only one thing between me and the next day. The night. And that was what was scaring me the most.

At least he didn't bore me with moral dilemmas – four days of agonising at Daisy's café had convinced him I knew what I was doing, and that this was a kind of destiny.

This time, it was him who took the lead. He kissed me, and I could see the clock on the mantelpiece, 8.35 p.m., which felt terribly early to be going to bed, but then again, why would you wait if you had the house to yourself?

He led me upstairs and into his bedroom, which was painted white, with a big wooden bedstead by the window. He switched off the lights, and sat with me on the bed, kissing me and stroking my hair, and murmuring my name. Then he started to undress me, carefully, down to my bra and knickers. He pulled the duvet down on to me, as he undressed to his underpants, and then we moved together, skin to skin . . .

The feeling of a man's body against mine, against the cotton sheets, in this silent, private room, is something I'll never forget. He smelled of a woody aftershave, and as I explored his upper body with my hands, I was surprised at how hairy he was – Gary was very different. Bob's skin was rougher, but in the dark it didn't feel like he was my teacher any more.

He was slow and methodical, working his way around every inch of me with his fingers, but with no sense of urgency. I felt excited but frustrated – sex was about lust, wasn't it, about explosions of need and passion? So I reached down to his pants, and touched his cock, and he whimpered.

He unhooked my bra, while I removed my knickers, and when he was quite naked too, we rubbed up against each other again . . . it was so different from the snatched moments of sex in impossible positions that Gary and I had been grabbing.

'Are you sure?' he asked me. I kissed him back.

When he entered me, it was familiar and yet different – better, more 'right', somehow. He was smaller than Gary, but I don't buy into the whole size matters thing, anyway. Especially

320

when Gary, like most sixteen-year-olds, had less self-control than a compulsive gambler or drug addict.

To start with I felt I should thrash around and make the noises you see in films, but he slowed me down, saying my name over and over again. And when I came, I opened my eyes and the light from the streetlamp lit up his face and I saw the look of satisfaction at what he'd done.

Afterwards he still kept saying my name, and we did it again and again till we fell asleep.

When I woke up, I felt different. For the first time I had actually 'slept' with a man, and I put my head on the pillow as close to him as possible, so I could take in the warm, bitter-almond scent of his breath. He woke up almost instantly, and when he saw my face, he looked shocked for a moment, then smiled.

In the morning, when we did it again, we could see each other in the daylight.

Bob fiddles with the control panel so there are two pools of light on the duvet, spotlights for the main attraction. I sit on the bed, and he moves around to my side, and kisses me. My body remembers and when he pulls the dressing gown open, goose bumps cover my skin.

'Oh, Tracey,' he says. 'It's been too long.'

CHAPTER FORTY

I wake up to sunshine pouring on to the duvet. It's the perfect day for ending a marriage.

Bob is still asleep. I think about leaving a note, but it seems underhand. It's just that now I know what must be done, I don't want to waste any time.

I tiptoe into the bathroom. My foot is throbbing, but the cut has started to heal. And I look exactly as you'd expect someone to look who's spent the night with a former lover. My hair is all over the place, there's stubble burn on my chin and around my lips, and my face is flushed and tired at the same time. I try to restore some order with Bob's comb, and I thank God for hotel freebies, because moisturiser and cologne just about tip the balance from dirty slut to plain old dirty stop-out.

I'm feeling quite pleased with the transformation, when I think about getting dressed. Shit. All I have is a pair of stupid pointy shoes, a leather dress and a ridiculous jacket. It is not an ideal outfit for a Sunday morning.

I carry the clothes back into the bedroom, and Bob stirs.

'Hello,' I say, as he opens his eyes.

'Hello.' He reaches out his hand to touch mine, but he looks sad. Or perhaps it's relief. He knows as well as I do that last night was a one-off. There will be no fairy-tale happy ever after.

'I ought to get home. Stuff to sort out, you know.'

'Can't I at least tempt you to breakfast in bed?' But he knows the answer. 'Then you must let me give you a lift,' he says, and pushes back the bedclothes.

'No, honestly. I've got the money for a cab. I don't want to drag you out of bed, especially when you've paid for this suite – don't leave until they throw you out!'

But I wish I hadn't said it, because what could be more miserable than having breakfast on your own in the most perfect bed, when the person you've spent the night with is no more than a dent in the pillow.

'Well, I'm not letting you leave like that.' He swings his body out of bed, and I look away. He doesn't belong to me; it seems wrong to see him naked now. He bends down to pick up his underpants and puts them on, then grabs a holdall off the floor, and rummages around inside. He pulls out a grey fleece, and a carrier bag. 'Here, wear this. Put the jacket in here. I'm sure you want to keep it as a souvenir – unless the TV company want it back?'

Shit. I've hardly thought about the programme since I walked out of the school gates, but what the hell did they do when I left? I take my mobile out of my handbag, and remember I switched it off when we got to the hospital. How many messages are there on it from Jenny and Alec? I drop it as though it's a grenade.

'Do you think they could sue me for walking out like that?'

He looks up from buttoning his shirt. 'I doubt it. Did you sign a contract?'

'Only something giving them permission to film me and the kids.'

'You'll probably be OK. I can't see them suing you, anyway, not exactly good publicity, is it?'

I pull the fleece over my head – it swamps me, which is a good thing. Only a short section of the leather skirt is visible. 'And what about you? The reporter and everything?'

Bob sighs. 'Can't stop them, if they really want to publish it. It's true, after all. I called our departmental press officer on my way to the hospital last night, so he's briefed.' He walks across the room to me, and reaches for my hand again. 'I'm sorry, Tracey. It might get messy. But I'll help out, you know. If the papers arrive, you ring me, and I'll arrange for you and the kids to go away for a while.'

'Don't apologise. It's my fault. Anyway, journalists don't scare me.'

'Atta girl,' he says, and rumples my hair. 'Are you sure about the lift?'

'Yeah . . . I mean, there could be reporters at home or anything. And if Dave's there, it could make things more unpleasant than they need to be.'

He smiles at me. 'I meant what I said about not settling for what you've got, Tracey. The prospect of being with your raddled ex-teacher isn't tempting, I'm sure, but do me a favour, and don't waste your life on that wanker.'

'OK,' I say, and I kiss him on the forehead. He winces slightly, and when I leave the room to call a taxi in reception, I think there are tears in his eyes. They make them look bluer than ever.

It's only eight o'clock, but Mum is looking out for me when the taxi pulls up. She's shaking her head as I walk up the drive.

'What the hell do you think you're—'

'Mum, I'm not listening,' I say, as I barge past her into the lounge. When she continues to rant, I stick my fingers in my ears, until her mouth stops moving.

'Put the kettle on,' I tell her. She looks shocked at being ordered about, but then meekly does as she's told. I wonder why I've never tried this before.

I look around the room, and it tires me out. It all feels like a compromise, with its washed-out colours and seen-better-days furniture. Now that Callum's growing up, maybe it's time to redecorate – white walls, beech tables. This time, I'll do it how I want it.

She comes back with two cups. The tea is very sweet, and makes me realise I'm hungry again.

'I'm not telling you where I went, Mum, so don't ask.'

'But you're a married woman—'

'It's irrelevant.'

She sighs, but gives a half-nod at the same time.

'Is Dave here?'

'No. I don't know where he is. I can't believe that you both abandoned your children like that, you're not kids any more, you have responsibilities.'

'I don't care what you think.'

'Now, there's no need—'

'Mum, I've decided to throw Dave out. He's unfaithful and he doesn't love me. And I don't love him. There's no point.'

She shakes her head. 'You have no idea how hard it is bringing up children on your own. You should—'

'I know exactly how hard it is. I've been doing it for the best part of a year. If anything, it'll be easier when I don't have to change my routines every time he heads back from Dublin on a whim.'

She tuts.

'Mum, I want you on my side. I'm going to need you. But I can't carry on with the marriage.' I pause until she looks up at me. 'Last night, I found him with Melody.'

'Oh.'

'I don't know if it's been going on since the wedding, or if they were just hooking up for old times' sake. I don't care, actually. If it isn't her, it's been someone else. Or lots and lots of someone elses.'

'If people split up every time the husband had an affair, there'd be no marriages left,' she sniffs. Poor Mum. She never had the option of standing by her man. She didn't see him for dust.

'Maybe. But I don't want to live like this any more, and I don't want the kids to grow up thinking it's normal for their parents to have nothing to say to each other.'

'I had to fight to bring you up,' she starts, and then stops. She's trying not to cry. 'I didn't want you to have to do the same.'

'I know, Mum. But if it's a choice between having two miserable parents under the same roof, or a single mother who's committed to you, I'd go for the second.'

She frowns. 'If I didn't know you better, Tracey, I'd say that was almost a compliment.'

I grin at her. 'Yeah. It almost was.'

If this was a movie, we'd probably fall into each other's arms, but instead we sit there feeling embarrassed.

'Oh, I forgot,' she says. 'That girl from the TV company came round last night, told me to get you to ring her as soon as you got in. She was very angry.'

I have a shower before I dare make the phone call. Compared to the jet-extravaganza at the hotel, it's a feeble dribble, but I still feel better for it. I put on a pair of brushed cotton pyjamas, which makes me feel less like a harlot, then I sit with my brush, trying to tidy up my barbed-wire hair.

By eight forty-five, I've run out of excuses. I take the phone into the kitchen, and then remember the packet of cigarettes I bought last night. I take them from my handbag, and dial Jenny's number.

She answers immediately. 'Fucking hell, Tracey. It'd better be good.'

'I'm sorry.'

'That's a start, I suppose.'

I know I've messed them about, but her attitude is already rubbing me up the wrong way. 'Look, I'm sorry I left, but there's no need to be so rude. It hasn't been an easy couple of days.'

There's a pause. 'OK. So what happened?'

'I found Dave with Melody.'

'With? As in . . . ?'

'Use your imagination. And then . . . I suppose you'll find out soon enough. One of the journalists at the press conference had found out something about the past. Something that's no one else's business, but anyway, there it is, it's out now.'

'Is it about Robert Carmichael?'

I nearly drop the phone. 'How do you know?'

'Something Gary said to you the day you met him at the pub. I did a bit of research, and it didn't take much imagination to work out what he was on about. It's OK, I didn't tell the others.'

'They'll know soon enough.' Last night feels like decades ago. 'How's Alec?'

'Oh, God, he was beside himself.' Jenny sounds amused. 'But seriously, Tracey, we're all in the shit over this. We carried on filming, did loads of interviews with people. But without you there, the film will be shit.'

'I know. I do feel bad. I'll do anything I can now, though. Maybe I should dress up again and do the interview as if I'm still there?'

I hear her laugh. 'You're a bloody fast learner, Tracey, I'll say that for you. And I suppose if this story about you and the teacher's going to come out, we might well end up with better ratings than we ever thought we'd get. By the way, any news on Boris?'

Boris. The one light at the end of the grimy tunnel of my life. 'Yeah. It's all fine. She's got a baby girl.'

'That's brilliant.' I'm sure I can hear someone else in the background.

'Are you all right, Jenny?'

'Yes . . .' More giggling. 'Yes, I'm fine. Look, I'd better go. I'll talk to Alec and we'll be in touch. Oh, and Jamie's just asked me to tell you he wants his radio mike back . . .'

I ring Boris's mobile. Brian answers.

'Tracey,' he says, and passes the phone over to Boris. She sounds knackered but elated.

'She's perfect,' she sighs, and I hope she is. If anyone deserves something beautiful, it's Boris.

'And what about you? Are you OK?'

'Hmm . . . the drugs are wonderful. I can't feel a thing.'

'And have you thought of a name?'

'Yes. We thought we'd call her Louise. The whole reunion thing got me thinking, and I always liked Shrimp, she was one of the good ones.'

She's such a bleeding heart, but I feel a lump in my throat. 'Lovely.'

'Anyway, what did I miss?'

Ten minutes later, I'm still talking, and when I get to the bit accusing Suzanne of being a scheming, manipulative bitch for inviting Bob, the line goes quiet, and I think she's fallen asleep.

'Boris?'

'Oh, Tracey . . .' she moans, and I worry that I'm tiring her out.

'What? Look, I'll leave you to rest.'

'No . . . no, the thing is, you see, it wasn't Suzanne that invited Bob. It was me.'

'You? But why?'

'I don't know. It does seem a bit insane now. Maybe it was my hormones. But I suppose I had a hunch that meeting Bob again might just make you realise how awful Dave really was. I'm so sorry, Tracey. I had no idea what was going to happen. Typical me, meddling where I'm not wanted.'

'No . . . no, don't apologise, Boris. It's probably the biggest favour you could have done me.'

When the kids get up, they head straight for the garden, and I drag out the paddling pool Mum kept from thirty years ago. This must be the first summer since Kelly was born that there hasn't been a hosepipe ban, so we fill the pool, and Mum and I take turns to watch them.

Dave finally turns up at two in the afternoon. I don't even realise he's let himself into the house until I see him through the kitchen window, taking a can of lager out of the fridge.

'What the fuck are you doing here?' I walk through the back door towards him. His face is unshaven, and there are dark circles under his eyes. I try not to think about how – or where – he spent the night. Though it's not as if I have any right to claim the moral high ground.

'Chill out, Trace,' he says. He's laughing at me.

'You're unbelievable. How dare you come back here after what happened last night?' I'm trying to keep my voice down, but the kids are watching from the garden, even though my mother's attempting to distract them by splashing.

'Er . . . because I live here? It's no big deal, Melody and me hadn't seen each other for years. It was meant to be a reunion, so that's what we were doing. Reuniting. Like you and your mate Suzanne! There was nothing to it. Don't tell me you haven't kissed anyone else in nine years . . .'

'Our marriage is over, Dave. I want you to leave.'

He doesn't even have the grace to react, but turns round to go outside.

'Did you hear me?' I shout. 'Are you fucking deaf as well as stupid?'

He turns back, and there's something about the long-suffering expression on his face that tips me over the edge. On the breakfast bar, Kelly's craft scissors are lying abandoned on top of a scrapbook. I grab them, and leap forward towards him.

'Trace?' he says quietly.

'I am not messing around. You leave NOW or I won't be responsible for my actions.'

He's shaking his head, but he doesn't know whether to take me seriously or not. 'I can't go now. I haven't packed any clothes or anything. Don't be hysterical.'

This time I jump even closer. 'I am not hysterical, I am fucking serious. GET OUT.'

He shrugs, and pushes past me on his way into the garden. Maybe it's my hangover, but when I walk outside everything is brighter, hotter, louder. The orange ducks floating on the magnified plastic-blue water in the paddling pool; the sunlight on my skin making me sweat and shiver at the same time. As Dave turns to sneer, I hear the click of the ring-pull on his can of lager, and the hissy release of gas as the beer bubbles to the surface. And the anger inside me spills over.

Before I really know what I'm doing, I rush towards him. I don't have a plan except to wipe that grin from his face, and it's only after I see this unfamiliar look pass across his eyes that I remember I still have those craft scissors in my hand, and I realise the look is fear.

I move backwards, shocked at myself, but it's too late for Dave to recover. He tries hard, but he's toppling backwards, fear replaced by confusion. Then he falls into the paddling pool. There's a satisfying splash of water followed by an 'ooof' as the cushion of air breaks his fall. It's like a clip from *You've Been Framed*.

For a second or two, we're all paralysed, and I notice that Kelly, Callum and Dave's mouths are pursed in the same 'O' shape. I'm just wondering what the hell to do next, how to stop this causing the kids some awful trauma that the bloody educational psychologist will blame for everything they do wrong over the next twenty years, when my mum comes to the rescue.

'Silly Daddy,' she says, and then starts to giggle. It sounds forced at first, but then Kelly and Callum look down at their father, and the sight of him wet through, his legs waving in the air like a beetle's as he tries to right himself, suddenly seems funny rather than shocking.

'Silly Daddy,' Kelly agrees, between giggles, and Callum points his fingers at the pool, as Dave finally manages to heave himself out. He forces his mouth from the 'O' to a kind of crooked smile, but his eyes are cold.

I look down at the scissors in my hand, and when I unfurl my fingers, I see that the metal has left indentations in my palm. As I let them drop on to the grass, I feel a kind of release.

'I think you should go,' I say, under my breath, as the kids try to stop laughing, clutching at their sides in pain.

Dave opens his mouth as if he's about to say something, but then looks down at his dripping clothes, thinks better of it, and starts trudging towards the back door. I spot Callum's Winnie the Pooh bath towel neatly folded on the plastic garden chair – Mum must have brought it out with her – and pick it up.

'Dave,' I say, and he turns. I think he's expecting me to beg, to have a change of heart, to apologise, something. But all I do is throw over the towel, and, instinctively, he reaches out his hands to catch it. 'You'll be needing this to dry yourself off.'

'Fuck you,' he mouths. But he knows he's beaten, and I hold

my breath until I hear the front door slam. I bend down to pick up his can, still trickling frothy beer on to the grass. I walk into the kitchen to throw it away. I go to the fridge, take half a dozen more tins of his favourite lager, and throw them in the bin, too.

The Trouble with Tracey . . .

'It's rude to stare,' my mum says under her breath, as we walk down the detergent aisle.

'Leave it.' I'm getting used to the attention, the sneaky looks and the nudges from people in the street. Four days after they showed *The Trouble with Tracey*, and the public attention I always craved is mine, in my home town, at least . . .

The reaction's been mixed. It certainly wasn't the programme Smart Alec Productions said they were going to make, but some of the critics (the ones who weren't too snobby to review a show on Channel 5) reckoned it was better for that. They changed the name from *Reunited!* to *The Trouble with Tracey* pretty much straight after the disasters of 21 July. I wasn't all that comfortable about it to begin with – I was worried they'd stitch me up, make me look terrible, but then Boris pointed out that I couldn't look any worse than I already did in the newspapers.

August is the silly season, so Andrew's exclusive, a story that at any other time might have been confined to the inside pages of one tabloid, hit the headlines in almost all of them. He waited a while to write the piece, and I wondered if someone had put pressure on him – I've watched enough thrillers to know that governments can cover up pretty much anything. But it seems Bob's reputation wasn't worth going to any trouble over, and as for mine . . . I guess no one was ever going to lose any sleep over that.

Bob's still in his post, though. I'd even hazard a guess that the whole thing won't do him any harm in the long run. Sure, shagging your pupils isn't recommended by the Department for Education, but things were different in the eighties, weren't they? Everyone was out for what they could get. We both survived the first wave of articles, and I was amazed that no one came out of the woodwork to put the knife in. Suzanne kept her mouth shut, and so did Dick Phipps.

It did mean that the last few weeks leading up to the programme have been mad. The press officer helped me choose the right interviews – I've done *Richard and Judy*, *Woman's Hour*, all the local radio stations and a couple of news programmes, plus a really fun makeover for a glossy magazine. I stopped short at Adam Ant jackets this time round.

All the publicity meant they got a huge audience for the programme; in Bracewell, there was a story going round that the electrical shops were getting loads of phone calls from people who still hadn't got round to tuning Channel 5, four years after it went on air, just so they could watch *The Trouble with Tracey*.

I quite enjoyed the editing, too. I had a few trips up to London with the kids, all paid for. Mum would take them to the Tower of London or the zoo, and I got to sit in a darkened room in Soho, eating free Danish pastries, and helping them write the script. They even took me for lunch at the Ivy, which is where all the actors go. Nicole Kidman was there, but I didn't even consider racing over to her table to ask for her autograph. That's how sophisticated I am now.

Instead of two shows, they made a single programme, a whole hour long. I don't know if it's an accurate picture of me – how can you ever tell? The guy from the *Sunday Telegraph* said I made Maureen from the *Driving School* programme look self-aware, but then the *Sun* said every bloke in the land would understand why 'Bonking Bob' (as he is now known, bless him) couldn't keep it in his trousers. Which is a compliment, kind of. And I've memorised what the nice woman from the *Daily Telegraph* said about me in the profile:

'Tracey's taken the knocks – from a marriage break-up to a summer of press persecution – but she's still the kind of woman you'd always invite on a girls' night out. Streetwise, witty, a true child of Thatcher's generation – and anyone who judges her as lacking in any way is simply a snob.'

She's right, though, it's been a hell of a summer. The divorce is coming along nicely, and Dave agreed to a very attractive maintenance deal on condition I didn't drag him through the mud on the programme. I was true to my word – there's not a snide script line about him in the whole thing – but he still comes across like a total scumbag in his interviews, without any help from me. And the beauty of it is, he doesn't even realise it. He rang me the other day and told me he's taking a VHS copy over to Ireland with him to show the lads. He really is a very stupid man.

The kids are doing better than I'd feared. They see about as much of him now as they used to, except now he has to make an effort to find things to do – the whole Sunday afternoon circuit of McDonald's, cinema, safari park, Wacky Warehouse. Towards the end of August, Suzanne got in touch to offer Kelly a place on some special week-long holiday for kids who've had problems, and Kelly said yes straight away. It hasn't turned her into a rampant extrovert, but she's made friends with another little girl who lives a few miles away, and she even had her round here for a birthday tea. She hardly ever talks to Jolene any more.

Perhaps I'll never know what makes my daughter tick, but

I'm trying to make up for what I lack. Suzanne said some deranged stuff that night – under that posh hair and flashy clothes she's the same screechy schoolgirl she always was – but I couldn't stop myself remembering a few of the things I said and did way back then. I wasn't a bully, *no way*, but . . . well, you need to be careful with kids. Throwaway remarks get taken the wrong way and then they remember it for ever and really, most of what I said when I was at school wasn't meant to be remembered. It was meant to make people laugh, to make the days go faster. They went too fast for me, eh?

So I don't feel guilty about Suzanne. No way. Though maybe there's the odd comment I regret, here and there. You don't expect people to store up your sentences like a stamp collection, do you? But I never meant to hurt anyone, not really. I was way too busy feeling hurt myself, about my dad and Shrimp.

She called me again last week, Suzanne did. Obviously still feeling guilty about the whole set-up with Andrew, because she offered to go into Kelly's school to do a talk before the programme went out, to make sure it didn't backfire. I'd never have thought of that, but good on her, seems to have worked. The kids think Kelly's appearance on telly makes her properly cool. Hope it lasts. It's so lovely being cool.

Oh, and I heard from Gary the other day. Well, from him and Gabby, actually. It was an invitation to their engagement party. The silly bugger finally decided to take the plunge. I won't go – I'm probably not the best person to celebrate the joys of marriage at the moment – but I can't help wondering whether the reunion might have helped him make up his mind. Even if it was just the shock of seeing me, and realising what a close shave he'd had . . .

'No, you can't have those, Kelly.' She's trying to sneak a

336

Barbie princess outfit on to the conveyor belt. It's emotional blackmail. But secretly I like the fact that she'll misbehave now. Who knows, maybe one day she might even get in trouble at school. Every parent has ambitions for their kids, eh?

We load the stuff into the car, and I drop Mum and the kids back. I've got a busy afternoon – including my first job interview in six years.

It's the strangest thing. On Tuesday, the day after the programme went out, I had a call from Beautiful Berkshire FM, the local radio station I've done most of my interviews with. The station director said that they'd been brainstorming and had had this idea for a new show, *Old School Ties.*

'It's going to plug into the whole reunion thing, and we're going to try to reunite listeners, mainly former classmates, but also people who used to work together, or old neighbours or whatever. And, well, we loved your interviews, you're so sparky and quick, and quite the local celeb at the moment, so we wondered if you'd like to audition as a possible presenter. Only if you're interested, of course.'

Well, it was a tough one. Was I interested in swapping my thrilling part-time job in the stationery shop for a job involving gossiping for an hour a day to a captive audience on five times the money? I really had to think about it . . .

It's not a done deal, but I rang Jenny and she said she thinks it sounds as though they've built the whole show around me, so my chances must be good.

'Don't undersell yourself,' she told me. 'The Tracey Mortimer name is worth a lot now, you know. You're a valuable commodity.'

How strange is that? I won't believe it until they give me a contract to sign. Or until I'm sitting in front of the microphone . . .

But then part of me also wonders if I wasn't always destined for more than life as plain old Tracey Brown. I've always loved to entertain people. OK, maybe I took a few wrong turnings, but I was never going to stay in my tedious life for ever, was I?

And no matter how horrible it's been at times over the last five months, I don't regret a second of it – not because of the job, or the designer outfits or the health farm, but because without the reunion I'd never have found Boris, or Bob. I don't know if I will ever see Bob again. He's called a few times, and it's tempting, but before I do anything about it, Boris thinks I need space, some time on my own, 'because you can't be happy with someone else until you're happy with yourself'.

I was tempted to tell her she was talking bollocks, that I'm the happiest person I know now, but then again, Boris doesn't often talk bollocks. And Boris is the best thing that's happened to me in years.

It's taken her a while to get fit again after the op, but Louise is amazing, a really jolly baby, and so charming that she's even managed to lure Brian away from spending so many weeks on the road selling software.

Smart Alec invited me to a launch party on the night the programme went out, but I decided I really wanted to watch it at home, with the kids, Mum and Boris. When Mum had followed Kelly and Callum to bed, and Louise was asleep in the travel cot, we sat up late drinking fizzy wine, and going over the stories that weren't in the programme. Shrimp. Melody. And Boris's favourite, the banishment of Dave . . .

'And I threw the towel at him, and I said . . .'

Boris picked up my cue: 'You'll be needing this to dry yourself off!' And we both collapsed in hysterics, until I started worrying that her caesarean scar wouldn't take the strain.

I had another swig of wine, and Boris grinned at me. It was the first time she'd been drunk since the baby was born.

She reached out to me, and kissed me on the cheek. 'Welcome back, Tracey Mortimer. I've missed you.'

And I realised I'd missed me too.

They say you can't rewrite history, but when the opportunity arose for my publisher, Orion, to reprint my first novel, the temptation to tweak this particular section of the past was too great.

It's seven years since I finished this book – I've written five more in the meantime – and I hope I've learned a bit about self-editing in those intervening half a million words. So I couldn't resist having a tinker here and there: this edition is *Old School Ties – the director's cut* . . . If you're interested in the process, I've blogged about it via my website (see following page).

I decided against updating the novel from 2001 to 2009, although it was surprising how much has changed in terms of our Web habits. It's unthinkable now that someone in Tracey's position wouldn't be online, yet just a few years ago millions of us were in the same boat. I remember my first trip online: it was terrifying. Now I can't live without it.

I hope you'll forgive Tracey her lack of Web experience (though she certainly has far worse flaws that need forgiving) and will enjoy her journey into her past . . .

I'd also like to thank all the lovely people who've helped me over the last six books. You know who you are. I am truly grateful.

Finally, I'd like to thank you for reading this. If you'd like to contact me, I'd love to hear from you at www.kate-harrison.com.

Kate Harrison, 2009